"If I Were To Ask My Lady For A Kiss, What Would She Say?"

Judith had hardly a moment to reflect how easy it was to play the theater doxy. "Is this the moment when she says 'ye

Lambert nod

"Then, yes,"

This seductiv  e needed, and in tha nd the bounds of play ms, gently but firmly. He kissed her, no need of script now or imagined roles to guide him in the enjoyment of the woman in his arms. As he shed his practiced pretense, so the background of the theater slipped away.

Judith melted in his arms. It was a remarkably sweet kiss, not quite shy but not quite sure of itself either. The embrace became more passionate. The kiss deepened. Every new sensation produced in Lambert a desire to go one step further, and Judith did not hold back...

And Heaven Too

ALSO BY JULIE TETEL

❧

For Love of Lord Roland
Swept Away
Tangled Dreams
The Viking's Bride

Published by
POPULAR LIBRARY

Julie Tetel

And Heaven Too

POPULAR LIBRARY

An Imprint of Warner Books, Inc

A Time Warner Company

POPULAR LIBRARY EDITION

Copyright © 1990 by Julie Tetel Andresen
All rights reserved.

Popular Library® and the fanciful P design are registered
trademarks of Warner Books, Inc.

Cover illustration by Don Case

Popular Library books are published by
Warner Books, Inc.
666 Fifth Avenue
New York, N.Y. 10103

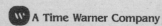 A Time Warner Company

Printed in the United States of America

First Printing: December, 1990

10 9 8 7 6 5 4 3 2 1

To T. L. C. Hagood

Many thanks to Mary Garrard for her book *Artemisia Gentileschi* (Princeton University Press, 1989) which inspired this novel. The central intrigue surrounding the fate of Gentileschi's *Judith Slaying Holofernes* is entirely the product of the author's imagination.

Many thanks to William Shakespeare for so generously supplying every quote used in this novel.

And Heaven Too

Chapter
1

SIR Robert emerged from the gloom of the stables and into the half-light of the courtyard. He surveyed the sky. "It looks to rain again, Miss Judith," he said.

Judith stepped out from the stables with him. The clip of hooves on cobblestone followed her as she led her mount out. "There's not a cloud in sight, sir," she said, looking up at a wide expanse of blue. "Not one rain cloud, that is," she amended, for several white masses were presently billowing to flock the morning sky.

"It's naught but an hour past the dawn," Sir Robert countered. "By day's end, now by day's end, I wager, by then—"

"I'll have been to Monmouth and back," Judith interposed.

"—the rains will be upon us again," Sir Robert finished. "And you will *not* have been there and back. It's five hours to Monmouth, one way."

"It's three hours one way at most, as you well know," Judith replied crisply. "And well you know, too, that I won't be persuaded from my errand by your shameful exaggerations. Now, if you wish to give me truly useful advice," she said, handing him the reins she held, "you may assure me that I have properly secured Barbary's saddle and bridle."

The Master of the Horse accepted the reins and responded

to the request by running a professional hand over the tackle harnessing the white maiden mare. However, he was not yet ready to concede defeat.

"That makes six hours in the saddle, by your reckoning," he said, "and I don't imagine you'll wish to enter Monmouth only to turn around again and return to Raglan. No doubt you will wish to visit with your cousins."

"No doubt!" Judith agreed. "And if rain is threatening by early afternoon, I shall certainly stay the night at Monmouth. If I do, you will receive word of it." She smiled persuasively. "I think you may count on me to use the good sense you know I possess."

"Your good sense should keep you at Raglan," he answered with a frown. "The roads are dangerous, Miss Judith."

"My good sense has prompted me to travel with four—yes, Sir Robert, four!—outriders *and* with Edith. Besides which," she continued, "it is perfectly obvious that I do *not* plan to travel by the road which *would* take me five hours but will rather take the path through the woods."

"The forest is even more dangerous," Sir Robert said gruffly, his frown deepening.

"Somerset Park?" she echoed with evident amusement. "My dear sir, *when* was the last time that a ride through the forest proved dangerous?"

"Miss Diana," he stated cryptically.

Judith smiled. "In recent memory, I mean. That little incident must have been all of fifteen years ago."

"Now it is you who exaggerate. It was ten more like, and it was no little incident, it was an abduction!!"

Judith laughed outright. "Only ten years ago, then?" she said. "Recent, in fact! A fearsome abduction it was, too, given that my cousin had arranged to meet the man who abducted her. Some might call that an elopement—or an attempted elopement, as it turned out. Some *did* call it that!"

"You were naught but a girl then, Miss Judith," Sir Robert reminded her, "and were not concerned to know all the details of the affair."

Judith's response was prompt. "You are perfectly right, and I am no more concerned with them today than I was all those years ago."

Sir Robert spluttered, then accused, wagging a finger, "You are taking advantage of his lordship's absence to do as you please!"

"Nonsense! My uncle gives me permission to do as I please whether he is here or not," she said, bending the truth only a fraction. "And since what I please to do in this instance is so entirely reasonable, I cannot think he *would* object! The day is fine, the journey is short, and I have provided myself with more than suitable escort."

"But the errand itself is an unnecessary one," Sir Robert persisted.

"Very true!" Judith acknowledged cheerfully. "Call it a whim! For weeks now, since my uncle set the date for my wedding, you know that I have been busily writing the invitations. It seems a simple reward for my industry to deliver the first invitation by my very own hand." She patted the thick envelope tucked away in the pretty pouch tied at her waist and smiled. "Where can be the harm in it?"

"I've just been telling you," Sir Robert muttered darkly.

"You have?" Judith echoed, frowning slightly in her turn. Then comprehension dawned, and her brow cleared. "Ah, so *that's* it!" she exclaimed. "*Now* I understand your references to the dangers of the forest and all that ancient history." Perceiving the expression on Sir Robert's face, Judith continued swiftly, "*Not* so ancient history—a mere ten years ago! Dear, *dear* man! How ingenious of you to think of it! You think you see a similarity, do you, between me and Diana?"

"She, too, had just been newly betrothed—to a very worthy man of his lordship's choosing!—before she was abducted," he said.

"If my memory serves, Diana did not desire the marriage arranged for her," Judith pointed out before taking the reins back from Sir Robert. "Would you feel better if I assured you that I am well content to marry Sir George? You must know that I count myself doubly blessed in that my choice of husband has the approval of my uncle.'' Impatient at the delay, Barbary began to shift and snort. Judith paused to nuzzle her horse affectionately. Then, with a glance back at Sir Robert, ''Beautiful though the day is for falling in love, sir, I am not planning an elopement in Somerset forest.''

''An abduction,'' Sir Robert corrected.

''Nor am I planning an abduction,'' Judith replied gravely.

Sir Robert growled. ''Rain,'' he predicted again and ominously. ''It's my last word.''

''You, Sir Robert, are a humbug,'' Judith said complacently. ''The day will be perfect.''

With that, she looped the reins around her left hand and reached her right hand up to grasp the pommel to mount the mare. Sir Robert, defeated, bent to grasp her left ankle to give her a leg up. With a swirl of skirts, Judith settled into the sidesaddle and hooked her right knee over the crutch on the left of center-saddle. Her left foot found the stirrup.

Judith beckoned to Edith who was just then leading her horse out of the stables, followed by Judith's favorite castle dog, Rogue, who was under the mistaken impression that he was to accompany his mistress for the day. Edith was a thin, spry woman who had had the raising of Judith and who was well known within Raglan walls for her inability to utter two sentences in a row on the same topic.

After Edith had received the same mounting service from Sir Robert, the two women took their leave of the Master of the Horse with repeated assurances of their safety for the day. Sir Robert accepted these grudgingly. For the next moment or two he watched the women leading their pretty mares through the stable yard and under the stone arch leading to a larger courtyard. He whistled once for Rogue who had been trotting, tail proud, alongside his mistress. When Rogue returned to him, tail down, Sir Robert shook his head and, muttering indistinctly, disappeared into the stables.

Once past the arch and in the Fountain Court, Judith discovered that her left stirrup was not properly adjusted and bent to fiddle with the buckle. As she moved to right herself again in the saddle, a rather ghostly bone-cracking creaking and groaning swept through the courtyard.

Judith laughed. "I thought at first those were *my* bones protesting!" she said to Edith whose face had wrenched against the horrible noise. "I shall never become used to Edward's inventions!"

"My heavens, they do make the most terrible racket, especially if you are caught next to one at the moment it decides to awaken!" Edith agreed, somewhat breathlessly. "Why, it is as I was saying to Elizabeth just yesterday—or was it two days ago? I don't remember now, but it seems that we were discussing the laundry. You know, it has been *so* difficult for sheets to dry properly with all the rain that I fear that all the beds will soon become mildewed! But as I was saying about the machines—Lord Edward's machines! —that my heart was like to stop when I heard that *terrible* noise—"

The rest of Edith's remarks were swallowed by a second, more prolonged and melancholy groan emanating from the bowels of Raglan Castle where many of Lord Edward's machines dwelled. Then a third groan wheezed and echoed eerily beneath the cobbles of Fountain Court. At this ominous sound, the women urged their mares to a brisker gait and passed quickly by the magnificent fountain in whose depths lived a mechanical monster of Lord Edward's making, which at any moment might begin pumping water for the day.

They crossed the remainder of the courtyard and under another heavy arch which housed a large buttery hatch murmuring with the sounds and smells of a household coming to life. They entered the grand Stone Court which served as the main entrance to Raglan. Around three sides of the Stone Court were the kitchen, the storerooms, and the residential chambers. The fourth side was dominated by the Great Hall which was defined by the buttery at one end and at the other by a paneled withdrawing room, or Solar, as Lord Somerset liked to call it. Above the Solar and the Great Hall ran the many fair windows of the gallery, the pride of the Tudor builders, glinting in the early morning light.

Judith did not glance up at the beauties of this splendid and luxurious palace for which Raglan was famous, but kept her eye on the gate house ahead. There, at the approach to the stone bridge arching over the moat, she discerned the four riders, her escorts, waiting to be off and loping across the hills of Gwent. Before them, the portcullis had already been raised at Judith's command, given confidently the hour before.

Miss Judith Beaufort had every reason for this confidence. She was, after all, the niece of Henry Herbert, Lord Somerset, the fifth Earl of Worcester, reportedly the richest, and most rigid, man in all of England. Judith had long ago adapted to her uncle's notions of correct behavior, for she had come as a very young girl, orphaned when her mother died, into her uncle's household.

In truth, Raglan Castle was less of a household and more of a court, for two knights served as Stewards and many gentlemen's sons, all bred in the castle, served him at his high table. In addition to these attendants and the many members of the extended Somerset family, Lord Henry's retinue boasted the Comptroller, the Secretary, the Master of the Horse, the Master of the Fish Ponds, the Clerk of the Kitchen, the Chief Auditor, the Clerk of the Accounts, the Ushers of the Hall, the Closet Keeper, the Gentlemen of the Chapel, the Keeper of the Records, the Master of the Wardrobe, the Master of the Armory, the Master of the Hounds the Master Falconer, the Porter and his man, two Keepers of the Home Park, two Keepers of the Red Deer Park as well as waiters, pages, and castle yeomen to the number of one hundred fifty persons, when the minor ranks were included. And the fully developed castle-palace of Raglan could shelter them all.

Over the years, Judith had perfected her role as the best of the Herbert daughters. She now wore the costume of well-laced respectability and exceptional privilege like a second skin, as naturally as she wore her handsome riding dress of royal blue embroidered silk. Even so, she regularly found ways to escape Lord Somerset's Rules for Castle

Life which were as numerous, it seemed, as his retainers.

Judith and Edith drew abreast of the four outriders. Judith addressed them by name and made her travel wishes known to the head scout. The small party of six proceeded past the gate house which consisted of two barbican towers and was flanked by the Library Tower. They came upon the bridge and presently drew into the shadow of the most distinctive and military feature of Raglan, the great hexagonal keep called The Yellow Tower of Gwent. Set in the middle of the moat, this tower was five stories high, with walls ten feet thick. One of those walls was disfigured by a tangle of machinery which propelled Lord Edward's waterworks, otherwise known as The Young Master's Folly.

Soon they had left behind the comforting, constricting bulk of Raglan Castle, and the undulating, dew-jeweled Welsh countryside rolled out before them. The traveling party broke up into its formation for the day, with two outriders cantering ahead and two dropping behind. Thus protected, Judith could truly imagine no difficulty arising to hinder her errand to Monmouth. The terrain she surveyed before her was open and unthreatening, for Raglan differed from all other castles in this part of the world in that it was designed to cover no pass; it forded and dominated no valley. It owed its splendor not to the ancient Norman scheme of holding down newly conquered land, but entirely to the family pride of a noble house of which she, Judith Beaufort, was a direct and happy descendant.

The traveling party walked their horses down the gentle rise on which Raglan squatted. The recent rains had left the ground damp. In the early morning freshness mists were still grazing the hillsides like the ghosts of old flocks, but if the mists were spirits, they were tame and friendly ones.

Following the lead of the scout, Judith and Edith did not take the main road leading to Monmouth but straggled instead down the muddy, deeply rutted main path of the castle village. Judith observed with contentment the neat tofts crowded with sunflowers and cabbages, waved benevolently at the rustics who, shouldering hoes, were emerging from their half-timbered thatches, and smiled rather distantly at the children who were already up and about and tugging at their mothers' skirts. She was conversing with Edith on indifferent topics when the peaceful morning air was rent by a noise of truly stentorian proportions.

Though startled, Judith had no difficulty identifying the source of this great shout. "We escaped just in time!" She shuddered good-naturedly. She turned to Edith, her eyes dancing. "Which of Lord Edward's brain-children do you think has just roared to life? The Bucket Fountain? The Water Screw?"

Edith had no opinion on the matter. "My heavens, how the young master's machines do terrify the entire neighborhood!" she exclaimed. "Some say it's the work of the Devil and, my heavens, I think at times like this that it just might be!"

"No, no. From the special groan, I would say it is rather the work of the *hydraulic machinery*," Judith teased and cocked a well-trained ear. "At a guess, I would say it is the Bucket Fountain."

"With the buckets going round and round to make my head spin if I look at it for more than a minute!" Edith exclaimed. "Why, it's the ugliest beast I've ever seen and we've an army of servants to raise water from a well, if it comes to that! I've a mind to tell Master Edward so, but with him gone from the Castle, there's not been an opportunity. Nor to speak with his lordship, for he's gone as well! And I'm not one to write letters, which is how Caroline must spend a great deal of her time. And such beautiful letters she writes! Why, the one we received from her only yesterday brought tears to my eyes!"

Judith was more than willing to pursue Edith's tangent. "I am afraid that Caroline's last letter did not quite move me in the same way."

Edith was surprised. "It did not? Why, I thought that everyone—even *you*, Miss Judith—must enter into the feelings that Miss Caroline expressed so . . . so beautifully! I thought that I must be falling in love again myself and was never so much reminded of the time when—"

Judith broke into what might have been a misty recollection of a lost love by saying prosaically, "It was a most beautiful effusion, I grant you that, and I am sure that I felt a palpitation in the region of my heart in the reading of it!"

"But—?" Edith began on a question.

"But, my dear Edith," Judith continued, "I remembered that my young cousin is somewhat inconstant in her affections and that this is the third time that she has found true love since being in London this month past!"

"Oh, no, no, no, no. *This* time is different! I am quite sure! Never has Miss Caroline described her love in such detail! He—now, what was his name again? Something like Herbert, but of course, it cannot be Herbert, for that is his lordship's family name. But as for the name of Caroline's love, I think it must be—"

"Lambert. James Lambert," Judith supplied, adding dryly, "Indeed, it *is* difficult to keep pace with Caroline's changing loves! And from the way she describes her latest, I am inclined to put him firmly in the category of *fop*."

"But his titles!" Edith argued.

"Titles?" Judith echoed, as if the word was a mild invective. "James Lambert's titles come without a penny or an acre of land, for his father gambled it all away years ago and died doing it!"

"It is such a pity when a son must pay for his father's sins," Edith said mournfully, with no rebuke intended at Judith's prejudice.

Judith had the grace to color a little. "Yes, it is—but not that I am actually *judging* the son by the father. It's just that . . . that when a son has such a father, one wonders about the upbringing he has received. Which leads me to think of Caroline's upbringing and the fact that one cannot be too careful with a young lady's reputation. Although I was initially in favor of her sojourn in London, I am beginning to think that she should return to Raglan. When my uncle hears that she is making a fool of herself over yet another handsome face at Whitehall, she *will* be brought home. And with no delay!"

"Oh yes, brought home!" Edith agreed, readily convinced by Judith's impromptu arguments. "You seem to know his lordship's mind so well, Miss Judith! That is exactly what his lordship will do when he learns of Caroline's attraction to an entirely unsuitable young man! It truly seems like the case of Miss Diana all over again!"

"Diana?" Judith asked, surprised by mention of her elder cousin for the second time that morning.

"Of course, Miss Caroline has *not* run off to Somerset Park the way Miss Diana did, and Miss Caroline has not been formally betrothed to anyone either," Edith explained, "but as for similarities in the two cases—Miss Caroline and Miss Diana being sisters, you see!—they both fell in love with the most unsuitable men. Why, now that I come to think of it, I wonder if James Lambert is related to Charles?"

Although well accustomed to Edith's conversational flights, Judith failed to follow the meaning of this one. "Charles? Charles who?"

"You were too young to have remembered it, of course." Edith's smile generously excused her mistress's ignorance. "And of course it was not talked about at the time. Very hush-hush! Then Miss Diana was married off in no time at all, so no harm was done! But I am thinking that—why, yes, I am quite sure that they are of the same family, though not brothers." Edith shook her head. "No, definitely not brothers."

From this disjointed discourse, Judith had sifted the essential nugget of information. "Was the man who ran off with Diana all those years ago named Charles Lambert, perchance?"

Edith nodded. "You wouldn't have known it, since you were so young at the time."

"And are you suggesting that Diana's 'abductor' and Caroline's latest love are related?"

Edith brought the conversational chaos into sudden clarity. "Charles Lambert must be James Lambert's uncle," she affirmed. "I'm quite sure of it!"

Judith digested this. Then, with disgust, said, "Perfect!"

"Just as I was saying: Miss Caroline is Miss Diana all over again!" Edith said brightly. "Sisters! And if that isn't exactly like Josephine, my third cousin, and *her* sister. . . ."

Judith listened with only one ear to Edith's ramblings. It was true that Caroline had never before written so heart-rendingly of a love: how James Lambert's lack of fortune was more than compensated by the true nobility of his nature, how he was worthy in character of the grand titles Marquis of Pembroke and Earl of Huntingdon which she, Caroline Herbert, would be proud to bear! Caroline had begged Judith's aid in persuading her father that his youngest daughter, at least, should not be sacrificed on the altar of family duty and should be allowed to marry whom she chose. Caroline had assured Judith that she was being circumspect, but she and James would not keep their secret forever. Soon they would have to announce their love to the entire world! *Remember Diana!* Caroline had written.

Remember Diana, indeed! What little sympathy Judith might have harbored for Caroline's romantic plight now vanished. How would her uncle react, were he to learn that his youngest daughter desired to marry the nephew of the man who had nearly ruined his elder daughter's reputation? After briefly considering the muddle of Caroline's affairs, Judith gave it up. She had never permitted herself the luxury of the wild, disobedient passion that Diana had apparently indulged in and that Caroline was immersed in now; and the day was too fine for worry.

Beyond the village, they waded deep into the vast fields between Raglan and Monmouth, fields so rolling that they seemed to be in constant motion. Great patches of color quilted the horizon, afar off with fields of poppies alternating with purple loosestrife and clover, closer by with fields of wheat and barley and rye. The heat was hazing the land with sweet smells, of campion and wild basil mingling with the grains. The air was abuzz with the hum of bees blundering from wildflower to wildflower. It was a glorious day and a glorious ride through glorious, sun-ripening fields.

White and fluffy clouds were amassing directly above them. Two shafts of light, churchlike in their angles and effect, cleft the high billows and blessed the prospect with sudden splendor. More clouds gathered, and several pillars of sunlight came down in straight shafts to earth to become golden columns of light holding up the delicate weight of the sky. It was, Judith thought, a magical summer's day.

The trees of Somerset Park loomed ahead, doilies of green against the sky, marking the halfway point to Monmouth. Soon enough they were surrounded by bird song and leaf, the branches on both sides of the path having met and married to create a filigreed canopy overhead. This, too, was glorious. What, Judith wondered, could Sir Robert have thought would possibly go wrong, for had she not already determined that the day would be perfect?

As if in answer to her idle question, the first drop of rain fell. One drop, then two, then three. Within moments of the first drop, the head scout, who had closed his distance for the ride through the woods, had turned back to assure himself of his mistress's well-being. That done, he helped the women dispose their riding cloaks across their shoulders.

The scout informed Judith that they were near a fork in the path that would lead them to one of the many sod cottages dotting the park, if she desired shelter. Judith shook her head, pointing out that Monmouth was not more than an hour away.

And if it should begin to rain harder?

"We won't melt," was Judith's response. "Besides," she argued, tempting fate, "how bad can it get?"

The head scout obligingly trotted off to resume his position. The travel continued uneventfully and not unpleasantly at first, for the rain was indeed light and intermittent. The party of six had entered the most densely forested and hilly section of the park. The path was twisting and difficult, but Judith and Edith were competent horsewomen. When the rain began to fall at a steadier rate, Judith began to reconsider her earlier command; but it was not until Edith's horse stumbled on a rock and tossed a shoe that Judith decided it would now be wise to seek shelter.

Judith turned in her saddle to look behind her, but the path twisted too much at that point for her to discern the backriders. The outriders ahead were also out of sight. However, she distinctly heard their horses. Strangely, though, the sounds seemed to be coming from beside her, off into the trees, but she knew well enough that dense woods often distorted sounds.

Untroubled, she turned back to Edith and said, "Stay here a moment and wait for the men behind to catch up with you. I'll go ahead and let the others know that we desire a change in plans."

Edith agreed, and Judith prodded her mare forward. The little business of a thrown shoe and the inconvenience of the light rain would not hinder her journey very much. She remembered having passed a fork in the path not too many minutes ago, and she surmised that this path would lead to a cottage.

Out of sight of Edith, two things happened at once. It suddenly began to rain considerably harder, and just as the irascible thought *Drat Sir Robert and his predictions!* crossed Judith's mind, a pair of arms materialized out of the dense foliage. They snatched Judith's reins from her unresisting hands and tossed them over Barbary's head. Another hand was brought down on the mare's flanks, and suddenly Judith found herself dragged off the path and away into the trees. She clutched desperately at the pommel of the saddle to keep her seat on the mare.

The terrain was immediately rockier and steeper, and it took all of Judith's attention and skill in those first few moments of panic to remain upright. Through the surprise, she registered a man's voice beside her uttering a rude oath, followed by the words, "Thunder and lightning! I thought she'd never go off alone!"

To which another male voice, on her other side, replied with an affirmative grunt and the practical observation, "Saved us a bit o' trouble, she did."

By the time Judith had recovered enough to call for help, the heavens had opened up like a tap and were pouring their fury down on forest, fell, and field for miles around, effectively drowning out her exclamations. Riding a precarious sidesaddle at a canter and not in possession of her reins, Judith was helpless. She quickly considered saving herself by jumping off the horse, but just as quickly rejected the idea. Once the initial shock had passed, she realized, with a greater horror, that it might be some time before anyone of her traveling party realized that she was missing and that when he did, he would have no way of knowing in which direction she had gone. Nor could anyone have easily found her. The thick curtain of rain falling on the already rain-soaked ground was combining with the summer heat to turn the forest into a steambath where visibility was low.

Although disoriented, she had a sense that they were heading in a direction opposite from Monmouth. In her alarming progress through the forest, she waged continual hand combat with the branches hanging low and was weighted down ever more by her skirts now dragging with water. She had not even had a moment to draw the hood of her riding cape over her head. It would have been a wasted movement anyway, for soon enough, a branch clawed at her and snatched the cloak from her shoulders. Its loss was a blessing, for without it she was lighter. A moment later, another branch grabbed and ripped the pouch from her waist and, with it, the reason she had undertaken the day's journey.

As the trees became less thick and the ground less rocky, the riders increased speed. Judith, already breathless, now had to contend with a full gallop. They scrambled down sloping, uneven trails, drove up muddy ones, and charged across lesser rises. They splashed through fords, and Judith was so soaked she no longer noticed the water spattering her boots and hem.

In brief moments, she assessed the two men who now held her life in their hands. The one holding her mare's reins looked squat and muscular and hideously ugly. Since they could not ride through the forest three abreast, Judith had no very clear picture of her other captor's face. What she did see of him suggested to her that he was as long and lean as the other was short and stocky.

Judith had lost track of time and was teetering on the edge of a certain, sodden despair when she saw, through the gray stew, a bridge in the midst of a clearing beyond which rose a gentle hill. Perhaps they had reached some kind of meeting point.

Hardly had her captors halted the horses before she heard wild shouts and curses pierce the fog. Then before her dazed and weary eyes she saw a half dozen horsemen swarm down a steep hill off to the side and thunder into the clearing where she waited, helpless and frozen, with nothing and no one to protect her.

One dark man, astride a raw-boned brute, directed his fellow riders over to the bridge. He shouted to Judith's captors and, liking what he saw, cantered over to them. He thumbed Judith's long and lean captor over to the group of riders heading toward the bridge.

The dark man drew rein next to Judith. Her heart quailing at the fate that might await her, she had only a moment to take his measure. He was as wet as she. His dark curls were plastered to his head and rivulets of water were coursing down the deeply carved lines of his lean face. He exchanged brief words with Judith's other captor. When he turned to look at her, Judith saw the gleam of satisfaction in the depths of his eyes rapidly change to genuine surprise.

"Good God!" he exclaimed, addressing the stocky man. "I asked you to bring back a beauty, and you have fetched me a drowned rat!"

Chapter
2

"SHE weren't bad looking before the soaking," the stocky man declared. "I got a good look at her through the trees before we took her. An eyeable lass!"

"How could this have happened?" the dark man snapped angrily.

"Oh, easily! We know her to be a wily wench but, thunder and lightning, not a mite of trouble did she give us! It was the simplest thing in the world to wait for her to break off from her traveling party and then she came with us"—the man snapped his fingers—"docile as a baby!"

Judith was making an heroic attempt to recover her wits. "Have I—have I been . . . *abducted*?" she breathed.

The dark man asked sharply, "Traveling party?"

"There were six of them," the stocky man answered. "We picked up their trail after you sent us to the south forest."

"We've never known her to travel before in a party," the dark man said, frowning.

The stocky man rubbed his nose. "Well, who's to say that this isn't the first time? We had to follow them for the longest distance. It's a wonder they didna hear us, but then, Allan and me, we've done it before and we'll do it again!"

"Was there another woman in the traveling party?" the dark man wanted to know.

The stocky man assured him cheerfully that there was. "But she was more of an old prune, and nothing at all to compare to this one," he explained.

"I *have* been abducted!" Judith exclaimed, still incredulous.

Ignoring this, the dark man flashed impatiently, "The woman we're looking for is *blond*!"

"I know that, but I thought she might be wearing a wig," the stocky man defended himself.

"Evidently not!" the master blazed, gesturing to Judith's rain-soaked locks which were unmistakably her own and unmistakably brunette.

"But you said—!" the stocky one began, then reversed himself. "Well, when I saw *this* one in the woods and no other, I thought to myself, 'She's a pretty one. Not a beauty, but she'll do!'"

"It's a deal of time we've wasted!" the dark man said, biting into his words. "And all for nothing!" Then, as if to himself, "Strange how her trail evaporated after London! But it was nearly certain that she was headed in this direction and most probably on her way to Holyhead."

"Well, this one's an eyeable lass," the stocky one insisted plaintively, with a rude nod of his head to Judith, "when her hair isn't matted down like that, and she's not shivering from the wet! And with her clothes damp and clinging, you can see well enough that she's—"

Judith had followed enough of the exchange to break in at this opportune moment. "Am I to understand," she said, "that it was your plan to abduct some poor woman and that you managed to abduct *the wrong one*?"

"Oh, no!" the stocky man answered, unabashed.

"No?" she echoed.

The stocky man rubbed his nose. "Not 'some poor woman' but a thief!"

"Well!" was all Judith could find to say to that. She returned her gaze to the dark man for a better explanation.

The master shifted in his saddle. "The devil's in it," he

said slowly. The fire had drained from his voice. It was edged now with disappointment. "There's been a mistake."

The rain was continuing to fall steadily. "A mistake?" Judith repeated, now fully outraged and gesturing to the heavens. "You call subjecting me to the terrors of a wild ride in company of two obviously deranged men through rough country and in a rainstorm a *mistake*? I don't call it a mistake! I call it an abomination!"

"Spirited, too!" The stocky man grinned appreciatively, still selling Judith's good points.

The master looked down at Judith. "And very wet," he said, a fugitive note of humor creeping into his voice.

"Not to mention angry!" she said. Although aching in every muscle, Judith pulled herself as straight in the saddle as her rain-soaked clothing would allow. "And since your idiot of a manservant," she continued, "seems to have made an egregious *mistake* with regard to the errand you sent him on—and I do not doubt that it was an unutterably foolish one!—I would like to know, sir, what you intend to do to untangle this mess to my satisfaction!"

The master looked abstractedly into the mist for several long moments, then over to the bridge where the group of riders were awaiting, restively, his next command. "Nothing more can be done today," he said to no one in particular. His eye fell on the very bedraggled woman before him. He seemed to come to a decision. "My house stands just beyond that stream," he said, pointing to the bridge. "Since we are all of us soaked to the bone, I'll offer you the shelter of my home until we can think what best to do with you."

Although she found fault with his phrasing, she found none with his suggestion. She nodded. Her gesture contained a hint of regal condescension, but the effect was somewhat spoiled by the rain trickling down her hair and face and into the neck of her dress. Once again in possession of her reins, she wheeled Barbary into step beside the raw-boned beast. As for the stocky man, the master sent him ahead with a few curt commands.

Judith put a firm guard on her tongue, onto which had sprung a fine bouquet of comments and criticisms. She decided that a demand for explanations of this abominable mistake would have to wait until she was in less undignified circumstances. The master must have come to the same decision, for, apparently feeling no need to explain himself, he gave Judith only the impersonal directions necessary for her to negotiate the pathway to his house.

Once across the bridge, they mounted a swell of earth which was banked by a brick wall with a low stone coping in disrepair. At the top of the path, they turned into an allee bordered by great elms and oaks and an overgrown yew hedge. At the end of it stood a crumbling brick gate. This opened onto a courtyard which was ringed by an old rose garden run riot. Through the gray gloom of the rain and the advancing afternoon, Judith perceived a large house, probably built in the previous century and evidently not maintained since. It was of dark old brick, hugged by ivy, with a pattern of stones climbing the corners to a high stone balustrade with carved beasts guarding the large, dark entry.

Although the house was not terribly inviting, Judith's very dampened spirits rose at the sight of dry shelter. The master halted in the center of the courtyard and swung easily out of the saddle in order to help Judith dismount. Strong arms encircled her waist to lift her and then set her down. The master threw the reins to a man who was standing ready to take Barbary and the master's steed to what looked to be a very dilapidated stable.

"This way, ma'am," he said. "I'm sure you will feel more like yourself when you are dry and have had something fortifying to drink!"

Standing beside him now, Judith had to look up to reply. His face was politely impassive, but his voice held a faint note of spurious courtesy. Judith confined herself to offering the conventional response. She followed his lead toward the house.

The path was overgrown, the entry cobwebbed, the heavy oaken door weather-scarred. Judith was hardly surprised when, with a push of the master's hand, it creaked open on rusty hinges.

With a "Welcome!" and a wide sweep of his arm, her

host ushered her in. Judith stepped across the threshold. Ready to embrace the dry warmth at first glance, she had to stifle a gasp at the overwhelming shabbiness of the Main Hall.

It might have been a beautiful room once, perhaps fifty years ago. The paneling covering the walls from floor to ceiling was rich but black with age and old smoke. The two spacious window recesses, jutting off from the long wall, were lined with large windows of stained glass and were probably once very charming on sunny and gray days alike, but now the majority of the little colored panes were gone and had been boarded up with rough-hewn planks. The ceiling was a masterpiece of molded joists which crisscrossed to form a coffered surface. The beams themselves were decorated with scrolling patterns of intertwined hop stalks, which provided an embroiderylike relief, without spoiling the pattern of the beams. However, the scrolls were so encrusted with dust and dirt that the delicate effect was lost. The most charming feature of the room must have been at one time the dais. It was quite cleverly contrived and ran the entire length of the far short wall. In the Hall's better days, it must have served as a stage for musicians or even players, for it was framed in a tattered velvet curtain which sagged on its cords with the weight of age and dirt.

The Hall was large and easily accommodated the dozen men or so in it. Several lounged in one window recess, one idly strumming a lute, another surrounded by curling sheafs of papers and busily scratching another sheet with a quill. At the near end of the Hall a low fire burned in the capacious fireplace, warding off the damp. There most of the occupants of the room were clustered in a raucous knot. They were evidently dicing. Above the heads of the kneeling men ran the chimney's wide mantelshelf, also made from carved wood, and above it there appeared to be carved portraits of the original owner of the house, his wife, and their children. They looked down their wooden noses in deep disapproval of the activity going forward on the unswept flagstones of the hearth beneath them.

At Judith's entrance, the men looked up from their occupations, faces alight with expectation.

To stem the flow of their various calls of "Good work!" and "At last!" and "The thieving wench!" and rather more lively, less genteel exclamations, the master held up a hand and announced that the day's mission had not been successful.

"And I'll ask you to mind your manners, lads," he admonished them, "for Will has nabbed us a woman who I'm guessing is nothing like the fair robber Rosamunda!"

He then issued a series of commands which sent a number of men scurrying from the room. He shooed the dicers from the hearth and bade the others continue with whatever it was they were doing. They did so reluctantly.

The master led Judith to the fireplace, peeling off his dripping wet doublet as he did so. "There's nothing for it, ma'am, but to dry yourself here. It's a bachelor establishment," he said without the slightest hint of apology, "and I've no woman to attend you." He hung the doublet haphazardly on a hook protruding from the mantelshelf. "Neither will I be able to bear you company until you dry, for I've left too much undone today as it is, and all for a useless errand."

These casual words and gestures instantly dispelled the awkwardness Judith had felt at sight of the room and the company of men. "Oh, no, no!" she said, stopping with her host before the fire. "Don't trouble yourself on my account! One does not expect a maidservant when one is abducted."

She was not surprised that her tone of derisive hauteur drew nothing more than an impertinent smile from her host. At that moment, one of the men who had been sent from the room reentered with an armful of white cloth. The master took several steps toward the man.

"In fact," Judith continued to her host's back, "I have come to see that when one is seized from a forest path in broad daylight, one cannot expect too much in the way of courtesy—"

What was to be a masterful condemnation of her host and his henchmen was never completed. The man carrying the armful of cloth said, "Here are the linens you desired. What next would you like me to do, Lambert?"

Judith stopped in mid-sentence. She blinked. "Lambert?" she said in disbelief. "You are Lambert?"

The man turned, his eyes suddenly curious and assessing. He took several towels from the man's arms and, bearing these, he returned to her side. He bowed carelessly. "Your Servant."

Astonished, Judith said the first thing that came to mind. "I thought you were at Whitehall."

"I am lately come from London," he affirmed.

Judith reappraised her host frankly and in disbelief. Could this be James Lambert, Caroline's latest love? Phrases from Caroline's letter—*My love has the greatest address of the most splendid cavalier at court!* and *He is as handsome in words and deeds as he is in countenance!* and *A more earnest love I shall never meet! He is all goodness, all seriousness!*—jangled through her mind. None of them seemed to describe, even remotely, the unhandsome, unchivalrous man standing before her. Judith found Caroline's judgment at all times imperfect, but even Caroline, Judith thought, could not err so dramatically.

Then, in that flash of a wide-eyed second, Judith saw the light in the depths of Lambert's eyes deepen into a distinct twinkle of amusement. A smile had come to hover at the corners of his hard mouth, transforming the harsh lines of his visage into a less forbidding arrangement. His eyes, she noted, were a deep gray. Suddenly she found them, his smile, and his whole face unexpectedly attractive, so that she wondered, in the next half second, whether Caroline's taste in men might not have strangely, subtly, improved.

"A towel, ma'am, to dry yourself?" Lambert asked, proferring her a large square of linen.

She took one wordlessly. Still captive to confusion, she watched him rub his own towel over his head and face and neck. Then she remembered Caroline's description of him that had given Judith the mental image of a fop. Even allowing for the drenching, no amount of liberal interpretation could call Lambert's dress modish, much less that of a splendid cavalier. To be sure, he was a well-built man, but rangily muscular rather than graceful. Stripped of his doublet and with his linen shirt clinging damply to his torso, she could see that he possessed a good pair of shoulders. However, his shirt had hardly a scrap of lace at the collar, and from the doublet hanging before the fire fluttered not one ribbon. His breeches were not fashionable but plain cut and tapered into leather thigh-boots that were well worn and unpolished.

His head emerged from the towel, revealing hair still damp but now curling at random. Judith was surprised into a blunt honesty. "*You* are Lambert? I find that very difficult to believe, for you are not at all what I expected!"

Lambert bowed again, perfunctorily. "Neither are you what I expected," he replied with every evidence of good humor. "On that score, at least, we are quits."

"Very amusing!" she said lightly. "Almost as amusing as my ride through the woods just now!" She composed herself and said with pardonable self-importance, "Before we bandy words any longer, I will take leave to inform you, sir, that I am Judith Beaufort!" When this information had no appreciable effect on him, Judith added, with dramatic emphasis, "Caroline's cousin!"

This news affected him. He said to his manservant, "Place the rest of the linens here, John, and that will be all!" When he turned to Judith, it seemed that he had forgotten all about his other, pressing tasks. He was regarding her with lively interest. "Are you?" he said.

"Indeed, I am," Judith replied, satisfied with his reaction.

"I was, of course, wondering who you might be!"

Judith smiled, a little pityingly. "I must suppose that you did not dream to have mistakenly abducted one of Caroline's kin!"

"You suppose correctly."

"Nor do I suppose can you imagine what she will say when she hears about it!"

"I have not the most distant guess," he replied. "What do *you* think she will say?"

"She will be greatly shocked," Judith said with composure.

"You mean to tell her about it?" he asked. "I am wondering why you would!"

"It is certainly none of *my* business why you should be careering through the countryside attempting to abduct some woman named Rosamunda," Judith said with a touch of scorn. "Ah, but Caroline! That is quite another matter entirely! As difficult as it will be for her to learn of it, she must be told! Do not think I relish the task, however. It will not be easy to explain such a—such an *outrageous* incident in a letter."

"Indeed not!" he agreed sympathetically. "On the other hand, you might simply tell her of it when next you see her."

"You would like that, wouldn't you?" Judith said, regarding him with a kindling eye.

Lambert seemed rather taken aback by this. "I can't say that I have a strong opinion on it, one way or the other!"

"As if I would be fooled by such a statement," Judith said, scornful again. "I must write her, since I won't be seeing her for some time yet. She is still in London, as you must know."

He did not respond to this but asked instead, "Do I gather you were not on your way to London, then?"

"I will not be going to London for another two months," she answered him, "*not* that it is any of your business! For your information, I was on my way to Monmouth!"

"Bad luck!" her host replied, a little too casually to Judith's way of thinking. "We're on the other side of the forest from Monmouth, near Abergavenny. Speaking of Monmouth, though, I wonder if you could tell me whether Sir Brian is still alive."

Judith gaped slightly at the question which was entirely tangential to their train of conversation. "Indeed, sir, the last time I saw him, he was very much alive!"

"And when was that?"

"On my last visit to Monmouth. A month ago, it must have been."

Lambert nodded. "And old Raymond?"

"The Gate Keeper?" Judith replied. "No, he died."

"Recently?"

"Five years or so ago," Judith said, still too surprised by this turn of subject to do more than simply answer his questions.

"A pity," Lambert commented. "But I've always been fond of Sir Brian. Now that I'm in the neighborhood, I shall have to make a point of seeing the old curmudgeon!"

Judith bridled. "I will desire you to speak of Sir Brian respectfully, for you must know that he is a relative of mine."

"Is he?"

"He is a cousin of Caroline's mother's sister," Judith informed him, "as if you didn't know."

"I didn't! But I wondered when we would come back to Caroline!"

"Soon enough, sir," she replied stiffly, "despite all your efforts to divert the subject."

"You can't blame me for trying," he said with a rakish smile.

He was toying with her! Judith was not at all surprised and, indeed, was almost gratified to have her low opinion of James Lambert confirmed. However, she had not expected him to be so self-possessed when faced with the knowledge that he had just abducted the cousin of the woman he wished to marry. And now having seen his house, Judith no longer doubted Lambert's motives in paying court to one of the wealthiest heiresses in the kingdom. Caroline was an attractive young woman, but her money was even more so. It was obvious to Judith that Lambert was no more than a fortune hunter.

Her thoughts diverted down this new path, she turned her head to look about the room and said, "This could not, after all, be the Hall of the Lambert estate!"

"It's not," her host informed her kindly. "It was formerly known as Speke Hall, and only a few acres come with it, making it more of a house than a grand estate."

She had heard of the place but had never before visited it. "*Speke* Hall? How came you in possession of Speke Hall?"

"I bought it."

"What do you mean?"

He smiled at that. "Squire Speke's heirs sold it to me."

"It's yours?" she asked skeptically. Now was not the moment to mince words. "I thought that the Lamberts had lost all their wealth."

"The old man gambled away the Lambert estates and fortune a good twenty years ago," he replied in a tone of unconcern.

"But this house—?"

"I said that I have bought it."

Before she had a moment to absorb this new information, a second man appeared at Lambert's side bearing a tray on which stood two glasses and a full decanter. Lambert bade the man place the tray on the fireplace seat. When the manservant withdrew, Lambert offered a glass to Judith, but she declined. She did not wish to prolong this encounter nor to accept too much hospitality from Caroline's latest love. She had also discovered that it had become difficult to maintain a dignified conversation while dripping wet. She began to mop ineffectually at her hair, her face, and her dress which was plastered rather immodestly to her body.

Lambert, meanwhile, had taken another linen and lightly rubbed his neck and torso, then slung the towel around his neck. He picked up a glass, raised it to Judith, and took a sip. Then, completely at his ease, he propped an arm against the mantelshelf. He leaned against it and meditatively watched Judith's efforts to repair her toilette.

"There now! You're drying out nicely!" he said.

Judith looked up to watch him watching her. Not to be undone by his appraisal nor drawn into unwise comment, she arched a mobile brow and returned to her ministrations.

"Though I think your dress may be ruined," he commented helpfully.

"It most certainly is, no thanks to you and your henchmen," she returned.

"Unjust! You would have received the drenching even without Will's intervention. You must have still been a good way from Monmouth when you, er, caught his fancy in the woods."

"Less than an hour away," she retorted. "In Will's good company, I spent at least three!"

"But even an hour in the rain would have ruined your dress," he observed.

The reasonableness of that remark did not improve her opinion of her host. "We were not speaking of the rain or my clothing," she confined herself to saying, "but of—"

"But of your family, I believe," he interrupted. "Tell me more about it!" he invited congenially.

"Not so fast! We were speaking of the illustrious Lambert family although even by your own admission the family titles are quite worthless!"

"They were never worth a thing to me, in all events," he said.

This bald admission momentarily disarmed her. She recovered. "Then why, may I ask," she said, thinking to catch him at his tricks, "should Caroline write so profusely about them!"

"Ah yes! Caroline again!" he said. "We seem to come back to her name with remarkable regularity!"

Judith was not diverted. "You have not answered my question!"

"I cannot imagine why she should write anything about them, or what they have to do with me."

It seemed to Judith that the man was perversely enjoying himself. "Because she is a well-bred young woman, as well you know, and . . . and quite *impressionable*, as you also know!" Judith paused for breath, then said determinedly, "Pray, excuse my plain speaking, but my family duty demands it of me. I am quite convinced that you have grossly misled Caroline about the . . . the nobility of your character!"

Lambert was surprised, even shocked. "I?" he said. "I have never, to my knowledge, misled her about anything."

"To your knowledge!" Judith jumped on the phrase. "Well, sir, just as I can see that you are not as young as I might have supposed, you, too, can see that I am considerably older—that is, I am *a few* years older than Caroline! So do not try to hoodwink *me* with innocent protests and disavowals. With your age and your experience and yes, sir, your charming smile!—no, no! do not think it will affect me!—I do not doubt that you were easily able to capture a young girl's affections! But to tell me that your titles mean nothing—! And all this after my abduction and my firsthand knowledge of your very casual manners! Well! I certainly cannot guess what Caroline will say to you when next she sees you!''

Lambert was listening with deep appreciation to this speech, but Judith's last phrase caused him to ponder a moment. ''If she is as well bred as you claim,'' he said reflectively, ''I imagine she will curtsy and say something like 'Pleased to meet you.' ''

Judith's still damp bosom swelled. ''Are you saying—'' she began.

''That I've never met Caroline.''

''Do you know who I am, sir?'' she demanded angrily.

''Certainly. You told me not too many minutes ago that you are Judith Beaufort,'' he replied. ''Caroline's cousin.''

''Then I fear for your understanding, sir! You *dare* to say that you don't know who Caroline is?''

''It is rather I who fear for yours, ma'am! I told you not a moment ago that I have never met her.''

''Are you not Lambert?'' she rapped out.

''That, too, I told you!'' he said, regarding her with considerable amusement. ''In fact, I told you who I was before you told me who you were. Though in all fairness, I should say that I have found this to be a damned confusing conversation, so perhaps you have not quite grasped the particulars of who I am!''

Judith was in so much sympathy with this view of their encounter that her anger threatened to sputter out on a laugh.

''Much better!'' Lambert encouraged.

''I *will* not laugh!'' Judith said, making an effort to control herself. ''And if you tell me now that you are *not* James Lambert, I will—''

''I thought it must be something like that!'' he interrupted. ''I never said I was James Lambert. Although I now gather that my nephew must be making up to your cousin Caroline. And to think that the last time I saw James, he was hardly breeched!''

"Your nephew—?" she began, aghast. "Then you must be . . . you must be—"

Almost before he said it, Judith knew who it was. "Yes," he said with another slight bow, "I am Charles Lambert."

Judith had thought that nothing in this extraordinary encounter could increase her astonishment. She was wrong. Her already deranged thoughts began to spin wildly. "But you are—But you are—"

Lambert cocked a brow and let her flounder.

"You are on the Continent!" she said, finding an admirable finish to her sentence.

"I am in Wales, not far from Abergavenny," he corrected.

Judith took a moment to put her reeling thoughts in order. Then, with admirable calm, said, "I think I would like that drink now, if you please!"

Charles Lambert was so kind to pour her a glass of wine. He handed it to her politely. She took a sip and felt her nerves steady. After another sip, she had recovered enough of her good sense to look over the rim of her glass and to say, "What inconsiderate treatment! You must have guessed I had mistaken your identity. You might have saved us both the confusion if you had said at the beginning that you had no idea who Caroline was!"

"It was more appealing to guess," he replied readily, "and you have a certain flair for the dramatic which I enjoyed. In any case, I was entertained by the prospect that anyone would claim to know me in the neighborhood after all this time. I knew we would sort it out eventually!"

"Meaning, I suppose, that in default of having tracked down your Rosamunda you decided you had nothing better to do than to amuse yourself at my expense?"

"Or you at mine," he replied. "You seemed to enjoy reading me the list of my shortcomings! My wits were fully engaged!"

"Then engage them to good purpose, sir," Judith invited. "We came to your house to sort out this miserable affair, and we have yet to discuss just what you plan to do to restore me to Monmouth!''

At this juncture, the stocky man who was the cause of Judith's present predicament entered the room and crossed to Lambert's side. He, too, was still damp after the day's excursion. "I found the trunk you wanted," he said. "Dick and Allan are bringing it in now!''

"Trunk?" Judith asked suspiciously.

"A trunk of clothes. Women's clothes," the stocky man answered. "You can't be wearing that gear. You'll catch your death!''

"But I do not wish to change clothes," Judith said, remaining calm. "I wish to be on my way to Monmouth.''

"Monmouth!" the stocky man exclaimed. "Never today. You'll wade no farther than the courtyard now mired in mud!''

As if to illustrate his point, the wind whipped up around the house just then and buckets of rain seemed to pour onto the roof.

"And the master has instructed a bed to be made up for you in one of the upstairs rooms as well," Will continued cheerfully. "You're going nowhere this day!''

Judith's mouth fell open. She turned to look accusingly at Lambert who smiled and said, offhandedly, "Dry clothes and a dry bed are the very least I can offer you.''

"This is *not* what I had in mind when I set off today!" Judith stated with justifiable indignation. "I should have been at Monmouth hours ago!''

An old trunk was borne in then on the shoulders of two men, evidently Dick and Allan, the former incredibly large, the latter long and lanky and whom Judith recognized as one of her captors. The men deposited the trunk at Judith's feet. They, along with Will, were dismissed.

When the thongs were unbuckled and the lid raised, Judith beheld a motley heap of garments, all of them women's clothing. "I thought you had a bachelor establishment," she said to Lambert on a puzzled note. She reached down into the trunk and drew out a bold, gaudy dress of crimson. Catching at the most plausible explanation, she said, "Am I to gather that you keep these clothes on hand for any chance abduction you might undertake?"

"Any chance abduction?" he repeated humorously.

"Today is a case of history repeating itself, is it not?" Judith said.

"I don't recall having abducted anyone before," Lambert replied.

Judith let the immodest dress fall and looked up at him. Although thoroughly displeased with her present situation, her face was suddenly alive with mischievous delight. "You don't yet know who *I* am, do you, sir?" she challenged with a little relish. "Or who Caroline is!"

Lambert raised a brow in inquiry.

"Caroline," she pronounced, "is Diana's sister!"

Charles Lambert's face was an interesting study in emotions. It was first blank, then startled, after which it dawned with understanding. He held up a hand. "No, let me guess! If you are Caroline's cousin, you are Diana's as well."

"Their father is my uncle."

"And if you were on your way to Monmouth," he said, "you must have been coming from Raglan."

"That is correct."

His reaction was not all that she had hoped, for he did not display the embarrassment she might have thought proper. Instead, Lambert bellowed over his shoulder, "Will! In the future you must be more careful whom you choose to grab in the woods! Don't you know it's bad for business to abduct Somerset's niece?"

Chapter
3

THE tone of his master's voice drew Will back like a magnet. "If my name isn't Will Puckett!" he exclaimed. "A gentlewoman!" He surveyed Judith critically up and down. "How could I have guessed?"

"How, indeed?" Judith replied with irony, almost enjoying herself. "You could certainly *not* have determined that from the fact that I was traveling in company of very sedate escorts! The kind of traveling company, if I do not mistake the matter, that your Rosamunda was avoiding!"

"You have a point there," Will admitted. "A woman like Rosamunda would not come in the way of gentlefolk, so I'm thinking. But we've been trailing her since—"

"Since London," Lambert broke in very smoothly, "and we've still not caught up with her, as you perceive. However, given that she has been so difficult to track down, you will have to excuse Will his belief that any traveling party—even a very respectable one—might be suspect as one in which she had chosen to hide herself."

Judith was not yet satisfied. "And my clothing?" she wanted to know, holding out her once elegant but now ruined skirts for Will's inspection. "Did you imagine Rosamunda to be wearing so proper an ensemble? I confess I do not!"

Will had the answer to that. "Oh, a professional lady such as she has no doubt played a strumpet, milkmaid, and a queen," he said, "and should be able to play a gentlewoman well enough!"

Judith had not articulated to herself Rosamunda's probable profession. However, hearing the range of this lady's repertoire momentarily shook Judith's self-possession. She blushed.

"I have reason to believe that Rosamunda's main profession is in the theater," Lambert explained.

Judith recovered. "She is an actor? A *female* actor?" she asked, justifiably cautious. "There isn't such in England."

"Rosamunda is Italian," Lambert said.

"Oh!" Judith turned the matter over in her mind. "But a woman on the stage—? It's a disturbing thought."

"It's a matter of perspective," Lambert replied. "In Italy, and Spain for that matter, they consider the spectacle of a man dressed in woman's clothing to be even more disturbing than that of theatrical women, and so they have made allowances for actresses to appear in public."

Although she was tempted to pursue this fascinating subject, she had become accustomed to her host's slippery ways and so inquired with great aplomb, "And just what does this have to do with *you*?"

The answer came from Judith's side. "We are, all of us, in the service of Thespis, ma'am," said a melodious, masculine voice.

She turned to see a smiling youth standing before her. He was a handsome young man, lantern-jawed with black hair tied back prettily and black eyes heavily fringed and beautifully browed. He was neatly but not lavishly attired, and he was holding a beribboned lute in his hand, which identified him as one of the occupants of the window recess Judith had noticed upon her entrance. He bowed gracefully.

"Good mistress," he said, "you see before you a man named Robin. To see me thus is to see a man of modest address and unassuming manners! But amongst these men—" he gestured about the Hall "—my fellow players, I become quite a different Robin entirely! In this company my hidden character is permitted to flourish, and I become a—'' he paused provocatively ''—a comedian! Oh, of the finest! Although the modest man in me admits,'' he said with a slyly apologetic smile and several sidelong glances, ''that even a lesser star shall shine the brighter in dim company! Still and away, I vow I could wring your heart by the smallest gesture and a whispered line, expertly executed and at just the right moment! Few leave my performances with dry eyes!''

Judith's eyes had widened considerably. However, at this point in her extraordinary adventure, she was in sufficient command of herself to accept this amazing, mellifluous speech along with the rest. Having followed the handsome young man's gestures and looks, she perceived that his sweet voice had lured the men in the room from their leisure and had drawn them to the fireplace around which they formed a loose circle. Lambert had taken a step back and was watching the proceedings.

A lean, active youngster elbowed his way past Robin, pushing him aside. ''Aye, Robin, they weep with despair at your wretched acting!'' he said. ''Why, I'll play my Widow Medler to your Mistress Lucre any day, and we'll see who makes them cry the more! Only *I* make them cry with laughter! It's my Puck that does it,'' he explained to Judith. ''Never mind that beardless youth,'' the boy continued, nodding at Robin, thereby dismissing a man who must have been several years his senior, ''for he's only so much talk and no action! But in one of *my* performances! Ah, *that's* worth the trip to Whitechurch or Marstow! The name is Tom, ma'am!'' he finished with a crisp bow.

''Enough, you braggarts!'' boomed the basso profundo of a burly, barrel-chested man who swaggered into the center of the circle. Judith recognized him as one of the bearers of the trunk. ''It is *I* the audiences come to see, for I am a—''

His dramatic pause was filled with the timorous, high-pitched taunt of ''Bully!'' causing everyone, including Judith, to laugh. The bully's face suffused a choleric red, he clenched his fists into the size of murderous eggplants, and seemed so entirely capable of violence that Judith knew a moment of fear. During a hushed, expectant moment the bully's bulging eye roamed the circle seeking his prey. Then, unexpectedly, he unclenched his hands, threw his fingers heavenward, tossing off his anger as if it were no more than a handful of powder. He turned to Judith and, in a voice modulated with geniality and self-control, commented on his own impressive performance, "A measure of my skill, mistress! The smallest measure! Is it any wonder that the audiences flock to see me? They cheer nightly for Richard!"

Judith was charmed. "Do I find myself in the presence of the fair Columbine, the lackey Harlequin, and the fearsome Rhodomont?" she asked, turning to Robin, Tom, and Dick in turn. "It's merely an educated guess, however, since I have never seen an improvisational troupe."

While the three players took their bows, suggesting that Judith had guessed aright, another figure made his way to the center. His hair was disheveled, his shirt and doublet askew, his breeches stuffed carelessly into his boots. His clothing hung on his finely boned form. He was also twirling a quill in one ink-stained hand.

"Improvisational troupe?" he repeated on a frown of displeasure. "They have not enough wit about them to improvise! No! We are not an *improvisational* troupe, ma'am!"

"You, sir, must be a writer," Judith said.

He performed a complicated bow of assent. "Harold Webster is the name. I believe my fame has spread. Perhaps, ma'am, you have heard of me?"

Judith had not, but did not say so, nor did she have the opportunity, for Mr. Webster was continuing. "I am the most versatile, the most dynamic of writers—the playwright! It is my dialogues that the audiences come to hear! My scenes! My plots! My poetry! My originality!"

Jeers and jests ensued. "Your threadbare plays would be nothing without us!" "My part in your latest farce was a dismal affair and far too short!" "Your last original piece was taken almost entirely from Tourneur!" and the like.

"You are a playwright, then," Judith said at the next interval.

"Yes, I am a true creative artist. Not for me the well-worn grooves of the old comedies that every market audience knows by heart!" Mr. Webster said with a proud toss of his head and a flick of his quill at the circle of men. "Although," he added, anticlimactically, "I have been known to make use of stock characters and plots when the occasion warrants."

Judith turned to Lambert. "And you, sir?"

"I've been a player," he admitted easily, "but I'm in another line of work now."

"Nevertheless, you continue to travel with the troupe," she observed. "Is it out of habit?"

"Hardly! I haven't traveled with this band of ruffians for years now," he said. "I engaged them only last week to help me find Rosamunda."

"Now, at least, the women's clothing is explained," she said, looking down at the trunk. "But tell me," she continued, for her curiosity had been mightily piqued, "what *does* all of this have to do with Rosamunda? I am still in the dark!"

After an infinitessimal pause, Lambert smiled and said, "It's a long story, ma'am. And as for the clothing, perhaps you had better choose a dress that will suit you for the evening. I would be a very poor host to allow you to remain damp for many minutes more!" He called to various men who had gathered to the circle. "You, Allan! Dick! Take the trunk upstairs to the room I've asked to have prepared for our guest! Mind that the fire is lit and the linens are dry! Be quick about it! John! To the kitchens! Not you, Will! Wait a moment!"

Lambert turned back to Judith. "Dry clothes, a dry bed, and a full meal is the most I can offer you." He cast his gaze out the window where the light of day was dying. "We shall sup as soon as you are ready. You have only to let me know."

Judith accepted both his dismissal and his subsequent invitation with what grace the occasion seemed to warrant. The weather outside had not abated, and she had come to feel that the atmosphere inside was considerably less threatening than she had originally supposed upon first sight of a roomful of idle, loutish men. She accepted, as well, the escort of Allan and Dick, the men shouldering the trunk, and left the room.

Lambert's eyes narrowed as they followed Judith's back. By the time Will reached his side, the Hall had emptied. Lambert slung an arm around his henchman's wide shoulders.

"Now, Will," Lambert said. His tone was companionable, his words were not. "Will, my friend, we have known one another a long time. You've seen me in and out of more trouble than I'll ever know, but this—! You've never before muddied the waters so badly! And here I had planned to deal with the old man neat as you please in London a month from now!"

Will showed some remorse by rubbing his nose. "Somerset's niece," he said with a wealth of meaning.

"And if she's half the stickler her uncle is, a very sweet deal may collapse."

"She does not seem to be," Will opined. "And she's a pretty thing, too, when she's dry. You'll see!"

"She might be as beautiful as her ravishing cousin Diana for all I care! What troubles me, rather, is what she will tell her uncle. I certainly do not relish the thought of Somerset sticking his long and well-informed nose into my business!"

"He'll never be able to guess the reason you have returned!" Will objected.

"True. But in my experience," Lambert said with a wry smile, "the old bastard has an uncanny knack of knowing everything. He's probably good for a deal or two, but I don't want to be at a disadvantage with him on account of his niece."

"Well, a good dinner set before her might turn her up sweet," Will suggested hopefully.

Lambert was shaking his head. "I'm trying to recall now what was said about Miss Beaufort recently at Whitehall. I wasn't closely attending, since I had never before heard of her." Unable to catch the memory, Lambert waved it away. "Whatever it is, I have the uneasy feeling that we must do much better than a good meal to 'turn her up sweet' as you say."

Judith, unaware of her host's misgivings, was led down a wide, central hallway that rambled off to a warren of rooms and up a broad staircase whose banister was thickly covered with dust. She was led down a hallway to a private alcove where a door stood open. The men entered that room, unloaded the trunk from their shoulders, then withdrew, closing the door behind them.

A fire soughed on the hearth. By its light, and in contrast to the rest of the house, she could tell that a rapid broom and dust clout had been sent through the room. The uncurtained bed had been hastily aired and looked dry and comfortable. A branch of candles stood on the table before which sat an upholstered stool and on which the thoughtful conveniences of a ewer of water and bowl had been placed. In addition, a comb and a brush had been conjured and a small, cracked mirror.

With a cry of dismay, Judith inspected herself in the mirror. Her face was smudged with dirt, and her hair was a tangled mass. She unpinned what remained of her coiffure to allow her hair to dry. She cast her eyes about the room, gazed a long moment at the closed door to the hallway, and stripped down to her chemise. She laid her clothing out before the fire, spreading it on an ancient, carved counterpane frame she found in one corner and shoved before the fire.

Judith dug through the trunk out of which cascaded dressings, purls, falls, squares, busks, bodices, scarfs, carcanets, rebatoes, borders, tires, fans, palisadoes, puffs, ruffs, cuffs, muffs, pulses, fusles, partlets, fardingales, kirtles, busk-points, stockings, stocking ties, and slippers. She held up in fascination one unsuitable dress after another. Then, toward the bottom of the trunk, she came across one style perhaps five years out of fashion. It had a pinked surface, a high waist, and full, elbow-length sleeves. It was evidently a theatrical costume, cut from a loud purple figured velvet of very poor quality that would have been eye-catching from a distance. Although Judith found no stomacher, she did find its matching skirt and, reaching the very bottom of the trunk, she even found some decent underclothes.

In a little under an hour, she had performed an adequate toilette. Very happy to be dry and thinking that she looked well enough, except for the fact that the dress's rather immodest bodice displayed more of her bosom than she liked, she emerged from her room. She swept down the hallway and the stairs with the confidence she would customarily assume going to a meal in the Great Hall at Raglan.

That confidence was soon put to the test by Lambert.

Upon arriving at the main Hall, she saw her host standing in front of the little stage, involved with several other men in the rigging of the tattered curtain. At her entrance, he quickly strode over to her. His hair was dry, and he had pulled his curls back with a black ribbon at the nape. He was freshly dressed, and his entire appearance confirmed her earlier suspicion that his dress, when dry, would be every bit as careless as his manners.

Crossing the room, he had as much opportunity to observe the details of her ensemble as she had had to survey him.

"Good God! What a color!" he said by way of greeting, running a disapproving eye over her toilette. "Not up to your usual standards, I warrant. Better this wretched dress, though, than wet clothes." He had apparently forgotten any intention he might have had to turn her up sweet.

Momentarily taken aback, Judith rapidly adjusted. She rallied him in turn. "Such an extravagant compliment! Trying to minimize the damage you did me earlier today?"

He smiled. "Have I offended you?"

"No, no! I am used to your opinions! At our first meeting, I believe you compared me to a drowned rat!"

He laughed. "Allow me to acquit myself by saying that the dress looks a good deal better on you than it does on Robin—despite his pretentions!" Thinking that Will had been right about the shapeliness of her figure, he offered her his arm. "Does that please you?"

"What woman could cavil at being told that a dress looks better on her than it does on a man?" Judith tossed off airily, accepting his escort.

Lambert laughed again, while Judith's attention was claimed by the transformations that had been wrought on the Hall. Tapers had been placed onto the wall sconces and lit. They cast a mellow glow around the room, enhancing it inherently pleasing proportions and aspects. The long trestle had been taken from its place near a wall and positioned in the center room. It was laid with a branch of candles and white nappery, indicating that supper was to be taken there. Three chairs from the scattering in the room sat straight on three sides of one end of the table.

"I hope you are hungry," Lambert said as he seated her so that she squarely faced the dais behind whose now-drawn curtain came a bustling of movement and whispers.

"Ravenous!" she replied. When Lambert seated himself on her left, she asked, "And for whom is the third place laid?"

"For the playwright," he answered.

Just then, Will scurried into the room, balancing on a platter two steaming plates. He placed these before Judith and Lambert with the words, "It's a mushroom soup! Not my best, but then you'll be knowing that having a guest was on short notice! Eat while it's hot!" Then he disappeared, mumbling something about preparing the next course.

"Do we start without Mr. Webster?" Judith asked.

"He's backstage," Lambert said, "instructing his cast. We're not to wait. He'll be here when he can."

"Oh, we are to be entertained this evening?"

"Entertained? I doubt it," Lambert answered. "But they do mean to present you with an example of their craft. I warn you that you have fallen in with a troupe of ham actors!"

Judith anticipated the performance—even a very bad one—with a modicum of pleasure, for she had little experience with the theater. Her uncle believed it to be immoral and permitted no performances at Raglan. She said nothing, but merely nodded.

Mr. Webster came from backstage just then to inform his future audience of his progress. He was working on script changes, he said, and was having trouble with several doltish men who called themselves actors. He said that if he could not join them for the meat dish, he would be there for the fish, and barring that, for the dulcet. "However, when I am consumed by the fires of creation," he told them loftily, "I am not hungry."

The soup was eaten with no further sign from Mr. Webster, nor was there any during the meat dish. If Judith had thought that the absence of the playwright might cause an awkwardness, her fears were soon allayed. Throughout the early part of the meal, easy, impersonal talk flowed. Through the meat dish and the second glass of wine, one topic led to the next to arrive, finally, at the topic of Speke Hall.

"And how long have you lived here?" Judith inquired.

"Today's the first day," Lambert answered. "We arrived only last night."

"Oh?" Judith said, then with sudden comprehension, "Ah!"

Lambert laughed at her tone and expression. "It is very dirty, I agree," he said congenially.

"Well, I *was* wondering how it was possible to live in such conditions," she replied honestly, "but now I understand. Have you recently acquired the house, then?"

"I bought it last week in London."

"So that explains it. I didn't think I had heard of any property changing hands in the region," Judith said. She looked about her with new eyes. "It's a pleasing room with great possibilities," she said, mentally cleaning and furnishing the Hall. "I wonder, however, why you did not have the house cleaned up, just a little, before moving in. It obviously has not been touched in years!"

"I bought it sight unseen," he informed her.

"Sight unseen?" she said, surprised. "How extraordinary!"

"Not really. Since I haven't been back to Gwent in fifteen

years, I bought the first house that I heard in London was for sale in the area. I didn't think it worth the trip to inspect it, and so—''

"Not been back in fifteen years?" Judith interrupted. "Not since—not since you—'' She found she could not finish the sentence.

"Not since I ran off with your cousin, you mean?"

"I would not be so tactless to mention it," Judith said primly.

Lambert laughed. "Tact, Miss Beaufort, does not seem to be one of your strengths."

"A failing that you, sir, apparently recognize without difficulty," she replied sweetly. "If I did not mention the incident, it was only to spare you pain."

"Pain? How so?"

"Well, one imagines that an elopement is precipitated by a strong emotional bond," Judith replied, "and that its failure was painful to you."

Lambert reached for his glass of wine and fiddled with the stem. "Diana and I were supposed to have been violently in love," he said dispassionately, "and ran off together when your uncle announced Diana's betrothal to another man."

Judith waited expectantly, hoping he would elaborate on the subject which had kept her brain seething with conjecture the evening long. "After which, you departed, never to return," she prompted after a moment. "That is, never to return until yesterday."

"I did not actually depart," Lambert said. "I was *removed*, and very expeditiously, I might add. You see, it was decided between your uncle and my uncle that so passionate and impecunious a youth as I should be sent as far away from the fair Diana as possible. Removing temptation, as it were. Diana was betrothed to a man whom she described as the richest, most respectable man your uncle could find," he said without rancor, "which is to say, very rich and respectable. In short, a dullard. By the bye, did she marry him?"

"Yes, and you didn't *know*?"

"No," he said. "Once I left Gwent, I never thought to find out."

"Diana's been married to Simon Stephens these past fifteen years," Judith told him, adding loyally, "and Simon is not dull. Not so *very* dull, that is! In addition, they have three children."

"Good Lord! Diana a mother!" was all Lambert said to this, taking a sip of wine.

When it seemed that no further display of emotion was forthcoming, Judith commented humorously, "Well, so much for the story of youthful passion blighted!"

Lambert laughed at that. He set his glass down, pushed his plate aside, and folded his arms on the table. He looked at her, smiling. "We've all heard it a dozen times before. Why, even Harry could write better!" he said, gesturing to the stage curtain which was quivering with the activity behind it. "But I'm thinking that there is some poetic justice in the world after all," he went on, "that my youthful follies should pass in review the day after I set foot again in Wales."

"Yet you seem to return with no regrets," Judith observed.

"None at all! It was the best thing to happen to me to be sent out on my own. I was a reckless and foolish lad and most foolishly reckless in love."

"But how sad for you then to have been sent off alone, without your lady love! How you must have missed Diana!"

Lambert disappointed her by saying, "How glad I was to have been *spared* her company, rather. Diana was the most indecisive creature imaginable and never knew her own mind, and so she yielded at first to my idea of elopement, for I was a persuasive young man. But, then, not an hour after we had met in the Park and begun our flight to London, she had dissolved in a flood of tears at thoughts of disobeying her father. I was heartily glad, I can tell you, when your uncle caught up with us. She missed some grand adventures, but then I don't think she had the backbone to have enjoyed them anyway." He caught himself up short. "What an absurd story! I am *sure* that Harry has written better!"

Judith had to laugh at this and privately thought that Diana had not changed much in fifteen years. Aloud she said, "After which you were 'removed,' as you say. You might not have missed Diana, but did you not at least miss your family?"

"No, why should I have?" he queried. He had picked up his glass again and was twirling it. "My mother had died years before, my father was old and irascible, and my uncle had gambled away the family fortune anyway and was trying to get in your uncle's good graces by packing me off. It's difficult to know what they were cutting me off from."

"Still, it's nice to be part of a family," Judith stated from her own experience. She raised her glass to her lips.

"Is it? As I recall, it's a long series of rules and obligations." Lambert glanced over at Judith, a mischievous gleam in his eye. "Take, for instance, the Rule Against Swearing."

Judith choked on her wine. She eyed her host with disfavor. "You know about that?"

"Somerset's Rules for Castle Life are as infamous as they are legion," Lambert said.

"The injunction against swearing at Raglan," Judith replied with dignity, "is not the least hardship on *me*, sir! And besides, not all of his rules are so—are so—"

"So ridiculous?" Lambert supplied helpfully.

"So specific!" Judith said. "Rules are necessary when the household is so large."

"You have *that* very pat," he commented. "All the more reason to be happy not to have a family."

"Ah! But what about your nephew?" Judith pointed out.

Lambert regarded her with a sardonic eye. "I gather you have not met him. I spent not above five minutes in his company last week at Whitehall. He's the most overdressed puppy I have seen in a long while. I can't imagine that I should wish his company or that I have anything in common with him."

"Only a taste for Herbert women," Judith remarked.

Lambert slanted her a glance. "Which your cousins have

obligingly reciprocated. But if I know your uncle, he will cure Caroline's taste for James before much longer.''

"He will naturally want what is best for Caroline,'' Judith retorted.

"What he wants is obedience,'' Lambert retorted, "pure and simple. He'll bring Caroline around—will she, nill she!''

"He is in a better position to determine what is best for his daughters,'' Judith countered, a little cross at the criticism.

"A better position than who? His daughters themselves?'' Lambert said, his brows rising. "Now, if Caroline does not have a better head on her shoulders than her sister Diana, you might be right. And if she has conceived an attachment for my nephew, I cannot doubt that you are right! But I have found, in general, that obedience to paternal authority is a damned unrewarding path to follow. Not that I am unhappy, mind you, that your uncle came to retrieve his daughter from my tender care when he did. My youthful passionate nature found its appropriate outlet in the theater where I began all my adventures.''

"But now you've found another line of work, I believe you've said, and I have been wondering what it is,'' Judith said, to change the subject whose turn against her uncle she had not liked.

The very topic of her uncle had caused Lambert to focus on Judith more closely. He had been trying, the evening long, to remember the phrase he had heard used in describing her at Whitehall, but he could not recall it, and the problem teased him. During his adventurous career, Charles Lambert had developed the knack of mentally stripping a person of title and wealth to judge the character beneath. Judith Beaufort, seen as the niece of one of the wealthiest and most powerful men in the realm, was a handsome young woman. She had thick dark hair, brown eyes, a masterful nose and feisty chin, a curvaceous figure, and beautiful alabaster shoulders that glowed in the candlelight. Imagining her as a young woman of no particular rank or distinction, Lambert found her looks nothing out of the ordinary, and he decided that he had liked her better before knowing who she was. Had she not been Henry Somerset's niece and had the circumstances been somewhat different, he would have taken the provocative dress as an invitation and would have looked forward to the hours ahead with pleasurable anticipation.

However, she was Somerset's niece, and the circumstances were not different. When Lambert did not immediately answer, Judith misunderstood his silence. She continued, "Your youthful passionate nature does not seem to have altered much in the past fifteen years, for here you were today roaming the Welsh countryside in search of Rosamunda! If that is not theater, what is it?"

"Art."

"Art?"

"Yes, art," he replied with a strange note in his voice, "and I have just realized the oddest coincidence! I was looking for Rosamunda today because she was going to lead me to a Judith. A Judith in oils and on canvas."

"I am afraid I do not understand!"

"I'm referring to the biblical Judith," Lambert said, "and instead what I found is a Judith made of flesh and blood."

"That is hardly an explanation!" Judith objected. "I think I'm entitled to a better one than that, after all!"

"Are you? I wonder," he said. "Perhaps you are entitled to know that I am searching for a painting of the Judith story."

"Any painting of Judith?" she asked. "Why, there must be dozens of such canvases. Hundreds, even."

He was shaking his head. "Not just any painting," he said laconically. "One particular painting."

After a pause, she asked, "Why is the painting so important to you?"

His answer was slightly evasive. "I purchase paintings for a living," he said.

Judith digested this information with difficulty. "Your new line of work is the purchase of paintings? That does not sound like much of a profession."

He heard the touch of supercilious Somerset scorn in her

voice. He smiled his truly charming smile. "Then I sell them again. For a profit. I have an eye for the best." He was regarding Judith lazily. "And I am beginning to see an interesting physical resemblance between the Judith on canvas and the one before me." His brows snapped together. "Are *you* a widow, as well?"

"I beg your pardon!" she said, momentarily bewildered. Then, after a moment, "Oh! You wonder whether I am a widow like the biblical Judith!" She shook her head. "No, I am not yet married."

Lambert's expressive brows rose. "How is it that you have escaped matrimony for all your advanced years?" he asked.

"All my advanced—?" she began with a touch of asperity.

"Yes, years," Lambert finished amiably. "You mentioned them yourself when you accused me of . . . now, what was it? . . . misusing my experience and my charming smile, I believe it was, to entrap the young innocent Caroline. Naturally, I wonder why it is that you are not married."

Judith was sensitive on this particular subject, but kept her dignity when she said, "It's not as if I have not received a variety of offers."

"As the niece of Somerset, I don't doubt it!" he responded with a laugh.

Now indignant, Judith began again. "If you mean to imply, sir, that no one would seek me in matrimony for myself—"

Lambert broke in smoothly. "I'll pay you the compliment of assuming that you do not cherish any false comparisons between yourself and your beautiful, pea-brained cousin Diana! Given the unnumbered years of your life and your family name, it's hardly a blot in your chapbook that you are unmarried. It's rather more of a miracle!"

He was right, of course: it was nearly miraculous; but while Judith had been eager to hear Lambert's romantic past, she had no desire to tell him hers. "The fact of the matter is, sir, I am but newly betrothed," was all she cared to say.

"Uncle Henry's doing?" Lambert asked.

Judith paused. "Officially, yes. That is, he approves of my choice."

"So the resemblance to the biblical Judith ends with a few physical traits," Lambert commented. "The Judith of flesh and blood is most obedient."

Judith had always admired her biblical namesake. Nettled, she said, "Implying that I, unlike the heroic Judith, have no backbone to stand up to paternal authority? For me, it is rather a case of obedience converging with inclination."

Lambert's memory jogged. He suddenly recalled what he had heard about Judith Beaufort at Whitehall. She had been referred to reverently by some as The Incomparable, and less reverently by others as Miss Perfect. How fitting, then, that the perfect Miss Judith Beaufort's choice of husband should converge so perfectly with her duty!

"And who's the lucky man?" Lambert asked.

"Sir George Beecham," she said a little stiffly.

Beecham. The name was familiar enough for Lambert to think he had met the man last week in London. Lambert searched his memory until he arrived at the image of a very rich, very respectable, and very dull young man.

"Congratulations," he said. "Nevertheless, there was no happy convergence of obedience and inclination for our brave biblical Judith," Lambert observed. "It took a most disobedient and defiant Judith to go into Holofernes' tent and slay the patriarch to keep her people free."

Judith folded her lips. Then, slowly, said, "Perhaps I am not cast in the heroic mold. However, few of us are ever called upon to act in so effective a manner." Will arrived to whisk away the remains of their meal and to offer a bowl of dressed fruit and nuts and a fresh bottle of wine, and Judith had the opportunity to turn the subject with an entirely conventional, "My, this looks delicious!"

"It's what I call ambrosia, ma'am," Will said, pleased with himself. "The master likes a dulcet with the wine."

"What I call aphrodisiac," Lambert said, feeling a return of his youthful recklessness. He reached for the newly uncorked bottle of wine. "Shall I fill your glass?"

Judith arched a brow. She sensed a touch of danger in this

situation and in her dress. She thought it better not to respond in kind and, in any case, this provocative comment had been offered only after she had declared herself promised to another man.

"Yes, a drop of sauterne would complement the ambrosia nicely," she answered calmly and held Lambert's slightly mocking regard with an impassive one of her own.

Lambert was relaxed and replete and prepared to pursue a flirtation with the woman sitting next to him. He was discovering that Miss Perfect had her charms—in the present setting, at least. Her proximity, of course, was the first stimulant; her unavailability provided a pleasant spur. (Judith had guessed aright.) However, just as he was leaning over to fill Judith's glass, the playwright stepped out from behind the curtain and announced with a solemn bow, "The players are ready."

Lambert was an adaptable man. He completed the gesture of filling Judith's glass, then placed the bottle on the table. Not more than mildly disappointed at the interruption, he sat back in his chair. "What's it to be?" he inquired.

"First we will present a comic scene from a well-known market day piece entitled *The Atheist's Tragedy; or, the Honest Man's Revenge*," Mr. Webster informed him. "It is not the most refined work," he said with a sniff, "but the players like it. After which will come a performance of a rather more elevating nature—the central scene from my newest moral tale *Every Man in His Hour*." He turned toward the stage and clapped his hands. "Players! Robin, are you ready? Allan, please to secure your breeches. Remember what happened last time! Places, everyone! Tom! Dick!"

"*Harry!*" the cast replied in chorus from behind the curtain.

Mr. Webster looked down his exquisitely boned nose at Judith and Lambert and said, "They will have their little joke." Then, taking the vacant seat at the table, he called for "Curtain!"

Judith settled back into her chair. When the curtain swept aside, her attention was fully engaged by the characters of

Flaminio and Mirabel, admirably played by Tom and Robin, who were embroiled in the trials and tribulations of the course of true love which never runs smooth.

It was a humorous piece and full of action, and Judith was amused by the raucous byplay. At one moment, Mirabel protested Flaminio's ardent lovemaking by clapping a hand to her heart and exclaiming, "How are we, frail women, to keep our ladies' own bodies pure?"

She was rejoined by the villains of the piece lurking behind the stage bushes:

"Bodice? Bodice?" said the Lecher, convincingly played by Allan. "A lady's own bodice?"

"Bawdies? Bawdies pure?" Peeping Tom called. "Is such possible? Show me!"

However, these immodest puns as well as the scene where the sight of Mirabel caused the Lecher's "appetite to raise" were so broadly played that Judith was not offended. When the players took their bows, Judith applauded her pleasure.

The next offering was a creature of Mr. Webster's imagination. It was certainly dramatic—if high-flown language and gestures and a story where the good were rewarded and the bad damned counted as high drama. With a delicious mixture of disbelief, amusement, and astonishment, she watched and listened as the improbable characters muddled their way through tragedy and triumph. When it was over, she clapped politely while exchanging a long regard with Charles Lambert whose face was maddeningly bland.

Mr. Webster leapt from his chair, wildly applauding his own work. He turned, his face flushed, his eyes sparkling. He challenged, "Dare to say that you were not moved by the events I have told!"

"Oh, indeed I was!" Judith said readily. "But perhaps I was more surprised than moved!"

Mr. Webster nodded with satisfaction. "All good playwrights blend the exotic with the familiar!"

"Oh yes, er—no!" Judith said. "I was rather surprised by some of the lines I heard. Some very good lines, in fact! It seems to me that I have read somewhere before: 'Love is blind, and lovers cannot see/ The pretty follies that themselves commit.' "

Mr. Webster was not the least put out. "No, no," he said. "*My* line scans: 'Love is blind, and lovers cannot see/ The pretty follies that *they* themselves commit.' "

"Ah! Now I see the difference!" she said, biting her lip. "But did I not hear another line, something like: 'Love is not love/ Which alters when it alteration finds,/ Or bends with the remover to remove'? Surely that is not your own!"

Mr. Webster composed himself, then said with dignity, "I borrow only from the best."

"Harry subscribes to the same playwright's line: 'There is boundless theft in my profession,' " Lambert remarked. "We let him get away with the petty larceny, since no one takes him seriously."

"If we are to quote, then let us ask 'What makes robbers bold but too much lenity?' " Judith tossed back easily.

Lambert enjoyed the shaft, but Mr. Webster did not. "You do not, I fear, madam, understand my art," the playwright said with a distinct chill.

Thereafter was elaborated a rather long conversation which was entered into with enthusiasm by Mr. Webster who liked nothing better than to defend his craft. In his defense, he was more interesting and indeed more eloquent than in his plays. On into the evening Judith, Lambert, and the playwright, with an ever-changing group of cast members who ambled in and out, spoke of comedies and tragedies and allegories and farces and romances and histories.

Presently Judith declared herself ready to retire and was escorted from the Hall. The night was uneventful, her sleep undisturbed. The next morning dawned beautifully clear, and Judith rose early, well rested but a little groggy. She dressed quickly and a little haphazardly in her own now-dry but certainly ruined dress.

She was in the courtyard checking Barbary's tackle, ready for departure under the escort of Will and Allan, when she next saw her host.

Lambert emerged from the stables leading a beautiful brute of a stallion, indicating that he, too, was ready to ride out that morning, presumably in his continued quest for Rosamunda. Seeing Judith, he approached her and greeted her. He helped her to mount, saying, "Give my regards to your uncle. And tell him that he once again has Lamberts as neighboring landowners."

Judith read the request as a challenge, which it was. She did not hesitate to cross swords. "Shall I, indeed, give him your regards?" she asked, settled and looking down at him.

"Do you deny me the courtesy?" he riposted.

"Not at all! I merely wonder that you should desire that I recite the details of my adventure, for they do not flatter you!"

"You do not plan to tell your uncle all?" Lambert queried on an exaggerated note of surprise. "That sounds disobedient to me!"

She had not yet decided how she was going to portray the events of the past day to Edith and to everyone else. She did not tell him that, however. Nor did she answer his question. Instead, she asked one of her own. "Why must you think the worst of me?"

"Sure now," Lambert replied, mounting himself, and meeting her eye to eye. "How was I to guess that the straitlaced Henry Somerset had such a right-thinking niece?"

"You wouldn't of course," she answered him. "I doubt you often guess aright!" When he smiled at that, she was emboldened to continue, "If you are *very* nice to me in the future, I shall put in a good word for you to my uncle. I am privy to all his most important business affairs," she said. She glanced at his house whose shabbiness prompted her to add with a touch of self-importance, "He has depended on my advice for years! Now that you are settling back down in Gwent, you may wish to call on him. If your eye for art is as good as you claim, you might find that you have much in common with him."

"I'll remember that," he said. He took her up on her offer to come calling if the opportunity presented itself, but he did not bother to correct her misimpression about his settling down in Gwent.

They exchanged parting remarks. Judith reined Barbary

away to join Will and Allan who showed themselves eager to give her every attention they had denied her the day before.

Lambert's eyes, narrowed in speculation, remained on Judith Beaufort's back and followed her progress until she was nearly out of sight. Then, abruptly, he took Scaramouche in hand and cantered off in the opposite direction.

Chapter
4

SOMERSET'S *niece*.

The phrase echoed idly through Lambert's mind as he traveled the forests of his native Gwent. He was riding west and north, to the Welsh coast. He had had it on good authority that Rosamunda's trail led to Holyhead and most probably on across St. George's Channel to Dublin. Would the strange journey that he had begun in Italy all those weeks ago finally end in Ireland?

The question, once raised, remained suspended. He felt no urgency to answer it. Although he sat astride Scaramouche who was riding forward in single-minded pursuit, Lambert had allowed his thoughts to wander for the day, giving them range to roam. They had risen to be absorbed in the cathedral of the forest, with the thick columns of trees soaring to Gothic heights, their branches thrusting and intersecting high above, crossing the leafy canopy with vaults. The sun bent and broke through the leaves and cast its light on the path before him in stained glass patterns of greens.

Familiar greens. Deep and secret greens. Cool greens and wet greens mingling with the sharp, dark green scent of peat and loam. The dense, thick greens of Wales. So different in shade from the parched ochred greens of Italy, where the sun, when vertical, dropped a flood of dazzling light across the land, leaving no room for shadows. So different in shape from the sculptured cypresses standing stark under the pitiless sun, studding the hills of Tuscany. So different in scent from the dry, sweet green of the rosemary wafting lazily on the still air and mingling with the hot breathlessness of the nights spent in the spreading gardens of his villa overlooking Florence.

Lambert breathed deeply. For a man who had not seen his homeland for fifteen years, he indulged in no nostalgia. Nevertheless, he was unexpectedly content to be traveling this corner of the earth; and now that he was back, it seemed both a lifetime ago and only yesterday that he had left. Horse and rider emerged from the forest to cross an abandoned, weed-choked field on a rugged hillside. The stretch was well known to him, and he made his way with steady purpose between the overgrown bushes and thick grasses, the hill rolling away to his right, upward until it merged with another line of woods to ramble over still another, undulating hill off into the distance. He waded into a fresh patch of smell and color. It was pungent and unlovely and strongly familiar. He liked it. He reached deep into a memory and identified wild campion.

Judith Beaufort.

She, too, was familiar to him, but oddly and elusively, as if he had seen her before, but only in glimpses. His eye caught several skylarks pitching jovially among the branches of a straggly clump of trees, but this time his attention was not diverted. His thoughts lingered on the woman he had left but several hours before. Judith Beaufort. Not a beautiful Judith, but a strong one. Not a painting, this Judith, but a Judith of flesh and blood.

Her blood was Somerset's blood. Lambert nearly smiled at the thought. He had had more than his fill of Somerset women. And her flesh? Despite the fact that he would most likely have nothing more to do with Judith Beaufort, Lambert considered this question with more interest. Her flesh was soft and white and pleasingly rounded and, in that one respect at least, highly reminiscent of the

Judith of oils on canvas he was seeking. Lambert frowned.
No, the Judith of oils and canvas that he *owned*. His frown
deepened. Not owned. Not technically. Not anymore. But it
should have been his. It had been his. By all rights, it
should still be his.

So deeply did he lose himself in thought that the heavy
crease marring his brow did not ease before Scaramouche,
startled by the sudden uprising of a pheasant from the
undergrowth, stopped dead. Only when the beast threw up
his head and snorted was Lambert jerked out of his mus-
ings. He admonished Scaramouche but leaned forward to
pat his neck as well, in understanding. "You wonder, too,
why Rosamunda stole the painting out from under my nose,
don't you, fellow?" he said. His brow lightened and he
smiled, appreciating anew the absurdity of his wild adventure. "You'd like to know, as well, who the devil she is, and
just whom she's working for." He laughed. "But that's not
the most pressing of our questions, is it? First, we'd like to
know what she's doing in England and what she's done with
the painting. But most of all, we'd like to know why she
chose that *particular* painting!"

They entered an open field. Scaramouche broke into a
trot, which became a canter that the beast would keep to
until the first meeting point Lambert had assigned with
Will and the ragtag troupe of actors he had hired for the
fortnight.

The central question still burned: Why, *why* that particular
painting? Why Artemisia Gentileschi's *Judith Slaying
Holofernes*? Lambert had examined that question from every conceivable angle in the past six weeks and more, and
he was still no closer to discovering the answer. Now, Judith
Beaufort had been correct in her estimation that hundreds of
paintings depicting the biblical Judith existed, and surely
dozens representing her moment of truth in the sleeping
Holofernes' tent. Had it been a painting of Judith—any
painting of Judith—by Rubens or Cigoli or Vouet or Van
Dyck, Lambert would have not given the incident further
thought. But no, it was a Gentileschi. Had there been some
confusion over which of the Gentileschis had painted it, he

could have understood it better. However, there had been no confusion, and the work had been explicitly auctioned as one by the lesser known Gentileschi—a mere woman and a very early composition of hers at that. Had the painting been vaunted as having been created while she had been under the tutelage of the great Caravaggio, then Lambert might have expected competition for its purchase. Yet, here again, the painting had been pointedly dated as having been completed before that apprenticeship.

Lambert had certainly been outbid for paintings before. He had also lost an occasional purchase, even after he had thought the deal had been sealed. Such were the vagaries of an always capricious marketplace, known for the temperaments of the artists, the arrogance of their banker patrons, and the jealousies and rivalries that characterized relations among the very small circle of independent professional art dealers, like Lambert himself, who were doing well for themselves in Italy of late in the golden sunset of the Medici power and influence.

It had been pure happenstance that day in April when Lambert had been sauntering through Florence heading down the Via Tornabuoni with nothing weightier on his mind than the evening ahead with the exquisite Elizabeth Marston. Since he had entrée everywhere, he had wandered into the dusty magnificence of the *grande sala* of the Palazzo Strozzi. There a lackluster display of paintings and sculptures and statuettes and carved ivories and medallions and gold pieces and a clock or two was being haggled over with little enthusiasm. Lambert had taken a cursory look around, had nodded to a variety of his cronies who were mildly engaged in the bidding process, and was about to depart when his attention had been arrested by one composition which had been adjourned to the margins of the bidding activity. His heart had stopped for a moment, then soared.

Lambert displayed none of his emotions. He did not even approach the painting for a better look. He merely scanned the official price list with a seeming disinterest, then took up a negligent position against one wall of the room. While awaiting the presentation of the painting, he bid for and bought several jasper goblets and vases, but his mind never left the painting. He had recognized it immediately as a Gentileschi—and not an Orazio Gentileschi, the famous father. It was not the subject of Judith slaying Holofernes that had attracted him, for it was a commonplace. Nor was it the composition itself. His discerning eye judged it to be studied and harmonious, but it was certainly nothing out of the ordinary.

Nevertheless, he had fallen in love with it on sight. His head could not have said why, but his gut knew it thoroughly. Perhaps it was the technical perfection of the chiaroscuro play of light and shadows which cast the muscular blue of Judith's bodice and sleeves into high relief; or perhaps it was the red of Holofernes' blood as it dripped and spattered the white sheets; or perhaps it was the strength in Judith's arms as she held the sword and bent with her entire body into Holofernes, not shying away from her task. Or perhaps it was the expression on her face which was not beautiful for its features but was gorgeous for its feminine determination. It was a virago Judith, a Judith who challenged other more timid representations of the same subject, a Judith who defeated the conventional expectation that even in the performance of so heroic a deed as the liberation of Israel a woman would stand at arm's length and look away from her deed.

The painting was finally brought forward. The bidding began low and unpromising. Lambert bided his time and waited his moment to enter. When he did, he soon found himself bidding against another voice in the room. It came from the opposite corner. He could not see its owner, but he did not make a show of discovering the identity of his counterbidder. On the slim evidence of the calling out of a few numbers, Lambert judged the accent of his counterbidder as not being Tuscan. Lambert's well-trained ear guessed the man to be from the province of Lazio, perhaps from Rome itself. It hardly mattered, though, and soon enough the bidding had spiraled to surprising heights. Lambert remained cool but determined and knew from the start that he would have the painting, at whatever cost. He had it eventually, at three times its supposed market value. However, since he intended the painting for his personal collection and not for resale, the scudi he paid for it did not matter. He left the palazzo a happy and satisfied man.

When he returned the next day with the requisite sack of silver to collect his *Judith*, he was told that the painting was gone.

Gone?

The Strozzi family steward shrugged apologetically and explained to Signor Lamberto that a woman had later come for the most lovely painting and had offered a better price.

Elaborately polite, Lambert pointed out that the woman had come forward too late with her price. The deal and the price had been sealed, as the steward well knew, the day before with Lambert's handshake.

The steward coughed into his fist and named the exact amount of money the woman had given him.

Even Lambert was impressed. He was prompted, of course, to ask after the woman's style and address.

It pained the steward most profoundly to inform Signor Lamberto that he did not know the identity of the woman. However, knowing the Englishman to be blessed with "the taste of angels" (as the saying went) and to be a dealer whose custom was good for the Palazzo Strozzi, the steward did describe the woman as thoroughly as he was able. He even hazarded the humble opinion that, "*Il quadro è già a Roma.*"

Rome. The painting was on its way to Rome. The painting had slipped out of his grasp. Lambert felt a loss, and it tasted bitter.

And what, the Strozzi steward asked, did Signor Lamberto wish to do about the so beautiful goblets and vases he had agreed to buy the day before?

Lambert declined the purchase in the grand manner, but he had hardly heard the question. As he left the palazzo, he was immersed in the regret at having made his presence in the *sala* so unobtrusive the day before. It would have helped him immensely to have at least seen the man who had been bidding against him, the man who wanted the painting as much, nay *more* than he did, the man who had sent a woman to steal it from him.

For that was what it was: theft, and Lambert never once considered *not* going after the painting to retrieve it. He had thought, initially, that he would have had the painting back in his possession within a few days. Now, all these weeks later, the adventure, so simply, almost whimsically begun, had become a quest in earnest for an insignificant painting bought for an extraordinary price. He had gone to Rome, of course. There, through the usual sources, he had learned some interesting and surprising information which included news of the sudden disappearance of a notorious Roman beauty whose description precisely matched that of the woman who had approached the Strozzi steward. She was reported to have connections to the world of the theater, and she was known among a certain fast and decadent set of *nobili* only as Rosamunda.

Although Will was well accustomed to his master's passionate caprices, he met Lambert's abrupt order to close the Florentine villa with a good deal of surprise; and although he never did grasp the fine points of Lambert's reasons for undertaking the extravagantly frivolous search for a painting of no particular value, he gamely followed. Their journey took them to all the large centers of artistic commerce, first to Milan, then to Augsburg, and then on to Antwerp, but it was not until one fine day in May when it became clear that Rosamunda's path led inevitably to London, that Will was moved to exclaim, "But you've said you never would go back to England! You've no business there!"

"I've brisk business in England," Lambert responded, "which I've conducted from afar for too many years."

"I know!" Will said. "Arundel and Buckingham! But they've never complained about your methods of doing business before!"

"Perhaps I've a mind to cultivate other clients," Lambert replied. Then, as if the thought had just struck him, "The divine Elizabeth left Florence last week with plans to return to England and, besides," he said, slanting Will a glance, "you're not objecting to the visit, are you?"

"You're wishing to see Miss Marston?" Will cried, surprised. "Well, she's not the first lady you've pursued at some length, though never quite *this* far! But it's a respectable family she comes from, and what's well and good for a dalliance in a heathen land might not be acceptable in the good neighborhoods of London! As for my own particular self, I'm not a sorry man to be going home!"

"Good," Lambert replied. Then, as if in speculation, "Do you think she'll refuse to receive me?"

"Never that!" Will answered promptly. "She's more like to fall about your neck. Or faint with surprise, for you never gave her the least. . . . well! But I'm thinking it's her *father* who's a rich enough merchant to have something to say on the subject, if he ever hears tell of your. . . your success! And speaking of which, never say that you mean to—that you are going to—" He was unable to complete the thought.

"Why not? I've played many a rôle in my varied career. Do you not think I am equal to playing the respectable suitor?" To his henchman's obvious confusion, Lambert added, smiling, "So you see, my dear Will, the journey becomes ever more logical the closer to England we get."

However, since arriving in England, the less logical it had all become. Lambert did not make the least effort to call at the home of his ladylove who lived in the newly fashionable neighborhood of Covent Garden but spent his time instead in a futile attempt to track down the painting on the London art exchanges. He came rapidly to realize that London was not, evidently, the end point of his journey.

However, England was his home turf, and Lambert had more resources at his command here than he had had on the road from Florence to Antwerp. He happened one day in London to run into his old theater buddies, and that encounter had given him the idea to hire the old troupe to help him catch the elusive Rosamunda. The idea had proved to be a good one. He soon discovered through underworld theater sources that a foreign beauty had recently passed through town and was now heading west.

Accompanied by the troupe, Lambert had thought he would soon have Rosamunda in his hands, and he had devised several excellent ideas for cornering her and unmasking her that made ample use of the talents of the ham actors. Yet, the closer Rosamunda's trail had led to Gwent, the less certain he had become of trapping her; and with her evident intention of now heading toward Ireland, his interpretation of her motives and movements had become even more difficult.

By this day's end in Wales, Lambert's calculations were to become infinitely more complicated.

In the late afternoon Lambert stopped on the main road to Holyhead at a well-known posting inn where he had instructed the others to meet him. The Craven Arms was justly famous for its ale, and over a tankard of foamy wet in the taproom Lambert satisfied himself with the story of how Will and Allan had deposited Miss Beaufort safe and of a piece (though "tetchy" as Will thought to describe her humor) at Raglan Castle. When the account was done and the laughter and jests exhausted, Lambert gave the actors permission to go into the village to amuse themselves as they saw fit. Only Harry Webster chose to stay behind at the inn, for he was deep into a new creation. Another tankard later, Lambert had the idea to check on the horses for the evening. He nodded for Will to accompany him to the stables.

Lambert bent first to exit the low-pitched door from the taproom. Will followed. The sun was sinking, and a rosy dusk was settling across the many-chimneyed roof of the rambling, half-timbered hostelry. Since the inn had grown haphazardly with the expanding trade, the odd angles of the building prevented Lambert from stepping directly into the yard, which was filled with activity. He was about to turn the corner of the building when a hardly registered glance into a far corner of the yard caused him to stop dead. He stepped back, hugged his back to the wall, and flung out an arm to prevent Will from proceeding further.

"What is it?" Will whispered, harsh, responding instantly to his master's gestural command.

"I think I just saw—" Lambert began.

"Our Rosamunda!" Will finished not unhopefully, bunching a fist. "Let's at her, then!"

"No," Lambert said slowly and peered his head again around the side of the building. "It is not Rosamunda."

"Who, then, man?" Will demanded, impatient.

Lambert shook his head to clear it of its confusion and turned to Will with a look of bemused disbelief. He had one word to say and that was, "Spadaccio."

This announcement was sufficiently stunning to check Will, his clenched fist arrested in midair. "Spadaccio!" he cried low and swore under his breath. "Unnatural man!" he said, indignant at the very mention of his master's old rival from his theater days. "You can't mean it!"

Lambert was having difficulty believing it himself. He slid his gaze around the side of the building a third time. His eyes had not deceived him. "Signor Spadaccio is a difficult figure to mistake," Lambert reminded his man.

A martial light sprang to Will's eye. "Right!" he said, his fist ready. "Let's at 'em!"

Lambert shook his head. "No, let me think first!" He considered this new twist. "Spadaccio!" he said again. "You take a look, Will. Perhaps my wits have fled after all these weeks of fruitless chase."

Will squinted cautiously around the side of the building. "Where?"

Lambert gestured with his head. "Over there. In the far corner. In the shadows."

Harry Webster was just then turning the corner from the yard, walking straight into Will's line of vision, and came face-to-face with Lambert. "Ah, there you are," he said, words fluent on his lips. "I have been thinking about it all night and all day—and I don't think that I can keep it inside of me any longer—" he began.

"Out of the way, man!" Will growled and pulled the playwright bodily around the corner and out of sight of the yard. "We're on the lookout for a man, and you're in the way!" Will bent his head around the side of the building and darted his eyes about.

"I am not interested in men at just this moment," Harry Webster replied with dignity, "but in women. One woman, in fact. Miss Judith Beaufort."

Lambert shifted his gaze to the playwright, brows lifted in inquiry. "What about her?" he asked.

The playwright gave vent to all the frustration that had been festering in him since the evening before in one explosive exclamation. "She did not understand my art!"

Lambert rolled his eyes. "What say you, Will? Is that our man?" he asked. Then, to the playwright, "Apparently her taste is at fault."

"To quote a minor character in my last masterpiece," the playwright said (here he cleared his throat): " 'In ways of taste, hers is a distempered appetite.' "

Lambert had certainly heard that line before—and not for the first time in one of Harry Webster's plays. He laughed, his attention momentarily diverted. "The trick, I think, is not to swipe too much from one source."

The playwright smiled deprecatingly. "Bad writers swipe," he intoned, "good writers *steal*."

"What, Harry, an original thought?" Lambert queried.

Before the playwright had an opportunity to divulge his source for that quotable line, Will turned back to his master and shook his head. "He keeps looking away, and I can't quite make out his face."

Although uncertain about the man's identity, when Lambert saw the man move away from his spot, he knew it was time for action. He held up a hand to stay further response from the playwright. "Will!" he commanded. "Go around the back and keep your eye on any back entrance, in the event that Spadaccio is going to stay at the inn. But don't let him see you! Harry, you go into the taproom and *mind your own business*! That should be easy enough. I'll go through the stable yard and follow Spadaccio around the front—if Spadaccio it is."

Will and Harry obeyed, and Lambert went off in the opposite direction, his mind fully focused on the possibility that the man in the yard was Spadaccio. Spadaccio. Lambert could not imagine what his old acquaintance from his early days in the Italian theater was doing in Wales. Lambert remembered having heard, years ago, that the exquisite Spadaccio had turned from the theater to politics—not an unusual transition for a man of Spadaccio's inclinations, to be sure, and one that he had reportedly made under the aegis of an obscenely rich, grotesquely fat politician in Rome.

Rome, again. Rome. Rosamunda was well known in Rome. The painting had originally been on its way to Rome. All roads lead to. . . .

Lambert had only the briefest time to consider that Spadaccio might somehow and mysteriously be involved with Rosamunda, for here he was far, far from Rome and on the same trail as she was. However, he had no time at all to wonder what possible interest Spadaccio—or whoever he represented in Rome—had poking his long, elegant fingers into an odd intrigue involving a little-known painting. Lambert knew only that he did not wish for Spadaccio to see him, in the unlikely event that the Italian was associated with Rosamunda. Lambert had been extremely careful, up to this point, not to have given Rosamunda reason to think she was being followed. He thought he had been successful thus far, and he certainly did not wish to reveal himself unnecessarily.

Nevertheless, Lambert took the risk of crossing the yard. He kept close to the front of the building and avoided any suspicious-looking behavior. He sought, and thought he found, the slim figure moving with willow-grace through the general commotion of the yard. He hurried to the other end of the stable yard and hid himself quickly behind one wall of the inn. It formed a curious angle with another wall of the inn and made a perfect hiding place from the yard. The wedge was open to a grove of trees, and no one from the yard would be likely to wander over in this direction.

Several coaches entered the yard just then. He cursed them for momentarily blocking Spadaccio's figure from sight. However, the second coach that entered passed within several feet of his hiding place, and Lambert saw the crests emblazoned on the doors pass right before his eyes. He recognized that crest without hesitation, and he watched, with great interest, as the ostlers jumped to the commands of the coachman.

A moment later, the occupant of the second coach descended the steps that had been unfolded for him. Its noble occupant paused on the top step, giving Lambert a full second to register the man's identity. He was older by fifteen years than when Lambert had last seen him, but age had not bent his carriage nor dimmed his aura of unquestioned authority.

In the next second, Lambert was witness to a fascinating little scene. The nobleman descended the steps and bumped—inadvertently, the casual observer would have said—into an exquisitely handsome, exquisitely dressed man who proceeded to beg the older man's pardon, rather profusely, and in a heavily Italian-accented English. Then, the young slim man moved on—but not before having slipped a note to the nobleman who had just descended from the coach.

Lambert stood, transfixed. Spadaccio moved back across the yard and a few minutes later left the Craven Arms in a carriage heading north. Sometime after that, when the noble gentleman's carriage had had a fresh team of horses harnessed to it, it had driven out of the inn, heading south.

Lambert suspected that he had seen something extraordinary. He would have been quite sure of it, if he had known that the scene had also been witnessed by a second person standing in one of the upper windows to the inn. If Lambert had looked up, he might have seen a slim figure with a delicate face framed by blond curls frowning meditatively over the little exchange between the elegant Italian and the distinguished nobleman. But Lambert did not look up, and a few minutes later that person, too, left the inn, however, not by the front door but by the back door. That person passed within a foot or so of Will who was guarding that entry and even wished Lambert's henchman a pleasant "good eventide."

The soft gouache of twilight was washing the sky when Lambert finally moved away from his hiding place. Many thoughts crowded through his brain, but uppermost was the memory of the words spoken to him earlier that morning: "If you are *very* nice to me," a lovely voice echoed in his memory, "I shall put in a good word for you to my uncle, for I am privy to all his most important business affairs!"

Well! Well! Lambert thought, *I may just have to cultivate the acquaintance of Somerset's niece after all!*

Chapter
5

TEN days later, Lambert was to have his opportunity.
In a swift and welcome change of her plans, Judith
found herself in one of her uncle's comfortable
traveling coaches, seated across from Edith, and approaching
the city gates of London.

Two days after her little incident in Somerset Park, Judith
had received a hastily written letter from her uncle which
directed her to travel posthaste to London to deliver several
sealed letters that he had included with his missive. Instructions for their delivery were given with minute, and characteristic, precision. Lord Henry expressed every confidence
that he could depend for the proper execution of this request
on his very reliable niece.

Now Judith sat in the coach, gazing abstractedly out the
window. The open country rolled past. The green fields
were stitched by lanes and punctuated by an occasional farm
or country house. The heights round about were crested
with windmills and dotted here and there with hamlets
clustered between sloping woods. As the coach moved into
such outlying districts as Hampstead and Shepherd's Bush,
the fields were divided from town by stretches of heath and
moorland which were the haunt of highwaymen. No such
thugs were daring enough to hold up the well-protected

Somerset carriage. However, Lambert, who had paid off the troupe and sent them back to London, had been bold enough to follow the carriage, at a discreet distance, all the way from Raglan. As the traveling party neared the river, where the principal theaters stood, there were gardens and groves of trees; and since the march of fashion was ever westward, new and handsome houses soon sprang up to meet them in their approach. Then they were within city walls.

With clear skies overhead and unmuddied roads beneath the wheels, the travel from Wales to London had been, to Judith's way of thinking, pleasant enough. However, the conversation had not, and in the confining space of the carriage, Judith's patience had been exercised to the limit. Edith's thoughts, which normally scattered as easily as the seeds of a dandelion puff in the slightest wind, had clung, perversely, to a single topic this past week.

When Edith began *again* to recount the night of worry and dread she had passed when Judith had been lost in the woods, Judith cut her off. Without looking away from the window, she said, "I *know*, dear Edith! For you have told me of the wild fancies that you entertained, with new and more vivid details at every telling! And while *you* may have worried about me for only one night," she continued crisply, "*I* have begun to worry about *you* this past week and your well-being! Instead of your continuing alarm over the . . . the *uneventful* night I spent in Somerset Park, you should be grateful that such a nice family of farmers offered me warm, dry shelter for the night and fed me so wonderfully!"

Edith had not quite exhausted herself on the subject. "Oh, I *should*, but I can't, and it doesn't seem possible that so . . . *extraordinary* an event should have had such an *ordinary* explanation!" she cried.

"Such is life," Judith said, with emphasis, "a succession of extraordinary events with entirely ordinary explanations!"

Edith was not diverted by this piece of wisdom. "But, no!" she protested. "Why, a thousand horrible images ran over and over in my mind during those hours when you were gone! I thought at first that your horse must have bolted with the sudden storm—which, of course, you said it *did* do, but Sir Robert is of the opinion that such was not possible! He did not say it in so many words, not Sir Robert, and not to you directly! No, when you returned and told your story, he said to me later, shaking his head—hours later it was, after I had been given a strong draught, which did not thoroughly calm me, I do not hesitate to say!—and this is what he said: *'Bolt?'* That is all! Just one word! *'Bolt?'* Well! It was as plain as day that he did not believe it! Not that he would say it!''

''He certainly did not express his doubts to me, in all events,'' Judith murmured.

''I have just said that he would not, mistress!'' Edith fired back. ''Well! So I told *him* then and there that I had feared the night long that a wild animal crazed by the storm or a band of ruffians must have snatched you right off the path in the woods. Or that the earth had swallowed you up without a trace! Or that fairies had come and taken you with them into the ether!''

Judith glanced, briefly, at her companion. ''Fairies?'' she repeated with a quiver, the image most humorously incongruous. ''My good Edith!''

That was enough to set Edith off in earnest. ''Better fairies than a wild boar, and how was I to guess that you had been properly sheltered?'' she defended herself. ''My heavens! To think what *might* have happened! And you newly engaged! Why, any breath of scandal might have—'' Edith did not finish her thought but continued without pause ''—*not* that Sir George would have raised any objections! But his mother! She is a very proper lady, and although I know she is *thrilled* that her son is to marry into the Somerset family, you know as well as I that she has mentioned more than once that your betrothal to Sir George is not the *first* for you!''

This, of all topics, was Judith's least favorite. Edith knew it, but she was too engrossed in her emotions to notice the warning look that had come into her mistress's eyes.

Edith continued, blithely, ''As if it was your fault that Lord Henry annulled the engagement to Lord Rockingham when it became known that he was—well, that he was *unsuitable*! Ten years ago it was, when you were but a girl! As if it was your fault that only two years later your second betrothed should have got himself killed in a riding accident! And *as if* it was your fault that you did not find another to your liking before Sir George! Why, his mother should compliment you on your good taste and discretion. She should compliment his lordship, your uncle, for allowing you to take your time and make your own choice! But, no! 'Never two without three,' Lady Margaret has been heard to say, along with sly comments about your age! Why, I've a mind to tell her myself that at four-and-twenty, you are not exactly *old*!''

Several pointed comments had sprung to the tip of Judith's tongue, and she opened her mouth to speak. It was well that she never uttered them, however, for Edith had worked her way to this inadvertently pithy thought: "But never mind Lady Margaret just now—although she is hardly a dame one can easily *overlook*—it's just that if some less . . . *unexceptionable* circumstances had befallen you, his lordship would not have asked you to jaunter to London to do his business! He is almost rewarding you, I would say, with this trip! My heavens, I'm thinking that if you had fallen in with a band of ruffians or the like, his lordship would not have let you out of sight of Raglan walls until the day of your marriage!''

This observation stilled Judith's tongue and restored her good humor. "I believe you are right,'' she agreed pleasantly. "How fortunate for me that such did not happen, for I hate to think how tedious it would have been to spend the next six months buried in Gwent! But I don't think that my uncle is intentionally rewarding me for all my good behavior. It's rather that he has some important business and knows he can count on me. Here we are!''

By that time, the carriage had crossed under the turreted gateway known as Whitehall Gate and was lumbering down a street flanked on one end by new gardens and orchards and on the other by the royal palace which, over the years, had spread its rambling wings along the banks of the Thames.

These boundaries marked the large physical space within London walls that constituted a royal village. The coach came to a heaving halt in front of the rabbit-warren palace that was Whitehall.

When Judith arrived at the suite of rooms she was to occupy, she discovered that her uncle had a letter waiting there for her. She stopped in her chambers only long enough to read that latest letter, to tidy her hair, and to change into the new deep blue silks she had had made for the trip. In among the mountain of traveling boxes containing her belongings that were being carried on the backs of a steady stream of pages, she found the several messages her uncle had sent her to London to deliver. She secured these, along with the new note, in the drawstring bag which she tied to the ribbons embellishing her stomacher and tucked it into the folds of her skirts. She then left Edith behind to settle into the half-empty suite.

Judith's first, self-appointed task was to contact Caroline. For this consideration, too, she thought her uncle would thank her. Judith knew her cousin's chambers were located not far from hers, down several long hallways and up a flight of stairs. It was Judith's idea to bring her flighty-headed young cousin under her wing as soon as possible. There at the door to Caroline's chamber, Judith learned from a tight-lipped Somerset servant girl that Caroline had been so thoughtless to go on an excursion at Hampton Court for the day. Now, even though Judith had not informed her cousin of her impending arrival, she felt a flutter of vexation that Caroline was not available to her. However, Judith was in such a good mood at being in London, since the opportunity came to her so rarely, that she thrust the spur of displeasure to the back of her mind and kept to the business at hand.

No, the serving girl did not know in whose company Miss Caroline might be other than that of her own tiring-woman and the party got up by Lady Mary Villiers. Yes, the serving girl was satisfied that the party was properly chaperoned. No, the serving girl did not know exactly when her mistress would be returning. Oh yes, the serving girl suggested, very respectfully, that Miss Caroline had lately taken to the habit of sleeping late in the mornings and should not be contacted until tomorrow afternoon at the earliest.

Although thwarted in the first of her missions for the day, Judith felt hardly defeated, and it was a wholly pleasurable experience to be making her way through the luxurious palace of Whitehall which, despite its several thousand rooms, was a crowded world of wits and wags, of poets and writers, of talents and beauties and courtiers, of servants' families and servants' servants. Indeed, it was positively uplifting to one's spirits to be passing through the halls hung in fine tapestries and noble paintings whose ceilings were elaborately painted and plastered and whose floors were paved with Italian marble. It was no less than a privilege to be alive and to witness the glorious sunburst of the Stuart monarchs.

Judith basked in the glow. Never had there been a prince in England whose genius and taste were more elevated and exact than that of Charles Stuart. He saw the arts in a very enlarged point of view. The amusements of his court were a model of elegance to all Europe; and his cabinets held only what was exquisite in sculpture and painting. None but men of the first merit in their profession found encouragement from him, and these abundantly. Inigo Jones was his architect and Van Dyck was his painter. Charles Stuart was a scholar, a man of taste, a gentleman, and a Christian.

But was he also, secretly, a Catholic? Judith hoped, of course, he was not.

She was considering just that question as she was crossing one gallery, particularly rich in Florentine bronzes, delicate ivories, and cut crystals. She was remembering a brief conversation she had had with her uncle before he had left for Ireland on the very subject of Charles's imprudent, possibly dangerous, Catholic sympathizing. Her uncle's dark pronouncements flew out of her head, however, when her eye was caught by a large canvas she had not seen on her last trip to Whitehall, which had been years ago. She surmised that the king must have just added it to his already enormous collection, and she paused to admire it. She was not Somerset's niece for nothing. Her well-trained eye guessed this new work to be done by the hand of Gentileschi; and sure enough, when she surveyed the sensuous, white-limbed feminine forms gracing a sun-dappled Parnassus, her guess was confirmed that the skillful interpretation of the "Nine Muses" was, indeed, inscribed with the name of the Italian master. It was just this painter, Orazio Gentileschi, for whose latest canvas she had reason to believe she had been sent by her uncle to London to negotiate.

A light voice broke into her critical appreciation of the composition. "Judith!" it cried.

Judith turned to behold the bold and handsome Lucy, Countess of Carlisle, an enchanting picture herself in her silks of pale saffron and coral pink, and her ringleted hair framing a plump, oval face.

"Have you been hiding yourself from me?" Lucy asked archly. "Or did you just arrive, my dear?"

"I have just arrived," Judith answered and returned Lucy's warm greeting and kiss. "This morning, but a few hours ago."

"I thought it very strange when I saw you just now, for no one told me you were here—nor even planning to come before next month," the countess said. "Not even yourself!"

"I decided that it would be more amusing to surprise the Court with my presence," Judith commented, "but I am now perceiving the foolishness of my ways." Since the Countess of Carlisle was an unerring vehicle of court information, Judith thought this encounter a happy one. "I did not write my cousin Caroline in advance to inform her of my arrival today, and I am disappointed that she is away for the day. My bad luck! I am eager to see her! Lucy dear, you who know everything, tell me: How does Caroline fare?"

"Like every other beautiful young noblewoman at Court!" Lucy replied with a delicious twinkle in her large brown eyes.

"That is not reassuring, my dear," Judith answered. "I understand that she is often seen in company of James

Lambert. Is it possible that he has accompanied her to Hampton Court, do you think?''

Lucy considered the question. "If Caroline is in the party that Mary Villiers organized, then I am sure he is,'' she said. "Yes, I am quite sure that James has gone with them.''

"Is Caroline often seen with him?'' Judith asked.

"Often enough,'' Lucy replied, "but not *too* often, if you know what I mean!''

Judith did. However, she did not think the Countess of Carlisle's interpretation of "often'' would coincide with her own. As casually as she could, she asked Lucy to tell her about James Lambert. "I have never met the young man, you know, and I think that Caroline is quite taken with him. I would be interested to know almost anything about him.''

Lucy searched her well-informed memory. Then her eyes lit, and she tapped Judith's arm with the gloves she dangled in her hands. "The latest news is that James has an uncle who has lately returned to England—from Italy, I believe. He left England ages ago over some scandal or another! His name is . . . Charles! I think. And he has just bought a house. In Wales. Oh! Have you met him?''

Judith hesitated momentarily before stepping neatly around the question. "In Wales, you say? I shall look forward to welcoming him. As I was wondering—''

"But wait!'' Lucy interrupted, her eyes suddenly alight. "There is more!'' She lowered her voice conspiratorially, and her eyes danced wickedly. "It is rumored that Elizabeth Marston—do you know her? No? I'd never heard of her, either. She's the daughter of a wealthy Londoner. Well, *she* has just returned—heartbroken, so the story goes!—from Italy as well. Florence, to be exact! And the name that hers was linked with in Italy, so it is whispered, is none other than Charles Lambert!''

"Oh?'' Judith said, unable to suppress a prick of interest.

"Elizabeth was supposed to be madly in love with him,

but he was said to have broken it off. And, my dear,'' Lucy said, ''she is *gorgeous*!''

''Oh?'' Judith said, interest growing, in spite of herself.

''But now that he has returned after all this time, there is some speculation that he has come for her! It also explains why he bought the house in Wales! To settle down at last!''

''Oh?'' Judith said again, frankly pursuing.

''There was some question how he managed to buy a house, for before he left England all those years ago, he was wildly extravagant, and no reports of his reform have been heard!''

From having seen the house herself, Judith did not doubt that he must have scraped together all he had to buy it.

''And he is supposed to be marvelously attractive!'' Lucy added.

''Are we still speaking of Charles Lambert?'' Judith asked skeptically.

Lucy winked. ''I've not met him myself, but I plan to do so without delay, for I have heard the naughtiest stories about him! I know you, Judith! Your taste runs to calmer, more predictable types! And let me be among the first to offer you congratulations on your betrothal!''

Judith thanked her kindly and the subject of her forthcoming marriage was bandied about until she could bring the conversation back around to her original concern. ''But really, Lucy, I am very curious about this James Lambert. Is he so very handsome and charming?''

''Very!'' Lucy affirmed gaily. ''But nothing to compare to his uncle!''

A few minutes later, Judith was continuing on her way again. Although hardly cheered by Lucy's disclosures, she resolutely turned her thoughts to the delivery of her uncle's messages. She sallied forth from Whitehall, eager for the rest of the day's adventures, for it was not yet beyond mid-morning.

Judith headed first in the direction of Holbein Gate which led from the Banqueting House to the street and out into the congestion where stalls of fishmongers and sellers of herbs and roots hindered the passages of coaches. It was her intention to deliver first those of her uncle's messages directed to Westminster. She was almost across the court-yard when, entirely by chance, George Beecham just then left the main block of Palace buildings. He was heading in the opposite direction, toward the Banqueting House. Judith's path intersected with Sir George's in the shadow of Holbein Gate.

"Sir George!" Judith exclaimed with evident delight at the unexpected encounter with her betrothed. "I was just coming round to send you, among other people, message of my arrival in London!"

Sir George, whose eyes were cast down to the ground and whose handsome face was marred by a frown, looked up. "Odds fish!" he uttered involuntarily with more evidence of surprise than delight. Then, "Miss Beaufort!" Belatedly remembering his manners, he doffed his elegantly plumed hat.

Judith held out her hands. "Are you not happy to see me, sir?" she inquired as her betrothed recovered himself enough to take the tips of her fingers in his and to bow over them. "You looked so fierce just now, sir. I'm afraid your preoc-cupation has not been wholly dispelled upon seeing me!"

Sir George straightened himself and released her fingers. "But I had no idea you were here," he said in a well-cultured voice that nicely blended self-defense with a hint of reproach.

"Of course, you did not," Judith said easily. "I arrived in London only this morning." Noting that Sir George cast his regard very discreetly behind her, she added hastily, "I left Edith behind in the suite to unpack and to attend to the delivery of our furniture, while I was charged by my uncle with several messages whose delivery I did not wish to delay!"

"Your journey was spur of the moment?" Sir George asked.

"Not entirely," Judith explained. "Some days ago my uncle requested me to undertake the trip. I made my plans this past week and—" She broke off, reading the expression on Sir George's face. Then, tilting her head, she said, "If I did not send you message of my impending arrival, it was only in the hopes of surprising you, sir!''

"You have, indeed, surprised me," he replied with a certain punctilious stiffness.

"But surely *this* surprise is cause for some pleasure?" she said with a coy smile.

Sir George's lips relaxed into an answering smile. "A most charming surprise, my lady," he said with a bow. He replaced his hat atop carefully groomed blond curls. "Allow me to suggest, however, that you send a message immediately to my mother, informing her of your presence at Court. Although I am glad for the surprise of seeing you a full month earlier than planned, I am afraid that my mother, at her age, finds the unexpected rather disconcerting."

The next instant Judith was to discover for herself just how disconcerting life's little surprises could be. Hardly had the words, "I shall lose no time in writing to her!" left her mouth, than a third party passed from the street to enter the Palace grounds through Holbein Gate.

Who should it be but Charles Lambert. He acknowledged Judith Beaufort and George Beecham with the meager salutation and bow that befits a meeting among unknown peers in a crowded public thoroughfare. Then, with a tiny start of recognition, expertly executed, Lambert checked his step and said, on a note of inquiry, "Miss Beaufort? Do we meet again?"

Speaking of unexpected encounters! Judith thought with her own little start of recognition. Hardly pleased, she said, with a curtsy, "Yes, Sir Charles. We meet again."

Chapter
6

LAMBERT had stopped. "I didn't recognize you at first," he explained. Running his eye over her, he said, "Pretty! Very pretty, indeed!" Then, meeting her eyes with his laughing ones, he murmured, "*Much improved!*"

Aware that she was looking her best, Judith was alternately pleased that Lambert had complimented her on her appearance and vexed that her husband-to-be had not. She chose to ignore Lambert's last, provocative comment and acknowledged his compliment with a modest "thank you."

"But what a happy coincidence," Lambert was continuing. He had touched his fingers to his brow as if suddenly put in mind of something. "I have some things of yours, Miss Beaufort, that I have been meaning to have returned to you. I confess that it had slipped my mind, but seeing you again has reminded me of it!"

Sir George, a man of fine manners, had not entered into the careless cordiality of this exchange. With some of his earlier stiffness returning, he addressed his future wife. "I perceive that you are acquainted with this gentleman, ma'am. I do not believe I have had the honor."

"Why, yes, Sir George," Judith admitted and rose to the

occasion by making Sir George and Sir Charles known to one another.

It was just this sort of coincidence that an old improvisational hand such as Lambert delighted in. New, dramatic possibilities for the scene suddenly opened up to him. He instantly said that he recalled having met Beecham at Whitehall several weeks previous. He explained his momentary lapse of memory by mentioning that he had recently returned to England after a fifteen-year absence. He apologized for not yet being fully reacquainted with all the court gentlemen.

To which smooth speech Sir George uttered the appropriate words to explain *his* lapse in not remembering Sir Charles which he attributed to the fact that their encounter had been extraordinarily brief. (The real reason stemmed from the fact that Lambert had struck Sir George as a rough, scruffy fellow too far beneath his notice to remember.)

During this polite, measuring exchange, Judith was aware of the strong contrast of light and dark the two men made: George Beecham, all lightness, handsome and muscular and resplendent in a superb suit of old gold, slashed and braided, with deep lace at neck and wrist, a circular three-quarters cloak held back by his dress sword, breeches tapering to the knee from which spilled more deep lace over the boot cuffs; and Charles Lambert, all darkness and unhandsome, with no hat, no lace, no color, nor anything to relieve his gray ribbed-silk suit of the stark, lean impression it gave of unadorned shoulder and sinew and thigh.

The niceties completed, Sir George turned to his betrothed on a note of puzzlement. "If you have just arrived at Court, and Sir Charles is only lately returned from fifteen years abroad, how is it that you could recognize one another at all?"

If Judith found herself at something of a loss to answer, Lambert did not. "I recently met Miss Beaufort at my house in Wales," he was happy to explain.

"In Wales, was it?" Sir George said. He turned to Judith, his tone reproachful. "You did not tell me any of this!"

Judith was determined to maintain her equanimity. "Of

course I have not told you any of this, for I have not yet had the opportunity," she said with a smile. "I will certainly give you all the details later!"

Sir George was not willing to wait until later for all the details. "When was this?" he demanded.

"Oh, about three weeks ago," Judith said rather airily.

"Three weeks ago—?" Sir George echoed. He turned to Lambert. "I am afraid that I am now more confused than before! How is it possible that you did *not* immediately recognize Miss Beaufort at a distance of only three weeks?"

"It was dark when we met," Lambert said. He gestured minimally to Judith. "Her dress, her hair, they were different."

"It was raining," Judith chimed in hastily.

"Dark and raining?" Sir George queried, frowning. "Her hair and dress different?" Then, brighter, he asked, "Did Somerset get up a welcome party to greet Sir Charles? Very neighborly of him, and too bad about the rain!"

"It was not exactly like that, Sir George," Judith said quite pleasantly, trying to pass over rough ground lightly.

"No?" Sir George returned.

Judith cast a sidelong glance at Lambert whose expression was one of polite innocence. "I shall explain it to you later, as I have said," Judith stated.

"Somerset wasn't there, then?" Sir George insisted.

"It was not a welcoming party," Judith answered evenly, aware of the ground shifting uncomfortably beneath her feet.

"Your serving woman must have been with you, at least," Sir George pursued.

"I said that I would explain it later, dear sir," Judith said very firmly now, with an undertone of real irritation.

Lambert had the irresistible urge to be of some help. "And you needn't worry when she comes to the part about having to spend the night at my house—" he volunteered.

Judith felt the ground crumble.

"—for it was unexceptionable, I assure you!" he continued. "I was most happy to have been of service to Miss Beaufort, and we spent an agree—"

Sir George broke into this easy flow with one explosive word. *"Night?!"*

Lambert stepped back from Beecham dramatically. His hand went to the hilt of his sword. "Do you question my lady's honor, sir?" he said dangerously.

Sir George's face had suffused a dull red. "Odds fish, man!" he ejaculated, his chest swelling with real indignation. "I take leave to inform you that I am Miss Beaufort's betrothed!"

"Ah!" Lambert uttered the syllable with pregnant understanding. Dropping his guard and his hand from his sword, he was instantly conciliatory. "Naturally, I did not know!" he said and begged Sir George's pardon.

Judith was unimpressed with Lambert's theatrics. Since there was no saving herself now, she held his bland eye and said dryly, "Thank you so much, Sir Charles, for having cleared that up for me." Then, hoping to give the conversation a dexterous turn, she inquired, "And those items of mine that you have been meaning to return to me?"

"It's nothing!" Lambert disavowed quickly, glancing at Sir George. "Nothing at all!"

Lambert might as well have said that he was prevented from answering her by the presence of her fiancé. Thinking that Lambert had done enough damage already, Judith said again, "Do not hesitate to tell me what it is, sir! I am sure that Sir George is as curious as I."

Lambert waved it away and recalled a pressing engagement on the other side of the palace grounds.

This was really too much for Judith. Her voice was calm, and her words precisely spoken. "I insist, sir, that you tell me what it is."

Lambert was all gracious reluctance. "In that case, ma'am," he said very smoothly, "it is your chemise and underslip."

The scoundrel! was Judith's immediate thought, followed hard by *I should have expected no better*! Judith had no clear recollection of how she responded. She was aware only that within seconds, Lambert, acting as if nothing out of the ordinary had occurred, had excused himself with a flourishing bow.

Thereafter Judith had to summon a good deal of patience and exert an uncommon amount of tact to smooth Sir George's sorely ruffled feathers. Over the next half hour she succeeded in allaying her betrothed's concerns and in redirecting most of his anger. However, she did not fully persuade him that she should receive none of the blame for having met Charles Lambert under such equivocal circumstances; and when he demanded that she repeat the details of her adventure, stopping her at several points for further clarification, she found that her desire to persuade him of her innocence was rapidly waning.

"This is a most fantastical tale," he pronounced heavily, at last. "Do you expect me to believe it?"

Stung, Judith replied instantly, "Indeed, I do!"

"And you had to *lie* upon your return? Well, that's what comes from not having listened to Sir Robert's good advice!" was Sir George's opinion.

Her resources of patience and tact depleted, Judith retorted testily, "Advice only becomes *good* in retrospect!"

"Permit me to quote my dear mother to effect that *recognizing* good advice is rather a question of good character," Sir George replied in a voice of awesome repression.

Judith bit her tongue. The reply that sprang to her lips would not have improved relations with Sir George—or with his mother. Judith thought herself much too dignified to allow the conversation to degenerate further. She took a deep breath and said evenly, "I have said all I care to say on the subject at present. If you wish to discuss the matter further, we may do so privately. I fear that here we are attracting unbecoming attention."

Sir George was far from finished, but at no time did he wish to make himself ridiculous in public. Following Judith's lead, he, too, took a deep breath which he expelled on the slightly pompous phrase, "You may expect me, ma'am, to call on you later this evening at your apartments, at which time, I hope, we shall be able to come to a more mutually satisfying interpretation of good advice."

Although Judith recognized the statement as conciliatory, she was not thereby conciliated. "Perhaps tomorrow would better suit a meeting, sir," she said frostily, "when our tempers have cooled."

Sir George bridled slightly at the rebuff but accepted it. He bowed, deeply, stiffly. "Until tomorrow, then, ma'am," he replied. He turned on his heels and walked off in what Judith could only describe as a huff.

The day, Judith admitted freely, had started off badly. However, since she prided herself on her cool head, she mastered her anger and left the shadow of Holbein Gate to proceed with her errands, assuring herself that she felt calm and controlled. She decided that her first errand would be the delivery of the messages intended for Westminster Hall. It was not until a good hour later, upon her return from Westminster and once again crossing under Holbein Gate, that she realized how badly her nerves must have been jangled. As she sorted through the remaining envelopes, she discovered that she must have misdelivered several letters at Westminster. In having to retrace her steps to redress her errors, her humor was not improved by the fact that the traffic had increased during the course of the morning, thus hampering swift progress over the ground she had just covered.

Neither was her mood improved by the discovery that one of the messages from her uncle was unable to be delivered as addressed. Judith suspected that this was the most important message, too. The sealed letter was directed to a Mr. John Smith residing in Thieving Lane. Once there, however, Judith learned that Mr. Smith no longer resided there. She might not have pursued the matter, but her uncle had mentioned this one message most particularly in the note that he had sent ahead and had waiting for her upon arrival at Whitehall. She surmised that her uncle was most concerned about its delivery and thus she persevered in discovering the current address of Mr. Smith. She demanded of a number of rather unsavory persons littering the open doorways of Thieving Lane the possible whereabouts of this Mr. Smith until she came across one highly questionable sort who informed her, with a kind of leer, that her Mr. Smith might, on a good day, be found in St. John's Street,

Clerkenwell. That is, if he were in the country at all. Vexed that this hamlet lay too far out of her path for the day, she resolved to make a point of traveling to Clerkenwell the next day.

She had no choice but to return to her chambers. To add to her frustrations of the day, she was greeted by Edith who was thoroughly discomposed by the fact that much of the furniture ordered for the apartment had still not been received. Edith told a wild, tangled tale that contained a good deal of irrelevant information and ample commentary on insolent pages, incompetent waiters, and something about the entourage of the Venetian envoy having ruined quite a number of feather beds and bolsters, thus causing a palace shortage in these valuable commodities. Thus it was that Judith spent the better part of the next three exhausting hours attending to the ordering and placement of the bedding and other furnishings upon which her comfort at Court depended and which Edith should have been able to have accomplished hours ago.

As if all that was not enough, she received an unadorned package containing her chemise and underslip to which no note was attached.

By the end of the afternoon, Judith was ill-tempered and out of sorts. She ordered a private supper in her suite for herself and for Edith. If there was anything for which Judith could be thankful, it was that no masque or banquet or dancing or any other amusement was planned for the evening and that she and Edith could spend a quiet evening alone.

However, Judith's evening was to prove far from quiet, and she certainly did not end up spending it alone. It was to be, quite simply, a case of a day going from bad to worse.

Judith's difficulties might be said to have truly started at the moment when the writing desk finally arrived at her door borne on the broad backs of two overworked pages. Laying eyes on this piece of furniture suddenly reminded Judith of a most disagreeable task she had left undone during the course of this most disagreeable day.

She gestured the pages to set the desk next to the long,

north-facing windows, placing it at right angles to the light streaming in. When the lads withdrew, Judith bade Edith fetch her pen and ink and paper. Then she pulled a Farthingale chair up to the desk, sat down, and opened the lid. She drummed her fingers on the leather-bound surface a moment, considering how best to begin the letter to Sir George's mother, informing that lady of her arrival. Judith's feelings toward Lady Margaret, which had never been fond, were not improved by Judith's current lack of charity toward her son.

Judith gazed off in thought to her left. Her eye traveled through the open door which led to her bedchamber where her eye fell upon the four-poster with its canopied tester, flock mattress, and luxurious counterpane. Finding no inspiration there, she swiveled on her chair and started off to her right and into Edith's similarly, though less luxuriously, appointed chamber. No inspiration there, either.

Instead, Edith entered, bearing the requested writing instruments. She placed them on the scriptor in front of her pensive mistress causing Judith to rouse herself from her abstraction with an effort. Drawing a deep breath, Judith decisively trimmed the quill. Then she dipped its tip into the ink pot, scratched out her message, sanded it, sealed it, and handed it to Edith without a second thought.

Hardly had Edith left the suite to deliver Judith's letter than there came a knocking at Judith's door. Thinking that Edith must have forgotten her key, Judith crossed the antechamber to the entry hall to open the door.

When she swung the door open, her smile froze. She was far from pleased by the sight of the man at her door.

"What do you want?" she demanded curtly.

"To come in," Lambert replied pleasantly, unaffected by her palpable lack of cordiality.

"I do not want to let you in."

"I'm sure you do not," he agreed suavely, "but you will, because I am going to stand here until you do."

"Then you may stand there all night," she invited, beginning to close the door in his face.

He looked up and down the hall. "At present, there is no

one," he said. "But who is to say who will come in by the next hour or two and report that they have seen me lurking outside your door?"

Judith checked her gesture. "Why have you come?" she demanded again, peering around the edge of the half-closed door.

"To apologize."

He had said the magic word. Judith reopened the door, prepared to be mollified.

"I thought that would work," he murmured as he stepped across the threshold.

Judith put a hand out against his chest to stop him from entering. *"You thought that would work?"* she said, her anger rekindling. "You try me too far! Is this your usual method? Deliberately insulting a woman in the morning in order to gain access to her chambers in the evening with a spurious apology?"

He had walked into her hand which splayed across his chest. He grabbed it with one of his own and held it imprisoned there. "But I did not know this morning that Beecham was your fiancé," he defended himself.

"I told you his name the night we met," Judith said, stalwartly refusing to acknowledge the tingle she felt all the way up her arm at his touch. "I remember it distinctly!"

"Alas, I forgot!" he said with a charming regret and, in one fluid movement, he had bowed gracefully over her hand, had crossed the threshold, and closed the door behind him.

By the time Judith had snatched her hand back, he was through the entry and in her antechamber. He was glancing around appreciatively. "Well done!" he approved.

"Thank you," she said, watching his back as he prowled her well-furnished antechamber. "I am so happy for your approval! Now, for the *third* time, sir, tell me why you are here, since you have apparently *not* come to apologize!"

He turned on his heel. "You are one of the few acquaintances I have at Court, ma'am," he said, as if surprised. "Just a social call!" He smiled. "May I?" he said, gesturing to one of the carved oak chairs standing beside the trestle table dominating the center of the chamber.

"Just a social call?" she repeated skeptically. "You shall tell me next that you are desirous of entering society!" However, since he was impervious both to her irony and her snubs, and since she could not bodily throw him out of her suite, she nodded assent that he be seated.

She crossed the room to close the doors to the bedchambers. She was about to seat herself opposite him at the table when there came another knocking at the door.

"That will be Edith," she said with premature relief, crossing the chamber again to the entry hall, "and it seems she *did* forget her key."

However, it was not Edith, but rather a Court waiter standing before a rolling table upon which sat a variety of covered dishes that she had ordered the hour before.

Momentarily nonplussed, she simply stood aside when the waiter wheeled the table into the antechamber. He bowed himself out of the suite before Judith had moved from her spot at the entry. She stuck her head out the door to look for signs of Edith. Seeing nothing, she closed the door.

She returned to the antechamber to find Lambert standing over the rolling table, uncovering each of the platters in turn and savoring the smells that rose from the steaming dishes.

Hands on hips, she glowered at her guest. "Do you mind, sir?"

He looked up innocently. "Not at all!" he said. "It is an excellently chosen meal."

"One chosen for Edith and me," Judith pointed out.

"Who is not here, I perceive," he replied. "And the food is getting cold. It will be simple enough to order a third meal when she arrives. The king's service is excellent. Now, where is the corkscrew—ah, here!" Lambert uncorked the bottle of wine that stood on the cart and poured out two glasses, unperturbed by Judith's continuing glower. Extending her a glass, he said smoothly, "You look as if you need some fortification."

"If I do, it's no thanks to you!" Judith retorted promptly.

·"How one's best efforts to help *do* go awry," Lambert said soulfully.

"*Help*!?" Judith bit off the word. "Do not—I repeat—*do not* try me too far!"

"Oh, were things very difficult with Beecham after I left?" he inquired solicitously.

Judith saw her error. She composed herself with effort and accepted the wine. She allowed herself to be seated in the chair he had drawn up for her to face him, saying, "Oh, no, not at all! Sir George is a very reasonable man and had no difficulty understanding the situation once I explained it to him!"

Lambert disposed himself in the chair opposite Judith. "All the better, then," he said, raising his glass to her before taking a sip. "No harm done!"

"None whatsoever," Judith said primly.

"It's just that he looked—how shall I say?—angry when I left," Lambert commented reflectively, "though perhaps I misinterpreted."

"Thus prompting your desire to call on me to *apologize*, perhaps?" Judith said sweetly, "which, I note, you have *not* done."

"And which no longer seems in order," Lambert said deftly, "since all's well that ends well!"

Judith saw that she was not going to win on that one. Neither did she have the least desire to thank him for the return of her chemise and underslip. Accepting defeat, she let the topic drop. It was just as well, for Lambert was presently absorbed in inspecting the various dishes again and uncovered the one that was intended as the first course.

To her pointed silence, Lambert said meditatively, as if dredging a memory, "If I recall correctly—but, then again, I have been out of circulation for so long—I think that the rules governing social calls require that the parties engage in conversation." When Judith made no reply, Lambert dished up the fish which she refused with a shake of her hand. He set her portion in front of her anyway and said, "Let me see, now. Perhaps this is the moment where I ask politely after the cause of your sudden change in plans."

"My sudden change in plans?"

"Why, yes," he said as he proceeded to shake out the two large linen napkins and handed her one before tasting the fish in a cream sorrel sauce. "I believe that you told me when we first met that you had not planned on coming to London for another two months. And here it is but a month later."

"I did?" Judith asked, eyes round. Then, eyes narrowing, said, "I did!" She folded her hands on the table. "You remembered the detail of my travel plans, yet forgot the name of my betrothed? Your memory is selective, I perceive!"

His smile was maddeningly charming and impenitent. "Evidently!"

She held his regard steadily, then mused aloud, as if thoroughly puzzled, "What *did* Diana see in you, I wonder?"

"I was accounted something of a handsome devil in my youth," he replied outrageously, and the attraction of the light in his now-laughing eyes nearly proved the truth of his statement. Before Judith could respond, he pursued idly, "And your change in plans?" He bit into his food.

She shook her head at him, wondering if Elizabeth Marston had found his dark, ugly handsomeness more appealing than conventional good looks. Seeing no reason not to answer his question, she said, "My uncle requested me to conduct some business for him that he was unable to attend to personally."

"Unable?" Lambert prompted politely.

"He's in Ireland," she offered. "Or was, I should say."

"Ireland, was it?" he asked. "Drink up," he urged, nodding at her untouched wineglass. "Was he there long?"

Responding to the power of suggestion, Judith began to sip her wine, reflecting on the question. "Four weeks, I suppose," she said. "No, a bit more. But he's due to return to England soon."

"Soon?"

"That is, he is already in England, for he should be arriving in London the day after tomorrow." She paused to calculate. "No. The day after that."

"Two or three days from now? Your uncle must have felt he had urgent business to send you ahead to take care of it."

"I take care of quite a bit of his business," Judith said with a certain dignity, "as I have also told you before! Although I can't think that the messages I have to deliver for him here are precisely urgent, I am most happy to oblige him!" She stopped and looked over at her guest who was thoroughly at his ease and enjoying his meal. "That is, I *was* happy until this morning!"

"Let's not pick dry bones!" he recommended. "You were telling me about your uncle's misplaced sense of urgency with regard to the delivering of these messages in London."

Judith inferred a criticism of her uncle. She remembered the conversation she had had with Lambert over dinner at his house. He had put her on the defensive then about her uncle's Rules for Castle Life. She felt on the defensive now, as well.

"My uncle likes to stay abreast of his business," Judith said, "even when it isn't urgent. I can understand it."

"And what might that business be?"

Judith thought she understood his drift. If Lambert was settling down soon in Wales, he would need some money to repair Speke Hall, and he was probably desirous of transacting some business with her uncle. To show him that she bore him no grudge, she decided to be helpful.

"Paintings and more paintings," she said, walking into his broad opening. She also thought to rectify the rather negative bias Lambert held against her uncle. "He more than compensates for all of his other strictures and economies by his passion for Italian art. He cannot seem to find enough paintings to buy or to spend enough on them. And the next more beautiful than the last! His taste is impeccable, I might add. Not to mention that his *other* weakness is Irish illuminated manuscripts—for more of which, I hardly need point out, he has been in Ireland all these weeks!"

Since Lambert was evidently interested, Judith warmed to her subject and waxed enthusiastic. "But the paintings!

When next you are at Speke Hall, you must come to the gallery at Raglan. You will see there a collection of paintings rivaled only by the king's! Which reminds me that today I admired a new Gentileschi in the South Gallery which I will be sure to tell my uncle about. Have you seen it?''

Lambert said that he had not had the opportunity, but that he, too, was very interested in paintings and would be sure to look at it.

"That's right," she said, "you buy and sell paintings for a living, I think you said." She could not quite keep the touch of amused condescension out of her voice, and she completely misinterpreted the gleam that came into Lambert's eye when she continued, "You must look to do business with my uncle. I fear you shall have to wait in line, though, for he is presently negotiating with a man who wishes to sell him a painting. Despite his passion, he does buy canvases only one at a time! This man—a Mr. Smith, if you please!—must be engaged in a profession similar to your own. However, this morning, I was unable to locate him, since the address my uncle gave me was no longer current. I hope that tracking him down is not going to prove to be too much of a wild-goose chase—" Here Judith broke off and was put in mind of another topic entirely. "Speaking of wild-goose chases, did you ever find your Rosamunda?"

"Not yet." Lambert smiled noncommittally. "And your plans for the morrow? Do you continue with the search for Mr. Smith?"

"Most likely!" Judith replied.

"And where does your search take you?"

Judith was about to reply that in the morning she was bound for St. John's Street in Clerkenwell. However, she was prevented from doing so when came a third knocking at her door.

"At last! Edith!" Judith said, immediately rising and crossing to the entry hall. "That woman never remembers her key!" she remarked as she crossed the room. "Strange, though, she is not in the habit of knocking so forcefully."

It was not, in fact, Edith, and the sight of the man at her door caused Judith's heart to drop.

"Sir George!" she croaked. Then, a second time and louder, "Sir George!" She cleared her throat and said, "I thought we had agreed not to see one another until tomorrow!"

Sir George looked extremely handsome and, more important, humble. "I could not wait, Miss Beaufort!" he said with a good deal of emotion.

Although she was delighted by this expression of passion from her betrothed (since it was, in fact, the first such expression), she did not think that his timing was all that it could be. Desperate, she raised a strong offense as her best defense. "I am not prepared to receive visitors, Sir George," she said sternly. "Edith is not with me! It is not proper!"

"I know that, Miss Beauf—Judith!" he replied, reaching out for her hands and grasping them in his. His throbbing voice was suddenly loverlike. "But allow me to explain! I see it all now! You were right, and I was wrong! I was too harsh! Too critical! I beg you to let me in and make it up to you!"

"Sir George," she said as calmly as she could. "I am sensible to your request and—and . . . thrilled by your appearance at my door. However, I must insist—I *do* insist—"

All Judith's words were for naught. Her impassioned lover pushed past her, bent on making his apologies and righting his wrong.

With a tiny, fatalistic shake of her head, Judith closed the door and followed her betrothed into her antechamber.

Chapter
7

THREE steps later, Judith reentered the chamber to find that Lambert was nowhere to be seen. She was profoundly relieved, of course, but also puzzled.

Sir George had stridden to the center of the antechamber. "Miss Beaufort!" he said. "Judith!" He had turned toward his wife-to-be, his hands held out in supplication. All his earlier stiffness was drained from his voice and his gestures. "Pray, excuse this intrusion, but it is necessary!" He paused dramatically. "I have come to explain myself. I have come, in short, to apologize!"

Unfortunately, this highly gratifying opening did not have the effect on Judith it might otherwise have had. "Well, it's not the first time I have heard *that* ploy this evening!" she said, almost at random. Now, where, she wondered, was Lambert hiding? She glanced at the bedchamber doors. They were both closed. Was it possible that Lambert had sought refuge behind one of them? Or could he have slipped through the open window? She looked back at Sir George. The stricken, uncomprehending look on his face suggested strongly that she had said the wrong thing.

She tried again. "You have come to apologize?" she said politely. "How nice!" This did not seem to be quite the appropriate reply either. "I—I am . . . I am honored and deeply grateful for this expression of your sentiment.'' She took several more steps into the room, giving herself time to compose herself. ''But I really do think that it was not worth the tr—I mean that you should not have troubled yourself—that is—'' She gave it up and said brightly, ''Won't you be seated?''

She had come near enough to Sir George for him to have grasped her hands again. He held them tightly. ''You are nervous, my dear,'' he said with a note of prideful pleasure. ''I have taken you by surprise!'' He looked down into her brown eyes, the light of possession warming his blue ones. ''Just as you took me by surprise this morning.''

She attempted a smile. She looked away hastily. ''Yes, indeed! So *very* much like this morning, and so many surprises in one day!''

''Say that it is a pleasant one!'' her love cajoled. ''Just as you bade me this morning acknowledge the same!''

''Oh, indeed,'' Judith said, obeying mechanically, and attempted to draw her hands from his.

Sir George let her hands fall the moment he felt her resistance. ''I see what it is, my dear,'' he said, smiling wisely. ''Your tiring-woman is not here, and you are embarrassed to receive me alone and unattended.''

Judith seized the opportunity. ''Yes, it is most improper that you are here while I am unattended. Perhaps you should go. Immediately! We can discuss this tomorrow.''

''You must know that I think the better of you for your delicacy! Your propriety!'' Sir George exclaimed.

''You do?'' Judith said in failing accents.

''And I should be whipped for having doubted you this morning!'' he continued, making no move that would hint of departure. ''Which brings me back to the reason I have come!'' He paused. ''Judith!'' he said again, seeming to like the taste of her name on his lips and the sound of it in his ears. Then, daringly, he said, ''My love!''

Judith had waited months to hear such words, so imploringly and sincerely delivered, from her betrothed. Unfortunately, given the circumstances, she wished that he had not said them so loudly. It was dreadful to think of Lambert overhearing them, if he were still anywhere in her suite; and she could think of no way to tell Sir George that now was not the moment to bare the secrets of his heart. On the other hand, if Lambert had escaped by the window, he would be well out of earshot. However, that left the highly problematic possibility that his unconventional departure would have been seen from the windows of the apartments opposite hers. Would a scandal have screamed through Whitehall by the morrow?

Words failed her. Judith could only gaze, dumbly, up at her betrothed. This was wholly satisfying to Sir George, for he was pleased to interpret her silence as a modest shyness he had not before detected in his wife-to-be. He had also had time to take stock of his surroundings.

With an abrupt change of topic and tone, Sir George said, "I see that you have ordered dinner in your chambers."

Judith affirmed this.

"For yourself and your woman?" Sir George asked.

"Yes," Judith could answer truthfully, "for Edith and me."

Sir George peered at the two plates of food on the table. "It's still steaming hot," he remarked. He looked about him. "Where *is* your woman, by the way?"

"I had to send Edith out on an urgent errand," Judith explained.

"Just now?" Sir George asked.

"But a moment ago!" Judith improvised.

Sir George frowned. "Then it is a wonder that I did not encounter her in the hallway. That is strange. Well! And what could have been the most urgent errand that would make you take your woman from her supper?"

Judith had the perfect answer. "To send your dear mother word of my presence at Court," she said, "as you requested of me! To avoid surprising her *unpleasantly*—which I am rapidly coming to see is a consideration that more people should respect! In any case, the moment I remembered it, I could do no less than write a message and have Edith send it round to her."

Sir George was impressed by his betrothed's obedience to

his wishes and her thoughtfulness toward his mother. It augured well. "My dear, *dear* Miss Beaufort!" he said and, catching her unawares, he moved toward her and kissed her.

Startled, Judith submitted to the peck. As much as she had been curious in the past several months what a *real* kiss from Sir George would feel like (and not just the chaste press of his lips against the back of her hands), she was not able to enjoy it with an audience—even an *unseeing* one.

She broke away hastily. "Sit!" she commanded without further reflection, adding belatedly, "If you please, sir!"

Insensibly responsive to her tone, which was masterful, Sir George obeyed, taking the chair that Lambert had lately vacated.

Judith cast about for a topic of conversation. "I suppose you have heard the latest, most disturbing news that traveled through Whitehall today, sir?" she offered.

"You refer to the trouble in Scotland?" he asked, a little surprised.

"I do."

Sir George smiled a slightly superior smile that indicated that he understood that, in her embarrassment, she wished for impersonal conversation, but that she was not to worry her pretty head with such serious concerns as political uprisings. "Of course I have, my dear," he responded. The congenial note in his voice suggested that he was not offended by her slight recoil at his kiss and was possibly even pleased by it. "But speaking of my mother, as we were doing, I have already taken the liberty of informing her of your arrival—*not* that I thought you would fail to inform her yourself, and I can see that I was not disappointed in that expectation! No, indeed! However, while your message will not now give her any news she does not already know, it will be received rather as a signal of flattering attention on your part toward her."

"And how does Lady Margaret go on?" Judith asked, happy to latch on to this topic until she could think of a way to end this interview as gracefully and quickly as possible.

"Excellently, thank you," Sir George replied, half bowing in his chair. "And you will be pleased to know, I am sure, that my mother is, in part, the reason I am here this evening.''

"She is?"

"Only indirectly. You see—and I think it may surprise you to know," he said in a manner strongly reminiscent of an elderly uncle handing a pretty child a sweet, "that my mother was in complete agreement with your position."

"My position?"

"About your encounter with Charles Lambert in Wales."

"Good heavens! I thought I had covered myself! Has that story gotten around so quickly and without my knowledge?" Judith exclaimed.

"I do not believe so," Sir George replied.

"Then how could she know about it?"

"Well, I was quite angry with you this morning when I left your side—" he began.

"Not to mention that *I* was quite angry with you, sir," Judith interpolated swiftly.

"—and was not quite myself," he finished, a little tightly, "and yes, yes, of course, you were angry with me. I have come to own myself at fault, have I not?"

Judith backed down with a gracious nod of her head. "And your mother?"

"As I was saying, I was quite angry with you. Angry and not feeling myself. Almost as if I were *transported* with feelings—which I can tell you I was not raised to be! So I went to Mother and vented my anger, so to speak, and she was not entirely sympathetic to my position! Are you surprised? I can well understand it! Nevertheless, Mother thought that you could not be held accountable for the events, and she did not think that Charles's...provocation, shall we say, was reason enough for me to lose my temper."

"You told Lady Margaret the story of our encounter this morning?" she asked, incredulous.

"I am accustomed to going to her for advice, since it is so unerringly good!"

"You told Lady Margaret the *whole* story?" she iterated, mouth slightly agape.

"You *are* surprised!" Sir George said with rare powers of

perception. "I don't wonder at it, for you have never had a mother and so cannot know the comfort there is in one! However, I did not quite tell her the *whole* story. I simply said that you had met Charles Lambert in Somerset Park one afternoon and that you were unescorted! That was quite improper enough for Mother, and as for the part about your having had to spend the night under that . . . that wastrel's roof and all the lies you told at Raglan about being sheltered by a farmer and his family for the night—well, *that* shall be our little secret!"

Judith's expression did not suggest that she was appeased.

"You must know that Mother is quite fond of you," Sir George continued blithely. "She—and I—are both looking forward to the day when she can be a mother to you, too, to give you advice, to counsel you, to comfort you!"

"To prevent me from not recognizing good advice when I hear it, perhaps?" Judith's voice held a smile that hid steel.

"I have come to apologize, and will not remind you of it a *third* time," Sir George responded in kind. "It is not that I think you headstrong. No, I am not saying that. And, if nothing else, I have come to realize this evening how modest you are! However, I *am* saying that had you had the care and counsel of a mother all these years, your unfortunate encounter with Lambert would not have happened! Well, in point of fact, it is not *I* who first advanced this enlightened view. The credit properly belongs to Mother. In short, I think we will all be easier when you may call Lady Margaret your mama."

"Oh, assuredly!" Judith said, who had never felt the lack of a mother and was quite sure she did not need one now. "Did Lady Margaret, perhaps, prompt you to come to me this evening?"

Sir George wore an expression that improbably mixed guilt with determination. "My mother," he explained, "told me specifically *not* to come to visit you this evening."

"You asked for her advice on that score, too?" Judith's tone was sweet. "And she counseled you against it? I wonder why?"

Sir George shifted uncomfortably in his chair. "It was not

precisely that she thought I would *spoil* you with the attention of . . . of so precipitously seeking you out and owning myself at fault. . . .''

"No?" Judith prompted with great interest.

"No, it was rather," Sir George continued awkwardly, "that since you had refused me this morning—yes, *refused* me! Now, don't argue with that, Miss Beaufort, for I remember saying that I wished to call on you later this evening, and you put me off! In any case, since you refused me, it did not seem to my mother as . . . as *proper* that I should force my attentions on you."

"And yet you came," Judith observed, "in defiance of your mother's unerringly good advice."

Sir George reassumed his confident smile. "I do not think that I have been wrong in coming to see you."

Before Judith had a chance to reply, there came yet another knocking at the door.

Judith rose, saying aloud, "That will be Edith," and thinking, *Surely she will help me find a way to get rid of Sir George!*

However, the person at the door was not Edith but rather a stately, handsome woman whose ample figure was elaborately swathed in purple silks.

"Lady Margaret!" Judith exclaimed with a jarringly contradictory mixture of emotions. "In a day of surprises, this is surely a—why, what a *pleasant* surprise!"

Lady Margaret inclined her head to acknowledge this apparently enthusiastic greeting and formed her lips around the words, "Miss Beaufort. Good eventide."

Judith peered around Lady Margaret and inquired, "Did you not come with Edith?"

"Edith?" Lady Margaret echoed. "Your dear little tiring-woman? No, I have not seen her this evening."

"But I sent her round with a message from me to you some time ago," Judith said. "I wonder where she could be?"

Lady Margaret was not interested in the question. She smiled and said instead, "There is an unpleasant draught in the hallway, my dear."

Judith promptly held the door open to allow Lady Margaret to enter her chambers. After that large dame crossed the threshold, Judith poked her head once more out into the hallway. Seeing no one, she closed the door again, shaking her head.

"You never received my note?" Judith asked, still perplexed by Edith's possible whereabouts.

Lady Margaret turned briefly. "No. However, I see that you are much exercised by the question. If you like, when Edith does return, you may send her to me and I may instruct her in the proper ways to serve you. All this is not, of course, the reason I am come." With a smile intended to be arch, she said, "It was rather my firstborn son, who, in point of fact, informed me of your arrival at Court."

"Speaking of whom . . ." Judith began, ushering Lady Margaret on into the antechamber, but stopped mid-sentence.

The antechamber was empty of Sir George.

The coward! was Judith's first thought.

Good God! Lambert! was her second thought.

Judith's eyes flew to the two bedroom doors. Both were still closed. Would Sir George have escaped through the open window? Judith dismissed the idea. And if Sir George had chosen the same bedroom door as Lambert—?

Lady Margaret commandeered the chair that her firstborn son had just occupied. She was talking without stop. Judith took her own chair, responding distractedly and smiling mechanically.

After a moment Lady Margaret halted her seamless stream of remarks, reached over and patted Judith's hand. "I see what it is, my dear!" she said with gracious condescension. "You are nervous and not quite sure of what to say to your mama-to-be!" She smiled with vast maternal understanding. "You have absolutely nothing to worry about! I am not a dragon, but the most indulgent mama imaginable! I am certain that we shall deal extremely! Like mother and daughter! You have only to relax, my dear!"

"Oh yes, relax," Judith repeated in a tone of almost comical dismay.

Relax! she commanded herself. Never mind the fact that

she was currently experiencing the most uncomfortable situation of her life. *Relax!* After all, the odds ran even that Sir George would *not* be behind the same door as Lambert. On the other hand, the odds ran even that they *were* behind the same door. That is, *if* they both had not escaped out the window in full view of all of Whitehall and were not now in the gardens, looking at each other, wondering how they came to be below the same window. . . .

"A devoted mother misses nothing!" Lady Margaret was continuing affably. "It's the little tiff you and my firstborn son had this morning, isn't it, my dear? It has made you nervous. Very proper in a bride-to-be! I can see that I used *very* good judgment in coming this evening, to explain to you how you must go on with Georgie. Sir George," she corrected herself. "But that is not my main objective for—Oh! What is this, then? Your dinner? I see that it is your dinner."

Judith snapped back to the conversation. "Yes, I am in the midst of my dinner," she said.

If Judith thought that her guest would take the hint to leave, she was doomed to disappointment. "But there are two plates," Lady Margaret stated, with her unerring powers of observation.

"For Edith and me," Judith said. "We are *both* of us in the midst of our dinner."

"But only one of the plates has been touched." Lady Margaret's brow furrowed. "I believe you have just told me that you sent Edith on an errand to deliver a note to me, did you not?"

"Yes, I did," Judith replied.

Lady Margaret considered this information. "I do not approve," she announced.

"I thought the message to you most important," Judith replied in a tone that was not entirely deferential, "and should be delivered without delay."

Lady Margaret smiled benevolently. "Of course, you did. However, I never approve of sending trusted servants off on errands without their meals, and never, never approve of interrupting one's own meal for any reason whatsoever."

"Well, in that case, perhaps I should resume—"

"Now the food is already getting cold, and you did not even recover your dishes," Lady Margaret went on instructively. "Food should always be eaten at the temperature at which it is served. That is very important. I will discuss with you in a moment the temperature at which my firstborn son, your betrothed, enjoys his food. However, I must repeat that never, under any circumstances, must one interrupt a meal. Now, you interrupted your meal and that of your dear Edith for what you considered to be a most worthy errand. I am sensible of your consideration! But here is my lesson: A meal should not be interrupted, even for so important a reason as sending a message to *your future mother-in-law*. Do you understand? I am sure you do, for you are a clever young woman, and I have the gift of being able to communicate my ideas perfectly."

Judith saw, with a sinking heart, that Lady Margaret was settling back into her chair, as if preparing for a good, long visit.

"However, I must say—and this is not a criticism, my dear," Lady Margaret continued, "that this evening, by interrupting the meal the way you did, you display just the tiniest bit of evidence of the inconstancy, let us say almost the *impetuosity*, of your character that has troubled me in the past—but only in the smallest degree. Yes, you see that I count among my virtues the ability to speak my mind forthrightly and clearly! So that no mistakes arise as a result! That is to say, when one sits down to dine, one sits down to dine and should *not* suddenly think to dash off notes—important though they may be! And by the same token, when one is writing one's correspondence, one should not be thinking of dining! If one engages in only one activity at a time, with no distractions, one is sure to accomplish it the way it should be accomplished! But, as I was saying, I have been *concerned* about the fact that Sir George is your *third* betrothed. *Not* that I have been counting! However, it is common knowledge that you had not one, but *two* previous engagements, neither of which came to anything. And you are no longer young. Although I am *not* saying it was your fault that your second betrothed went off and got himself killed, it does, nevertheless, cause people to talk when they remember that you were quite outspoken in your refusal of your first betrothed because he was so *unsuitable*—"

A thudding noise and muffled groan emanating from behind her bedroom door caused Judith's heart to sink to her stomach.

"—which is not to say, of course, that I reproach Lord Somerset for having contracted such a betrothal in the first place. His judgment is as vast as his fortune, I am sure! And he could not have known that the young man drank as much as he did or that you would take such a disliking to his habit! Nor do I reproach Lord Somerset for having acceded to your wishes in crying off! However, your previous engagements *do* occur to one when one hears that—" Margaret broke off. "What *was* that noise, my dear? It sounded like something coming from behind that door. Is that your bedchamber, perhaps? How odd! How very odd! Now, I know you are a dog lover. Did you, perhaps, bring one of your dear little creatures to Whitehall with you? I adore dogs, I assure you, but I do not approve of taking them on trips. There's that noise again! It sounds as if it is coming from directly behind that door! I hope you will not tell me that you have brought one of your dogs with you from Raglan!"

Judith was rapidly coming to the conclusion that the worst of her fears were being realized just beyond her bedchamber door. "No," she replied with a smile that recognized impending doom, "I did not bring any dogs from Raglan."

"I am, of course, glad to hear it, and this brings me to the purpose of my visit to you this evening," Lady Margaret said with an approving nod, "for I did not come to discuss dogs or dining procedures or even how my dear firstborn son likes the temperature of his food—which is important, but I shall save that for a future discussion. Only one topic of discussion at a time is my rule! Yes, you must have guessed by now that I have come to speak with you about that little incident that occurred between you and a man whose name and reputation I hope shall never again be said in conjunction with yours! His is a name that should not be uttered in polite company! His is a name that should never again be linked with a Herbert or a Beaufort! Now, since you were such a very young girl at the time, you cannot be aware of the *scandal* that man caused—and in your very family! I will *not* mention the unfortunate woman's name, for she is well known to you. However, I will say that *he* was sent from England! And for a very good reason! I hesitate to pronounce the word 'abduction,' but there it is! Now, he is lately returned, and I am afraid, yes, *very* afraid, Miss Beaufort, my dear daughter Judith, that you have had the misfortune through your own ill-considered actions and poor judgment to have had an 'incident' with him. I have come, in short, Miss Beaufort, to speak to you about that very unsavory character, that very wicked man—''

Accompanying these final words, a crash emanated from behind Judith's bedroom door that could have been caused only by her chest of drawers toppling over. Judith jumped up from her chair at the same moment that her bedroom door opened and a very disheveled Sir George hurtled through it.

Lady Margaret's head had whirled around. She, too, stood and barked, ''Georgie! George! George Augustus Beecham! *What* is the meaning of this?''

Sir George was unable to reply immediately, for he was having to work his jaw with one hand and to shake his head clear.

Immediately on the heels of Sir George, Lambert emerged from the bedchamber, and Judith felt a kind of helplessness wash over her.

It was Lambert who replied to Lady Margaret. Smoothing down the sleeves of his doublet, he said with remarkable impudence, ''I am afraid that this fellow here does not know how to conduct himself in a lady's bedchamber.''

''*Who*, may I ask, are *you*?'' Lady Margaret demanded.

''Charles Lambert, ma'am,'' was the reply, punctuated by

a smooth bow. "I do not believe that I have had the honor . . . ?"

Lady Margaret's mortification was profound. She turned to Judith, riveting her with a quelling look. "And what have you to say for yourself, Miss Beaufort?"

Judith said the first thing that came to mind. "I do wish Edith were here," she answered. "Everything would be so very much less *complicated* if Edith were here!"

Lady Margaret was not going to waste her time with lesser prey. She returned her basilisk eye to Lambert. She intoned with majestic indignation, "So! Charles Lambert! And *what*, may I ask, were *you* doing in Miss Beaufort's *bedchamber*?"

Lambert was unmoved. "I am not sure you may ask, ma'am, but Miss Beaufort has the right to know that my retreat to her bedchamber," he said with the righteousness of one who believes himself to be on the moral high road, "was an attempt to spare her embarrassment. However, it would seem that my motive," he said with an insolent nod at Sir George, "differs significantly from this fellow's here."

Never did Lady Margaret allow indignation to overcome her powers of speech. "'This fellow,'" Lady Margaret shot back, "is my son!"

Lambert looked from mother to son. "Ah!" he remarked with composure, "so his motives *did* differ from mine!"

Sir George recognized an insult when he heard one. Flourishing his bruised chin and thrusting aside all his hurt and humiliation, he flung back, "Upon my honor, I should call you out for that, Lambert!" he challenged impetuously. His hand went to the hilt of his sword.

Lambert's hand did not follow suit. "Keep it sheathed, Beecham," he recommended without heat.

"You refuse me?" Sir George's tone was ominous.

"I refuse you nothing," Lambert replied.

At that, Lady Margaret collapsed into her chair, clutching her bosom, finally rendered speechless at thoughts of her firstborn son skewered at the end of this disreputable man's sword.

"I recommend that you do not call me out, however," Lambert continued, unperturbed, "for I would not refuse you, and an open duel between us would only cause Miss Beaufort more trouble than you have already given her this evening."

The extreme good sense of Lambert's remarks was not lost on Sir George. Far from cooling the flames of his unreason, however, it fanned them. "I? *I?*" Sir George ejaculated. "*I* caused her trouble? How so, sir? *How so?* When it was *you* who started it!"

"If only Edith had been here," Judith murmured, "none of this would have happened. Where *can* she have gotten to, I wonder?"

Lambert measured Sir George with an eye in which scorn and surprise were nicely blended. "If you wish to say, Beecham," he replied, ignoring Judith's interjection, "that I started it when my fist hit your jaw after yours missed mine, I will not take exception."

Sir George felt angry and defeated but not silenced. "I found *you* lurking in her bedchamber!" he cried, stepping forward, brandishing his fist in Lambert's face.

Lambert was unimpressed with the argument and the gesture. "You took refuge there as well, my good fellow."

With the quarrel threatening to come to blows again, Judith stepped into the breach. Desperate to reaffirm control, she began in her most authoritative accents, "Gentlemen! Gentlemen! And Lady Margaret! All this has such a *simple* explanation! Listen to me!"

The evil star that was crossing Judith's evening continued to exert its nefarious influence. Before she could offer her admirably simple explanation that would set all to rights, another knocking came at the door.

This interruption was enough to divert her. "Now *who* on earth could that be?" Judith cried in real exasperation. "I wish they would go away!" When the knocking became insistent, she propelled herself to the entry door.

To Judith's profound surprise, she opened the door to Edith, with Judith's wayward cousin Caroline in tow.

"I forgot my key!" Edith said brightly, holding up her

empty hands. "Oh, and I have not yet delivered your message to Lady Margaret, but I *have* found Miss Caroline!"

"Too late!" was all Judith could think to say. "I already have visitors!"

"Oh, a party! That is very fine!" Caroline said happily and fell on her cousin's neck, kissing her soundly. With the tide of events firmly against her, Judith simply stepped aside while Caroline and Edith chattered their way happily across the threshold.

Caroline stopped short her bubblings when greeted by the scene in Judith's antechamber. She bobbed a curtsy and wished a polite "good eventide" to Lady Margaret, Sir George, and the man in the room who was unknown to her. Caroline was an exquisitely pretty young woman who had not above the average powers of perception, but even she was able to discern the charge in the atmosphere. In a question not calculated to soothe matters, she characteristically blurted out, "But, Judith, what have you been *doing*?"

Lady Margaret had risen from her chair. She had recovered from any vision of her firstborn's tragic and ignominious death at the tip of Lambert's sword. Her tongue had been restored to her. "What Miss Beaufort has been doing," she replied majestically, "is exhibiting her hoydenish ways which, I do not hesitate to say, includes the entertainment of men in her bedchamber!"

Caroline rounded her pansy eyes and formed her cupid's lips into an O. "Judith!" she said, surprised.

"Not one, but *two* men," Lady Margaret clarified.

"Judith!" Caroline iterated, now with a pretty frown.

"It was not enough that she saw fit to entertain a man to whom she has been honorably betrothed," Lady Margaret pursued ruthlessly, "but she has included in her court a man whose name has already besmirched that of the Somerset family!"

"*Judith*!" Caroline repeated, the one word now full of reproach. "That is very bad of you! I see that I have come none too soon! I did not think it would have been necessary to tell you not to entertain Sir George privately—or any other man!—but now I think that I must instruct you in the ways of Court without further delay!''

"It needed only that!" Judith exclaimed, casting her hands heavenward. "A lesson in social conduct from Caroline!"

"Well, Edith did persuade me that you were eager to see me," Caroline said, "and now I understand!" She looked about her at the principals in the present drama and said seriously, "This is not the kind of party you should be having, my dear. I am afraid that you will have given your future mama-in-law the wrong impression!"

Lambert recognized his cue to leave. He approached his hostess, bowed, and said, "Miss Beaufort! I am sorry!"

Judith met his eye. He did not *look* sorry. "You have been nothing but trouble since I met you," she said.

"So it seems," he acknowledged with another bow. "You must tell me how I can make this evening up to you."

Judith knew exactly where to lay the blame of the entire episode. "You will oblige me immeasurably by never crossing my path again."

"Just so, ma'am," Lambert said, deeply respectful, and took a graceful leave.

Lady Margaret was not as graceful under pressure as Lambert. She had been shocked and mortified and was unable, or unwilling, to overcome her shock and mortification. She did not deign address Judith. "As for *wrong* impressions, Miss Herbert," Lady Margaret said in majestically reproving tones to Caroline, "I will leave you to the instruction of Miss Beaufort. Come along, George. I must agree with Miss Herbert's great good sense that this is *not* the kind of party to which the House of Beecham is accustomed!" Lady Margaret almost snapped her fingers.

Her firstborn son obeyed. He left the room in his mother's wake, lingering only long enough to cast Judith a long, soulful regard and uttering, "Odds fish, Miss Beaufort!" in a voice compounded of betrayal and desire.

"I shall speak to both of you on the morrow," Judith had the presence of mind to call out to their backs, but no response came from either.

Judith drew a deep breath and turned to Caroline and

Edith. Before either of those two ladies could speak, Judith held up a hand. "Do not, I beg of you, say a word! Not a word!" She drew a deep breath. "I am in no condition to receive any comments or criticisms just now! Attribute it to a failure of nerves and my very hoydenish ways!"

For all of her other faults, Edith did know, on occasion, when to hold her tongue. Caroline took charge. "There, now, Judith!" she said, taking her older cousin's elbow and leading her to a chair. "You will feel better if you sit! We shall speak on the morrow, and there will be time enough then for me to tell you of Court ways! You needn't worry about this evening! You are not accustomed to the manners here and think you are at Raglan where you can command everything to your liking! You have always made it a point to stay at Raglan where you do so much to insure Father's comfort! There, now! I am sure that it was all a stupid misunderstanding. Don't you feel better now?"

Judith's composure threatened to desert her. Her voice began to wobble when she said, "Oh, assuredly, Caroline! Much better! But I feel, yes, I really do feel that I need some moments alone!"

Caroline was all understanding. "You do, indeed, my dear. I shall return on the morrow after you have had a good night's rest to tell you how to go on at Whitehall! It is not so very difficult." She leaned down to kiss Judith and bade her a "good night" to which she appended numerous soothing platitudes.

Edith was torn between her duty to her mistress and her duty to her younger charge. "I am not sure that Miss Caroline should go unattended through the hallways," Edith said, biting her lip.

Judith had covered her eyes with one hand. With her other, she waved Edith out of the room. "Go, Edith, do!" she urged, her voice still wavering. "And don't forget your key!"

Edith exited, with the assurance that she would return on the instant.

A very few minutes later, the well-trained member of the King's Royal Service returned to finish his duties at Miss

Beaufort's suite. When he presented himself at his mistress's hallway door, he found that it had been inadvertently left ajar. After a light knocking produced no response, the waiter stuck his head inside and called out his presence.

A muffled, unsteady voice replied with something that sounded remarkably like, "Good God! Dare I ask who it could be?" Then, "Come in, come in. Nothing more can possibly go wrong, for the worst has already happened."

Hesitantly, the waiter entered the antechamber. There he saw the mistress of the suite slumped in a chair, her shoulders shaking, one hand lying in her lap, the other covering her eyes.

"Begging your pardon, my lady," the waiter said, hushed and embarrassed, "but the hour has passed, and I've come to inquire whether you have finished with your dinner."

At that Judith looked up. To the waiter's surprise, he saw that she was not crying but laughing.

"Dinner? Am I finished with my dinner?" Judith replied, unable to keep her voice from quavering. "You might say that I am *quite* finished with it! Yes, indeed! You may take it away! Not a bite did I eat, but I am most certainly done with dinner!" An unsteady merriment lit her eyes. "*Un*done, rather!"

Chapter
8

LAMBERT was in a good mood. He had concluded a
tidy transaction at the Banqueting House the hour
before. He relished dealing with men whose passion
for painting equaled his own and who would not be deceived by the certificates of authenticity which were peddled
so promiscuously by less honest dealers. Nevertheless, Lambert did not place the same demands on great canvases as
did some at Whitehall who seemed to subscribe to the
current maxim: "The trumpet of art blows louder through
time and space than any other trumpet." Although Lambert
was not an ardently political creature himself, he would
have said, shrewdly enough, had he been asked to assess the
future of Charles Stuart's monarchy, that a skillful collecting
was no substitute for skillful governing.

None of these thoughts weighed on him as he made his
way down St. John's Street, heading toward The Red Bull
Theater. Absorbed in the moment, he was reveling in the
sights and sounds of the narrow lane which was thronged
with a motley marketday crowd whose number was being
swelled at every moment by more marketers who mingled
into it from the debouching labyrinth of equally narrow
streets. The jostling crowd flowed between the cobbles and
the shops which stood gable-end on to the street, with their

deep eaves and carved corbels, projecting upper stories, lattice windows, and their signs of the Golden Fleece or the Three Lutes or the Spread Eagle swinging over their doors.

Lambert wove his way between the drays and packhorses, the sumpter mules and porters who competed with each other and the marketers. With a shake of his head, he passed by the outstretched hands of 'prentices crying from their shop doors, "What d'ye lack, gentles? What d'ye lack?" He eyed with fleeting interest the outstretched hands of the gaudy strumpets who cooed in mimicry, "I have what ye lack, gentles! I have what ye lack!" His ears rang with the melodious sounds of the men and women on the street corners who sang, "Hassocks for your pew!" or "Sweet Lavender!" or "Cherry ripe!" He savored the changing palette of aromas, both fragrant and fetid, that assailed his nostrils with each new step.

It was not a wholly fashionable throng, the one Lambert traveled in, but it was colorful; and as he approached the vicinity of the theater, the crowd became even more of an ever-shifting medley of colors, all jostling, laughing, cursing in the summer sunshine under the blue sky where pigeons circled.

Only once did Lambert have to stop, when he was elbowed—quite by accident, one might have supposed—by a muscular youth with an acorn haircut.

"Easy, stripling," Lambert said softly into the youth's ear. He had grabbed the young man at the wrist. "I carry no purse." In a viselike grip, Lambert withdrew the pickpocket's hand from inside his doublet.

The young man displayed no chagrin at being caught, and Lambert continued on his way. At the bottom of the lane Lambert spied the establishment of entertainment known as The Red Bull Theater. Like all other London theaters, this one was built of wood and open at the top, save for that part immediately over the stage which was thatched. Its construction was suited to performances in the daytime and when the weather was fine. Today was such a day, and soon the flag with the cross of St. George upon it would be unfurled on the roof to signal that a play was in progress.

Lambert plunged unhesitatingly into the crowd of theater-goers who milled in front of the ticket booth. This crowd now included women whose masks and fine clothes indicated that they were from the middle or upper classes and that they had come to this place of liberty in search of adventure. Lambert bought his ticket and paid for a box. He then made his way past the booth and diverted his path down the side of the building.

He passed to the left of the main entrance above which was hung a banner announcing, to all who could read, that the day's performance was Philip Massinger's *The King and the Subject*. The banner proclaimed it to be "A Spanish Historie, Acted by the Companie of the Revels." For such a subject, the theater crowd was an unusually large one this day.

Lambert darted into a clump of trees between the theater and the street. In the shade, he found Will, as had been prearranged. Lambert's brows had raised in question. "Any sign of her?" he demanded of his henchman.

Will shook his head. "Not yet, and I've been here the better part of the morning."

Lambert glanced to his left. There he had a good view of the back entrance to the theater by which the actors entered the wings. The open door was hung with a dirty woolen curtain that was drawn to one side and held back by a man whose insolent demeanor indicated that he had been bred and breeched in the backstage world of the theater. There was the usual activity at that entrance befitting the half hour before a performance. Off to his right, Lambert spied the entry to The Old Dun Cow, the locale known to be frequented by thirsty players before a performance.

"She might well be in disguise," Lambert suggested as he gestured minimally first to the stage door, then to the tavern. "But," he added wryly, "we have thought that from the beginning."

"I've had my eye out, right as rain," Will assured his master, "for my name wouldn't be Will Puckett if I couldn't twig to her tricks!"

"Our Rosamunda has led us on a merry chase," Lambert agreed.

"Until now," Will replied stolidly.

"That remains to be seen," Lambert said. "Rosamunda's trail certainly leads here, and good work you did to discover it."

"It were Dick what heard the news that a woman fitting Rosamunda's description had just taken to plying her trade at The Red Bull in the past few days," Will confessed, for he was never one to steal another man's thunder. "But as for nosing out news, it's a damn sight easier when you're among men what speak the tongue! Faith, it's good to be back in England!"

Lambert nodded. "Nevertheless, following her trail here is one thing. Getting her to comply with our wishes is another."

Will assumed his characteristically pugnacious stance. "I've got what it takes, master. Never you doubt it!"

"I don't, my dear Will," Lambert reassured. "However, you lack delicacy. I've told you often enough that brute force is not the answer to everything. Ingenuity often serves better."

Will knew nothing of delicacy or ingenuity. He grumbled a response that expressed a heartfelt desire to draw Rosamunda's cork.

"I've never liked blood, Will," Lambert said. He smiled. "Except on canvas, of course."

In that case, then, Will offered to simply crush the hapless Rosamunda's bones.

"Poor, gentle Rosamunda," Lambert remarked.

"Hah!" Will pounded his fist into his open palm. "I says: let's hunt her down and deal with 'er like a man!"

"That," Lambert replied, "would be most satisfying. But if it's a man's blood you want, you might rather lust after Spadaccio's, for his stake is at the bottom of all of this. Somewhere. Somehow. His appearance in Wales was too extraordinary to be a mere coincidence with Rosamunda's tracks. Ah, Spadaccio! Always wearing one mask or another! Too bad he is not a figure known to the English theater world, as our Rosamunda seems to be!" Lambert paused in reflection. "Yet he is known to Somerset." He shook his head. "What the devil does Somerset have to do with him? And what, I wonder, is the precise relationship between the two of them and my painting—if any?"

Will could not answer these extremely abstract questions. Since their return to England, Will had listened in some awe to Lambert's assessment of the current situation in the English Court. Will did not understand all the particulars, but he knew that Lambert had a quick ear for news and an uncanny way of piecing together unlikely bits of information, and Will knew that Spadaccio's appearance on the scene had roused Lambert's suspicions that the king was secretly negotiating with the Vatican. Will had vaguely grasped the idea that King Charles was playing a dangerous game with Rome, exchanging compliments and agents between his Court and the Vatican. Lambert had explained to him that the king's affection for his Catholic wife and her friends was making him indiscreet; that the king harbored the hope that the Vatican would make the necessary concession to the Anglican Church so that there might be, once again, a unified Catholic Christendom; that the king's favoring of the Papists and persecution of the country's Protestants was not only foolish but also possibly deadly; that the king was blundering badly, if events the day before in Scotland were any indication.

Lambert had explained to him, as well, that Somerset was, to the depths of his Puritan soul, a loyal supporter of the Stuart king. Somerset was no doubt well aware of the pitfalls that lay ahead if the king remained on his present course. Somerset would not have underestimated the strong, militant Puritan dislike of the Catholic-sympathizing Charles. Somerset, Lambert guessed, had received straight from the hands of Spadaccio some important message from Rome that day in the yard of The Craven Arms.

Mention of Somserset did prompt Will to ask eagerly, "And Somerset's niece? You visited her last night, did you not, to discover what you could of her uncle's interest? What did you learn from her?''

All Lambert's seriousness vanished. His very engaging smile flashed. ''I learned that she has a prig of a husband-to-be and a formidable future mother-in-law!''

Will had never been able to keep up with his master's nimble moods. ''You don't mean it!'' he said.

''Oh, but I do!'' Lambert said, laughing. ''However, I believe with a little practice Miss Beaufort will be the equal of the cross, overbearing, battle-ax of a woman who goes by the name of Lady Beecham.''

Will interpreted this as a criticism of Miss Judith Beaufort who had won his admiration that day in the rain in the woods of Gwent. ''Miss Beaufort, a battle-ax?'' he demanded, half astonished, half angry.

''Perhaps one day!'' Lambert replied cheerfully, still laughing at the memory of the previous evening's entertainment. ''Furthermore, I predict that she'll have brought the husband-to-be to heel by this evening and have him whimpering and wagging his tail by the morrow.''

Will hardly knew how to respond to these disclosures. ''And Somerset?'' he ventured.

Lambert turned his empty hands palms upward. ''I know little more now than I did a week ago.'' He shifted his gaze back to the stage door and the procession of tuppenny theatricals. ''Miss Beaufort is either a consummate actress or completely ignorant of her uncle's affairs. She did give the glimpse of an idea, however—''

Before he could complete the thought, Will had grabbed his master's arm and exclaimed in suppressed tones, ''There she is! Over there! Just beyond the ticket booth! Tell me if that's not our dainty Rosamunda!''

Lambert obeyed Will's directive. He saw a woman's back whose curves and movements were strongly familiar. Even on so warm a day, her cowl was properly arranged to cover most of her head, thereby obscuring the color of her hair from Lambert's view. The color of the hair hardly mattered, however, for Rosamunda was known to favor wigs. The general bustle at the ticket booth also prevented Lambert from a direct look at the woman, but he had trailed her from Italy from far greater distances and with far less to go on.

Lambert had received the reliable information about how and where Rosamunda was earning her living in London. He might have known that this stage-whore would do nothing so obvious as to enter by the stage door. Here she was, at the ticket booth, displaying an understated hesitation, as if she could not decide whether or not to purchase a ticket. A lovely acting job—just in case anyone was bothering to watch her.

"Do you think—?" he said to Will, his eyes suddenly alight. "That just might be the woman I am looking for."

"Oh, aye, that's her!" Will agreed, craning his neck to keep his eye on the woman's back, although it was hard to do with the throng bustling about her.

"I can't quite tell," Lambert hesitated.

"I'll take care of this," Will announced. "And a pleasure it will be, too!"

Lambert stayed his henchman with a strong arm. He shook his head. "Once she buys a ticket and enters, she'll be lost to us, and I don't want to miss this opportunity." He then commanded Will to stand pat. "I'll take care of it my way! Brutalizing a woman in the marketplace will not advance our cause!"

"Don't go soft on me, man!" Will admonished, thoroughly disappointed, for his idea of making the most of the opportunity included the rearrangement of Rosamunda's facial features.

Lambert began to walk off. "Soft?" He looked back over his shoulder at his henchman. "Soft is exactly what I intend to be, my dear Will!"

At the ticket booth, Judith had been dithering over whether to attend the performance of *The King and the Subject*. Her ability to decide was not improved by the jostling crowd of extremely rude men who seemed to find almost any excuse to rub up against her. Since entering the market in St. John's Street, she had found herself to be forever in contact with somebody or another. It was most annoying. Added to which, of course, was the fact that she had been, once again, unable to deliver that most important letter entrusted her by her uncle.

Not ten minutes before, Judith had presented herself at what she had been given as the present address of Mr. John Smith. There she had been told that the mystery man only occasionally stayed in St. John's Street and was, in any case, not there just then.

Did anyone know where Mr. Smith could be found? Judith asked. Today, for instance?

No answer to this question had been immediately forthcoming.

Judith had, by then, gathered that she was standing at the door to a brothel; and it was hardly a quality establishment at that, if the raddled beauty with whom Judith was speaking and whose uncorseted curves were running to fat was any indication. Although reluctant to enrich this lady of pleasure by so much as a farthing, Judith withdrew a silver coin from her purse, and this douceur produced information that was as startling as it was puzzling.

"*Mr.* Smith," the beauty said, leaning forward, "might best be found performing his sport at The Bull." The beauty elbowed Judith suggestively. "If you see what I mean."

"The Bull?"

The beauty nodded her head toward the street. "Across from The Cow."

Could Mr. Smith be described, Judith wanted to know?

The answer to this question required the exchange of another silver coin. "He's a lovely beardless youth, he is, with his yaller hair," the beauty explained. She surveyed Judith critically. "About your height. About your build, think on!" The beauty opened her mouth to add something to this description but apparently changed her mind, for she closed it again and nodded a dismissal.

Judith thanked the woman and headed down the street in the direction the beauty had indicated. A few more steps, and Judith had put two and two together to arrive at the sum that Mr. Smith could be found at The Red Bull Theater. Standing in the bright, bustling crowd outside the theater, Judith had determined that Mr. Smith must be an actor.

Although Judith was not squeamish or otherwise shocked by her encounter at the brothel, she could not help but wonder: *What sort of business is my uncle engaged in? And what sort of people is he involved with in it?*

After much hesitation and strongly aware that she had wandered into territory that should be out of bounds to her, Judith decided that she very much wanted the answer to these interesting, forbidden questions. And the answers lay inside, not outside, the theater.

She stepped up to the booth and attempted to position herself in the throng of last-minute ticket buyers. She was almost at the wicket when a body—a thoroughly masculine body—slid up behind her and pressed its length to her back. One strong arm slipped round her waist while the other bold one found her breast. A low voice, deeply familiar, whispered a suggestion and a price, both of which were very flattering.

The surprise and surge at this man's touch was powerfully immobilizing. It took a second for Judith to recover. Then she whirled around in the man's arms. Her color was high, to be heightened further by the sight of the man who held her.

"I might have known!" she exclaimed.

Lambert was no less astounded than Judith. His embrace slackened. His hands fell to her waist. "There's been a—" he began.

"*A mistake*?" she finished swiftly, hot anger, mixed with a kind of relief and something else again, blazing from her eyes.

Lambert looked down into Judith's angry, upturned face and lost the impulse to beg the lady's pardon. He grinned. "Perhaps not, after all," he said.

"*Not* a mistake, then?" Judith continued. Experiencing acute embarrassment, she summoned anger to cover it. "Your manners, sir, are at all times extraordinary! But do not tell me that you have been away from England so long as to think that this—this *greeting* passes as acceptable!"

The grin did not leave Lambert's face. His imp of

mischief prompted him to explain, truthfully, "No, in fact, I was searching for Rosamunda."

Judith was incredulous. "You confused me with her *again*?"

"No," Lambert said, "Will did."

Judith blinked.

"He's over there," Lambert directed smoothly, plainly enjoying himself, "under the trees. Do you see him?"

Judith turned her head slightly and caught sight of the man she remembered as Will standing in the shade of trees, with a sheepish expression on his ugly face. When he saw Judith look over at him, he slid his cap respectfully from his head, smiled meekly, and trilled blunt fingers in salutation.

"You are blaming this most . . . *outrageous* incident on Will?" she demanded, anger flaring again.

"Yes," Lambert replied, without hesitation. While Judith assimilated this further information, Lambert gestured to Will to enter the theater by the stage door. Will disappeared. "And lucky you were that I took the situation in hand, so to speak," Lambert continued. "If I had let Will have his way, you might have had your nose broken."

"Oh, I see!" Judith exclaimed tartly, "I am to respond to your . . . your . . . *behavior* by thanking you?"

Lambert smiled. "If your response is to thank me," he replied with mock, exasperating seriousness, "I suggest you choose a less public place."

"You are—I repeat—outrageous!" she exclaimed.

The look Lambert bent on her was unrepentant. She saw that it was clearly impossible to disconcert a man with as little moral fiber as Charles Lambert—which thought led her to realize that she was still imprisoned in his arms. She looked down and said, with steely sweetness, "Do you mind, sir?"

"Not at all!" came the prompt response.

"Your hands, sir!" Judith snapped.

"Ah yes!" he replied and let his hands drop, reluctantly, from her waist.

Judith readjusted her cloak across her shoulders. In an attempt to recover her composure she said, "I see what it must be. Since Will thought to abduct me in Somerset Park at your instigation, you thought it only fair to . . . to *manhandle* me in the marketplace at his behest. Have I got that right?''

"Speaking of which," Lambert said conversationally, "and in the press of all the other events yesterday, I never had a chance to ask how things went with you when you returned to Raglan after your, er, abduction.''

Given the magnificent disaster of the preceding day, Judith did not think her dignity could suffer any more abuse. "There were no unpleasant repercussions from my uncle, if that is what you mean, who was very understanding of the sequence of events when I wrote him of them," Judith said. Since she had no desire to embroider on that patent lie, she continued,"However, the similarities in the two incidents is *not* what I find most striking at the moment!''

"No?"Lambert inquired politely.

"No," Judith replied. "In fact, what I find most singular just now is the fact that I requested of you—at the low point of the 'other events,' I think you are phrasing it, hardly twenty-four hours ago, sir!—*not* to cross my path again! And you agreed to stay out of my way! What more must I do to insure that happy state of affairs, I wonder?''

"First, you must stay away from the theater crowd," he said instructively, "and secondly, you must understand that those were merely our exit lines.''

"Exit lines?''

"From a bad scene," Lambert began.

"A bad scene—?''

"—in a bad play," Lambert finished, nodding sagely. "You see, since I have been in so many of Harry Webster's remarkably bad farces, I am well acquainted with the rôles." Lambert had noticed that the crowd was thinning, and he did not want to miss a moment of the performance. He took Judith's hand, slid it through his elbow and guided her, unresisting, another step or two toward the theater entrance. "Let me see. There was Outraged Propriety— admirably played by Lady Beecham. I was almost impressed. The Befuddled Suitor. The Youthful Beauty—''

"The Youthful Beauty?" Judith asked, suspicious.

"Your niece," Lambert explained. "Caroline, isn't that her name? The one who is taken by my nephew? Yes. Lovely girl. And The Mouse—your tiring-woman, I believe. Indeed," he said, "all the elements were there, and rather well cast!"

"And myself?" Judith demanded.

"Why, the Butt of the Joke, of course," Lambert said.

Judith snorted. "I am not accustomed to such a rôle, sir, I assure you!"

"Which is, perhaps, why you fell somewhat short," Lambert said sympathetically, "of rising to the pitch of humor that the scene demanded of you!" He surveyed Judith critically. "You might think yourself better cast as Queen of the Castle, but I'll share with you a piece of theatrical wisdom. It's often the case that those who take themselves the most seriously make the best comedians! However, I do not mean to criticize, for with practice comes improvement."

Judith was eyeing her escort malevolently. "And *your* rôle, sir?"

"Why, I was there to give the piece a bit of dignity, to save it from a descent into true bathos," he said with a touch of hauteur, instantly in character. Then, anticlimactically, "Although I would have loved to have broken Beecham's teeth."

"You wouldn't have!" Judith exclaimed.

"Yes!" Lambert replied without hesitation, but then added reflectively, "Fortunately for you, my professionalism was too great to have allowed the scene to degenerate into a common brawl."

So absurd an interpretation of the most exquisitely embarrassing situation of her life brought an inappropriate laugh to Judith's lips. She quickly suppressed it. "The only fortunate part of the scene for me was that it engendered no scandal!" she said. "I truly expected to have disapproving eyes and mouths whispering behind hands following me this morning when I traveled the corridors of Whitehall!"

Arms still linked, Lambert and Judith had been slowly trailing the last of the ticket holders approaching the entrance. At that he stopped and looked down at Judith. "No," he said, "news of a king embroiled in grave affairs of state always takes precedence over a personal scandal, does it not?"

"The king embroiled himself in no grave affairs of state yesterday," Judith said cautiously.

"Merely an uprising in Scotland," Lambert tossed off, "as a result of the new prayer book Charles so imprudently imposed on the Presbyters. And he a Scot himself! He should have known better."

Judith could affect as much unconcern as he. "Since when does an uprising in the North qualify as 'grave affairs of state'?"

"When it breaks into civil war," Lambert said, serious now.

"The king will, of course, need to exercise control in Scotland, if that is what you mean," Judith said, suddenly uncomfortable with the dark turn in the conversation.

"The king exercising control! There's a topic for theater!" Lambert said, his tone once again light. He looked down at her quizzically. "I must suppose that you are come to The Red Bull today for the same reason that I am come!"

Judith thought it unlikely. "And what reason might that be?" she inquired, meeting his eye.

"A trifling case of censorship," he said. "Surely you have heard of it?"

"Of course," she replied, tight-lipped.

He could not determine her reaction, but he did heartily wish to know the reason she was at The Red Bull today and unescorted. "Like everyone else—and you perceive the crowd that has gathered," he said, gesturing about, "I've come to see whether the playwright has bowed to the royal request to rewrite that passage in the first scene of his history *The King and the Subject*."

"Bowed?" Judith replied. "The king found the passage most objectionable, I understand. If he has asked Massinger to alter it, he is merely testing the playwright's loyalty."

"The king is testing his own ability to censor," Lambert said.

"The king found some of the playwright's lines offensive," Judith said, loyal herself, "and it is widely known that the king's taste, in literature as in art, is impeccable. His taste should be respected."

"The king is most certainly a gentleman of taste," Lambert acknowledged readily. He continued daringly, dangerously, "However, he does not seem to act with as much discernment as he reads, and as for knowing the arts, I would say that the art of reigning is the only one of which he is ignorant. He has governed for ten years now without a Parliament and will not last another ten without one." Before the niece of one of the king's most trusted advisors could condemn his words as treasonous, he was remarking, "Yet the crowd has come for one reason or another—and most probably not for the high moral tone of the entertainment." He held out the ticket he had purchased. "Speaking of high moral entertainment, do you join me?"

Judith hesitated. She looked back at the ticket booth just as the shutter was being closed across the wicket. She had developed a many-sided interest in the day's production. She raised a skeptical brow. "With you as my escort?"

"With me as your escort," Lambert said. "For protection."

At that moment, the trumpet sounded thrice, signaling that the play was about to begin.

"Somehow, I think, sir," Judith said, "that *you* are the very one I should be protected against!"

Interpreting that as a "yes," Lambert merely laughed and ushered Judith through the stile and into the theater.

Chapter
9

JUDITH and Lambert were among the last to enter the theater. Behind them the heavy beam was set across the wooden doors. It would be lifted only after the curtain fell on the last act or in the event that some fool started a fire, for men of rank smoked freely here.

Inside all was abuzz with what was the real business of the afternoon. In the main arena, the fine young sparks were indulging in rough jokes, drinking beer, eating fruits, playing cards as well as beckoning to the prospects in the gallery which ran around three sides of the building. In this structure, reserved for the better portion of the public at prices ranging from sixpence to half a crown, sat the respectable middle class of merchants as well as the unmasked ladies who enjoyed the flattering attention of the ''groundlings,'' as those who paid a penny to stand in the pit were known. According to their interest, these bold damsels responded with taunts and coarse rejections or with come-hither looks and cloaks now open to reveal broad, white Puritan collars whose cut displayed anything but Puritan intentions. Several covered boxes crowded close to the stage. Known as lords' rooms, these were occupied by more dashing cavaliers who were already seriously engaged with another class of lady whose coquettish black linen masks were now askew. Matrons of refined taste and morals also appreciated the theater and were lodged in such boxes, though always escorted by a man and never accompanied by their giddy daughters who would have been prime targets for the "groundlings." Above these boxes was perched a higher gallery for the orchestra, and the stage was separated from the audience by palings and a woolen curtain on a rod which would be drawn apart in another minute or two.

"And our ticket?" Judith inquired, looking about, surveying the open commerce with a mixture of fascination and disapproval.

Lambert gestured toward the stage and to the left. "I bought the last of the boxes." He drew her in the direction of their box by placing his hand lightly at the small of her back.

"Good." Judith nodded, accepting his guidance. "I would not want to miss a moment of the action onstage—or a good view of any of the actors."

"If we attend too conspicuously to the performance," Lambert said, eyes twinkling, "we shall draw unwanted attention to ourselves."

Judith stopped short and looked up at him. This provocative comment brought vividly to mind the manner in which he had greeted her not ten minutes ago. If he were trying to disconcert her, he would fail. She had to put a stop to such nonsense right from the start. "Not a thing, sir," she threatened, low. "Do not try a thing."

The twinkle in Lambert's eyes deepened to something warmer. He bent down to whisper into her ear, "You must wait until we arrive at our box to tempt me so."

Not for a moment was Judith fooled by this apparently amorous byplay. Her voice was firm. "I shall try to contain myself, sir."

Lambert released his hand and drew himself upright. "Oh, I see!" he said, feigning sudden understanding. "I thought that you—but you could not know—! That is, you are unacquainted with what I find attractive in a woman. I see now that your sharp set-down was not to spur me on but to stop me. Perhaps you confused me with a dog, eager to heel to your commands." Then with a dazzling change of subject, he asked, "By the bye, after last night's fiasco, how goes it with Beecham?"

"At least you call it now by the right name!" Judith replied, "But in point of fact I predict that all will go smoothly."

"Predict?"

"I sent Sir George a message this morning and requested an interview with him later today, before this evening's masque," she informed him. "I am hopeful that he will agree to it. In fact, I am sure that he— Just a moment, sir!" she said, when a thought struck her. "Do you compare Sir George to a dog, implying that he will heel to my commands?"

"I? Whatever would have given you that idea, ma'am?" Lambert replied. He appeared to give the matter some thought. "Although I would venture—upon reflection—that, in your case, a well-trained husband is surely to be desired!"

Judith reined in her tongue, with an effort. The less said about her betrothed, the better. She forced herself to smile. "I wonder why it is," she mused pleasantly, "that the word 'outrageous' springs to mind so readily when I am in your company?"

Lambert bowed and intoned, "You are too good, ma'am."

Judith had no opportunity to reply. At that moment, they had to hurry on, for the curtain was being pulled back to reveal a nearly barren stage strewn with rushes and hung around with tapestry. The tapestries could represent the interior of a private house behind which villains might lurk, or they could be used to represent the actual exterior scenes depicted in the tapestries themselves. The central and largest tapestry was most probably intended to represent a splendid Spanish countryside. The Red Bull Theater evidently depended on the vivid imaginations of their audiences to produce that illusion, for the tapestry itself was of no high level of craftsmanship or design and featured a rather trite representation of the rolling meadows of an idealized English landscape.

Above the central tapestry and at the back of the stage was the stage balcony. It rose some eight or ten feet above the floor. It would be from this structure that murderers would leap down on unsuspecting tyrants; or where the ghosts of murdered persons could later present themselves; it could be made use of by a lover to climb; it served as the hint of a city street, a distant hill, or could be wreathed in leaves to suggest a forest scene. It might even be used as privileged seating for persons of great consequence who attended a particular performance. It seemed as if this last possibility was the use the stage balcony was being put to today, for as Judith and Lambert were sliding into their semi-private box, the curtain had been drawn back enough to reveal on the stage balcony a full complement of finely dressed gentlemen who did not look the least theatrical and who were attended by a small constellation of pages.

Judith had given nothing beyond the briefest considera-tion to these privileged theater guests before Lambert held her chair and seated himself at her right. Once settled, Judith gazed out over the stage. Her attention was instantly arrested by the sight of one man on the stage balcony.

The man's bearing was erect and haughty, as befitted a man of age and consequence. He was turned, his long, aquiline nose in profile to Judith. He was magnificently dressed in an embroidered paned and stamped white silk doublet and kneed Venetian breeches. His matching cloak was cast back across the back of his chair to reveal a lining of palest blue. He was seated, his back straight, his hands one atop the other and palming the hilt of his sword which was stuck at a right angle to the floor. His head was tilted back and up, and he was instructing one of his no less meticulously groomed pages who was well known to Judith. As the man spoke, Judith's eye traced his profile from the tip of his well-clipped beard, up his sharp, patrician fea-tures, to the white shock of his still-thick curls held back by a white satin ribband.

The man was her uncle.

Judith was both surprised and amazed. Hardly realizing it, she gasped and thereby drew Lambert's regard to the stage balcony. His eye, too, fell irresistibly on the distinc-tive, resplendent figure of Somerset. Lambert's brows rose, and the thought came: *Stuart affairs of state must be in worse case than I had realized!* followed by the swift question, *And what* other *interests does the old bastard have in the theater today*?

Although disconcerted by her uncle's unexpected appearance, Judith was, at first, willing to interpret his presence at the theater positively. She had been concerned by the news of troubles in Charles's reign that had arisen almost overnight, and she had been disturbed by Lambert's interpretations of those same events. For a monarch who had, a scant year ago, professed himself to be the happiest king in Christendom, the recent outward turmoil of his dominions must have been affecting his inward tranquillity enough to have wished to censor this play at The Red Bull. However, if her uncle saw fit to frequent the performance, Judith surmised that this was a sign to all that nothing was to be made of the king's disapproval. If Somerset could enjoy himself here and now, then everyone might breathe easier as well.

In the same split second, a less sunny interpretation occurred to her. Her uncle's arrival in London two days ahead of schedule might instead indicate that something more urgent was afoot; and this possibility seemed to be underscored by her uncle's very presence at the theater, which was the last place she would have expected to find him under almost any pretext, given his comprehensive disapproval of this form of entertainment.

These vague considerations gave way to a more immediate worry. As she gazed idly around the theater, her eye fell on the lively figure of Lucy, Countess of Carlisle, seated far off to the right. Now, she had told Lucy the day before that she had never met Charles Lambert, and while Lucy might not know who Judith's companion was today, she would be sure to discover his identity by nightfall, if she had a mind to. Judith might have severe difficulty contriving a story plausible enough for Lucy's ears to explain what she was doing in public at the theater with Charles Lambert. She would, no doubt, have no success persuading Lucy not to spread the story.

And now that Judith was fully aware of the pitfalls of her

decision to attend the theater, she was considering the possibility that her uncle might not be completely sympathetic to her presence either and might not fully understand how she had become acquainted with Charles Lambert or came to be seated with him.

Hardly had all those thoughts taken shape in her brain than she eased herself into the shadows of the box. She fussed with the hood of her cloak, pulling it up over her ears. She folded back the selvage to obscure her profile from both the stage and the far right where Lucy sat. The point of these little maneuvers was certainly not lost on Lambert.

Neither did Lambert wish to be seen by Somerset. Not at this particular performance and definitely not in company of his niece.

Then Somerset nodded to his page, as if in dismissal. At the fraction of a turn of Somerset's head toward the audience, Lambert performed the only defensive ploy against detection he had at his disposal. He stretched his right arm across Judith and ran his hand up her left arm where it came to rest on her shoulder. This maneuver partially blocked his face and hers from the stage. Then he leaned over into the shadows and put his mouth against hers. But he did not kiss her.

Judith was at first too startled by these actions to protest. His words slew all her desire to do so.

Any trace of his usual banter gone, he said, "Do not cry out or struggle against me unless you wish to draw anyone's eye to our box." As he spoke, his lips moved across hers in the promise of a kiss. "To make this truly believable, return my embrace."

Judith considered his suggestion, then made shift to comply.

So close to him, she saw the flicker of laughter spring to life deep in the gray of his eyes. She felt his lips curve upward against hers in what must have been a smile. "No, your *other* arm," he said, his serious tone slipping. "Your left arm. To shield our faces completely from the audience. Yes, that's right. Lay your hand on my shoulder." After a moment, the humorous tones now evident, he commented, "You might try to make the caress convincing. We are at the theater, after all."

For a response, Judith pinched his shoulder, hard.

"Ah!" he said low, his breath mingling with hers. "The lady favors me!" His lips now became insistent.

At that, Judith attempted to push back away from him, possibly spoiling the ploy. He countered her swiftly with a bolder action. He pressed her farther back into the shadows of the box, causing her chair to stutter against the floorboards, and pushed her against the paneled wall of the box. In the same movement, with his left hand, he pinched her plump backside, very lightly. This made her buck against him slightly, an action which would have appeared to any casual observer as an ardent response to her cavalier's lovemaking. Then, he grasped her other shoulder, thereby pinning her to the wall.

"My gallantry has its limits," he informed her, his lips moving again against hers.

"Your *gallantry*!" Judith exclaimed under her breath, helpless and indignant.

"Yes. You do not want to be seen by someone here today," he stated, "and perhaps not with me." His gallantry did not, however, extend to divulging *his* reasons for not wishing to be seen by Somerset. "Or do I mistake the matter?" He made as if he would release her.

"No," Judith admitted quickly, "you do not mistake."

He reaffirmed his grip. "Then it's a disobedient Judith who has come," he taunted lightly and with satisfaction. "Perhaps you are more like your biblical namesake than I had thought." He pressed his lips to hers in an imitation of a real kiss. "And perhaps I can urge you to more disobedience still."

"This," Judith managed, turning her face away, "was hardly the nature of Judith's heroic disobedience."

"Nevertheless, I feel a certain righteousness," he said, in between kisses to that part of her face that had presented itself to his lips, "in exerting myself—you have a very lovely ear—to protect the heroine from the harsh patriarch's notice.''

"How can you be so sure that I fear my uncle?" Judith asked, for she did not wish him to think her so craven.

"It is not from your uncle that you wish to shield yourself?" he demanded, his eyes narrowing slightly.

She shook her head slightly. "It's Lucy, the Countess of Carlisle. Behind you," Judith replied. "She is known to talk."

Should he believe her? "Well, then," he said, "allow me to shield you from the countess's notice."

"Putting yourself out on my account?" she said, attempting an acid irony, but losing the effect in her breathlessness.

Lambert took her chin with his free hand and turned her face back to him. His lips curved up in another smile. His lashes lowered. "Yes," he said, contemplating her mouth. "Any other action on our part would be highly suspicious. If we sat down only to leave again, many eyes would be drawn to us. A public display of intimacy in this setting is the only way to conceal our identities."

"How . . . convenient!" Judith managed. Although this was hardly a true embrace, she had been taken by surprise and was unable to prevent herself from feeling the effect of his touch down to her toes.

To maintain appearances, Lambert trailed his mouth down her throat. "Isn't it, though?" he agreed.

"But somewhat extreme," she said.

He kissed her. "Not at all. The most ordinary thing imaginable—" He kissed the corner of her mouth. "—at the theater." He kissed the corner of her eye. "Not even very original."

Judith firmly resisted the force of his arguments, which were particularly persuasive, and it occurred to her that Lambert must have his own reasons for not wishing to be seen by someone in the audience. However, this hazy idea was submerged in the further realization that here she was, now seated in the theater, hiding herself from her uncle and the countess, being thoroughly kissed by Charles Lambert, and that all of this was the inadvertent result of the impulse to ride to Monmouth one fine morning hardly two weeks earlier.

"What would please you into kissing me back, I wonder?" Lambert asked, kissing the corner of her mouth again. "An idle question, of course, but since we find ourselves captive to the needs of the moment, I see no reason not to enjoy it. Do you have any ideas?"

Judith quirked a brow. "None," she said, and this time she achieved her acid effect.

Lambert returned her quizzical look. " 'Teach not thy lips such scorn, for they were made / For kissing, lady, not for such contempt,' " he quoted easily. His eyes lit with an idea. "Ah! But that is it, of course! You have an ear for the poetic, as I recall." He bent to graze her nape with his lips. "Let me see. Yes." He adjusted his embrace to something quite tender and kissed her. " 'Come, sit thee down upon this flowery bed,/ While I thy amiable cheek do coy,/ And pluck up kisses by the roots/ That . . . that are . . . that are . . . are. . . .' " Intent on the curve of her neck, the last line failed him.

"A flimsy poetry," Judith mocked and quoted back, "That are . . . that are . . . are?"

"A copulative verb," he said.

"Sir, you take liberties," Judith rebuked him and attempted to draw away.

He prevented her escape. "License," he tossed back. "Poetic license."

"Poetic licentiousness, more like," was Judith's response.

Her words were as sexy to Lambert as a bared breast. " 'And pluck up kisses by the roots/ That grow upon thy lips,' " he finished on an inspired note. He was suddenly pleased with himself and his kissing partner, and bent to pluck her flowers.

But it was not flowers that grew upon her lips. Lambert found something different there, and more interesting. Judith Beaufort was an unexpected flavor, like the discovery of an almond among the walnuts or a sprig of mint where one had expected parsley. Or pepper, perhaps. He decided that he liked her taste. His embrace shifted again and became more purposeful. He kissed her so that his lips could not be denied. It was a provocative kiss, a flirtatious one, a thoroughly delightful one from his point of view, and an entirely successful one.

Judith began to kiss him back. Really, she had no other choice, and she was not experienced enough to know how to forestall his advances. Nor did she know how to douse the little flames that had spurted up of their own accord deep inside her. Since, as he had pointed out, they were committed to this course of action, it did seem a waste not to fan the flames a little, to feel the heat, to enjoy his lips and hands and muscle. It was an indulgence, perhaps. Certainly improper. Actually a little wicked. Even potentially more than a little wicked, if they were to continue in this pastime.

Judith's wandering thoughts halted. "Surely we cannot keep this up for the entire performance!" she said, struggling free of an embrace that threatened to become *very* wicked.

"No. Most couples so engaged at the opening of the first act find that they must excuse themselves before the beginning of the second," he replied. He resumed his wicked kissing.

"I mean it, Lambert!" Judith breathed, a little desperately.

"This is only a tactic to give you time until you decide how best to resolve your predicament," he argued.

Judith was finding it difficult to think, much less decide anything. "Your hand, sir," she said weakly. His left hand had slid down to her breast where it had stayed, and its pressure was causing her thoughts, not to mention her heart, to behave erratically.

Ever a man of the moment, Lambert was warming to the role that circumstance and his wit had fashioned for him; and he was willing to acknowledge that, on one score, at least, Judith Beaufort deserved the epithet Miss Perfect. Events and the woman in his arms intoxicated him. Intoxication made him impudent.

"I agree!" he replied at once. "What is needed is a little more realism." His hand caressed her breast through the material.

To her surprise and alarm, she felt the tip peak in response to his fingers. She said on a strangled note, "That is not what I meant!"

His impudence carried him along. "A complaint, I perceive. We've already explored that territory outside the theater and need to seek something more interesting." With that he removed his hand from her breast and slid it along her right leg, bunching her skirts until he came to the hem, and his kisses suddenly became more compelling.

When his fingers touched her bare thigh, Judith froze. If she had been in danger of succumbing to his lovemaking (whatever that might ultimately have meant in the context of a semiprivate box at the open theater), she drew herself back from this wholly unexpected precipice of passion.

"If you make one more move, Lambert," she said, her voice at its crispest, "I will bite your lip." Her teeth caught his lower lip. "Until it bleeds."

Her words had an effect. His hand stopped its progress. "If you bite my lip," he returned slowly, "I cannot be accountable for my actions." His voice was every bit as self-possessed as hers, but his speech was not very clear. His lower lip was still between her teeth. "Rough and tumble is exactly the way I like it. You may take that as a recommendation—or as a warning. Either way."

Judith let go of his lip. Lambert withdrew his hand from her thigh. They had reached an impasse.

Keeping his right arm in place, he drew slightly away so that he could look at her. A delicate vein throbbed beneath the white skin of her throat. He liked what he saw. A strong woman, flushed and responsive. Somerset's niece. Whose kisses mixed honey and vinegar. He liked what he had tasted. Miss Perfect. Plump and piquant and all feminine flesh. He liked what he had held. Miss Judith Beaufort. A damned distracting woman. What was she doing here? Could she conceivably be here with her uncle's approval?

He drew a deeper breath to steady himself. He had not expected this. He slanted a glance over his arm and down on to the stage. The opening bit of the first act was being played, and he had not been watching out for any signs of

Rosamunda in the wings. He glanced up at Somerset on the stage balcony. The old man gave every evidence of mildly enjoying the action taking place below him.

Lambert's eyes lingered on Somerset a moment. Somerset glanced up and out over the audience, briefly. Lambert saw his eye pass over their box without the slightest hesitation or change of expression.

Lambert shifted his glance back to Judith. "Do you care to look?"

Judith, recovering her breath, shook her head slightly.

"What is it to be?" he asked. "Do we stay or do we go?" He focused a moment on the problem of Rosamunda. Perhaps Will, or one of the others, could be trusted to catch her. "Our best chance to exit without being seen will come at the end of the first act. It's your choice. I know the way through the back."

Judith's eyes rested on Lambert's harsh, unhandsome features. It was perverse the way this disreputable man's kisses had drawn from her an unmistakable answer while Sir George's circumspect attentions had left her so—

"And if we leave now—?" she asked.

"We're close enough to the stage to draw attention from others in the audience," Lambert replied. "It's a risk."

Judith nodded understanding. While she thought about it, Lambert kept watch a moment or two on Somerset's eyes. As before, Somerset divided his attention between the stage and scanning different sections of the audience. No doubt he had come to discover the extent of Massinger's obedience. It must also have been of interest to him, Lambert decided, to see who else was in the audience.

"We had better stay," she said, "at least through the first act."

Lambert nodded and glanced into the wings. No sign of anyone resembling Rosamunda. He glanced back to Judith. He was finding the woman at hand of far more immediate interest. His eyes dropped to contemplate her mouth. "If we're to stay," he said, "you had better fight me off."

Judith was torn between disappointment and bewilderment. "Fight you off?"

"I have been too forward," he explained. "Too precipitate. Now, I will drop my right arm when you lift your left against me. Always keep our faces protected."

Judith thought she understood, but when she began to struggle with both arms to break free of his embrace, his arms clamped down on hers with immediate force to resume their original position.

"You're to fight me off playfully, coquettishly," he said, a little harshly into her ear, "so that I am sure to come back for more."

Judith tried again to fight him off as instructed, and was, again, unsuccessful.

"Have you no experience?" Lambert demanded, disgusted. "Here. Let me show you."

Judith writhed to break free of him but succeeded only in finding his arms more closely entwined about her.

"Much better!" he approved.

"That was not acting," she retorted, harsh in her turn. "Aren't we being unnecessarily realistic?"

"I take a professional pride in all my rôles," he said, and kissed her again, this time with interest to show how very accomplished he was.

"Ever the actor, Lambert?" she replied scornfully.

"And your performance is still a bit rough around the edges," he said, unscathed by her tone, "but might improve, as I suggested earlier, with practice." At that, Judith began to squirm again. "Very good. You're learning!" he encouraged. "We would give ourselves away if we did not keep this up. We are one of several sideshows whose progress various members of the audience are watching with idle interest."

"Including, no doubt, the Countess of Carlisle," Judith said.

"Including, no doubt, the countess," he said. Lambert lifted Judith's cowl more firmly over her head and bent to kiss her again. "And so we are in deeper than ever and must continue for you to escape her notice. However, the more compelling reason, from my point of view, for continuing this pleasant scene is that I find myself in company of a very desirable woman who kisses delightfully."

With a wry turn of humor, Judith was amazed to find how very effective such words were, even knowing them to be playacting. Still, she resisted him. "But this is so . . . so public!" she protested, struggling against him.

"Ah, so you, too, my lady, are aware of the limitations of our little scene," he said smoothly. "Now, for the lesson. Allow me to show you how to fight a man off while leading him on."

Keeping his right arm ever in place, he crossed his left hand over to grasp Judith's left hand. He opened her palm and put it against his right cheek. "Now, caressing my chin, push me away," he directed. "Always keeping my face turned away from the audience, of course. Slowly. With a caress. Yes. Very good."

His left hand sought her right. "Now lace your fingers in mine," he commanded.

Judith obeyed. When his fingers slid through hers, she felt a tiny fire blaze in the palm of her hand and scorch her arm.

"Guide my hand toward your body," he said. "Slowly, my dear."

She did so, and suddenly his hand, still intertwined in hers, had slid under her armpit and around to her breast.

"This cannot be for show," Judith breathed. "No one can see the maneuver."

"It is very subtle, yes," he agreed. "It's the little things that no one sees that lifts a performance above the ordinary."

Judith's hand attempted to stop his from sliding under the lace of her bodice. The strength of his exploring hand overruled the defensive gesture of hers.

"Just keep pushing my face away, as if you don't want me to kiss you. Yet. Use both hands. That's it," he encouraged and, when she had both hands so engaged, he used her defenselessness to his advantage. In the next moment, he had unbuttoned part of her collar from her bodice and had slipped his hand under the material. Her chemise was pushed aside by his probing, and suddenly his hand had grasped a bare breast.

Judith gasped at the unfamiliar, exhilarating sensation,

and the reflex of her arms seemed as if she were drawing his head back to hers.

"Not yet. A little longer. I think you have a future in this. Yes. Very nice," he cajoled. "And if I were to ask my lady for a kiss? What would she say, I wonder?"

Judith had hardly a moment to reflect how easy it was to play the theater doxy. "Is this the moment when she says 'yes'?"

Lambert nodded.

"Then, yes," Judith said.

This seductive affirmation was more than he needed, and in that moment, he stepped well beyond the bounds of playacting. He bent first to kiss her breast and was enchanted by the soft swell of flesh. Then he drew her into his arms, gently but firmly, his earlier impudence replaced by earnestness. He kissed her, no need of script now or imagined rôles to guide him in the enjoyment of the woman in his arms. As he shed his practiced pretense, so the background of the theater slipped away.

Judith joined him in the abandonment. She responded, all earnestness, too, all playfulness gone. It was a remarkably sweet kiss, for two such pungent personalities, not quite shy, but not quite sure of itself either. The embrace became more forceful, as Lambert felt a long red carpet of desire for this woman unfurl inside of him. He did not hesitate, gauging her response, to run his tongue experimentally inside her lower lip, and the kiss deepened. Every new sensation produced in Lambert a desire to go one step farther, and Judith did not hold back.

This abandon could not last. The theater reasserted itself. The very circumstances that had brought them there and had nudged them to this embrace intervened and brought to a momentary halt this unexpected passion.

The first act was nearing its climax. Although the play was set in Spain and featured a King Don Pedro, no one in the audience believed that it was the Spanish monarchy Massinger had in mind when he wrote the play. The critical passage had come, the one that King Charles had proclaimed was "too insolent and must be changed." The audience knew it. The wits in the pit ceased talking and drinking; the young bucks laid down their cards; the ladies and their cavaliers paused in their flirting; the merchants sat forward; the gentlemen on the stage balcony sat erect and expectant.

The altered atmosphere of the theater audience drifted into the semiprivate box to the left of the stage. Judith and Lambert broke off their kiss, regretfully, but Lambert's hands did not leave Judith's curves. Their eyes locked, neither looked down at the stage. They did not need to do so, for the hush that had come over the theater made every word said on the stage easily audible.

They heard the character of Don Pedro step forward and, in an attitude of a true tyrant, utter the words:

Moneys? We'll raise supplies what ways we please,/
And force you to subscribe to blanks, in which/
We'll mulct you as we shall think fit. The Caesars/
In Rome were wise, acknowledging no laws/
But what their swords did ratify, the wives/
And daughters of the senators bowing to/
Their wills, as deities.

The speech was a shock. Massinger had not unsaid his words. He had not obediently changed his portrait of the lawless Don Pedro. Excitement rippled through the pit and the gallery and the boxes. It was an audience composed of mixed sympathies. Thus, contradictory murmurs could be heard to the effect that "Massinger's audacious!" and "Down with the king!" and "Long live King Charles!" and "A pox on all Stuarts!" and "Massinger will pay for this!"

These reactions were followed immediately by a dead silence in expectation of what would happen next. Judith, with her back to the stage, could feel her uncle's disapproval cramp her muscles all the way down her spine.

The loyal subject, Miguel, next stepped forward and, with a scraping bow, pleaded with his cherished lord:

Unsay these fateful words, my lord and only master/
I beg of you, Say you do not mean it!

Don Pedro turned. In that one dramatic moment lay the fate of the play, the fate of the playwright, and perhaps the fate of the nation. Don Pedro paused. He said, flippantly:

Not a word of it.

The tension in the audience broke as quickly as it had crystallized. Quiet, rather muffled sounds of "Bah!" could be heard, but mostly there was a sense of relief. The playwright had kept his censored words but had recanted them. Judith's spine relaxed.

A new character came onstage then, a messenger bearing news from the Emirate of Cordova. The action moved forward, and the audience eased back into their seats, eager to take up where they had left off.

So was Lambert. He was at all times a passionate man. At present he was also a lustful one. "That's settled," he commented, indifferently, in reference to the political business that had interrupted a far more fascinating conversation. Seeking to recapture the moment and Judith's lips, he readjusted the embrace which he had not fully withdrawn. He put his mouth to hers and with the power of his lips and his intermittent words, her kisses quickened and came alive.

"Soft kiss," he said. "Dainty kiss." "Reasoned kiss." "Righteous kiss."

Chapter
10

"RIGHTEOUS kiss?" Judith queried lazily.

"Very."

Judith shook her head. "Not righteous, Lambert," she said between kisses.

"What then?" he asked, willing to follow her lead.

"Faithless, I think."

"Where is the faithlessness?" He kissed her. "In me?" he asked. "Or you?"

"In you," she said, "for are you not promised elsewhere?"

Lambert attempted to conjure an image of the dazzling young Englishwoman he had pursued in Florence but found he could not. Nor could he, at the moment, remember her name. "'Promised,'" he answered, "is a very strong word."

"In me, then," she stated.

"I pray you permit me persuade you otherwise." Lambert was enjoying himself. He was finding many interesting points of persuasion on her face and neck and hair and breast.

Judith shook her head again. "Faithless on my part, then," she said. "I am promised to another, and nothing you can say or do will alter that."

Lambert had a genius for improvisation. He rose to

Judith's challenge. "Faithless in your future condition," he conceded readily. "You mistake, however, the subtlety of your present condition. In my embrace."

"Subtlety? No. Idle seduction, more like," she returned.

"We're at the theater," he reminded her. He kissed her lightly, but fully, lips lingering. "My lips dress yours. These are costumed kisses." He knit her hand in his. "A glove, you perceive." He drew their intertwined hands to her breast. "Now here is lacing." He pressed his leg against hers, calf to calf, thigh to thigh. "Now you wear a boot." He smiled against her smile. "A fitting kiss." He kissed her.

A fitting kiss. A costumed kiss. She had, indeed, underestimated the subtlety of her present situation. At the theater. In his embrace. She slipped her hand from his and placed both hands on his shoulders. The tips of her fingers felt the nibs and nubs of the texture of his doublet smoothed over skin and sinew. His lines were lean and strong and taut as cords. His hands replaced the lacing at her bodice. His lips had the feel of velvet. They fashioned of her mouth a slipper for his tongue. Muscle and skin and mouth and moisture and hands tightened around her as corseting. His lips and fingers and knees fit hers, became a second clothing, a costume. Should her clothes be discarded, she would let the fabric of his skin clothe her, fit her. The inner stays and lacings of the respectable Judith Beaufort began to loosen.

The loosening dissolved into a melting. Her silks dripped and dissolved into a puddle at her feet. Just a few spurts of moisture at first, then a pool at her toes, then swirling up around her ankles. She wondered if the water would rise up over her knees and eventually engulf her. It was like drowning—but what a welcome drowning! She wished for the drowning, desired it. The level of the water rose to compel her, to envelop her, to submerge her, to fit her. A costumed fit, a passionate fit, a fitting fit, a *married* fit—

Judith snapped upright. With an effort, she broke through the surface of the water. She looked hastily down to survey herself. With great relief, she saw that she was still at the theater and that she was still wearing her clothes. She gave herself a mental shake. Of course, they had not melted from her body. She was not drowned. She pushed Lambert away and quickly dammed the floodtide of her emotions. Her sterner fabric rose to subdue her watery self.

"Costumed kisses," she said with a trace of derision. Surely she was not so easily seduced with poetry and practiced kisses!

Lambert laid his head to rest in the curve of her neck. His lips grazed her neck. He composed himself, with effort. This passage had gone much farther than he had forseen. He composed himself, with regret. When he lifted his eyes to hers, he, too, had taken control of his passions and was regarding her with some cool study. "To doff and to don at leisure," he replied, easing himself slightly away from her.

The moment was charged. Two wills strove with each other, divided against each other and their own doubt and desire.

It was fortunate, then, that the first act drew to its close. *The King and His Subject* was not a tragedy of the blood and thunder order, for which audiences had a very keen relish. It did, however, have the requisite minimum of suicide and murder, and so at the end of the first act, there was indeed a corpse lying upon the stage for the spectators to gloat over. Just as the last lines of the first act were being uttered, a roar of conversation erupted from the audience, not in response to the murder but rather at the playwright's decision to blunt the portrayal of the high-handed Don Pedro several scenes before.

Had not Judith and Lambert already broken their embrace, the commotion occurring at the end of the first act would have certainly halted it. As they disengaged their arms and bodies, they struggled to diffuse the passion that had overcome them.

Judith was relieved by the separation. She shifted her attention outside of the box. Since the curtain was never drawn between the acts, her eye went immediately to the stage. There, the final words were ringing from the actor who had committed the hideous, bloodcurdling crime of murder. As he spoke, he was looking down with triumphant evil at the body at his feet. The voices of the audience were rising to overpower his.

Her eye fell first on the large, faded central tapestry. Then, from her excellent vantage point in the box, her attention was caught by some movement in the wings opposite. She thought she saw a woman in the shadows, behind the curtain, just offstage. She saw the woman look anxiously behind her, as if afraid of being detected by someone backstage. Then the woman glanced up at the stage balcony. Judith could have sworn the woman was looking straight at her uncle. The anxious expression did not leave the woman's face, and Judith noted that she had cleverly hidden herself in the folds of the curtains and so might remain undetected either by anyone backstage or by anyone onstage.

Judith gave no more than cursory notice to the woman and her surreptitious actions. An even more dramatic moment in the day's entertainment had come. When the last line of the first act had been uttered, Somerset, in his position of privilege and power on the stage balcony, rose to his feet. Age had not bent his posture. He stood straight, his hand ver the hilt of his sword whose tip touched the floor in a line parallel to his rigidly erect body.

Resplendent in white, Henry Herbert, Lord Somerset, fifth Earl of Worcester, stood motionless until the initial excitement of the audience had subsided. It might have been five seconds. It might have been a minute. Judith could not have said. He stood there, serene, surveying all before him, smiling beneficently down on the actor who was obliged to drag his now-lifeless fellow actor off the stage. Lord Somerset's smile patently approved of Massinger's decision to unsay Don Pedro's words. Lord Somerset sheathed his sword, slowly, deliberately, significantly. This gesture of peace seemed to help quiet the roar of the audience, like drops of oil upon turbulent waters. Lord Somerset gazed out over the audience, swept his glance around the theater. Then he nodded his approval, bowed minimally, as if taking his leave from the audience as a whole. He departed the stage balcony and, presumably, the theater.

Judith shrank back into the box. Her uncle's eyes had swept across her face, but she did not think that he had registered her presence. She knew that gaze of his, his seignorial gaze, seeing without deigning to recognize. He would not have been looking for her. He would not have expected to see her, not here, not today. Just as she had not expected to see him. Whether her uncle fully approved of Massinger's compromise, she did not know. She guessed that her uncle would have been far happier had Massinger removed Don Pedro's offending speech altogether. Knowing her uncle's deep and secret Puritan heart, she guessed that his most complete happiness would have been for Massinger to have recanted the entire play or, better yet, for him never to have written it. Indeed, Judith knew that her uncle would have thought the world a better place were all theaters summarily closed. Nevertheless, the approval her uncle so dramatically displayed served his higher cause, his even deeper and never secret loyalty to the king.

For all Somerset disapproved of the theater, Judith realized that, with his gesture on the stage balcony, he had shown an excellent sense of theatricality. She gave a mental snort. Theatricality. There was a word. She cast a glance through lowered lashes at Lambert next to her as he briefly surveyed stage and theater. His eye seemed to have been caught by something offstage, in the wings opposite.

She used Lambert's absorption to consider him. A theatrical man. A fully, avowedly, professionally theatrical man. She had almost recovered now from the passionate folly that had possessed her during the first act. With her recovery but with the memory of the passion still fresh, came an understanding of her uncle's comprehensive disapproval of this place of entertainment.

Her thoughts on the theater in general and Charles Lambert in particular were diverted by the sibilant sounds of the name "Somerset" hissed about the theater and hushed in the wake of her uncle's departure.

Lambert heard the syllables, as well. He knew that this stern and noble lord's presence at the theater was as the proxy for King Charles and that the fact was understood by the majority of the theatergoers. Somerset's departure after the first act was now open for interpretation by the members of the audience. It was an equivocation: By sheathing his sword, Somerset had condoned the playwright's compromise solution; by leaving, he was signaling that the rest of the play was not worth another moment of his time.

Lambert had further reason to wonder at Somerset's abrupt departure from the stage balcony. Did it mean that Somerset had no other business today at The Red Bull? Lambert glanced back into the wings, opposite. The spot was now empty. There was no time to lose. Lambert leaned an arm across the front railing of the box and turned toward Judith.

"The first act is over," he stated. "We were agreed to wait until this juncture to exit. What is your pleasure? Do we stay, or do we go?" Although he was itching to get his hands on Rosamunda—for surely she was the woman he had seen in the wings just now—his voice betrayed no eagerness to leave.

To Judith's slight hesitation, Lambert suggested, "Or we can continue where we left off."

His ploy worked. "I think we had best leave," Judith decided.

Lambert nodded agreement. As he drew her to her feet, he glanced down at the stage. The second act was starting. He darted his gaze back over into the wings, opposite. Nothing. He peered out over into the wings closest to the box, but the angle was not good enough for him to see well into it.

"Perhaps we should depart through the back?" he suggested. "So as not to be seen by anyone you might possibly know?"

Judith agreed readily, and Lambert took her hand and pulled her out of the box, saying, "I know the way."

He led her behind the gallery and down a rickety wooden staircase that deposited them in the midst of the backstage hustle and bustle. Since Judith would have no knowledge of the most direct route out of the theater, Lambert was free to take her on as circuitous a route as pleased him. He was curious to inspect the wings closest to the box they had lately occupied, to discover whether Rosamunda might be hiding within the folds of that curtain. He took Judith down the hallway off to the right of the stairs, but Rosamunda was nowhere to be seen on this side of the stage. He had an unobstructed view of the front of the stage, however, where the play was going on, across to the opposite wings. There he thought he saw a woman's figure pass through the shadows. Why was Will not following her?

"We'll have to cross behind the stage," he said to Judith, "and exit by the door on the opposite side of the theater."

Still holding her hand, Lambert led her through the back maze of dark, dusty hallways, the only illumination coming from the daylight that squeezed through the chinks in the old, warped planks of the scaffolding. There was the usual commotion of stage whores and actors milling about, along with those with financial interest in both classes of theater folk. They passed by the staircase that led to the stage balcony. Judith looked up briefly. It was empty. It seemed certain her uncle had left the theater, and Judith naturally welcomed the thought.

Lambert negotiated another turn and another hallway, and soon they were behind the stage. They were headed straight to the wings opposite and would be there after another right turn.

Suddenly, Judith heard familiar voices off around the corner to the right and farther down an adjacent hallway that intersected with the hallway that she and Lambert were traveling. The voices were whispering, but by some trick of acoustics, every word could be heard distinctly.

"Not a trace of him, sir," said the voice that Judith unmistakably recognized.

The footsteps stopped. A voice replied. "Not a trace," the man agreed. "He has been most unobliging."

"But are you sure he was to be here today?" the page asked.

"Quite sure," was Somerset's confident reply. "I received a message from him saying that he was to be here this afternoon." A small pause. Then, harshly, "However, I have not brought the amount of money he is now demanding.'' The footsteps began to echo again, coming closer. ''Mr. Smith's price increases daily, it seems, but I will pay only the original price.''

Mr. Smith? Judith froze. Before hearing that name, she had been rapidly considering how she was going to face out this meeting with her uncle. Now, however, she felt it imperative to avoid a confrontation with her uncle. Perhaps it was the tone in his voice as he spoke the name of Mr. Smith that chilled her. Perhaps she thought that if her uncle was involved in serious business, he would not welcome an unexpected, awkward, possibly embarrassing meeting with his niece.

Whatever the reason, she shook herself of her immobility. Recent events had taught her that only one evasive tactic was open to her. She pulled up her hood. She pushed Lambert against the wall in a corner of the hallway, deep in the shadows. In one movement, she took his hands in hers and placed them at her waist. She held her hands up and drew his face to hers. She placed herself against his length and kissed him soundly.

Lambert's fuse was short. His response was fast and fiery and more realistic than Judith had expected or intended. Gone were his genteel, practiced kisses and caresses. This response was of another order entirely, and Judith discovered in the first instant that it was far, far more intoxicating and dangerous to be passionately kissing a man when pressed fully to his length than when seated next to him. In the next instant Judith felt the balance of power change with dizzying rapidity, for the aggressor leapt out of Lambert. He flipped her so that her back, instead of his, was against the wall. Her arms were trapped about his neck. His arms pinned her fully into him.

''No, Lambert!'' she whispered urgently. ''My uncle!''

''He'll never detect you in this embrace,'' he replied thickly.

His hold left Judith little room to protest. She managed, at last, ''That was my point.''

Something in Judith's tone brought Lambert to his senses,

but control of his passion lagged far behind. He did not have himself in hand. He was aware that Somerset and his entourage were about to round the corner. "Ah! I had flattered myself that my manly charms had overpowered you," he said. "But you said earlier that it was not your uncle from whom you wished to escape notice."

"That was *before* the play began," Judith replied. "It might be more difficult now to explain my presence here. With you."

He understood. His embrace became less savage. He took a deep breath, to steady himself. "If this is to work, you must, nevertheless, bear with me."

The footsteps and voices turned the corner.

"One more, Queen of my Thoughts," Lambert urged in a throaty stage whisper. "You may trust me, my lady."

Somerset and his entourage passed within several feet of the couple locked in a scandalous embrace. Somerset's steps did not check, but Judith was fully aware that her uncle had taken notice of the couple in the shadows. She felt the flick of her uncle's eyes down Lambert's back, but she did not dare open her eyes to see.

"One more sweet kiss, Queen of my Heart," Lambert continued, still in carrying tones. He accompanied his words with some very bold gestures (entirely for effect) that would have convinced any casual onlooker that Lambert meant to have his lady, and on his terms.

"Soon the theaters shall be closed," Somerset pronounced to his attendants as he continued down the hall. "Soon." Further words drifted back down the hall to Judith. "And now, for our Mr. Smith. If he has double-crossed me or demands a further increase in price, he shall be very sorry. Very sorry. What say you, gentlemen? Shall we essay the nether region. . . ."

The rest of his sentence was lost as her uncle disappeared into the gloom of the backstage hallway. Judith sagged against the wall, still encircled by Lambert. They remained motionless against each other for another moment, each attempting to recover from the heightened effects of this second short, strong wash of passion.

Judith felt herself sinking ever deeper into a morass of deception and desire, with Lambert as her unlikely partner in deceit. Lambert's thoughts took no similar course. With a wry turn of mind, he was coming to realize the curious delights and real frustrations of helping well-bred ladies maintain their reputations. He felt uncharacteristically noble. It was a feeling he was beginning to experience with some regularity in Judith Beaufort's company.

He pushed himself away from the wall and regarded her through slightly closed eyes.

Judith resisted the scrutiny. " 'Queen of my Heart'?" she quoted ironically. It was a shaky humor.

"Conventionally trivial," he explained, "and completely in characer for the theater rogue. Let's go."

He took her hand and led her down the remaining hallway. They turned right then jogged left around some scenery that butted against this side of the wings. He was about to turn right again when he spied a door across which a curtain had been pulled. The daylight that glowed beyond indicated that it was one of the backstage doors. Lambert saw a woman's figure move toward that door. It might have been the woman she had seen from the box. If she were hiding from someone, she might have wished to wait until Somerset's entourage had passed before departing. She might be thinking that the coast was clear.

The woman, lifting the curtain, was framed for a moment by the light from outdoors. Lambert saw her unmistakably as Rosamunda. He need only hurry a little to catch up with her. What he would do with her once he got his hands on her, he did not know, given Judith Beaufort's presence. But catch up with the woman he would now, he could now, and with very little effort. She was almost within his grasp.

Just then, the woman cast an anxious glance over her shoulder, to see whether she was being watched or followed. Perceiving Judith and Lambert, she lifted her skirts and hastened her step. The next moment she had disappeared behind the curtain.

"The backdoor," Lambert said to Judith. "That's the exit."

They hurried to the door. Lambert drew back the curtain to allow Judith to pass through and caught a glimpse of the blond beauty moving with unladylike haste away from the theater. Before Judith crossed the threshold, her way was blocked by a tall, thin figure who had held up an arm across the door to bar their passage.

"Rubbish! Tripe!" the figure said to them in accents of outrage. "*This* is what packs a theater! A little notoriety! Censorship! Why, *I* might cast aspersions upon the king and see the attendance at my plays improve!"

"Mr. Webster, is it?" Judith ventured.

Harold Webster swept a deep bow. "Miss Beaufort," he said. "And Lambert. Good day to you," he added with a nod. He quickly put his arm back across the door to bar their passage when he saw that they both desired to move on. "Yes. You appreciate the theater, as I recall—after your own fashion. And as it happens, I have a bone to pick with you."

"Save it for later, Harry! Out of our way!" Lambert snapped, as he saw the figure of Rosamunda turn toward the half-timbered buildings that crowded up to the yard of the theater. Lambert realized that physical violence against the playwright to effect their passage would unnecessarily raise Judith's suspicions about the woman he was trying to follow.

"Eh?" said the startled playwright, unused to such brusque commands from Lambert.

"Miss Beaufort desires to leave!"

"She may, of course, but not until she hears that Massinger received six pounds for this play!" Mr. Webster said with suppressed passion. "*Six* pounds! Can you imagine it? When *Every Man in His Hours*—my new moral tale—and a fine tale it is, too, as you know, for you have seen its most glorious climax!—well, *it* received a mere three pounds. Three! *Three!*" he spat.

Rosamunda was nearly at the corner.

"Dear me, three!" Judith said, as eager as Lambert to get out of the theater.

While Harold Webster relieved himself of his thoughts on

the inequities of the world and on the crass tastes of the London theatergoers, Lambert saw Rosamunda slip around the corner and out of sight. No doubt she had been instantly and anonymously absorbed into the marketday throng.

Lambert leaned against the doorjamb and exhaled at length. Judith had followed the direction of his gaze, and was frowning in puzzlement. Her thoughts were at first too confused to be sure whether Lambert was truly trying to catch up with the strange, elusive woman or to speculate what his interest in her might be; but as Mr. Webster concluded his little speech with his plans for the betterment of society, Judith was putting some of her ideas in order and was gazing at Lambert with a long, wordless, wary regard.

Looking down on her flushed face and into her bright, assessing eyes, Lambert was considering just how much Judith guessed about him, just how much he could trust her, and just how much he desired kissing her again.

Decidedly, Lambert thought, Judith Beaufort's company provided curious delight and great frustration.

Chapter
11

JUDITH was outwardly calm as she waited for the door of her uncle's suite to open.

Edith was inclined to fuss. "Your collar, Miss Judith. It's askew. It will never do to present yourself to his lordship with your collar askew! It will make him think of Rowena in the buttery hatch who can never keep her apron pinned properly!"

Judith thought that possibility unlikely in the extreme, but she was too preoccupied with the coming interview to do other than submit, silently chafing, to Edith's ministrations.

"Oh, your hair!" Edith squeaked. "A ringlet is out of place! If I were to tuck it behind your ear, perhaps an effect can be achieved. There! Now, let me look at you, Miss Judith!"

I am being punished! Judith thought, and she knew why. She had left her rooms this morning, indicating to Edith only vaguely that she intended to deliver one of her uncle's messages. She had firmly, even imperiously, declined Edith's generous offer of escort. She had stayed out far longer than she had anticipated, causing Edith (by her own account) to entertain a wild variety of improbable stories to explain her mistress's "disappearance." To make matters worse, upon her return, Judith had vouchsafed few details of her outing.

Edith had been sorely, and volubly, offended, and she was, just now, at her irritating worst.

"Edith," Judith said sternly, "your efforts are quite unnecessary! You have already seen to it that my toilette is perfect! Now, I understand that you were upset when my uncle sent for me before I returned from my outing, and I understand that you have somehow conceived that it is *your* fault that I have made my uncle wait this past hour or more, but I must point out—once again!—that he could not have expected me to be awaiting his arrival today. So, please, I beg of you, *cease*—"

The heavy, carven door swung open. Judith stopped mid-sentence. Somerset's most faithful and senescent steward, Sir Albert, bowed and nodded and ushered Judith and Edith into Henry Somerset's suite. When Judith crossed the threshold, her heart wobbled uncertainly, but she denied that this minimal aberration resulted from any fear she might have felt at having lately come from the theater and Lambert's arms to face her uncle.

Of one thing Judith was sure. Her uncle was vexed. Judith knew him well enough to interpret the precise minute that elapsed between her knocking at the door and its opening as a token of his displeasure that she had kept him waiting. It was unreasonable, of course, for him to have expected her to be at his beck and call fully two days ahead of his announced schedule. However, if that was the extent of his displeasure with her, Judith would be well satisfied.

Sir Albert gestured to Edith to take a seat in the spacious entry hall where she would wait out her mistress's interview. He then motioned Judith to enter the antechamber. She stepped into the large room which was filled with late afternoon sunlight streaming through a bay. It opened out onto a direct view of the Thames and a variety of boats skimming past. Although the appointments of the chamber were elegant and Italianate and in the modern style of King Charles, the room retained an old-fashioned aspect that hinted at the earlier, grander time of Charles's father, James, or that of the Virgin Queen before him. A half dozen pages, like so much movable furniture, hovered here and there attending to their tasks.

In the middle of the chamber sat Lord Somerset, like the sun, with his servants orbiting quietly about him. At Judith's entrance, he rose from his chair. He did not cross to greet her but stood straight and still as his niece approached him.

He was, Judith noted, still dressed in his superb white silk suit. It had hardly a crease in it, and his white, flowing mane was perfectly coiffed, with not a hair out of place. His face was impassive. Judith could not gauge his mood.

He did not say anything, as was his custom, until Judith had bowed before him. Judith kissed the hand he held out to her. It was old but still strong and commanding. He placed a kiss atop her head. Still touching his fingers with hers, Judith curtsied low, letting out her breath, very slowly. She always held her breath when her uncle kissed her.

"My dear," he said. "You have answered my request. I thank you."

"I give you greeting, my lord," Judith murmured, as her knees sank to the ground before him. She raised herself and looked into his eyes. They were blue, startling for their translucent paleness and the lucidity of their expression. She chose the offensive. "But request, dearest uncle?" she said. "I read your message as a summons!"

Somerset condescended to smile. "Did it sound so to you, my dearest niece?" he asked, but apparently had no desire to pursue the subject, for he begged her to be seated, "and tell me how it came about that you have made me wait." He withdrew his hand from hers and seated himself in his heavy, turned walnut chair.

"Sheer inability to read your mind, sir," she answered as she disposed herself in the less important chair arranged on his right. "Your last communication to me stated plainly that you were to arrive at Whitehall two days from now."

"My plans changed," he said.

"So I perceive!"

"But my evident change of plans," he continued, dispassionately, "does not explain your movements this morning, my dear.'' Before Judith had an opportunity to offer the pat answer she had planned for that question, her uncle explained with a thin thread of amusement in his voice, ''Your Edith—so it was reported to me—was most discomposed when she heard the message that you were to present yourself at my chambers. She delivered herself of quite a number of astonishing utterances—again, so it was reported to me—to the effect that she did not know where you were, nor when you would be back, and that she was beginning to believe in the existence of fairies, for this was the second time in the month that you had vanished into thin air!''

''There is no telling what manner of thing Edith said, for she is a nervous and excitable woman,'' Judith said to this. She held her uncle's eyes steady and willed her hands to remain relaxed and motionless in her lap.

''Indeed.'' He nodded. ''It was a most nervous and excitable effusion, according to Jonathan, who has a gift for transmitting messages with unerring accuracy. He has an ear for intonation and a memory for exact wording, which is why, of course, that I have him in my employ and pay him so exorbitantly! The importance of a faithful messenger in one's employ is often underestimated, I fear. The transmission of a message—accurate to the word and to the inflection—can avoid many a misunderstanding.''

The import of this gentle piece of seignorial wisdom was not lost on Judith. ''I stand ready to confirm to you the extent of Jonathan's talents,'' she said lightly, ''for I have known Edith to invoke fairies at any slightest opportunity!''

''Dear me. She does not precisely reflect your style, does she,'' her uncle remarked. ''I have often thought her mismatched to you, but you are such a reasonable young woman that a tiring-woman of another temperament would be, almost, redundant.'' Then, reflectively, he said, ''One wonders now, however, whether your Edith has not been at her position too long. What say you, Judith?''

The conversation had taken a decidedly disagreeable turn. She shrugged with just the right amount of indifference. ''Been in her position too long? I don't think so, sir. It is true that Edith and I have been together a long time, but I am well accustomed to her, and her temperament does not bother me, if that is what you mean. As you say: a more reasonable tiring-woman would be redundant.''

Somerset's gaze was particularly penetrating. ''Yes. Well. I am glad to hear that she does not bother you. I merely thought that you might, perhaps, prefer now a woman who was better capable of keeping track of your movements and, thus, better capable of representing you to others. A woman who was more . . . reasonable, like yourself. But I have made too much of nothing.'' He waved the subject away with a negligent sweep of a heavily beringed hand. ''I did not request your presence to speak of strange, nervous tiring-women and their possibly inaccurate and certainly incomprehensible messages. We were speaking, rather, of your movements this morning and early afternoon.''

Judith had nearly given herself over to the surge of anger she felt at her uncle's veiled threat to remove Edith. However, his sudden dropping of the subject made Judith reconsider her uncle's intent. Perhaps her own guilty conscience had prompted her to misread his words. Whatever the case, Judith did not think it wise to let this negative characterization of Edith go unchallenged. She could, at the same time, evade the answer to his implied question as to her whereabouts earlier in the day.

''Perhaps her message to you,'' Judith said, without hesitation, ''was no more inaccurate than yours to me informing me of your arrival two days hence.''

''I do not think you mean for me to repeat to you that my plans changed.''

''No, sir,'' Judith said easily. She was rarely intimidated by her uncle. She did not permit herself to be so now. ''I must insist, however, that since I was not expecting you today, I had no reason to remain in my chambers, nor to have informed Edith of my particular activities. I am not accustomed to having to account for myself.'' Judith smiled and took, again, the offensive. ''I am rather more interested in the account of *your* movements, sir. When did you arrive at Whitehall? Have you been here long?''

Her cleverness did not serve her. "Long enough to have received a visit from Lady Margaret," her uncle said languidly.

Judith blanched. She had not been expecting it. The events of the day—beginning with her unsuccessful search for Mr. Smith and ending with her near encounter with her uncle backstage at The Red Bull—had crowded out the memory of the tangle of her affairs involving Sir George and Lady Margaret. And Charles Lambert.

Her sangfroid must carry her through. "It was a most unfortunate episode," she said with dignified regret.

"Most."

This terrible monosyllable chilled Judith more thoroughly than any criticism he might have offered. Although he posed no question about the incident, Judith felt compelled to explain. "I cannot know, of course, how Lady Margaret portrayed the events of last evening to you, sir . . ." Judith began.

Somerset smiled. The effect was not warm. "Her interview with me bore a strong resemblance to the account of your affairs given by Edith."

Things looked bad. "Surely not, sir!" Judith said, attempting mild, insouciant humor.

"Surely not." His tone was not encouraging. Neither was his attitude. He had steepled his fingers under the trim V of his clipped beard. His elbows were propped delicately on the arms of the chair. His eyes were fastened, unwaveringly, on Judith. The small nod of his head invited Judith to tell her version of the previous evening's events—if she dared.

She dared. "It all began—quite unfortunately!—yesterday morning, sir. I had just arrived in London and was most eager to execute the commissions you had sent me to discharge—oh! and while I am on the subject, let me tell you that—"

The small shake of his head indicated that he would not be diverted by a tangent.

Judith resumed her story. "Well, it was yesterday morning when I was standing at Holbein Gate, and there I ran into Sir George. It was a most pleasurable encounter! Then, as it happened, a man crossed our path.''

"A man?"

"Yes, a man. Lambert.''

"James Lambert would that be?''

"No, sir. Charles Lambert.''

"I see. Charles Lambert. And how could it be that a chance meeting—it was a chance meeting, was it not? —with Charles Lambert at the Holbein Gate could have led to the 'moral outrage and ethical offense to all good feeling'—I quote Lady Beecham—last evening in your apartment?''

Judith swallowed. "I believe that Sir Charles insulted Sir George,'' Judith explained.

"Ah. Insulted?''

"Yes, well—'' Judith hesitated. Before committing herself, she thought it strategic to hedge. "Did not Lady Margaret give you the background of the incident yesterday evening?''

Not one muscle in Somerset's expression had changed. "The background, as you say, to her story was very murky. Very murky indeed. Pray, continue. We were at the part where you were describing the nature of the insult Sir Charles delivered to Sir George.''

Judith drew a breath. "I believe the nature of the insult had something to do with Sir Charles failing to recognize Sir George. They had been introduced not three weeks before and—well, the fact of the matter was that Sir George was offended!''

"And did Beecham recognize Lambert?''

Judith glanced up at the ceiling. "Not that I recall, but I do not think that Sir Charles was thereby similarly offended.''

"Indeed not.''

"Then, Lambert came to my chambers to apologize to me—''

"Apologize? Most interesting.''

"Isn't it? That was his stated purpose in all events,'' Judith said, regarding her uncle directly again. She was not, as she had said, accustomed to giving an account of herself, and she hated doing it now. "But then Sir George came to call on me and when he saw Sir Charles, he jumped to an incorrect conclusion. Sir George exacerbated, if I may say, the animosity toward Sir Charles he had experienced that morning, and into the midst of that . . . that quarrel stepped Lady Margaret! I must say that the situation was beyond my explanations! Lady Margaret, too, jumped to incorrect, and unflattering, conclusions.''

Judith resisted the strong impulse to unsay this string of half-truths. She let the story lie.

Her uncle considered this recital in silence. Then, he said, "How do you interpret Lambert's desire to call on you at your private chambers to apologize for an insult that was apprehended by Beecham?''

Judith picked an explanation from thin air. "Sir Charles deemed it a courtesy to make amends with his neighbors at Raglan.''

Lord Henry betrayed a flicker of emotion. It might have been surprise. "Neighbors?''

"Charles Lambert has bought Speke Hall,'' Judith said, adding hastily, "so he said!''

A blaze of interest flared deep in the pale blue of Henry Somerset's eyes. As quickly as it was lit, it was extinguished. "Recently?'' he asked with just the proper amount of common curiosity.

"It is my understanding that it was within the last two weeks,'' Judith informed him.

"That means he must have been in Wales within the last few weeks as well,'' he said, "visiting his property.''

"It is likely,'' Judith said noncommittally.

"I received an unconfirmed report to the effect that he had been seen—'' Lord Henry broke off. He waved away the thought, as if it were a trifle. He paused to recompose his already very composed face. Judith had an uncanny sense that the direction of the interview had just, very subtly, changed course. Whatever Judith had imagined her uncle's reaction to her tale might be, Somerset's next words were most unexpected. "Thank you for this account. The situation has become greatly clarified.''

Judith smiled cautiously, not daring to examine what lay

under this mild acceptance of her story. She hoped that her smile betrayed none of her guilt.

"I had been wondering just how it all fit together," he continued, "for Caroline shed little more light on the incident than did Lady Margaret."

"Caroline?" It was Judith's turn for surprise.

"Caroline. Yes. She had the privilege of arriving at your suite at the end of the little scene yesterday evening, is it not so? Earlier today, when you were reported out on your unspecified activities, I sent for Caroline directly after having received Lady Margaret. Yes. Caroline. You look surprised, my dear."

"It is only that I had not realized that you had spent enough time at Whitehall today to have . . . that is, that you had been in London long enough to have already had two interviews!"

"I have had four, not including the present one."

"You are efficient, sir!"

"Always. My devotion to my family is second only to my devotion to the king, as you know, Judith."

"Of course, sir! I never doubted it! And what of Caroline?"

"She will soon be on her way back to Raglan." Somerset cast his eye out the window. It was mid-afternoon. "Perhaps the coach is readying for departure now."

"I had no idea she was planning to depart today," Judith said involuntarily.

"She was not, in fact, planning it. I planned it." Somerset let his hands fall to his lap where they rested. Judith thought the pause owed a great deal to the theatricality she had seen him display not two hours before at The Red Bull. "Caroline has been indiscreet," he said tonelessly. "I have sent her home. I do not care to have her name linked with that of James Lambert."

Judith felt an inseparable mix of anger and foolishness and fear that Caroline's ignominious fate was to befall her now, as well.

"You know, my dear," he said without emotion, "the Lambert family is impoverished. I would not usually object to Caroline finding her affections engaged with a man with no fortune, but poor judgment is a sad family trait among the Lamberts. You see, Caroline is not the judge of character that you are, my dear. She needs a strong man—not necessarily a rich man, for surely she has enough fortune for both, but a man with sense and judgment. A man like Sir George Beecham, in fact. I have recently found the ideal man for my beautiful youngest daughter. I feel fortunate that his family is well disposed to Caroline, and she shall be formally betrothed within the next several weeks. In order for her to prepare for that happy event, I have returned her to Raglan." He paused. "She was most compliant. Even eager, I believe, when I described to her the young man's countenance and character. He is very like Sir George. I think you will agree, my dear, that I have chosen well for Caroline."

"I am quite sure of it, sir," Judith said while contradictory thoughts collided and locked in her brain: that Caroline was, indeed, unable to judge character; that her uncle's high-handedness was not, thereby, justified; that Sir George was far from a model of good sense and judgment; that Charles Lambert had been right when he predicted that her uncle would remove Caroline from his nephew's reach without a second thought for Caroline's own opinions or feelings.

"I was confident that you would agree with me, my dear," Somerset said. "I am also confident that you will agree that even the most . . . sensible man—I am thinking here of Beecham—can be pushed too far. And no man likes to look the fool."

Judith was not in perfect charity with Sir George. "If Sir George has looked the fool, he must surely accept some of the blame!"

"Yes. You are right. Yet we must make allowances for the depths of a man's feelings"—Somerset paused—"when he is in love."

"As to that," Judith said swiftly, "I have arranged to meet Sir George early this evening. To smooth over the rough spots!"

"That will not be necessary."

Judith was startled. "Sir?"

Somerset smiled. "Among my other interviews this afternoon, I have received Beecham," he said.

Judith's eyes widened.

"He is an excellent young man," he continued. "A man of sense and judgment, as I have said. However, I believe that, in this instance, he has shown himself to be too quick to perceive an insult where none may have been. I attribute that, naturally, to the affection he feels for you. You are fortunate in your choice of betrothed, as I am persuaded you know. Thus, it will not be necessary for you to seek Beecham out in private to discuss this matter which might possibly produce awkwardness or even misplaced passions of remorse or apology. Beecham has assured me that he has already put the incident behind him.

"As for Lady Beecham. . . ." Here Somerset paused. "As for Lady Beecham, she is an estimable woman. She, too, has been persuaded that her son showed himself to be too quick to take offense. Herself, as well. She assures me that it will not happen again. Also like her son, she is rueful over her behavior to you last evening. Although she is pained, I have persuaded her that she need not discuss the matter further with you. We discovered to our pleasure that we shared many similar ideas on the subject of the festivities to be provided at your wedding. When next you communicate with her, you will wish to pursue with her this happy subject. She understands that you will want to set your own personal tone, of course."

Somerset's face was expressionless when he finished this speech, saying, "Lady Beecham is extremely receptive to the idea that a dower house shall be built for her on the Beecham estate. One does not exist at present, and I believe—although I do not think she had considered the matter at length—that she had assumed she would live on in the manor house with you after your marriage. She now has a craving for personal privacy, and she has conceived a variety of projects for the improving of the estate that will best be administered from the dower house."

Judith was too stunned for the moment to respond to

these extraordinary disclosures. Lord Henry had meddled deeply, unforgivably, in her personal affairs. However, he had defended her at every turn. He had put Sir George in the wrong. He had shown Lady Beecham the error of her ways. And he had not questioned Charles Lambert's role in the affair, nor her curious, unexplained association with him.

Her uncle had been decent and trusting. His next words displayed his forgiveness and love. "You say nothing to this, Judith." A sunbeam of warmth penetrated the cool blue of his eyes. "I had hoped to please you with my actions, my dear, for you are the best of my daughters."

These words of approval, simply and sincerely spoken, suddenly made Judith glow inside, and she sunned herself in his approval and enjoyed the sensation of being anchored under the wing of his strength and love. She felt calmed and centered and stabilized in his presence, a feeling that made her realize that, by contrast, she had been queasy and lurching before this interview. It was Charles Lambert who had unsettled her, who had nearly overwhelmed her in the box at The Red Bull Theater with his tide of passion and desire. In Lambert's arms, she had felt herself drowning, and happily so. His waters were deep and choppy and scalding. It was no wonder that, when away from him, she had felt rudderless and adrift. After leaving the theater and Lambert's arms, she had returned to Whitehall very slowly and very thoughtfully, and she had indulged some very heretical ideas, chief among them being that George Beecham would no longer please her as a husband.

Now, however, for the first time since leaving the theater, she felt buoyed, even steadied, confident, once again, of who she was. Seated with privilege at her uncle's right, Judith felt a renewed sense that the plan of her life was good and decent and straight. Her uncle supported her. He stood behind her. She, and no one else, had chosen her future. She, and she alone, was mistress of her fortune.

"I am grateful," Judith said after a respectful little pause, "and humbled by your favors, sir."

Somerset smiled. "I have often been accused of favoring

you, my dear," he replied. "Perhaps I love you too well." His smile was tender. "I do not think that my reason has been clouded in the past. Nor do I think so now."

She gazed up at him, her love for him shining from her eyes. "I thank you for your trust."

"Which extends to my belief that you will not be so uncircumspect in the future as to be seen again with Charles Lambert," he said.

Judith gasped. "But—" she began to protest that she had engineered none of their meetings, not in Somerset Park, not at Holbein Gate, not in her suite, not at—

Somerset's voice sliced across hers. "Anywhere."

The finality of that utterance caused a ghastly thought to occur to her: Had he seen her at The Red Bull with Charles Lambert? No, it was impossible. And yet, there was something in his tone which suggested the possibility. She looked at him. There was something in his eye that told her he knew more than he was telling her. He had vowed his love for her. He had given her his unqualified protection. She would not protest her innocence. She would not push her luck.

Suddenly he seemed to be standing above her, not behind her. Suddenly she did not seem to be mistress of her fortune, after all. "Of course not, sir." She had bowed her head in a gesture of acquiescence, but she was not fully acquiescent. A thin shoot of rebellion had taken root in her during the course of this conversation and prompted her to ask, "Is Charles Lambert so bad?"

"Independent, uncommitted men," he said, "are dangerous."

With that, the subject of Charles Lambert was closed. Her uncle had moved on to a new subject. "You were about to tell me of my commission. Had you any difficulties delivering my messages, Judith?"

Judith raised her eyes to meet his. "Yes. With one."

"Not an important one, I trust."

Judith bit her lip. "The one directed to Mr. Smith."

The smallest fraction of a second passed before her uncle said, "I am relieved. I was afraid lest you tell me it was the one for Lord Chamberlain. I had written him that I was unable to obtain for him a certain Irish manuscript. A very beautifully illuminated manuscript. It was a pity I was unable to locate it, for he was very keen to have it in his collection. I believe he gave me incorrect information about the location of the manuscript.''

''Oh! But I had gathered that the one to Mr. Smith was . . .'' Judith trailed off, halted perhaps by something in her uncle's expression.

''You were under the impression—?'' he prompted.

''Well, it's just that you had mentioned his direction twice. You are not usually so . . . anxious in your instructions. So, I interpreted that to mean that you regarded Mr. Smith's message as the most important.''

Somerset smiled wanly. ''Anxious?''

Her uncle was sparring lightly. He was not going to extend his love for her into divulging a confidence. Judith felt the rebellion sprout into a reed-thin shoot inside her. ''I assumed it was about the purchase of a painting, sir,'' she said, attempting a light laugh. ''A Gentileschi. I was under the impression that you were eager—that is, wishing to purchase—I mean to say that before you left for Ireland, your correspondence centered on—oh, I don't know!—the king's relations with the Vatican, and that you had heard of a painting he wished to buy—is that not right?—and that it was a Gentileschi and that you wished to purchase it for him—to give it to him—as a surprise. I know that you have many contacts in Italy as a result of your trips there! But perhaps I am mistaken—?''

Somerset listened to this artless recital with no change of expression. ''Your story strikes me as a flight of fancy more to the style of your Edith,'' was all he said, but some inflection in his voice gave Judith the satisfaction of thinking that she had guessed aright on a number of particulars. ''But you have relieved me that the most urgent missive to Lord Chamberlain has not gone astray. Now, about Mr. Smith. Were you given a newer address? Did you seek him out?''

Something swung in the balance. Taking a step down a

path whose ending she could not foresee, she said, "No."
She felt the jolt of the lie down to her toes, but she did not
wish to retract it.

"And the missive, my dear?"

"Here, sir." Judith reached into the purse at her waist to
withdraw the letter.

As she made to extend it to her uncle, he raised his hand,
thereby bringing Sir Albert instantly to his side. With a
negligent wave, he gestured to Judith to hand it directly to
his steward. Her uncle evidently did not care to bother
with the missive, as if his interest in it did not survive the
telling of its misdirected fate. Neither did he spare a glance
at the letter, to see whether it was still sealed, which it was.

Nevertheless, Judith felt as if something sizzling hot had
left her hand, and her fingers tingled with a burning sensation.

"Albert," Somerset said to his man before he had taken
a pace away, "I have just bethought myself of an urgent
message." He turned to Judith with a faint smile. "You
will excuse me a moment?" Immediately Albert placed a
portable writing desk across his master's knees. Somerset
efficiently scratched a brief note, sanded it, folded it, sealed
it, and scrawled a single bold name across the front. He
handed it, along with the writing tray, to the waiting Sir
Albert who nodded solemnly. Sir Albert passed it to a
courier page who sprang to duty.

Somerset returned his attention to Judith. "We have not
yet discussed your plans, my dear."

"My plans?"

"Whether you desired a return to Raglan. You have
accomplished my commissions, and I am now in London to
take care of the rest," he said.

"But I was not expecting your arrival until two days
hence," Judith reminded him.

"Yes. That is correct." He paused, as if coming to a
decision. "Perhaps you had anticipated attending the masque
this evening."

Judith had had no great desire to attend the masque, but
neither would her pride swallow a summary banishment to
Raglan. "Naturally I had anticipated it," she said.

"Naturally. It shall be so," he said by way of granting her her wish. "By all means, you must attend the masque. You shall certainly see Sir George, and although I do not think he was expecting to see you again at Whitehall, I believe his understanding sufficient to accord you the utmost public respect and attention. Yes. You shall attend and meet Sir George amicably, which will silence any wagging tongues that might have heard a misreported story of what occurred in your apartment last night."

It seemed she was supposed to thank him for allowing her to stay. "Thank you, sir," she said, but the words tasted bitter.

Somerset merely nodded to that. Then he rose, thereby bringing Judith also to her feet. "Such a lot of business for one day," he said, almost wearily.

"Have you had other engagements today?"

His gaze was particularly piercing. "Have I not already indicated to you how I have spent this afternoon?" he said. Then, with an abrupt return to the opening subject of the interview, he said, "You will want to consider, very seriously, engaging a new tiring-woman when you become a married lady. That will be soon. You have little time in which to ponder the matter. I am afraid that Edith does not represent you to best advantage, and her unreason, after all these years, may well have affected you."

"You attend admirably to details, sir," Judith said, with an edge.

"A want of attention to details," Somerset said, "usually results in ineffectiveness. Take, for instance, the misdirected letter to Mr. Smith. A small affair. Of no importance. However, a want of attention to details can bring a reign—even the most stable and agreeable one—to an end. When unpleasant events occur—you have heard of the uprising in Scotland, I must suppose—the details become ever more important. I will look forward to seeing you at the masque tonight, my dear Judith." He added, almost as an afterthought, "Perhaps there will be several people whom I shall introduce to you."

She was dismissed.

She curtsied low, kissed his outstretched hand but received no answering kiss on her forehead. She left his chambers, then, feeling mightily confused. She had emerged unscathed. She was not to be treated like Caroline who had, no doubt, been far less indiscreet with the unacceptable James Lambert than she, Judith, had been with his far more disreputable uncle, Charles. Had she not been so vulnerable, had she not been so relieved, had she not been so hungry for her uncle's love, had she been less dazzled by his skillful handling of Sir George and Lady Beecham, Judith might have wondered why her uncle would wish for her to remain at Whitehall. She might have wondered why he wished her to attend the masque, to circulate publicly in harmonious accord with her betrothed and her future mother-in-law. She was not, however, considering her uncle's ulterior motives. For all that he had insured that she would save face, she left him feeling nevertheless bereft, knowing that some of his earlier approval had been withdrawn. She felt as if she had been slapped, then hugged, then slapped again.

The manner of her dismissal actively worried her on her return to her chambers, and her wounded feelings were only exacerbated by Edith's irritating chatter. The queasy, lurching, unstable sensation returned, but it was weaker. At her center, she felt spurts of anger and rebellion and independence. She clung to these new feelings, was steadied by them. Her uncle did not like independence. He did not like disobedience. He did not like her interpretation of the importance of his letter to Mr. Smith. That was why he had withdrawn his earlier approval.

But, no. The chill had entered the conversation before mention of Mr. Smith. Yes, it had entered with the subject of Charles Lambert. A dangerous man, her uncle had said. A man, he implied, he could not trust. Her uncle's attitude had struck her at the time as unduly prejudiced, but now that Judith thought back on it, could she herself trust a man who could play the rôle of casual theater lover with well-timed precision? And, what, after all, did she know of Charles Lambert or his reasons for being at The Red Bull Theater?

What she did know of him and his strange pursuit of some woman did not inspire in her great trust, either.

The shoots of anger and rebellion were too fragile to sustain themselves in the strong, contradictory winds that blew through her. Gnawing at their tender roots was the threat of loss and fear, hard and cold. She was afraid of the loss of her uncle's unexpected generosity and discretion of the afternoon. She was afraid that his protection and trust and love for her could be withdrawn as easily as it had been extended.

Her spirits had sunk very low by the time the day had dissolved into evening. Though she anticipated it with little pleasure now, she was ready for the masque, coiffed with stylish ringlets around her face and dressed in a magnificent gown of emerald green which set her coloring off to perfection, making her almost beautiful. It was a lovely confection whose gorgeous falls of lace gracing the low neckline, pinked and puffed sleeves and slim stomacher enhanced her pretty, rounded curves. Even so, the evening ahead in public and in company with Sir George and Lady Beecham seemed more of a trial than a pleasure.

Then, at the very moment she and Edith had finished their preparations, one of Somerset's messengers came scratching at her door to request of her the honor of presenting herself at the masque on the arm of her uncle.

Judith's spirits soared. Her uncle must have reconsidered and regretted the cold manner of her dismissal. When Judith had draped the ends of her long train over her arm and, with Edith in her wake, was following the messenger down the long hallway to take her rightful place at her uncle's side, she was feeling far from unloved. Rather, she felt triumphant, and thought that the signal honor her uncle bestowed on her was no more than her due.

Chapter
12

AS his afternoon wore on, Lambert felt no similar surge of triumph. If he had begun the day with a profitably satisfying business transaction followed by an exquisite interlude in the theater box, he was ending the day with a sense of empty-handed irritability.

Lambert gazed up into the gloom of the rafters of the now-empty theater. He had a clear view of the rickety landings where a stagehand could draw ropes from above to raise and lower objects onto the stage. As for any signs of a person lurking in the ancient scaffolding, there were none. Lambert swore softly but fluently.

If he could just lay his hands on Rosamunda, he would have some of the answers he craved, even if it meant throttling the schemer's slender neck. Lambert was convinced that Rosamunda not only knew the whereabouts of his precious painting but also held the clue to Somerset's very curious role in this baroque piece of intrigue. Although Lambert had not seen Rosamunda return to the theater after her narrow escape at the end of the first act, he had a hunch that her secrets lay within the theater walls and that she would return, if she dared. And of Spadaccio, no wisp of that elegant figure had been seen since Wales. For all Lambert knew, Spadaccio might well have been back on his way to Rome, his mission to Somerset accomplished.

To compound his frustration, Lambert had a strong hunch that Judith Beaufort might, unwittingly, hold some important clues. However, as far as Lambert was concerned, she was now rather more part of the problem than a key to the solution. A taste for Judith Beaufort he deemed to be bad for his health and well-being.

Shaking his head clear of her, Lambert descended the upper scaffolding by a derelict ladder. He leapt down from a half-landing jutting out over the apron stage, as it was called, to land below on the stage proper.

At the thud of boots on the floorboards, the door of a trap in the stage floor flipped open. A grisled, ugly head popped out. It was scowling.

"Damned, plaguey, *bloody* female!" it spat.

"Now, Will," Lambert admonished. He crossed the empty stage to the trapdoor. He stretched out a hand to help his henchman up and out of the opening in the floorboards by which many an evil character was sent to perdition. "I'll beg you to watch your words."

With his master's helping hand and a grunt, Will hauled himself out of the hellhole, delivering himself as he did so of a far ruder series of epithets. Standing straight and brushing himself of the cobwebs he had gathered in the world below stage, he met Lambert's eye. "And I'll not be apologizing for the sentiments, neither."

Lambert was relieved of the necessity of reprimanding Will his crudity, for other characters, still in Spanish costume, wandered out from the apron stages to join them. Young Tom and Robin and Dick and Allan and the others indicated that their searches of The Red Bull, too, had failed to produce the elusive Rosamunda.

Harry Webster materialized from the backstage shadows, as well, but if he had been scouring the nooks and crannies of the theater for anyone, it was not apparent from his comments. The playwright was volubly criticizing *The King and His Subject* in a long oral review bristling with phrases such as "titillating jaded appetites" and "the jolly themes of incest and perversions'' (irony was not unknown to Mr. Webster) and ''violence and brutality added to censorious notoriety.''

Finding themselves at center stage, the actors fell into posturing and characterizations. Robin, ever beautiful in his skirts (he had played an exquisite, tragically fated señorita), flirted prettily with his fan and his eyes and attempted to enthrall Dick. However, since Dick preferred to spar with Allan and was unresponsive, Robin snapped his Spanish fan shut with decided pique and taunted provocatively, ''What, Dick, always a bit player? Your time would be better spent learning a trick or two from the one true *actor* among us.'' Robin swished his hem and shrugged one white shoulder. ''I, at least, can offer you practice for the performance at tonight's masque.''

Though directed at Dick, this soft-spoken insult was heard by all; and since it held an element of truth that applied to all of them, it was even more unforgivable. Surely, Robin did not need to remind his fellow players, yet again, that he was the only one of them to have been cast by the Companie of the Revels with a speaking part.

Dick, who excelled in theatrical rodomontades onstage, was the mildest of creatures offstage. ''We've all of us equal parts tonight at Whitehall,'' he pointed out, taking little offense. The boom of his stage voice was, in normal conversation, lowered to a muted roar.

Allan was more choleric. He stepped forward to air his views on the subject of ''true actors.'' He flicked the lace collar at Robin's breast and said, ''A trick or two, my lad? The only tricks a man could learn from you are—''

Lambert intervened. He had had enough experience in the theater to know how to handle restless actors still strung high after a performance. Hardly had the insult left Robin's mouth than Lambert had gone behind the curtain and returned a moment later with two dueling foils. Thus, when Robin was poised to counter Allan's aggression, Lambert said, opportunely, ''Have done, Allan.'' He tossed a foil to Robin, inviting, ''Exercise your wrist to some purpose, lad.

I like to keep mine in practice. Come and have a bout with me.''

Dropping the fan, Robin caught the hilt. Allan fell back to let the master tame the bitch in Robin. Slipping easily into his new rôle, Robin slashed the air experimentally several times. Then he turned to Lambert, assuming the fencer's stance.

The swords saluted. Though intended as stage props, the foils were real, and the flash of steel glinted in the light of the dying day. Lambert took the defensive, in order that his opponent might work the edge off his ragged nerves. He drew Robin into a series of lunges, which he deftly parried, and allowed himself to be driven back from center stage to the rim of the apron. It was, thus, an odd sight that would have greeted any passerby to The Red Bull, to see onstage a large, agile man driven to continuous retreat before the tip of a foil held by a golden-curled, petticoated damsel.

The sight effectively diverted and delighted their fellow players whose jests urged the strange contest on and provided fitting accompaniment to the sound of scurrying steel and the hollow echo of feet shuffling across the floorboards.

''By the saints, Lambert! Don't be such a woman!'' called out several who did not, at first, understand Lambert's tactics. A volley of ruder oaths followed, along with several crude observations on Robin's satisfactions.

''A woman besting a man in a swordfight? It is unnatural! It has never before been seen! I wonder if I can use it? Quick! My pen! Some paper! I feel the first breath of an inspiration!'' the playwright cried.

When Lambert butted against a post supporting a beam of the stage balcony so that his back was literally against a wall, he dropped his guard momentarily. Robin, who had been excited by his success, was thereby lured into a daring attack. When Robin lunged, Lambert parried and also caught Robin's right wrist with his left hand. Lambert drew his opponent so close that they were nose to nose. However, given their relative positions, it was difficult for the spectators to have said who had the upper hand.

''Had enough?'' Lambert queried.

Robin was panting. "That—should—have—been—my—line." He drew a ragged breath. "Do you—upstage me—even in defeat?"

Lambert's grip on Robin's wrist tightened. "Defeat?"

Robin smiled, with some regret. "The word is—relative. I have never had—this much success—with you, Charles."

"It was your skirts," he replied, "that unmanned me." Lambert released Robin's wrist.

Robin withdrew. The slight respite had helped him to recover. "My advantage," he said, piqued anew at Lambert's words, "is also my disadvantage." Robin smiled prettily. "Why, look you, Charles. You are not even sweating. 'Tis prodigious unfair. You have put me to shame."

At that, Robin pulled the heavy wig from his head and let it fall to the floor. Beads of perspiration glistened on his forehead, and he wiped them away with the delicate lace of his sleeve. He stripped off the offending skirts to reveal plain-cut breeches and hose and, with a practiced gesture of one hand, unhooked the costume bodice to expose a bare torso of a surprising muscularity. Manfully transformed, he nevertheless threw Lambert a flashing glance that retained something of the Robin dressed in skirts. He hissed the fencer's "Sa-sa!" and flexed his foil experimentally.

Lambert obliged by shoving himself off the post and saluting Robin's blade a second time. Robin fenced more cunningly, no longer encumbered by yards of material, the edges of his earlier irritation somewhat smoothed. With a few rough edges of his own to file, Lambert fenced incautiously and with flair, letting his emotions flourish with his blade.

This time Lambert had chosen the offensive. He engaged in tierce and led the attack by a beat and a straightening of the arm. He expected the demi-contre, which came, and promptly countered by a thrust in quinte. This was countered again, for without his woman's skirts, Robin was in better form. Lambert answered by reentering still lower and was again correctly parried. Then Lambert lunged, swirling his point into carte, and got home full, touching Robin's bare breast above his heart. The execution had been neat and precise and had looked too easy. It brought a scattering of applause from the onlookers and a "Bravo!" and a "That's more like like it!"

Robin bowed gracefully, accepting momentary defeat. "Do you think to give me a fencing lesson, O Master?"

"Those who wish to give lessons," Lambert answered piously, "should also be able to take them."

Although Robin smiled pleasantly in response, a determination to defeat Charles Lambert seized him. Robin raised his foil to engage again, and the salute he offered Lambert's blade this third time was ruthlessly purposeful.

Lambert easily checked Robin's opening thrust and was further inspired, rather than intimidated, that he was finally fencing man to man. With a series of feints and parries, he was luring Robin into giving him an ever-wider opening and driving the handsome youth back toward the tapestries that hung under the stage balcony.

Their little audience was shifting and shuffling around the line the duelists drew. After some minutes, the jests and jeers had ceased, and a certain earnestness had overtaken the atmosphere onstage.

Robin was clearly losing. When his back touched the tapestry that hung center stage, he knew he could retreat no farther. If he were to step back, he might hope that Lambert might entangle himself in the arras, but he also knew that the stairs leading to the cellar behind the stage lay open several feet behind him. He had failed to close the trapdoor after his earlier search for Rosamunda after the performance. He knew that he could not step backward without possibly breaking his neck.

When Lambert thrust in and broke Robin's guard, he remarked, a little breathless but far from winded, "What a pleasure it is—to fence with the man in you. Most days—it's hide-and-seek—with you. I confess—it's a trial to me."

Robin hated this losing game and suddenly knew how he could best Lambert. "You should—be better—at that man-woman game—by now—Charles," he taunted, "for all the practice—you've had at it—of late."

"What mean you, lad?" Lambert asked as his blade teased Robin in return.

Robin's expression was coy. It was almost as if he were holding the fan again, and not a sword. "Only that—you've been chasing a man-woman—for days now."

Lambert had been about to tip the foil from Robin's hand. At this curious disclosure his concentration wavered enough for his guard to drop and for Robin to pink him briefly before he flicked the lad's sword away. Having lost his momentum, Lambert also had to retreat a step and was subjected to a furious offensive by Robin the man.

"Do you suggest—" Lambert began, giving up the ground he had lately won.

"That Rosamunda is—no woman," Robin finished, pleased with himself and his attack.

"The lovely Rosamunda—is a masquerader?" Lambert pursued.

"We are—all of us masqueraders," Robin said. "And men—as we know—play women."

"But not—offstage," Lambert replied. He retreated several more steps. "Rosamunda a man? Can you—be sure?"

Robin smiled seductively, savoring his success. "Do you—doubt me?"

Lambert did not. Neither did the actors in their attentive little audience who had been listening and were now laughing and commenting freely on what Rosamunda had been hiding all this time under her skirts. Will was volubly outraged by the possibility that a man would dress as a woman *off the stage,* while the playwright was inclined to think that a man in woman's dress was an old ploy but one he just might have use for in a farce.

Lambert pulled himself together. So Rosamunda was a man. That explained at a stroke why Lambert had had such a damnably difficult time trailing the Italian all the way from Rome.

Lambert was still in retreat, only now it was strategic. He said, "Doubt you?—No. Only your source—or is your knowledge of—Rosamunda's manhood—firsthand?"

Robin's success had gone to his head. He divulged, laughing, "Rosamunda?—Let's call him Smith—more like."

Smith?

Lambert's brows snapped together, and he stopped dead in his tracks. He had lately overheard that name on Somerset's lips backstage. The teasing, taunting dueling game was over. With a quick flick of his wrist, Lambert tipped Robin's sword from his hand. It fell to the floor with such suddenness that Robin was wholly surprised.

Robin stood there swordless, expressionless. The other players were hushed and expectant.

"Smith is his name?" Lambert queried, the point of his sword at Robin's heart. "That does not sound very Italian."

"He's not Italian."

"Not a woman. And not Italian," Lambert remarked. "A skillful actor, when all is said. Most skillful."

"Not fully Italian," Robin said. "Though I'm told he speaks the tongue like a native."

"Ah," was all Lambert said. Then, with determination, "I asked you if your knowledge of Smith's manhood is firsthand."

Robin had never seen such an implacable look on Charles Lambert's face before. Perhaps Robin had miscalculated. When Lambert pressed the tip of his sword into Robin's flesh, he was sure that he had miscalculated. He nodded slowly, obediently.

"I have it from—a source," Robin answered evasively.

"Is it reliable?"

"Most."

"No tricks?"

Hands empty, Robin taunted, at his most seductive, "Tricks?"

"Who is it?" Lambert demanded, unamused.

There was a code in his world that Robin would rather not have broken. However, Lambert was toying with him now, and Lambert was driving him back again, step by step, into the central tapestry. Robin held no sword. He chose to avert complete humiliation by divulging the name of his most recent lover—the one who knew the deception played by the man named Mr. Smith.

Lambert stopped abruptly. He was convinced. Robin had given him the name of a high-placed lord who would have reason to know intimately the underbelly of court politics. Lambert lowered his sword. He nodded. He had one more, extremely important question. "And Somerset's part in the play?"

Robin's liquid black eyes were suddenly shrewd. He was massaging the tendons that ribbed the muscular surface of his sword arm. "The beautiful man in white?" he asked.

Lambert's voice was flat. "Is he known to you?"

"It's a strange and complicated world we live in," was Robin's response.

Lambert smiled congenially, but he jiggled the hilt of his lowered sword in his hand and made the gesture threatening. "Excessively strange and complicated, and becoming more so by the hour. Do you know the man?"

"Ask his niece," Robin said testily.

"The lad's jealous!" called several from the sidelines.

Lambert ignored this, as well as his flare of anger that sprang inside him at mention of Judith Beaufort. "Do you know the man?"

Robin relented. His gaze was unshadowed when he replied with a simple "No."

Lambert bowed perfunctorily. "Thank you." Then he shook his head. "Such a lot of work for so very little, Robin."

Robin rapidly recovered his customary impudence. He smiled saucily. "Feeling better?"

Lambert indeed felt better. Of the soothing of his nerves during this passage at arms, Lambert said nothing. Instead, he laughed. "That was my line, stripling," he replied.

Harry Webster, quill in hand and scratching furiously on some scraps of paper, walked over to them, saying, "Very good! Very good! Now, I would that you execute that last sequence—just a little slower, if you please! I am afraid that I did not get it all down! I think it has possibilities. Yes, distinct possibilities!"

When Lambert looked over his shoulder at the playwright, Robin took the opportunity to slide away. Lambert was in fine fettle now, all his acting instincts roused. Without moving from his position, Lambert flashed his blade out over the few feet separating him from the play-wright. He crossed the playwright's quill with his sword.

"En garde, Harry!" Lambert said.

The playwright looked up, startled. "Eh? I did not mean for you to 'fence with *me*, dear fellow," he explained unnecessarily, "but with *Robin*." When Lambert tickled the pen with the tip of his blade, the playwright caught on. "Oh, very amusing!" he exclaimed, but he withdrew his quill from Lambert's reach. "I am afraid, however, that my poor feather is no match to your steel."

"Impale me with your words, then," Lambert challenged.

There was laughter. The men watching were delighted. This was a fine jest, one that blunted any sharpness that might have been felt at Lambert's defeat of their comrade, Robin. The playwright needed encouragement.

"Set to, Harry!" they called. "Show your stuff!" and "Make good on your skill!" and "Words, now, Harry! Skillful words!" and "You've bleated long enough over the strength of your craft! Show him how strong is your quill!"

The playwright was a good enough sport, and responded to his players by raising his pen into the air and tapping it playfully against Lambert's sword.

"Show 'im, Harry!" they hooted. "Show your pen to be stronger than his sword, Harry!" and "Make the sword fall before the pen!" and "The quill bests the blade!" and "Harry's mighty quill!"

"There's material for you, Harry," Lambert pointed out, twirling the tip of his sword around the feather. "Can you use it? 'The quill bests the blade'?" Lambert turned to address the audience. "What say you, lads? Harry needs a quotable line. Can you help him out?"

"The mighty quill is better than the blade!" tried one. "The quill is mighty and better than the sword!" tried another. Then, someone produced the phrase, "The quill is mightier than the sword!"

Lambert laughed. "An admirable line, Harry! What can you do with it?"

The playwright had furrowed his brow in concentration. "The quill—perhaps 'the pen' would do better here—is mightier than the sword," he repeated slowly. "Hmmm. Yes. It *is* an admirable line. I wonder . . ." He trailed off. He disengaged his quill from Lambert's sword. " 'The pen is mightier than the sword,' " he experimented aloud. He began to write the line down but stopped himself. He shook his head on an afterthought. "No, I think not."

Lambert placed his sword, tip down, into the floorboards and leaned against it. "It scans, Harry," he said.

"It does," the playwright acknowledged, "but it still lacks a certain sort of something."

From the sidelines came again calls and taunts to the effect that "Aww, Harry, you never use anything we suggest!" and "That was a good one, Harry! Don't pass it up!" and "It's your chance for immortality!" and "It's a play on words, the pen and the sword, don't you see?"

With great dignity, Harry Webster looked at the actors surrounding him. He said, "Let us leave the wordplay to the writer, and the swordplay to the . . . inarticulate." He stopped, transfixed, blinded by his own brilliance. "Why, that's *it*! What a line! 'Leave the wordplay to the writer and the swordplay to the inarticulate,' " he repeated with deep satisfaction. "Now *there's* a line that will echo down through the ages! Yes, yes! I shall write that one down!" He scratched out the beginnings of the previous line and scurried his pen across the page, saying, "You see! You *are* helpful in your own particular ways! There! Perfect!"

Lambert was regarding the playwright with amused affection. "Will you be using the line tonight?" he asked.

Harry looked up. "What? Oh! No!" he said. "The masque at Whitehall tonight is not to be one of my creations but Davenant's *The Temple of Love*. Perhaps you did not realize that I am working as a consultant to Davenant tonight." He waved his hand, anticipating a question that was not asked. "No, no! *Not* that I am to be paid for the service. I am working free of charge. Gratis!" The playwright had worked himself into one of his flights. "Not for money, that is! I am certainly working for recompense. For the rewards given to me—and everyone—from great art. From creation! From . . . genius!"

"And you don't think it will hurt your career any to have your name linked with that of Davenant's," said Allan, who never minced words.

The playwright felt compelled to respond to that, this time on a less exalted note. "That is true," he said.

Lambert laughed. "You'll doubtless be rewarded by posterity, Harry—one way or another!"

The playwright took Lambert's words as the mere statement of truth. "A foregone conclusion," he said, not very originally, "but *not* if we are not at Whitehall soon to begin rehearsing!" He looked up at the sky. "It's late, men, and we'd best be off! Allan! Richard! Thomas! Shake a leg! And Robin, please to fetch your shirt. I do not wish for you to excite the ladies too early. Yes, the ladies! For you are playing a man tonight. A fair damsel's lover, no less, and I hope that you are equal to the part!"

Robin affected a masculine swagger and assured Harry Webster he would "make the ladies swoon."

Harry shooed the players off the stage, recommending them to be about their business. Before turning to go, he addressed Lambert. "I'll be needing a hand from Will to help me transfer the boxes of costumes from the theater to the Banqueting House. May I borrow him for the rest of the afternoon and evening?"

Lambert gave his assent and nodded to Will to follow the others. The stage emptied of everyone but Lambert who stood, still in the center, idly twirling his foil, listening abstractedly to the sounds of the men leaving the theater, staring in supreme vacancy at the tapestry before him.

Then the theater was silent, save for the occasional creakings and twinges characteristic of an old wooden structure. Lambert noted that the shadows had lengthened and deepened, but he did not move, nor did he remove his eyes from the tapestry. He was lost in contemplation of Robin's stunning disclosure.

Despite his deep thought, his eye for art was never completely dormant, and little by little the tapestry hanging not four feet in front of his face came into focus.

He took a step toward it and critically surveyed it. Its

colors and design were chosen to look good at a distance. On closer inspection, however, Lambert judged it to be cheap and poorly wrought. It was not a new weaving either, as Lambert could see from the frayed edges on the lower right border. But, no, those were not frayed threads. Rather they had been cut. Idle curiosity prompted him to lift his sword and with its tip to play experimentally with those cut threads. He caught the veriest glimpse of something hidden inside the tapestry. It was ivory colored and certainly thin but obviously sturdy. Perhaps it was a piece of parchment or muslin or even old canvas sometimes used to line poorly woven tapestries to give them body.

At the moment that his blade touched the weaving, Lambert gave voice to his overall judgment of the piece of craftsmanship before him.

"Hideous."

At the word, as if by magic, a tall, slim, and very elegant figure appeared from behind the tapestry causing Lambert's sword point to fall away from its probing of the cut threads of the tapestry.

Lambert was face-to-face with an extraordinarily handsome man. An Adonis. Truly a painting come to life, for the man's face and figure graced many a famous canvas. Lambert knew it well.

A pair of beautifully molded lips said, in Italian, "Your taste, Carlo, is ever accurate, I perceive." Dark, piercing, passionate eyes gestured to the tapestry, then flicked, measuringly, back to Lambert. "Or is your comment rather the realization of the, ah, difficulties of your present situation?"

When the first flash of surprise had passed, Lambert transferred the tip of his blade from the tapestry to touch the button on the man's doublet nearest his heart. "You speak of difficulties, Umberto?" he replied smoothly, also in Italian.

The man did not flinch nor display any other sign of discomfort. He smiled. Then he held up a hand, and a deep froth of lace fell from his wrist to lie against the peacock silk of his doublet. He snapped his fingers once. There materialized from the now very dark shadows of the apron stages several hulking presences. Lambert looked about him and saw four threatening bodies, hovering at the four corners of the main stage.

The handsome man smiled again and, with fastidious fingers, removed Lambert's blade from his breast. Lambert did not resist. This was not the time for bravura. He might be able to skewer the man before him. If he were quick, he might be able to outmaneuver the four men who ringed him on the stage, but he had no way of knowing how many reinforcements had been marshaled backstage for this occasion. In any case, none of these risky actions would win him anything or gain him any knowledge. He felt himself close to the heart of the matter, close to the pulse of blood in this strange affair. One false move might cause some of that blood to spill. He would take care that it would not be his own.

Lambert slid the steel slowly into its case. Though the sword was sheathed, he liked the feel of it against his thigh. He held up empty hands in a gesture of peace. Still, he was not completely helpless and here was an excellent opportunity to have some of his questions answered.

"*Grazie*, Carlo," Spadaccio said politely, inclining his head. "For all your hotheaded ways, you have your own brand of reason. Speaking of which, have you yet perceived the depths of your difficulties? 'Hideous,' I think, may well describe them."

Lambert assumed a relaxed posture. He was at home onstage, in England, after all. He shook his head. "I'm new at this. Explain to me the depths of my difficulties."

Spadaccio made a moue of irritability. "Look about you and you shall see."

"A threat?"

"Call it a warning."

"Ah."

"You have always been an astute man, *caro* Carlo."

Although Lambert had temporarily discounted the use of physical force, he did dare a verbal thrust. It was more of a stab in the dark. "Astute enough to know," he said, affecting a hint of boredom, "that you have come to England for the same thing I am after."

"And what might that be?"

"A painting."

Spadaccio's shapely brows rose involuntarily in surprise. He was a skilled actor, however, and turned his reaction to good account. "What say you, dear Carlo? A painting. You talk in riddles." He clucked his tongue. "And here I have just called you an astute man!"

Lambert pursued his advantage. "Allow me to dazzle you further with my intelligence, Umberto. An unnamed person knows the whereabouts of a seemingly worthless painting. The painting, so far from being worthless, is, in point of fact, extremely valuable. Its value is determined, of course, by the large sums of money that certain parties are willing to pay for it. You are one of those parties."

Spadaccio's polite mask of disbelief remained in place. "Your love of art has distorted your perceptions of reality, I am afraid. How came you by such an interesting interpretation of my presence in England?" he said at length. "It is entirely your own. I wonder at the way you arrived at such a fanciful interpretation."

"The same way a Puritan scans nature to find signs of God," Lambert hazarded daringly.

Something distinctly unpleasant lept into Spadaccio's beautiful eyes. He did not bother to hide it and kept his gaze fixed on Lambert. His response was slow in coming. "You mean, of course, that you see the interpretation everywhere," now Spadaccio's tones were somewhat harsh, "but I fear you have changed the subject."

"I think not."

"Ah, but we were discussing paintings. Religious conviction was not the topic."

"I am rather persuaded that religious conviction is at the center of our conversation." Lambert paused. "You see, Umberto. I have kept up with your career. I know you are in Rome and in the employ of the Vatican."

Lambert's gamble had worked. Spadaccio did not bother to deny the guess. "So," the graceful Italian said, "it seems I never really knew your hidden folds and recesses. You have more than one error of taste, after all."

"Why, Umberto, I would have said that our tastes converged in every way," Lambert replied, thinking of the Italian actress they had both wooed years ago and who Lambert had won.

"If you still have that ugly little cur, Guiglielmo, in your employ, I fault your taste a thousand times."

Lambert laughed. "Will never liked you."

Spadaccio acknowledged the comment with a little bow. "But we wander from the subject, *caro Carlo,* which you have identified as religious conviction, and despite all your other errors of taste," he repeated, "I would not have guessed that you harbored, deep in your heart, Puritan sympathies!"

Lambert laughed again. "I come from a family that has never been famed for rigidity in religious matters, Umberto! Don't deprive the Lamberts of their one virtue!"

Spadaccio paused. "I see. Then perhaps you might explain to me what interest you have in the—how shall I say—hypothetical painting."

"It is simple. I consider it mine. Someone stole the painting from me," Lambert replied.

"I am not a child, Carlo."

"Six weeks ago, in Florence, at an auction at the Palazzo Strozzi to be precise," Lambert continued. "I outbid my competitor by offering three times its market value."

Spadaccio considered these details. "*Ecco,*" he said softly, after a moment, apparently convinced. Then he shook his head and murmured, as if to himself, "Such a minor detail. Such a little hitch. Who would have thought any dealer would have wanted that painting?"

"I have already owned my taste at fault on several scores," Lambert stated flatly, "and I want the painting back."

This brought Spadaccio's head up and a flash of Roman hauteur to his liquid eyes. "You have become a rich man, Carlo. Yes. One hears of you from time to time, and I confess that I have been interested in your career, as you have been interested in mine. But even you do not have enough money for this deal.''

Lambert stood impassive. So. The Vatican *was* making overtures to Charles Stuart. Lambert was now certain that the painting was more than a gift. Perhaps it contained something else, a communication from the Pope with a dispensation to the Anglican Church and an invitation to help reestablish a glorious and unified Catholic Christendom.

''Unless, of course, you are willing to pay for it with your blood,'' Spadaccio continued, taunting, to Lambert's silence. His handsome face had gone quite cold and hard. He had never been a playful Robin, to tease and to flirt and to accept defeat gracefully; and Lambert did not mistake the man before him as anything other than a deadly enemy. ''But you have never liked blood, have you, Carlo? You see. I remember much.''

Still, Lambert did not respond.

''Or you might wish to pay by naming the unnamed person who you think has the painting? Or, even, where it might be?''

Spadaccio's desperate, Lambert reflected calmly. So, the Vatican's secret agent did not know where the painting was, either, and it now seemed likely that Rosamunda was double-crossing Spadaccio the way Mr. Smith was balking Somerset. Were Spadaccio and Somerset, who would usually be natural adversaries in this affair, now allies against the double-crosser?

When Lambert said nothing, Spadaccio snapped his fingers again, and the brutes ringing the stage began to close in on Lambert.

Spadaccio smiled then. ''It is my opinion that you really do not know the answers to these most interesting questions. Otherwise, I would have you killed. Yet, I have a sense of justice and a lingering fondness for you,'' he said, ''and will give you fair warning. It is only your ignorance that is saving you. Keep it that way. Leave London tonight. Go back to Italy, if you will. Go to Antwerp or to Augsburg. I don't care. But leave. Tonight. Now. You have no further business at Whitehall, and if you are seen there, you shall be killed.''

Spadaccio drew a dagger from his waist and advanced on Lambert. When Lambert's hand went to the sword at his side, Spadaccio merely shook his head and gestured with his knife that Lambert keep his hands up. Spadaccio stood inches from Lambert, a blade's length away. Then, swiftly, he unbuckled Lambert's sword belt. The sword clattered to the floor, leaving Lambert naked of defenses.

Spadaccio snapped his fingers a third time and said to his curs, ''I have orders to get rid of this man. Batter him a bit, boys. Nothing too unsightly. A fair warning, as I've said, but one he will take seriously. A little blood will do. Not too much.''

Spadaccio turned on his heels and a second later had faded into the shadows behind the tapestry. A second after that, Lambert was set upon by the four brutes. It was not a fair fight, but Lambert gave a good account of himself, for a minute at least.

When the first fist landed on his jaw and the sticky taste of iron and salt spurted in his mouth and the stars began to spin, he recognized how wise it would be to heed Spadaccio's warning. The painting was essentially worthless. Lambert's chances for retrieving it were receding. The intrigue was taking a nasty, brutal turn. He was vastly outnumbered, and on all sides. The forces of the Vatican were against him. So were those represented by Somerset, as well as those of the king whom Somerset was trying to protect. Lambert's part in the intrigue was now known to the principals, and his knowledge of the details was no doubt considered dangerous. His life would not be worth the price of a Raphael cartoon if he continued to pursue what could never be his. He had no political or religious stakes in the matter. Civil war threatened. A wise man would draw back.

When the thugs were done raining blows on his body, when his knuckles were raw, his ribs bruised, his head cracked, his jaw stiff, his eye swollen, and his gut wrenched, there was no doubt about it: He really must attend tonight's masque at the Banqueting House.

Chapter
13

SOMERSET patted Judith's hand. "I hope, my dear," he said, "that you will enjoy yourself this evening." Judith turned a dazzling smile and sparkling eyes on him. "I know so, sir." With that, she trod the last of the steps to the Banqueting House and passed under the imposing portico.

The facade of the royal palace was a kind of manifesto of the new purely classical style sponsored by Charles Stuart. This splendid entrance set the tone for the more splendid interior. It was the king's Arcadia, and it had been designed by Inigo Jones who had planned it after a long tour of Italy and executed it after a meticulous study of Palladio's drawings.

When Judith entered the grand apartment, she was instantly swallowed, but not diminished, by the size of it, for the room ran 110 feet in length and 55 feet in breadth and height, making it a double cube. Descending the interior steps, she looked across the vista which was divided harmoniously into seven bays by Ionic and Corinthian wall-pilasters. The expanse was given unity by a slight but subtly contrived projection of the three central bays and further interest by the use of varicolored masonry. The floor was paved with marble; the ceiling held nine great panels of

Rubens's paintings of the apotheosis of King James and the blessings of the Stuart monarchy; and the vast apartment was ablaze with light and abuzz with talk and laughter and music.

At the opposite end of the hall, centrally placed, was the "Great Niche," where the king sat enthroned on state occasions. The throne was empty, for the king was circulating among his guests. Beyond the Niche stood the masquing room that had been newly erected in the courtyard space between the freestanding Banqueting House and one of the wings of the royal palace with which the new room now communicated.

Lord Henry moved with stately procession through the crowd, nodding and bowing and pausing on occasion to exchange several words with his vast acquaintance. Judith had a considerable acquaintance herself and greeted many friends, among them Lucy, Countess of Carlisle. Judith breathed a sigh of relief that, during this greeting, Lucy had betrayed no evidence of having seen her at The Red Bull earlier that day.

Somerset did not seem to have a particular course in mind. At one moment, he drifted to a knot of courtiers, suggesting that he wished for Judith to make their acquaintance. The introductions were made. The faces were unknown to her, but certainly not their noble names, and after the customary greetings were exchanged, Somerset slipped Judith's hand once again through his arm, and they moved on.

As they left that group, a startlingly beautiful young woman, unknown to Judith, came into her direct line of vision. The young woman was standing some twenty feet away and was engaged in what appeared to be a soft and seemingly involved conversation with George Francis Villiers, the Duke of Buckingham.

"Good heavens, sir," Judith said impulsively, "and who might that extraordinarily lovely woman be?"

"What woman, my dear?" Somerset asked. Their steps had taken them past a small group that partially obscured the beautiful woman from view.

One step farther brought the woman back into their vision. Judith cast her eyes to the right and gestured slightly with her head. "Over there. Speaking with Buckingham."

Somerset obligingly glanced in the direction that Judith had indicated. "Ah. Yes. That is Elizabeth Marston," he replied. He looked down at Judith, an unreadable expression on his face. He cataloged, "She is the oldest of three daughters. Her father is a dear friend of the Lord Mayor Garroway and heads, incidentally, the Merchant Adventurers Company, although Marston himself, of course, is not a tradesman. He has become a rich and powerful man. Her mother is from Yorkshire."

Just then, Miss Marston glanced up at the Duke of Buckingham, and Judith caught a glimpse of the most heavenly blue eyes she had ever seen. Her unreflected thought was: *Why, she is even more beautiful than Diana! Lambert's taste runs to the exquisite!* Aloud, she said, "Shall we not go over and meet her?"

Somerset appeared to consider the matter. Then, he waved a negative hand. "Perhaps later, my dear. I will certainly make a point of speaking with Buckingham this evening. However," he said, looking down at his niece with what might have been a trace of humor, "at the moment I would guess that he would not welcome my intrusion. He is no doubt deep in discussion of the artistic glories of Italy. I believe that Miss Marston is lately come from abroad. Italy, in fact. She must be fresh with observations. I believe that she spent much of her time in Florence." He paused to reflect. "Yes. Florence."

"Miss Marston," Judith repeated and remarked, with a casual inflection, "Unmarried."

"As yet," her uncle replied. "One has heard rumors that she might have an attachment and may contract an engagement soon, but like so much of what one hears, it might be merely that: rumors. Speaking of which, look, my dear. Over there. It is Beecham. I think this an excellent opportunity to greet him and cry—shall we say?—*pax?*"

At that, he wheeled Judith gracefully away from the side of the room where stood the Duke of Buckingham and the exquisite Elizabeth Marston. The unspoken name of Charles Lambert wafted in the air, as real, but as intangible, as an intriguing aroma. It curled seductively through Judith's senses a moment until she resolutely shook it off.

When Somerset glanced down at his niece, a look of satisfaction crept across his patrician features, as if he had achieved a purpose. He said, "Beecham will be speechless this evening at your loveliness, my dear, and ready to forgive all."

Judith held few illusions about herself and her world. When she replied to her uncle, she did so in the spirit of the Judith he knew best. "We were agreed earlier, I believe, that Sir George has nothing to forgive me for."

"We were almost agreed on that point, my dear." her uncle replied, patting her hand, "but I am willing to concede you anything this evening, for you have never looked more fetching," and his voice sounded sincere.

Sir George's reaction to Judith's presence confirmed Somerset's assessment of Judith's appearance and was all that was flattering. As predicted, Sir George gawked a moment before finding words and gestures adequate to the occasion. Judith accepted these and offered her own words and gestures in return. Thus were the bad feelings and the hurt and the misunderstandings smoothed over and all under Somerset's benevolent eye.

As Somerset's good fortune would have it, at the very moment that all the expressions of regret and pardon had been uttered between his niece and her betrothed, two people happened by to bridge the possibly awkward pause that had fallen. The first was a good friend of Sir George's, and Somerset managed to send the two men off on an errand on the other side of the grand apartment.

The second was an extremely elegant man who wore his cobalt silk Florentine doublet and breeches with a Continental air.

"Signor Umberto," Somerset said, laying a hand on

the man's arm to stop him. "It is a pleasure to see you here tonight. I wish to present you to my niece, Judith Beaufort." Somerset turned back to Judith and presented her to Signor Umberto Spadaccio, identifying him as the envoy of the Duke of Orsini in Rome. Her uncle informed her that Signor Spadaccio had arrived but a day or two ago in London.

While Signor Umberto made an elegant leg and Judith returned the courtesy with a bob, she judged the Italian to be the most handsome man she had ever laid eyes on. His hair was black and thick and wavy, his eyes were black liquid fire, his nose was straight, and his lips were perfectly carved.

When the opening formalities were complete, Judith queried as a standard opening gambit, "You have come from Rome? Attached to the Vatican, perhaps?"

Signor Spadaccio had obviously fielded this question many times. "No, my lady. Although I am a representative of the House of Orsini which is famous for its ties to the Vatican, those with the Papal connections form another branch of the illustrious family entirely."

"Then you have come on secular business," Judith said with a smile, accepting the encounter as an entirely casual one.

Signor Spadaccio bowed. "Very secular. I am here, in your England, to locate a misplaced piece of Italian artwork."

Although Signor Spadaccio addressed Judith, she had the distinct impression that he was speaking to her uncle. Something pricked along the back of her neck and down her spine.

"A misplaced piece of artwork?" she said and hazarded, "Is it a very small piece of artwork, one that might easily be mislaid? A very small painting, perhaps? A miniature?"

Signor Spadaccio smiled politely. "Did I say, dear lady, that it was a painting?"

"No," Judith said, surprised by what she interpreted as a rebuff. "Perhaps you mean something more like the beautiful diamond cross that was sent to our queen as a gift from her godfather, the Pope.''

"Your understanding is quick, my lady," Signor Spadaccio replied with a bow. "That gift, as you will recall, should have helped to change the mind of all Englishmen who, erroneously, believe that Roman priests take, but never give.''

Somerset was not going to let this one pass. "Your mission is a secular one, dear Umberto," he reminded the handsome Italian, his voice extremely mild, "but while we are on the subject of religion, let us acknowledge, as friends, that what Urban VIII has to offer the English is little less than national turbulence and possible civil war. But let us not speak of such unpleasant possibilities at this most enjoyable of occasions.'' Somerset turned to his niece. "As for the misplaced artwork," he explained, "the Romans misjudged the character of the messenger who was to have brought the artwork from Italy to England. For some reason, there is a belief that the artwork went astray in England. Signor Spadaccio has been sent to repair the mistake. Let us hope that Signor Spadaccio will soon find to his satisfaction that the lost artwork also represents a lost cause, and that he will be able to return to his homeland with a clear heart.''

"My heart will be clear and my return to Italia will be assured, dear Enrico, when I have retrieved the artwork and placed it in the hands of the person for whom it is intended." Signor Spadaccio's manner was of the utmost cordiality, but his voice was not wholly pleasant.

The figure of the king, moving sedately through his Court, came into view of the threesome. His small, fastidious, royal figure was dressed, never with vulgar ostentation, but with the elegance and ceremony that reigned in every other aspect of his life. It drew and held a moment all three pairs of eyes.

"I wish you nothing but success, dear Umberto," Somerset said, bowing deeply.

Judith's discomfort and suspicions had grown apace during this strange passage. Were Signor Spadaccio and her uncle friends or foes? It was difficult to determine, for although their words were cordial, their messages seemed barbed. Their next exchange was to confuse Judith further.

"I have yet to persuade you to cooperate with me in order to insure that success," the Italian said.

"Speaking of cooperative enterprises, Signor Umberto," Somerset replied smoothly, "did you receive my note this afternoon?"

"Indeed."

"And were you successful in conveying the nature of my wishes to the appropriate party?"

"Entirely."

Somerset permitted himself to smile. "That is excellent. I agree with you that it is always easier to achieve admirable goals when we cooperate. Perhaps I might be able to persuade you to cooperate with me in my position."

"That may be difficult."

"It may," Somerset conceded graciously, "but not, I hope, impossible." He stepped back a respectful half pace, as if to signal the end of the encounter. "There is much more to discuss on this issue, and I fear I keep you from enjoying the further pleasures of this very pleasurable evening."

Signor Spadaccio echoed the gesture. "At least, Signor Enrico, we are agreed that cooperation holds its advantages." He, too, bowed formally and withdrew.

Somerset drew Judith's hand to his arm again, and they resumed their measured paces through the crowd.

"Keep an eye on him, Judith, my dear," her uncle said, low, after a minute had passed. "We can trust no one from Rome these days. Not even ones who disavow ties to the Vatican." Judith's wide eyes were pinned on her uncle's face. He continued, "I have other business to conduct and cannot make a spectacle of myself by dogging Spadaccio's footsteps. But you can help me, my dear. You can keep track of Spadaccio's movements this evening—very discreetly, to be sure—and tell me whether he leaves the room or speaks with unusual people or engages in any generally suspicious behavior."

Judith asked, reasonably, she thought, "But what is this all about?"

Just then Somerset nodded and murmured greeting to a passing lord and his lady before turning back to Judith. He said, completely ignoring her question, "I have every confidence in you not to fail me. You whom I trust and love above all others in this room."

She felt slapped and hugged again. She felt like a puppet whose strings he was deftly pulling. She felt angry. The heat of her anger felt good. "Yet your trust and love do not extend to telling me what all this is about? I am to ask no questions. Is that what you expect?"

Somerset's steps checked infinitesimally, and his eyes narrowed to slits. He slanted Judith a chilling regard. "What I expect, dear Judith, is obedience. Unlike certain Romans I might mention, I do not expect to have misjudged the character of my intimates of whom I request simple favors. Do you understand?"

Icy fear replaced her fledgling anger. She held his cold gaze without blinking. "I do."

Somerset's demeanor thawed a little. "Obedience and understanding," he said. "I see that you understand. Now, let us locate Sir George. Yes. There he is. Near the far bay. I am sure you are wishing to be restored to his side."

Until that moment, Somerset's evening might have been charmed, and all his careful orchestrations might have succeeded. However, he had misjudged his niece and had issued one order too many. By instructing Judith to return to her betrothed, he had caused that little rebellion—one that had been growing with the day's events—to rise unbidden in her breast. The strength of it surprised her.

She subdued it for the moment and obediently followed the direction of her uncle's nod. When Sir George came into focus at the far end of the room, she happened to catch a glimpse of a bone-thin, distinctive figure whose presence here this evening captured her interest. The rebellion clamored.

She separated from her uncle sedately, even meekly, and made her way across the crowded room as if straight to Sir George, but in the end, she cleverly avoided her betrothed's notice. When she reached the door to the masquing room and slipped into that chamber, she was not then seeking to sever ties to Sir George. She had every intention of returning to his side at some point in the evening. Her only desire was to snip some of the strings that made her dance to her uncle's tune.

The masquing room, with its semipermanent stage, its potential for elaborate scenery, and the complicated layout of the seating bore testimony to the fact that this form of courtly revelry had evolved far beyond the glorified form of amateur theatricals acted by members of the Court that it had been in the time of Elizabeth. The masque would not be performed for another little while yet, but still before the courtiers were thoroughly jaded with the evening. In the room reigned the muted chaos that preceded every such performance.

Women were allowed to play women's parts in the private court masques, and so Judith's presence in the masquing room at this premature hour went unnoticed. However, since these women were French like the queen, any immorality was to be expected of them. Hardly had Judith penetrated the chamber than she was accosted by a bold young man who mistook her for a theatrical lady. Judith handily disabused him of his misimpression.

She advanced to the stage which was erected with three sides and set like a mirror on a lady's dressing table. It was low to the ground and raised by only three steps behind each of the two side panels. Between the sets of steps ran a little covered hallway that served as the backstage. The stage itself was hung on all three sides with the customary tapestries and wreathed in front with a flowered trellis.

"I thought it was you, Mr. Webster," Judith said, coming up to the figure she had seen from the main room.

Mr. Webster whirled around, an expression that improbably combined surprise that any of the noble company would know him and satisfaction that his fame had evidently preceded him. However, when he saw that the person who spoke could not be counted among his most ardent admirers, his tones held a certain disappointment. "Oh, it is you, Miss Beaufort."

Judith held back a laugh. "Here we are again, Mr. Webster, together at the theater! Do you never tire of it?"

"Never. I am here this evening as a consultant to Davenant's *The Temple of Love.*"

"It is an honor for you," she remarked.

Mr. Webster saw an opportunity. He smiled a singularly superior smile. "My reputation is growing daily, Miss Beaufort, and Davenant had the great *good taste* to accept my services."

"Did he?" Judith said, biting her lip.

"Yes, he did. Davenant's work is good, but not so good that it is above criticism. His characters, for instance, are too complex, too convoluted. I—now I—like characters who represent simple characteristics and present contrasts of light and dark among themselves. In *Every Man in His Hour,* for instance, I took great pains to paint my characters—"

"A delightful play!" Judith broke into this. "A superior production! I remember it well! Tell me," she said, looking around her, her eye dizzied by the flurry of activity and the pre-performance jostling and jesting, "are Allan and Dick and Robin and Tom and the others here?"

"They are all here," Mr. Webster replied proudly and then returned to the important topic. "And I agree with you that *Every Man in His Hour* is most elevating." Mr. Webster lowered his voice discreetly. "I am pleased to be a part of tonight's production. Never think otherwise! However, I do not wish for my name to be associated too closely with this production, for it is really very gruesome. *The Temple of Love* cannot compare in moral tone to any of my more elevating pieces. And yet, despite the title, *The Temple of Love* is about incest and violence. Do I shock you?"

"Profoundly!" Judith said, her eyes dancing and finding that the evening had just taken a turn to the more amusing.

"Yes! Incest and violence! None other! Still, I am a fair man, and I will say that Davenant's little play is somewhat redeemed in that he has never attempted to justify his work on the ground that it is really a moral tract against the subject matter dealt with.''

''Oh, no! Er—yes!'' Judith agreed.

Mr. Webster had really worked himself up now. ''I believe,'' he said, his voice rising with his passion, ''that representation and endorsement go hand in hand. I stand behind everything I write, and if a person behaves immorally, I wish all my audience to know that his—or *her*—actions have been immoral! I do not equivocate!''

''I admire your integrity,'' Judith replied, her lip quivering. She queried smoothly, ''And Charles Lambert? Is he with the troupe tonight?''

Mr. Webster's demeanor fell from its high flight with a thud. He hissed a quick, quiet ''Sh!'' and made little nervous gestures while looking around him furtively. This behavior was completely incomprehensible to Judith. When she opened her mouth to speak, the playwright's eyes bulged alarmingly, and his face went rigid. He drew an acutely uncomfortable breath between his teeth and pulled her away from the stage. If he was trying to be unobtrusive, no series of actions could have been more suspiciously noticeable.

''Don't say his name!'' he whispered harshly into her ear as they walked away from the stage. They crossed in front of the wall of floor-to-ceiling windowed doors. These opened from the masquing room onto a terrace overlooking the gardens which rolled away from this corner of the palace. ''It's a secret!''

''It's a secret? The name of—''

''*Ssshhh!* He is in grave danger, and if he's seen here, his life will be forfeit.''

''Is he here, then?''

''Of course he's here!'' the playwright squeaked. ''Where did you think he was?!''

''I didn't see him in the Banqueting House, although it is very crowded, and I might have missed him. Neither have I seen him in here, among the theater people.''

Mr. Webster made a noise of disgust deep in his throat

and rolled his eyeballs. "He's *hiding!*—but I don't know where."

As Mr. Webster led her down an unlit wall of the room, passing several dark alcoves as they went, Judith considered the information. "Was he in danger this afternoon during the play at The Red Bull?" Judith asked, trying now to account for Lambert's actions at the theater and his desire not to be seen.

"How would I know that?" Mr. Webster demanded irritably. They were approaching what looked like a shadowy door that led, presumably, to the main palace block. Mr. Webster thought it safe to explain, in a high-pitched whisper, "You see, it all happened at the theater this afternoon—"

"The Red Bull?" Judith asked quickly.

Mr. Webster clucked his tongue. "Of course, The Red Bull! He was accosted—*after* the play, mind you—and was told to leave London. He was threatened within an inch of his—"

Mr. Webster never finished his sentence. As he and Judith passed in front of the dark doorway, one pair of hands reached out and grabbed him. Another pair of hands grabbed Miss Beaufort, one iron hand clamped over her mouth, the other encircled her waist. They pulled her into an adjoining antechamber lit only by the moonlight which shone through the high windows.

"You really are trying to get me killed, aren't you, Harry?" said a voice that belonged to the hands imprisoning Judith. It was Charles Lambert.

"Shut your potato trap, Webster, and give your red rag a holiday!" was Will's succinct response to the situation as he tightened his grip on the playwright.

"Good God!" the playwright squeaked. "I had no idea that you were sulking back here! You nearly scared me witless!"

Will seemed to have something to say to that, but Lambert forestalled him with a quick, "It isn't worthy of you, Will, and we've enough trouble on our hands as it is!"

In her brief, fruitless struggle with her attacker, Judith

had inadvertently collided with the wall of the antechamber. Now she was too stunned and too breathless to attempt to speak. With Lambert's hand over her mouth, she could do little more than glare at him anyway.

"I know!" Lambert said, responding to the look in her eyes that he could perceive even in the dimness. "You and I have already been down this road once or twice before! Only this time, I'm sorry to say, it's not quite as playful as it was earlier in the day!"

Since Will was not restraining Harry in the same way that Lambert was holding Judith, the playwright was able to respond to the variety of indignities he had just suffered. He twitched his doublet into place and took a deep, disapproving breath. "Your violence," he said, looking down his nose at Will, "is most unnecessary. And Lambert," he said plaintively, "I am not trying to get you killed at all! On the contrary, I was trying to protect you!"

"I see! By telling the first person to walk through the masquing room door that I am here at risk of death? I wonder, are you planning to be selective or will everyone be informed that I am *not supposed to be here?*"

"The first person to walk through the door—?" the playwright protested. "Miss Beaufort is not just anyone!"

"That," Lambert said significantly, "is true."

Mr. Webster chivalrously defended what he correctly interpreted as an insult to Miss Beaufort. "Well, her taste in literature is in profound error, but I doubt that her character is similarly flawed. I do not for a minute think she is the one who is trying to kill you."

When Lambert laughed at that, the grip of his hand across Judith's mouth slackened enough for her to bite it. He grunted with the pain, snatched his hand away, and had to let go of Judith while he nursed the hurt with his other hand.

"To steal an admirable line from the playwright," Judith said, now free and pretty huffy at his handling of her, "'Your violence is most unnecessary.' Although I don't feel like killing you, I would love giving you a swift kick in the shins, but I refuse to meet violence with violence."

"An uplifting sentiment, Miss Beaufort!" he mocked.

Her eyes had adjusted to the pale moonlight, and she could discern the bruises on Lambert's face. "Besides, it appears from your general condition," she continued with spirited relish, "that enough violence has already been done. What happened to you?"

Lambert did not answer. Regarding Judith steadily through his good eye, he motioned Will out the door, gesturing with his head. "And take Harry with you. As little as I welcomed this intrusion," he said, "I'm beginning to think now that Harry might have done me a favor, after all, and that something valuable has fallen into my hands. Perhaps it's time Miss Beaufort and I had a little talk."

"Don't be taking out on her what's happened to you," Will advised. "It's not her fault."

"That's exactly what I intend to find out," Lambert replied and placed his two hands flat against the wall above Judith's shoulders, effectively pinning her in place. "Will. Harry. Go."

His henchmen left, then, reluctantly, with the playwright in tow.

"I must be gone, as well," Judith said. "I'll be missed."

"If you were free enough to come along to the masquing room just now," he answered her without hesitation, "you'll not be missed anytime soon."

Judith had no answer to that. They regarded each other a long moment in silence, memories of their last meeting at the theater fanning and firing the embers that remained of their last, passionate kiss. Silver moonbeams crept across the parqueted floor but faltered before they reached the doorway, leaving Lambert and Judith submerged in velvet obscurity. The room was warm, and the air was caressed with the perfumes of the gardens that lay soft and green and hushed beyond the open windows. Judith stared steadily into Lambert's face which, in great contrast to the scene, was most unpoetic. His gaze was unwavering and searching. Hers was unafraid. Although her heart was pounding terrifically, the rebellion in her breast that had brought her to this pass was strangely calmed. A rather different kind of excitement had taken its place.

"Well," he said at length. "How do I look? Are you pleased?"

She was, curiously, not repulsed by his unsightliness. Nevertheless, she hardly liked his implication. Within the confining space of his arms, she tried to shrink back form him. There was no room to maneuver, and she still found herself but a sliver's space away. "And why should I be pleased?" she demanded.

"Had you no hand in this?"

She countered question with question. "What motive would I have, sir?"

"Perhaps Borgia blood flows in your veins," he offered. He glanced away, then back to look straight into her eyes. "Or perhaps, in your uncle's."

She liked that implication even less. She regarded him coolly. "And *his* motive?" she wanted to know.

"To defend your honor," Lambert suggested casually, "if he had happened to see us at the theater together. How does that strike you?"

"Implausible." Judith felt the heat crawl up her breast and throat. "We were, as you will recall, engaged in evasive tactics at the theater, and so it is not likely that he saw us."

"Perhaps once outside the theater, you had a change of heart and decided that I had misused you. You might have gone to your uncle and told him what happened."

"The subject did not come up," she said coldly.

"So, you have spoken to him, then," Lambert pursued.

"Of course, I have spoken to him. What are you implying exactly?" Before he could answer that, she continued, "I don't know why you are so quick to think the worst of him!"

However, even as she said these words, the unwelcome suspicion arose that Lambert might be justified in suspecting her uncle. Something in her uncle's demeanor this afternoon had made her uncomfortable. But what would have prompted her uncle to order Lambert's beating?

"One reason, of course, is that your uncle has never liked me," Lambert said with a touch of humor.

That was reason enough for Lambert's suspicions. "I suppose not!" she agreed roundly. "But I resent your implication that I, or my uncle, would have anything to do with your beating. He is certainly not one to hold a grudge—especially after fifteen years!" Lest Lambert think her sympathetic to his plight, she continued, "If you go about accosting and accusing people as you have done with me, you no doubt deserved the drubbing! Whoever did this to you thought you warranted it, and far be it from me to question this right-thinking person's motives!"

"Four," he corrected.

"Four what?"

"Four right-thinking persons, you might say."

"You were set upon by four people?" she said, aghast.

"Brutes, more like," he said, "in the service of a fifth person who, I presume, was not acting alone."

"Then my uncle certainly did not have a hand in it!" Judith laughed, the sound divulging more of her relief than she knew. "He's not the kind to employ bullies! He's much more likely to talk, rather than beat, you into conforming to his wishes! But it's a wonder you're still alive," she said, still gasping in horror at the injustice and brutality of Lambert's treatment.

"Oh, I don't suppose I was meant to be killed—this time," Lambert said. "The solicitous attention I received this afternoon was something more in the way of a kindly warning to leave town."

"Which, I perceive, you have chosen *not* to heed?"

"You perceive correctly," he said. Then, abruptly, "Why were you at the theater today?"

The question sparked all those uncomfortable thoughts about her uncle that had troubled her since the early afternoon. She could not answer with the full truth without also risking betrayal of her uncle, but she could answer with partial truth.

"It was a case of disobedience, I think you might say," she answered. "I had never been to the theater, and I was not expecting my uncle to arrive in London until day after tomorrow."

Lambert laughed, causing his jaw some pain. "A handsome admission, that!" he said, "and as simple an explanation as I could hope for."

One question thrust itself out of her spinning thoughts, like the tall mast of a ship on storm-tossed seas. Almost desperately, she asked, "Does this have something to do with your wretched *Judith* painting?"

He disarmed her by replying, frankly, "Yes."

Chapter
14

"I T does?" she said, surprised. She looked at him with suspicion. "And does it have something to do with that Rosamunda you were looking for?" she pressed.

He nodded slowly, holding her eyes.

"And is it connected with your beating at the request of a person unknown?"

"So it would seem."

"And is there some problem," Judith said slowly, formulating her question with care, "concerning the whereabouts of the painting? Has it, perchance, been misplaced?"

"That is exactly the problem."

"Well, if it is not a particularly small painting," she said reasonably, "I wonder how it could have been misplaced. Do you know where it could be?"

Lambert emitted a sound halfway between a grunt and a laugh. "No, and I was hoping you might have some clues to that!"

"Well, I don't!" she retorted, anger flaring up again, but at least now she did not think he was accusing her of anything. "Nor do I have any clues about the instigator of the beating you received!" She deployed an argument that followed a peculiarly feminine logic. "I never would have berated you as I did, or said you deserved such an unequal attack, or bitten your hand—although I do think you deserved *that!*—had I even suspected that you had lately been set upon so . . . so ignominiously!''

A slight smile lit Lambert's open eye. ''A spark of sympathy from the damsel?'' he said, ever alive to the possibilities of a situation. His fingers slid down her arms to capture her hands behind her back. ''Ah! Sympathy and moonlight. It seems a shame to waste them,'' he remarked, half teasing, half seducing, ''after what my poor face has endured. Would you kiss it and make it feel better?''

Judith blinked, finding it mightily incongruous that he should accuse her one minute of being a party to his beating and then desire her to kiss him the next. Still, the suggestion was not wholly unappealing. She felt an undeniable attraction to him, to the feel and smell of him, and it was not an attraction inspired by sympathy. It was pulled by something deeper, more elemental, and drew from a part of her that had long been dormant and was now awakening. The new self inside of her seemed alien and frightening.

''What, no protest?'' he said when she did not respond. He put his lips experimentally against hers, then winced away again on a groan. ''The cure in this case, I fear, hurts worse than the malady,'' he exhaled on a shaky laugh. He was, however, a resourceful man. ''What about nuzzling your neck?''

What about Elizabeth Marston? thought Judith.

''Ahhh. Just right.'' Lambert sighed into her neck. ''Such a lovely throat.'' He rubbed the side of his face that was least injured against her warm, soft skin. He breathed in deeply, deliciously. ''And such nice skin, too.'' The tip of his nose grazed her bare shoulder. ''It glows. I have always admired it.''

''You have?'' she asked dreamily. Then her eyes opened wide, and she was alarmed by how quickly she was softening in his arms. ''You have?'' she repeated, this time with sterner stuff. ''Well, then, you will have to admire it from afar! Just what do you think you are doing?''

''Stalling for time,'' was Lambert's lazy response. With

his cheek, he was exploring the dark pool of shadow at her collarbone.

She freed herself of the embrace, trying hard not to further hurt him. "I might have known you had an ulterior motive! What *is* this all about? Stalling for time for *what?*"

Lambert looked up. "To ask you a favor."

Judith's slightly giddy senses sobered. "What is it?"

"I'd like you to meet someone tonight," he said. "A very wily Italian fellow by the name of Spadaccio."

Judith's eyes widened. "Do you suspect him of having given the command to have you beaten?"

"I do not suspect. I *know,*" Lambert said. "What I don't know is whose orders he was following."

"Well, it certainly could not have been my uncle's!" Judith said with a kind of passionate relief washing over her. "Signor Spadaccio and my uncle are not exactly friends!"

Lambert opened his mouth to speak, then thought better of it.

"The fact of the matter is, I've already met Signor Spadaccio," Judith explained, misinterpreting Lambert's hesitation. "It was before I came into the masquing room—to speak with Mr. Webster! Well, Signor Spadaccio and my uncle had just had a conversation which indicated to me that they are not on the best of terms! It is unlikely that they should conspire together against you this afternoon and yet be so unfriendly to each other a few hours later!"

"Does it? Perhaps. In any case, you have already assured me that your uncle was not involved," Lambert commented easily.

Judith sprang to her uncle's defense anyway. "But my uncle isn't a . . . a devious man, and he doesn't have a motive to wish to harm you!"

"I'm not criticizing anyone's motives," Lambert clarified, "only his methods, particularly when it involves the necessity of getting rid of me! But we are wandering from the point."

"Which is what, exactly? The painting you are after?"

"The painting," Lambert confirmed. "Spadaccio is desperate to find a painting."

"Yes," Judith said slowly, "that is entirely possible."

"So, too, is your uncle."

That was very true, and Judith recalled having told Lambert herself that her uncle was trying to buy one. However, she did not consider her uncle's desire to be a desperate one. "It is unlikely," she said after a moment, "that all three of you could be after the *same* painting."

"So many unlikelihoods!" Lambert murmured.

Judith chose not to pursue the comment. Throughout the course of the day, she had been sinking ever deeper into this business. She would not extricate herself from it by refusing Lambert's request. "So," she said. "You wish for me to meet Signor Spadaccio? I have already done so. Now what?"

"I want you to keep your eye on him," Lambert said.

Judith chuckled involuntarily. What could be easier than keeping her eyes on Signor Spadaccio, when she was already engaged in doing so for her uncle?

She relaxed against the wall. "And?" she prompted.

"Tell me to whom he speaks, what he does, where he casts his eyes, how he comports himself. He's an excellent actor, but he's also desperate, as I said, and I think he will have to reveal himself tonight, one way or the other."

"And report all this back to you?" Judith queried. "Do you think the information will lead you to your painting?"

"Possibly."

"Before I accept such a responsibility, I would like to know what, in your estimation, is the particular value of the painting."

"A reasonable question," Lambert observed. "My guess is that the painting was intended to be a gift from Pope Urban to Charles Stuart," he said. "My guess is that the gift includes more than just the painting. Perhaps it bears with it an overture or an invitation to bring the Anglican Church back into the Catholic fold. My guess is that the invitation, if delivered, might appeal strongly to the king's ideals of unity and uniformity to urge him to enter into the establishment of a Catholic Christendom. My guess is that the painting is being offered to any number of interested persons, and that it will be sold to the highest bidder.'' Lambert paused. ''Do you need to know more? Shall I spell out for you the consequences of a joining of Stuart ideals to Roman authority? Shall I name the interested persons and the varying reasons for their interest?''

Judith shook her head. It all made sense, too fearfully much sense. She was impressed that Lambert had trusted her where her uncle had not; although, of course, Lambert had no choice but to risk her trust.

She asked speculatively, ''If I help you, what do I get in return?''

''The assurance that I won't tell your uncle how you spent your afternoon at The Red Bull,'' Lambert replied promptly and with a hint of mischief.

Judith shook her head. ''No good.''

''I suppose my heartfelt gratitude and a place in my esteem might not entice you either?''

''Not,'' she said with a cool smile, ''quite.''

The bargainer in Lambert took over. ''You shall have a token,'' he said.

''What kind of token?''

It was Lambert's turn to smile coolly. ''That, Miss Beaufort, you will know when you receive it.''

He's tempting me! ''A hint, perhaps?''

Lambert shook his head. ''Rest assured that it will be a token appropriate to the favor.''

''It is a small favor, after all,'' she said, ''merely keeping an eye on Signor Spadaccio and reporting his activities to you.''

''Very small,'' Lambert agreed, ''with the possibility of a very valuable return.'' Lambert restated the terms. ''A token of my choosing, then, one appropriate to the favor. Take it or leave it.''

What did Judith have to lose? ''I'll take it,'' she said.

''Very well,'' he said, betraying no emotion other than the satisfaction of a bargain concluded.

She held out a tentative hand. Lambert considered the gesture, then accepted her hand. They shook, once.

''When shall I receive it?'' Judith asked.

"That, my lady, shall be at your discretion. Tonight, if you insist," he offered gallantly.

Judith was not an unreasonable woman. "It is hardly a matter to risk your life over," she said. "I shall be returning to Raglan soon, within the next day or two. If it is safe for you to travel to Speke Hall, you might deliver it to me in Wales. I shall not press you to hurry but will expect that you will deliver it as soon as your life is no longer in immediate danger."

Lambert agreed. "As soon as my life is no longer in immediate danger," he repeated.

"How will you be sure that I will be keeping a watchful eye on Signor Spadaccio?" Judith wanted to know. "Do you plan to keep an eye on me as well? I don't see how you can do it without being seen yourself."

"I know the Banqueting House well enough and the masquing room," he said. "This anteroom, too, if it comes to that. During the spectacle, I'll be backstage. Otherwise, I'm familiar enough with the nooks and peepholes."

"You know Whitehall well?"

"It's been fifteen years, but I've quickly reacquainted myself with the barracks in the past few days."

"You have chambers at Whitehall?" she asked in disbelief.

"Where did you think I was staying in London?" he asked.

"I didn't know! It did not occur to me to wonder. But I never would have thought Whitehall!"

Lambert shook his head. "Better and better, Miss Beaufort! Your opinion of me is as consistent as it is unflattering!"

"How was I to know?"

"You did not guess that I might have rooms here at the invitation of the king?"

"The king favors only correct gentlemen, not vagabonds and wastrels," she said slyly.

"He's made an exception in my case," Lambert replied dryly. "And now to your duties, Miss Beaufort, before you bring a blush to my manly cheeks with your high praise!"

"I only thought that if we are to be partners," she retorted, "we might as well be honest with each other."

"If we are to be honest, we might as well acknowledge that we are conspirators," he said.

"Very true!" Judith admitted. "It seems that I am never myself when you are around and am always in some kind of trouble! I do not know where it will end!"

"I become ever more curious to discover the limits of your disobedience," he replied provocatively.

"My sanity, more like," she retorted, "for I am in league with a man who will risk his very life over a painting!"

She left him then by slipping out the doorway and into the masquing room.

There was a great flurry of activity on and about the stage, and as Judith crossed the masquing room she did not see Mr. Webster or anyone else she recognized; however, she did come face-to-face with a rather intriguing woman as she passed by the stage. She very nearly ran bodily into her, and Judith was able to look the woman straight in the eyes since they were of a height and about the same build. The woman's eyes registered some strong emotion at the near collision, but it was quickly masked. The woman lifted her fan and fluttered it before her face, dropping her eyes, so that little of her face could be seen. It was a graceful, shy gesture and very feminine. A man called over to her. He spoke in French. The woman looked over her shoulder, replied in French, and without a further glance at Judith, turned away and moved toward the man.

The encounter was over almost before it had happened, and Judith did not give it another thought.

She was drawn to the light and chatter of the royal gathering beyond the masquing room doors. Her thoughts whirled, and something in her veins bubbled and foamed. Before her meeting with Lambert, the evening had seemed flat. Now it sparkled or, rather, it glinted dangerously.

She regained the main apartment of the Banqueting House. She found Sir George's side, a safe harbor, and smiled and laughed and danced and kept her eye on Signor Spadaccio who was behaving with the utmost circumspection. Once, Judith happened to glimpse her uncle at the moment that a young man handed him a folded note. She saw her uncle dismiss the lad with a nod, excuse himself from his party, and move several paces away in order to scan the note. He did so with no change of expression, then refolded it unhurriedly and slid it into his doublet. Some minutes later, Judith exchanged a glance with her uncle. His brows rose imperceptibly in inquiry. Judith nodded, in response, smiling her cooperation with his wishes. For a man who did not wear his emotions on his face, he looked unusually satisfied.

The moment for the masque's spectacle had come. The several hundred guests made their way toward the sets of large double doors that had been thrown open to allow unrestricted passage into the masquing room where all was calm and in readiness.

The long wax tapers in the wall sconces cast a glow over the room where fantasy and imagination were soon to come to life on the stage. Since the purpose of such entertainment was to whet the courtiers' appetites for the further pleasures of the evening, the stage was set up in front of the long bay of doors that opened out onto the terrace overlooking the gardens which pulsed from their secret depths and beckoned and stretched out endlessly into grassy malls. Even in the summer, masques were often held indoors. Other times in the summer, they were held out-of-doors, with music supplied by the king's trumpeters and rather saturnalian torchlight processions down to the river and fireworks. There were even, on very grand occasions, waterworks displays at the fountains ringing the gardens. Such an event was planned several weeks hence and was to be orchestrated by Judith's cousin and Somerset's eccentric, mechanically minded son, Lord Edward.

Amid the chatter and the scraping of the chairs, Judith took her seat next to Sir George. She had maneuvered the seating so that she could have Signor Spadaccio in her line of vision. He sat in the front and at the outer edge of the seating to the far right of the stage, which afforded him, if he cared to use it, easy access to the backstage. Judith had chosen seats halfway back from the stage and on the left. Her uncle, she noted, was seated center stage, behind the king and queen who, of course, enjoyed pride of place. Her uncle's stiff posture suggested to her that he tolerated this decadent form of entertainment only because he had no way of stopping it.

Every other candle was snuffed, and the candles at the foot of the stage were lit as the curtain drew back. An eager, excited "Ooooh!" arose at the sight of the setting, and the audience settled back into their seats to enjoy the spectacle. Dramatists such as Johnson and Davenant had made the masque more than a glorified charade. They had given words to the courtly actors, significance to their speeches, and something approaching a plot to the theatrical action. Still, the masque remained little more than pictures with light and motion—a frame for the spectacle and a platform for the masquers. Davenant's *Temple of Love* promised to be a sensuous, titillating piece with plenty of feminine flesh bared by the French whores who performed upon the stage.

Judith was not, in any event, expecting to have to engage her intellect during the next hour and a half. However, from the moment she bent her idle gaze upon the stage, she would have been unable to pay heed to the most involving of entertainments anyway, for her attention was fully arrested by a strange item of stage property.

It was a tapestry. An unremarkable tapestry. One totally at variance with the rest of the beautiful stage decor. It was faded and represented an idealized English landscape. Judith sat straighter in her seat, struck suddenly by an idea.

She was sure she had seen that same tapestry at The Red Bull earlier in the day. It had been the central tapestry on that theater's stage. Judith remembered with startling clarity that it had been hanging directly below where her uncle had been sitting on the stage balcony. The tapestry was not center stage now, for it was not nearly beautiful enough for that. It hung on the side of the stage that jutted off to the right, so that Judith had a full view of it. Judith reckoned that from Signor Spadaccio's perspective, the tapestry, along with the entire right side of the stage, would appear severely foreshortened, even unrecognizable, if indeed Signor Spadaccio had any reason to recognize it.

Unlike Signor Spadaccio, Somerset had the perfect

view of the masquing stage. However, her uncle would never have been able to recognize that tapestry as having been at The Red Bull. He had been perched over the stage and that very tapestry, with no perspective whatsoever from which to have seen it.

It was all Judith could do to sit serenely in her seat and give every appearance of enjoying the froth of the action and the costumes and the speeches and the music and the stage "machinery" which provided, during the course of the spectacle, the raising and lowering of Greek columns, of an entire gazebo and of a platform of singing angels to attend the happy ending. Judith monitored Sir George's changing reactions and responses to the action going forward and thought it prudent to laugh when he laughed and clap when he clapped. She would later not remember one single detail of the evening's lavish production upon which had been wasted an infinity of time and money.

At last it was over. Judith rose and smiled and chatted and expressed every delight at the spectacle. The group followed the general movement of the rest of the audience which was toward the terrace overlooking the gardens. Judith's group approached the stage which they had to skirt in order to leave the room, and there Judith saw Signor Spadaccio exit the room by way of the terrace. She should have no difficulty maneuvering Sir George into taking a path that would follow the Italian, but she needed to discover an essential piece of information first.

When Judith's group had wandered close enough to the three shallow steps that led to the little wings backstage, Judith hastily excused herself on the pretext of suddenly remembering that she needed to say something to her uncle.

Sir George stayed her with a hand on her arm.

Judith looked up at him quickly, almost angrily, for she was expecting him to thwart her.

Sir George seemed startled by the look he encountered in her eye and let go of her arm. He bowed, formally, and said, "I merely wish to beg you, Miss Beaufort, to return to my side with haste."

Judith smiled in relief. She attempted to dismiss her

initial reaction to his gesture by returning a light remark in kind. When Sir George moved on with his group, she disappeared behind the stage. There she was pleased to see amid the backstage hubbub the figure of Mr. Webster.

"Lovely masque," she complimented him and could not resist teasing him. "It's curious, though, that I do not recall having heard one line taken from any previous work."

"Very amusing, Miss Beaufort," the playwright replied with all his dignity. "It *is* Davenant's piece, after all, but that is not, I think, what you are referring to. I am an honest playwright," he explained seriously, "and only, ahem, borrow from another author when I am *truly* without ideas about how to develop a plot or a character. Speaking of which, Robin did an excellent job tonight, did he not, along with Dick and Tom? I was rather proud of them. Even Allan might be said to have interpreted his part with some skill."

"Oh yes!" Judith agreed, although she could not remember having noticed one of the actors or actresses. "And the scenery! Most fascinating! In addition to the actors, were you commissioned by the Court to provide any scenery from The Red Bull?"

"No," Mr. Webster informed her, "we were charged only to provide a few costumes. The scenery at Court is quite of another order than that at a mere theater, as you must know."

"But that tapestry," she said, leading Mr. Webster by the arm so that he would have a perspective from the wings onto the right wall of the stage where hung the tapestry. "Did you not bring that over from The Red Bull?"

"Ah!" he exclaimed. "Now *there* is exactly the kind of composition one should admire! I certainly discern that it is faded. Yes, I see that. But the lines, the serene depiction of the landscape, the harmony and symmetry of the rolling mountains! No, I am sure that my troupe did not transport it here. You must be mistaken. That was never at The Red Bull. As I say, it is a very fine composition, although," he said, lowering his voice confidentially, "I am a bit surprised to see such on this stage. Not because it is somewhat faded, as I say, but only because the purity of its lines are not in keeping with the rest of the scenery, which, I do not mind saying, in all of its elaborate detail is not at all to my taste!''

Judith, too, had thought the tapestry discordant with the other stage property, and what she wanted to know was who had brought it from The Red Bull and why.

"You are right, Mr. Webster," she agreed with a straight face, "I see now that I was mistaken. It is a lovely composition, and I do not know why I singled it out for remark."

Mr. Webster nodded with satisfaction. "I see that my ideas have taken with you, after all. Let us continue this discussion in the gardens, where I am to join the others."

Judith thanked Mr. Webster for his invitation, declined gracefully, and escaped the backstage before anyone thought her presence suspicious. Her brain was whirling. She must keep track of the location of that tapestry. She must not let it be removed from its place on the stage or, even, from the masquing room itself before she had an opportunity to examine it. She must keep her eye on Signor Spadaccio as well, and he seemed now to have gone to the gardens.

Judith paused on the steps that led down from the platform erected behind the stage. Her eye scanned for the familiar faces of Robin or Thomas or Dick. Could she ask any player from the troupe to stand guard over it? Did she dare risk enmeshing anyone besides herself in this strange affair? She thought to find Lambert and alert him, but that was not part of their bargain. She owed her loyalty to her uncle, but she could hardly tell him her suspicions without also divulging the fact that she had been at the theater that afternoon. Perhaps she would find another way of communicating with him.

But first, she must discover Signor Spadaccio's location. To that end, she hurried out of the room through the windowed door and out onto the elegant brick terrace. She tripped lightly down the broad, stone steps, and hardly did she have her two feet on the garden path than a pair of arms reached out from the black shadows and grabbed her.

"Good heavens!" she hissed low and angrily, thinking she knew exactly who held her. Before fully turning to face her captor, she began to scold, "Enough of this! Besides, this is a highly public place and you might be seen—! Oh! Sir George! I didn't know it—You startled me!"

Sir George's grip on Judith slackened, and he was looking down at her, surprise and disapproval stamping his handsome features. "Are you nervous this evening, Miss Beaufort?" he asked.

"Why, what could make you think so?" she countered, in truth, a little nervously, drawing back from him. "It's just that it is so dark, and we might be seen, and someone might think that we . . . might think that we. . . ."

"I see what it is," Sir George said. "You are still suffering from the effects of the . . . unfortunate episode in your chambers last night." He continued gravely, "When you have recovered, I would dearly love to give someone reason to talk about us and what we choose to do on a garden path."

The thought came unbidden: *Then why don't you take me in your arms for once and kiss me senseless like Charles Lambert? Or at least nuzzle my neck!* Her eyes widened at her own brazenness.

Sir George interpreted her expression as shock. He stepped away. "Do not fear that I shall force unwanted attention upon you," he said at his most formal. "I wished to detain you just now only to inform you that I have been called away on an errand for my mother. The others of our party have wandered down to the first fountain beyond the flower garden. Shall I escort you to them before I leave?"

Judith assured him that that would not be necessary. She bade him attend to his mother's wishes directly and told him that she would be waiting for his return with eagerness. He replied in kind and bowed before withdrawing from her.

She stood in the blackness, looking up at the Banqueting House which blazed with light. She watched Sir George climb the steps, disappear through the doors and into the palace. She turned and looked down the intersecting pathways that were laid out through the gardens and lit by intermittent torches. She decided that she would wander through the gardens, unescorted, until she could catch up with Signor Spadaccio. However, just as she was considering which of the paths to follow, she saw the handsome Italian suddenly materialize out of the shadows on the other side of the broad staircase, some thirty feet away.

Signor Spadaccio was alone. He paused, looked to both sides, then very casually began to mount the staircase with the evident intention of reentering the Banqueting House. From deep in her hiding place, Judith saw him reach the wide terrace that spanned both the masquing room and the grand apartment of the Banqueting House. It seemed that he hesitated, not knowing which door to enter. It might have been that he was ill-acquainted with the layout of the palace and had momentarily lost his way, but Judith thought the hesitation held a hint of calculation.

When Signor Spadaccio chose to enter the main apartment for whatever reason, Judith lifted her skirts, bounded up the steps two by two. On her way up, she bumped into a man going down the steps. It was an odd encounter, not unlike the one she had had with the French actress in the masquing room before the performance. The man was evidently in a rush and upset to have been hindered. The man at first said nothing, but as Judith excused herself, she was able to look him straight in the eye since he was of a height with her. He seemed to her oddly, elusively familiar. Before she could place the resemblance, he had murmured his pardon and had hurried on.

Judith had no time to consider the incident further. She entered the masquing room. It was deserted now. A few candles still burned in their sconces, casting the dimmest of light in the room. She quickly mounted the steps to the backstage and walked through the blackness of the little hallway. She made her way to the entrance to stage right and emerged out onto the unlit stage. She perceived, with relief, that the tapestry was still hanging, innocently, where it had been all along.

Then she heard Signor Spadaccio's voice at the door to the masquing room. He was evidently speaking to a footman, saying that he had not lost his way and needed no further help locating his party. Judith surmised that he intended to enter the masquing room, and perhaps even approach the stage.

She tiptoed slowly across the stage to hide behind the tapestry. A floorboard creaked beneath her step. At that she sped her light step, heart hammering, and decided that her best course would be to leave the masquing room by the door to the anteroom where she had earlier met Lambert. At the moment she darted behind the tapestry, she collided with a masculine body that was coming at her from the opposite direction from behind the tapestry.

Her cry of exclamation was muffled into a groan by the man's hand that clamped her mouth. Her heart stopped cold, then thundered away with a clash of relief and fear when she perceived that the man was none other than Charles Lambert.

Lambert, upon recognizing Judith, instantly released her, too hastily, for his fingers had entangled themselves in the curls at her ear, and when he drew his hand away, roughly, several tresses tumbled down and the lace at her breast tore slightly.

He bent and whispered, almost inaudibly, into her ear. "I'm sorry if I hurt you! I've been shadowing our Mr. Smith this hour past and thought I had him just now. Instead it's you. I don't think it's safe for you to be here just now."

Footsteps were crossing the masquing room from the Banqueting House.

Judith was not thinking of Mr. Smith or her own safety. She drew Lambert's ear to her mouth. "Signor Spadaccio's coming!" she breathed. "You're in worse danger than I am!"

Footsteps were heard on the stairs to the platform that served as the backstage. Judith and Lambert looked across the dark expanse of the stage, then at each other. Without another word, Judith shooed Lambert behind the tapestry and arranged her skirts and train so that his breeches and boots would remain unseen below the lower edge of the tapestry. She turned to face the stage. She ran a hand up the tapestry. She grasped the edge and leaned against the tapestry, not quite pulling on it.

Just as she positioned herself casually against the tapestry, footsteps fell on the stage. Signor Spadaccio strode out into the middle. He looked about him in the dimness, as if expecting to see someone.

Then he saw her. He approached her and said, in Italian, "*Eccoti, puttana.*" Although Judith did not understand the words, she did understand the satisfied intonation to mean, "Ah, there you are" or "At last I find you" or "I have been looking for you."

Judith did not know how to respond and so remained silent.

Once the Italian had come close enough to identify the woman draping herself coyly against the tapestry, his entire being froze momentarily.

Then, with a flowing bow, he recovered enough to say in English, "Miss Beaufort, is it not?" His voice was smooth. "I thought I heard some movements upon the stage and came to investigate." His tone was chilling and dangerous. "What are you doing here?"

Chapter
15

"SIGNOR Spadaccio?" Judith replied, hesitating over the name, giving herself time to think. She had to find a way to explain her presence at such an unlikely place, and she decided that she could use her slightly disheveled appearance to good advantage. She cocked her head and slanted him a glance she hoped was suggestive. "It is not obvious?"

"It is not obvious to me," he said flatly. "You must be more explicit. Tell me what you are doing here."

Judith quelled the impulse to inform him that he had no right to interrogate her. Instead, she held fast to the one rôle that might see her and Lambert through this tricky passage. She fingered one of the curls that had tumbled across her breast and said with a hint of pique, "How can you ask such a question? Surely, a man of your understanding is aware of a delicate situation when he confronts one."

"Delicate? What do you mean, Miss Beaufort?" Signor Spadaccio said, his voice at once both cautious and suspicious.

"Why, Signor Spadaccio, I had thought you a man of the world," she chided gently. She tried to pout prettily. "Whatever could I mean besides that you have caught me?"

The Italian's eyes narrowed with one possible interpretation. From across the stage, Judith felt the force of the malevolent glint that sprang to his eyes.

"Caught you?" he repeated.

"And might be persuaded to . . . look the other way?" she suggested.

"I am not inclined to look the other way," he said. His voice was harsh. "I am surprised and, I must say, sorry that I find you here. I did not imagine that it would be you." Spadaccio took several slow steps toward Judith. He looked capable of murdering her. She felt an icy hand clutch her heart. "I assume," he said, stopping several feet away from her, "that there is someone behind the tapestry."

Judith did not move, nor did her eyes leave Spadaccio's face. She noted that he did not once look at the tapestry itself. Perhaps he entertained no suspicions about it. She had guessed that he had come to meet the very slippery Mr. Smith, whom Lambert had trailed into the masquing room, but she did not know how Signor Spadaccio could have confused her, even in the darkness, with the figure of a man.

She could not distract herself with the insignificant details. It was much more important that she focus her attention on her all-important rôle.

"Of course, you are right, Signor Spadaccio," Judith said, suppressing her fear and emphasizing brazen, honeyed tones.

"And do I also assume correctly that you made your assignation with that person earlier this evening? Perhaps after having met me?"

"Well, as to that," she said, "I made the assignation just a few moments ago in the gardens."

Spadaccio seemed surprised by that. "Just now in the gardens?"

"Well, everyone is there," she said, as if it were a matter of course.

"Indeed," he said with chilling finality. "That is, almost everyone, except you and me and . . . the person who is behind the tapestry."

Judith attempted a guilty smile.

Spadaccio nodded and took another step toward her. "And your uncle?" he asked. "I do so wonder where your uncle is at this moment."

Now was Judith's best chance to lead Spadaccio down the false trail she had laid out. Her face, whose look she hoped had been one of fragile sophistication, crumpled into little-girl confusion and anxiety. Deliberately misunderstanding him, she flung up a hand in a protective gesture and begged, "Don't tell my uncle, Signor Spadaccio! Don't, I pray you! He would never understand!"

Spadaccio's beautiful black brows snapped together. "He would not understand?" He regarded her speculatively. "Does he not know you are here?"

"Of course, he does not!" Judith's voice held the hint of a wail, and she was pleased. "It's worse than you think!"

Puzzlement was rapidly overtaking Spadaccio's suspicions. "It's worse than I think?" he echoed, uncomprehending.

"You cannot know, of course, that I have been newly betrothed," she said in a rush. She clutched at the torn lace at her breast, as if suddenly embarrassed. "To Sir George. Sir George Beecham!" She glanced nervously to the tapestry, as if referring to the person—a man!—who stood behind it. "How shall I explain it to you, a man whose sensibilities are of the highest order? For did you not tell me from the very start, when it became clear that you had caught me, that you could not overlook my . . . my indiscretion?"

Judith had warmed to her rôle now and was encouraged to continue by the look of dawning understanding on Spadaccio's face. She became one with the character of an ashamed young woman, newly betrothed, caught in amorous adventure with a man who was not her husband-to-be. She pleaded passionately for mercy. "How shall I explain it other than to tell you that a little while ago in the gardens my . . . betrothed was called away. I found myself bathed in moonlight and surrounded by the sweet smell of flowers and summer air. Suddenly I was not alone on that beautiful dark path. I looked up to see—but I dare not tell you his name!—him!"

Judith was delighted to see that Spadaccio's face had not only lost its murderous look but also its puzzled one, and that he had taken on an expression bordering on a disbelieving frustration. Her feeling went beyond delight and crossed over into the euphoria that surges when an actor convinces and captivates an audience. Had she been familiar with the term, she would have known that she was stagestruck.

Judith embroidered on her affecting story. "It was a shock to see him. Yes! But only for the first moment. I should tell you that *he* has paid me court in the past. Last year it was!" Judith lowered her eyes in pain. When she raised them again, charming, heartrendering tears sparkled at their corners. She was truly inspired. "But he is not rich enough for my uncle. No! And yet, will you not believe me that his lack of fortune is more than compensated by the true nobility of his nature, how his name is worthy in character of the grandest titles in the land which I, Judith Beaufort, would be proud to bear, even penniless? As much as I had been denying it to myself these many months, I now admit to myself and to him, that my love for *him* is true!"

She paused, seeming to savor the ring of these fine words for a moment, then, as if suddenly aghast at this burst of defiance in herself, she said in the accents of rawest youth, "But don't tell my uncle!"

Spadaccio had begun to look acutely uncomfortable. "I won't," he assured her with an expression of distaste. He took a step away from her. When he asked, "But why on earth, Miss Beaufort, did you make your assignation for the *stage*, when the gardens were so, shall we say, inspiring?" He sounded frankly exasperated.

Judith smiled mistily. "Because it was tonight's masque, *The Temple of Love*, that made *him* realize the true depths of his feelings for me, and we thought to seal our love, to commemorate it here—upon the stage." She added, on a practical note, "Also we were worried about being seen in the gardens, since they are positively swarming with people we know, and we never thought anyone would come inside again." She bit her lip. "May I count on your understanding and discretion, sir?"

Spadaccio was tapping an impatient hand against his thigh, darting his gaze off here and there into the blackness of the backstage corners. She guessed that he was attempting to figure how best to remove her and her abashed swain lurking behind the tapestry from the scene as quickly as possible. Almost, she heard his mental snort.

"May I, Signor Spadaccio?"

Spadaccio looked back over at her as if he had momentarily forgotten her existence. He nodded absently.

Judith took a further chance. She needed to take aggressive action if she was to get him to leave the stage for the few moments it would take Lambert to exit without being seen. She ran across the small space that lay between them and flung himself on her knees before him, grabbing one of his hands and kissing it reverently in thanks. Although she had exposed Lambert's legs and feet by moving from her spot, she reckoned that her action would divert Spadaccio's attention and keep it on her.

Her gamble worked. She came to her feet again and looked up, her eyes shining with heartfelt gratitude, to find Spadaccio staring down at her, as if she were a loathsome bug. His handsome face bore a highly gratifying mixture of expressions: boredom with the story of young love thwarted, frustration at the disruption of his careful plans, indecision about what action to take next, great desire to get away from Somerset's troublesome, meddlesome niece.

Judith did not move but stood gazing, dumbly, beatifically, ridiculously at the man to whom she was eternally indebted for not exposing the secrets of her heart to her uncle.

Only a few seconds of this treatment sufficed for Spadaccio to gather his wits, take a step back from her, bow stiffly, excuse himself hastily. He quit the stage, muttering violent curses in Italian under his breath as he left.

Judith flitted back to the tapestry, sighing, just above a whisper, "My love! We are safe! The kind gentleman will not tell my uncle! But what are we to tell Sir George on the morrow—and the rest of the world? Shall we never be together as one?"

She peeked quickly behind the tapestry and found the

spot empty. Clever man! Her distracting maneuver had paid off, and Lambert had removed himself without being detected. She knew they were far from being out of danger, and although she heard the last of Spadaccio's footsteps leave the masquing room, she did not dare sigh with relief.

What to do next? She was alone on the stage with the tapestry hanging before her. Without a moment to lose, she ran her hands over the weaving at several places. It was just as she had thought. She felt something inside it, bolstering it. Something stiff, yet pliant like a canvas. She had a shrewd intuition that it must be Lambert's *Judith* lining the tapestry. Mr. Smith—or whoever he really was—must have hidden it there, must have had it at The Red Bull in the hopes that her uncle would have been willing to meet the newer, higher price. Perhaps Spadaccio had come to bargain with him. Or was her uncle now willing to pay the better price?

The calm of discovery overtook her; her heart slowed to its normal tempo. She knew that she must think fast and clearly if she were to save the king or her uncle—or Lambert.

She glanced up to the two hooks that kept the tapestry suspended. She would never be able to unhook it alone and carry it away. And even if she could, where would she take it, and what would she do with it?

She shook her head. Her eye was drawn to the lower right corner, which was frayed. No, she saw, as Lambert before her had discovered, that the threads were not frayed; they were cut. She stepped to the right side of the tapestry and quickly slipped her hand into the opening provided by the cut threads. Her fingers touched a surface that was unmistakably canvas. She worked her arm into the tapestry as far as it would go. She felt along the back and the front of the canvas. In the lower left-hand corner of the tapestry, her fingers felt another object, this time parchment.

Now Judith's heart leapt into her throat and threatened to suffocate her. Not more than a few seconds had elapsed since Spadaccio left the room, but Judith figured that he would return as soon as he thought it safe, and she could waste no more time. She withdrew the parchment, fingers trembling now. Hardly glancing at it, she slid it into the neck of her gown at the place where the lace was already ripped. She stuffed it down her front to lodge it where the lacings joined the bodice to her stomacher.

She fled the stage. In hopes of finding Lambert, she headed off to the door that led to the anteroom. She was hurrying next to the wall where she and Mr. Webster had earlier strolled and which was scalloped with several alcoves. Before she reached the door, a hand reached straight out from the wall, so it seemed, and pulled her off her path.

"If this happens to me one more time—!" she began low but with emphasis.

None to her surprise, she found herself entwined in Lambert's arms.

"It's me," Lambert whispered into her ear.

"I know that!" she whispered back angrily. She looked about her in the darkness. She determined that she was in an alcove, but not one she had previously seen. "Where are we? I thought I was walking next to a solid wall on my way to the anteroom, but your hand seemed to come out of nowhere!"

Lambert was destined to show her rather than tell her. Sounds of voices and heavy, rapid footsteps entered the masquing room from the Banqueting House.

"Quick. Pull the train of your gown back," Lambert said, his voice nearly inaudible. "I don't want it to catch."

Judith obeyed, and Lambert fiddled with a mechanism on the wall. A door appeared out of the wall to slide quietly across the alcove, thus cutting them off from the masquing room. Tiny points of light penetrated the door at regular intervals. Judith peered through a pair of holes and was surprised to discover that they were intended as peepholes which afforded a pretty good view of the room.

"We're in one of the secret alcoves," Lambert informed her, speaking directly into her ear.

"It's minuscule!" she complained as quietly as she was able.

"I was in here for a good deal of the masque, until I

discovered Mr. Smith among the players," Lambert whispered back, "and it wasn't too bad. Of course, then again," he said pointedly, "I was alone."

"Oh, it's my fault we're cramped now? Could you be so kind as to take your arm off me?"

"I can't," he apologized, "there's not enough room for me to get it down from around your shoulders."

"Cozy!" she remarked under her breath. "There must be some way to arrange ourselves so that both of us have more room."

"We could take off our clothes," Lambert suggested. "Your gown is taking up quite a bit of space. I am sure we would be more comfortable without all the yards of material around us."

Judith turned to him, her mouth open. "You can't be thinking of *that* at a time like *this!*" she hissed, but her breathlessness at the suggestion, coupled with being pressed up to his length spoiled her intended effect of indignation.

"How can I not?" Lambert countered reasonably.

It was true. He had shifted slightly. Instead of making their positions less intimate, Judith now only fit all the better against him. Thoughts of Mr. Smith, her uncle, Spadaccio, the painting, and the sealed and folded parchment she had retrieved from the tapestry flew right out of her head. She was aware of nothing but the smell and heat of him, the planes of his chest and stomach and thighs against her curves, and the feel of him responding to the scent and heat of her.

"Of course, we cannot really undress," Lambert chuckled softly. She felt the roll of his stomach muscles, and a flame ignited inside her. "No," he continued, his free hand traveling from her shoulders to her bodice where he played a moment with the torn lace, then slipped his hand over her breasts, down to her hips, where it rested. "You could never get that dress off. There's not enough room to accomplish the feat, even with my help."

At his handling, a tingle spread from her neck down to her toes and was replaced by the sensual flush that rushed up her body from the opposite direction. The alcove was very tiny and *very* hot, and she was finding his neck a comfortable spot to rest her lazy, languorous head. However, the feel of his neck and his hair against her face roused her senses and made her feel, not lazy and languorous, but flushed and fiery.

These pleasant, confusing, dangerous sensations lasted but a moment. The noises of low, angry voices and boots stomping around on the stage penetrated their secret alcove and made them aware of the far less pleasant and far more dangerous situation they were in. Judith and Lambert suppressed what they could of an extremely ill-timed passion and pressed their faces to their respective peepholes.

"I knew it!" Judith breathed. "It's Signor Spadaccio returned. But who are those men with him?"

"The four trained animals who decorated my face earlier in the day," Lambert informed her gravely. He grunted significantly.

From their vantage point, they could discern the stage and the five people prowling around it. They pondered their present, precarious situation several more seconds before both murmured aloud, and at once:

"If Spadaccio still thinks he is looking for a woman, then Mr. Smith has led him on a merry chase."

"I wonder if Signor Spadaccio knows that the painting is hidden in the tapestry onstage, the one that was at The Red Bull this afternoon?"

They glanced at each other, speechless, only their eyes highlighted by the dim beams penetrating the peepholes. When they spoke again, it was in unison:

"So that's it!" she breathed, superimposing her memory of the French actress in the masquing room onto that of the man in a rush on the steps just now. "*She* and *he* are one!"

"In the tapestry? Not bad!"

It was not prudent to say more, even whispering as they were. Spadaccio and his men were swarming all over the masquing room. They were speaking harshly and low to one another in Italian. Judith could not make out their words. Lambert, however, fully understood their exchange, but it would not have taken a knowledge of Italian to know that Spadaccio was out for blood—anyone's blood—if that person stood between him and the painting.

By the thumping on the walls and the clattering of the swords, the five men seemed to be engaged in a thorough and relentless search of the room. One brute was running down the side of the room where stood the secret alcove, thumping on the walls as he went.

Wrapped as she was in Lambert's arms, her heart beating with his, she was aware of the increased tension in his body even before he breathed the stricken words, "Good God! *No!*"

The next second brought the horrified "Yes!" to Lambert's lips when the brute happened to thump the place on the wall where was lodged the secret catch that opened the door to the alcove from the outside.

The secret panel began to slide back, and Judith and Lambert were increasingly exposed to view of the masquing room. In that first second, the brute's dumbfounded surprise was all that saved Judith and Lambert from being skewered on his sword. Judith's heart nearly failed her, for they were effectively trapped in a tiny alcove, with no room to maneuver and nowhere to run.

It was Lambert's quick wits and fingers that saved them in the next second. The moment the brute thumped the wall at the fatally perfect spot, Lambert fumbled with his free hand and found the inside mechanism that controlled the door.

Almost miraculously, as soon as the door to the masquing room had opened, it began to close. Simultaneously, the back of the alcove against which Judith was resting began to move! That back wall was also a door, this one opening out onto the very anteroom where she had met Lambert earlier in the evening.

Judith was prevented from falling backward into the anteroom by Lambert's supporting arm.

"Glad I thought to experiment with these knobs earlier in the evening!" he remarked, rather pleased with himself. Then he grabbed Judith's hand, uttered a succinct "Let's go!'' and ran across the anteroom, pulling Judith ungently behind.

By then, the brute in the masquing room had realized what had happened and had called out to his comrades and his leader. By the shouts and the noises coming from the masquing room, Lambert and Judith realized that they would have five people after them as soon as Spadaccio and his men discovered the door farther down the wall that led to the anteroom.

"Our only advantage," Lambert said, dragging Judith to a door across the room and plunging down a very dark corridor, "is that we know the palace better than they do."

"And all this," Judith managed to expostulate, giving vent to a thought that had occurred to her earlier in the day, "because of a rainstorm in Somerset Park!"

To that, Lambert merely laughed and pulled her along faster.

They ran for a minute or two, Lambert leading them unerringly through a maze of hallways. When they arrived at the intersection of two corridors at whose joint there was another alcove, they slid into it and paused to catch their breath. They could hear the muffled shouts of the men behind them in the anteroom and one of the first corridors they traveled down.

"They've fanned out," Lambert said.

Judith nodded. "Some have gone into the gardens, by my guess."

They listened carefully for a few seconds. No sound could be heard coming down either hallway that stretched out immediately before them. Still, they did not relax.

"Where to?" Lambert asked, thinking aloud. "I doubt it wise to seek my apartment. Both Spadaccio and Somerset must know where it is by now."

"We certainly cannot go to mine, either!" Judith said quickly.

"I would not put your life at risk with my presence in it," Lambert said gravely with a bow.

"Noble of you!"

"Isn't it, though?" he agreed congenially. "I was actually thinking your apartment the perfect refuge. However, since you refused it, I thought I may as well get credit for gallantry."

Judith took a very deep breath and said with a certain majestic indignation, "And what do you call the present situation, sir, if it is not one that has put my life at risk?"

"No one will guess it's you. With any luck, Spadaccio and the others will have mistaken you for Rosamunda who—as you now know—is otherwise known as Mr. Smith," Lambert said. "He has proven himself a remarkably fine performer. Speaking of which, I must compliment you on your own excellent performance a few minutes ago. Much improved over your efforts last evening!"

"Over my rôle as the Butt of the Joke, you mean?" she asked, acid dripping from her voice. "I thank you very much!"

"Not at all!" he returned. "You were entirely convincing in your portrayal of a young woman in hopeless, guilty love. I was lost in admiration. Particularly at the part where you were pleading for your love—let me see, how did it go?—yes! 'And yet,'" he quoted, "'will you not believe me that his lack of fortune is more than compensated by the true nobility of his nature, how his name is worthy in character of the grandest titles in the land which I, Judith Beaufort, would be proud to bear, even penniless?'" Lambert looked down at her. A faint smile curved his lips. "Impressive!"

"The line was straight out of one of Caroline's letters," Judith said, biting back a laugh, "extolling the virtues of your nephew, in fact."

"Ah, that accounts for the ring of authenticity!" he commented. "Horrible stuff! But effective, as was apparent. You have great potential for comedic personalities, as I think I told you earlier in the day." He chuckled. Judith liked the sound. "Which is not to say that Spadaccio found you particularly amusing. If I correctly interpreted the import of his remarks when he returned to the masquing room, when next he sees you, he will have difficulty restraining himself from wringing your pretty neck!"

Judith smiled in response and looked up at him in the darkness. She was breathless now, but not from the running. "You know something?" she said. The wild exertions of the last minutes and the danger had released the sealing stone over the well of spontaneity that bubbled deep within her. "I was thoroughly *enjoying* myself!"

His smile deepened. Then the laughter in his eyes stilled as he placed his hands on her shoulders and slid them down under her armpits so that they could come around and caress her breasts in a full grip. She felt the strength of his touch down to her toes. She knew it was wrong to be feeling what she did for this man, yet she did not move away. Instead, she placed her hands on his shoulders and raised her face to him, her desire written plainly upon it for Lambert to read. She was ready, eager, even flaming for the kiss she was certain that he wished to bestow upon her.

The kiss never happened. The echo of footsteps, far away, but descending one of the nearby corridors, broke the expectant, aching span of desire that drew Judith to Lambert.

He released her breasts and grabbed her hand again. They took to running down another hallway. "I think we will have to get out to the gardens eventually," he said. He led Judith up a staircase. "Lift your skirts. That's my girl! Yes. The gardens. I had been planning on meeting Will and the others there. Down this way. There's another staircase at the end of this hall, leading back down to the ground floor. We've got to get to the first set of fountains by the tennis courts. I know a way to a side entrance from the wing to our left."

Judith could only nod her agreement with this plan. They ran several minutes more, down the staircase Lambert had indicated and around several more bends and turns in the labyrinthine palace. Judith had developed a severe stitch in her side. All at once, she halted abruptly and sagged against the wall of the corridor. She sobbed for breath. The full consequences of this evening's work were crowding in on her unpleasantly.

"Now that—you know—where the painting—is," she gasped, "what are—you going—to do?"

Lambert had actually dismissed the idea of retrieving the painting now. "So near and yet so far," he replied, exhaling heavily, "and definitely out of my reach."

Judith slanted him a glance. She gulped for air. "You mean—you are giving—up?"

Lambert was catching his breath, too. "Yes," he said, then, "Yes," and again, "Yes," as if coming to a decision. "The trick in my business," he reflected, "is to know when you've well and truly lost a sale." He laughed softly, shaking his head. "It's taken me longer than usual to realize that I cannot make this purchase, but as of this evening I'm finally convinced."

"You're serious," she said.

"I'm serious." His gaze lingered on her. "It affords a strange satisfaction, though, to know where the painting has been hidden all this time."

Judith returned his gaze. She had caught her breath. She pushed away from the wall. "Now what?"

"I suppose I shall leave town, as I should have done several hours ago, although I imagine it will be a good deal more difficult now to take that wise course. However, I have no regrets. Had I left earlier, I never would have experienced the delights of the interlude in the alcove with you."

"Any further such delights and I may expire on the spot!" she declared.

Lambert had a pretty provocative rejoiner to *that* but was prevented from uttering it by the sounds of footsteps, far off, coming down the hallway. He took Judith's hand again, and they moved on, less quickly, but still with haste. One more turn led them to a door, and the next steps took them outside.

They had entered one of the side gardens. It was evidently an herb garden, since they were immediately assaulted by the powerful odors of borage and bugloss, fennel, parsley, dill, balm, and succory.

"By boat," Judith said.

Lambert had raised his brows, attempting to understand Judith's comment.

She turned toward him. "By the Thames," she said.

"You must leave by way of the river. Signor Spadaccio will not think of that escape route. He will assume you've hidden in the palace or will attempt to leave by way of the gardens and the street. You can take one of the Somerset sculls."

"Good idea," Lambert agreed. "Now, first to find Will and the others at the fountains."

They left the herb garden and found a path that led them among the hawthorn and the ivy and the climbing roses. They passed arbors and leafy bowers which were fashioned of bush firs and juniper and which were designed for love on warm, summer nights with the sweet breezes rustling and scenting the air with flowers. Wreathed trellises shadowed their path and filtered the starlight and the moonlight into particles of silver dust.

They proceeded with caution and approached every intersection hesitantly, lest they come face-to-face with Spadaccio or one of his men.

Suddenly, Lambert stopped. He looked down at Judith and exclaimed in disgust, "I've never had a day with so many missed opportunities! First the theater. Then the alcove. Now this!"

Judith blinked up at him, not understanding.

"To quote yourself, ma'am: 'I found myself bathed in moonlight and surrounded by the sweet smell of flowers and summer air,' " he said, " 'and suddenly I was not alone on that beautiful dark path. I looked down to see *her!* ' "

"I said that?" Judith said, surprised. Then, laughing, she recalled, "I *did!* Explaining to Signor Spadaccio how it came that I found myself on the stage with my love hiding ignominiously behind the tapestry. Only I am quite sure I said: 'I looked up to see *him*'!"

"So I should hope, and now you see what a perfect setting this is. Damn! How I hate to waste a great scene!"

"A pity," Judith said dryly. "Now, shall we get moving again so that you will live to see the morrow?"

Lambert would not budge. The poet in him kept him rooted to the spot. He put his arms around her and drew her to him very gently. "Such a waste when the night is made for wooing and winning your very charming kisses." He frowned. "Unfortunately, I can't recall one line of poetry for wooing and winning them." He looked about for inspiration. "Hawthorn. Holly. Gardens. Well-knotted gardens. No. Nothing comes to mind."

Haloed in moonlight, Judith was shaking her head, in tenderness, in desire, in disbelief at this odd start.

He was looking down at her, an arrested expression on his face, holding her in his arms, melting her with the answering passion that lit his eye. He kissed her and said, entirely prosaically, "And there is more than enough room here to get your clothes off."

Judith attempted to push him away but was unsuccessful.

"Mine, too," he said and joined thought to deed by beginning to unbutton and unlace his doublet.

"*Keep your shirt on, Lambert!*" squeaked a nervous, high-pitched voice from the nearby bushes.

The sound so startled Judith and Lambert that they sprang apart.

Out through the hedge of box bushes came the playwright. "The Italians are everywhere," he continued to squeak, "and they're looking for *you!*"

"Let's *go!*" Judith urged him.

Lambert complied with Judith and the playwright, albeit under duress. Judith heard him muttering indistinctly about wasted scenes, bad timing, and how, throughout the course of this day, his feeling of nobility in preserving a certain young woman's virtue was wearing excessively thin.

The next quarter of an hour was to prove most harrowing. There were near misses and narrow escapes and comical mistimings, but finally all the players were rounded up, and the entire group, led by Judith, found their way down to the wooden quays where the boats used by the noble residents at Whitehall were moored.

Fortunately, this night there were no fireworks organized that would have brought the courtiers down to the river and that would have illuminated any sailing vessel on the water. Also fortunately, Judith had guessed aright that Lambert would not be sought down by the river, thus making the escape almost leisurely. Their greatest hazard would lie in negotiating the inky murk of the Thames, for although the oyster boats, the hay boats, the hatch boats, the pilot boats, the colliers, the luggers, and the City Company's barges were safely docked for the night, there was no telling whether a Dutch galliot, an East Indiaman, or a West Indiaman might not be hitching a ride on favorable nocturnal tides.

It was several more minutes before one of the Somerset sculls had been loaded with its disreputable cargo and had shoved off from its mooring. Relieved and winded, Judith heaved a great sigh of relief, placing her hand over the lacings of her bodice at the intersection with her stomacher. She felt the parchment within, which she had previously forgotten in the press of their pursuit.

She called out softly across the few feet of water separating her from Lambert. "You never told me exactly what your interest in that painting was, you know! Why did you want so badly to get your hands on it?"

Judith could just discern the smile that stretched across Lambert's bruises. "Because when I discovered it at an auction in Florence," he called back across the darkness, his voice striking a sweet note of simple truth, "I fell in love with it on sight!"

Judith stood there, motionless, considering his words.

Not so the playwright. He apparently wished to invest the departure with more dignity than would customarily attend a troupe of ham actors ignominiously slinking away from Italian thugs under cover of night. Rising from the plank where he sat, he said, "This reminds me of one of my better passages in a similar scene of embarkation. You will recall the poignant moment aboard ship in my early tragedy *The Hero's Song*." He declaimed. "'We will not from the helm to set and weep/ But keep our course though the rough wind say no,/ From shelves and rock that threaten us with wreck.'"

Mr. Webster would have continued in this elevating vein, had it not been for the fact that, at one time or another, every man in the scull had had a bit part in Shakespeare's Henry plays, one of which, of course, had provided Mr.

Webster with these exact words. Thus, they had heard these lines in their original setting dozens of times.

As one, they recommended him, succinctly, to "Shut up and sit down, Harry! You're rocking the boat!"

Chapter
16

MUCH later, snuggled down into the comforting depths of her bed, Judith struggled to surface from an exhausted sleep. She heard a distant voice calling her, but the sound was distorted, as if it traveled through water. She felt her body responding to that attractive call, moving through the water, trying to reach the voice. She was a mermaid, a beautiful mermaid, swimming happily upward, toward the voice. She broke the crystalline surface of water, causing it to splinter and scatter. Several bright shards of water lodged in her eyes as she opened them. Standing over her she beheld—*a handsome prince*.

She blinked. The drops fell from her eyes, and the prince was revealed to be a horrible monster who was violently rattling her body. One of his eyes was swollen shut.

Judith moaned awake. She felt more like a limp fish now than a beautiful mermaid. "Good God, Lambert," she said, consciousness partially restored, "What on earth are you doing here?"

Lambert ceased the gentle shaking of her shoulder. "I thought you'd never wake up. I had just about decided that I would rouse the whole of the west wing shouting into your ear before you responded. However, I am delighted to discover that you don't snore, and you look delicious while asleep."

Still groggy, Judith had grasped the fundamentals of the situation. In one reflexive movement, she sat straight up, threw the covers off, and sprang out of bed, her unbound hair tumbling riotously down her back in charming disarray. She had moved too quickly. She swayed on her feet. Lambert reached out to steady her. His touch was electric. She jumped back from him and grasped the poster at the foot of her bed.

She looked wildly about to confirm that she was indeed in the bedchamber of her apartment at Whitehall and that it was the dead of night. She looked back at the closed door to the chamber. First things first. "How did you get in?"

"Through the window," he said, rather pleased with himself. "The shutters weren't latched."

Judith's sleep-hazed mind was trying to recall what she had done just before dropping into bed only a few hours before. "Usually Edith latches them for me as I prepare for the night, but I don't remember where she was when I returned to my chambers. Tonight was so confusing. . . ."

The events of the evening came to her in fragments: the excitement she had felt upon the stage; the feel of Lambert embracing her in the alcove; the danger of their exposure to Spadaccio and his men; the way Lambert had looked down at her, just so, in the gardens; how Sir George's amorous attempts in the same gardens some time later fell so woefully, ludicrously short by comparison; her realization of a true dilemma with regard to her impending marriage; the welcome escape into sleep.

"Confusing?" Lambert said. "I found it particularly illuminating myself."

She shook her head, attempting to concentrate on the present situation. "Do you have a ladder?"

"No, I remembered that the brickwork on the facade of this wing is made for climbing."

"Remembered?" she said. Her conscious self was sweeping away the tattered fog of sleep. "I take it this is not the first time you have climbed into a lady's bedchamber at Whitehall?''

''No, but I admit that I haven't had to resort to these methods in years,'' he acknowledged.

''Not in, say, fifteen years?'' she queried.

''That's about right,'' Lambert said, almost nostalgically, ''and I had forgotten the charm of these late-night maneuvers. Or perhaps it's you who brings out my youthful recklessness. More to the point, however, was that it was lucky for me that your shutters were unlatched, for it made entering your chambers that much easier. Why, anyone might have done so tonight.'' Here an idea occurred to him. ''Come think of it,'' he said, taking several paces over to the window where the moonlight was streaming in, ''I wonder if—no, not a sign of him,'' he finished, satisfied.

''Is Spadaccio still after you?'' Judith asked anxiously.

Lambert shook his head. ''I doubt it. No, I was rather thinking of Beecham. The last time I was in your bedchamber, he was here as well,'' Lambert reminded her. ''Although I doubt it would occur to him to enter your bedchamber by climbing the outside wall.''

''Not being infected by youthful recklessness,'' she interpolated a trifle sarcastically.

Lambert was hardly ruffled. ''Or that it would occur to him to enter your bedchamber at all.''

''Indeed not!'' Judith retorted frostily.

Lambert walked back over to Judith and smiled down at her. ''No, his mother wouldn't approve.''

Judith ignored the fact that her heart turned over at his smile, even the disfigured one that stretched the ugly bruises on his face. ''If you have come here to insult my betrothed—'' she began.

''That, as a matter of course,'' he acknowledged. ''However, since I thought it best to return the Somerset scull once it had served its purpose, the occasion seemed opportune—'' Here he slid a hand inside his doublet. ''—to bring you this.'' He withdrew his hand and was holding it out, palm up and open.

Judith peered into his hand. "What is it?"

"Your token."

"My token?" She looked closer and saw a miniature whose dainty, gilded frame winked back at her in the dark.

"Our bargain. I was to give you a token of my choosing in return for your keeping an eye on Spadaccio. It was a very small favor, I think you said, and I assured you that the token you would receive would be commensurate to the deed." He took another step toward her so that they were almost touching. "It's a miniature of Judith."

"Of Judith?" she said, unable to suppress her delight, but she did not immediately take her token. She looked up at him. "If your purpose was to know Spadaccio's activities to lead you to your painting, I did not achieve for you what you wanted."

"No, you merely saved my life with your portrayal of the lovelorn lass upon the stage. And, in any case, I do know where the painting is—or was."

Judith accepted the miniature and held it up. It was exquisite. "A Cooper?" she hazarded.

He nodded.

"A valuable token," she said.

"Again, I think it appropriate to the ultimate service that was rendered."

"But I wasn't expecting it until much later! You were to give it to me when you were no longer in immediate danger," she said with a delicious mixture of emotions that included both anxiety for his safety and undeniable happiness that he had braved the dangers of Whitehall and the wall to be with her.

He was shaking his head. "The danger is no longer immediate."

"If you mean that the thugs are no longer breathing down our necks, I will agree, but aren't you being a little too . . . too cavalier about your safety?" she said.

"Spadaccio must have figured that I am long gone from Whitehall," he said, taking her chin in his hand, "and safety's a pale companion."

"What about my safety, then? What if Spadaccio becomes suspicious of my presence on the stage at exactly the wrong time and comes to my chambers to question me?"

"I would imagine," Lambert said shrewdly, "that he has already had your apartment thoroughly searched."

Judith paused. It was entirely possible that what Lambert had suggested was true. After seeing Lambert and the actors off at the dock, she had quickly found Sir George again and had spent the rest of the evening conspicuously in his presence. She had seen no further sign of Signor Spadaccio. When she had returned to her chambers, she had noticed that some of the furniture in her bedchamber looked as if it had been moved. In her tiredness, she had assumed that the slightly different arrangement was a lingering result of the disarrangement that had occurred in her chamber the evening before as a result of the fracas between Beecham and Lambert.

Instead of being relieved by the knowledge that Spadaccio had already rummaged through her chambers and had found no trace of Lambert or anything else, her anxiety doubled. "He could come again! You should have *sent* the miniature to me! I must thank you for it deeply, but you have been unwise! You need not have brought it to me in person!"

"Oh, but I did need to come," he said meaningfully, still holding her chin and placing his other hand behind her head in preparation for a kiss.

Something in his voice made her suddenly aware that she had been standing in front of him all this time in a froth of transparent cambric and lace, its modesty tied loosely with satin ribbons.

"You did?" she said, unable to move away from him.

"I did. You see, the moment after we had shoved off in the boat, the lines suddenly came to me."

"The lines?"

"The ones that had eluded me in the gardens," he explained. "In a day of lost opportunities," he said, moving his lips toward hers, "the underplayed scene in the gardens— with the moonlight and the scent of flowers and a desirable woman in my arms—struck me as the most egregious waste. I found I could not rest this night until I had come to play the scene right. To its completion.''

"To its completion,'' she repeated, more dazed than apprehensive, for the import of his words had not fully sunk in.

He bent and feathered his lips against hers. The contact was so light that he did not wince this time, but neither could he hold the kiss nor could he deepen it. Because of his wounded lips, he had to make do, as before, with nuzzling her neck. With her skin still warm and fragrant from sleep, this course of action was not a hardship.

"I did not expect, of course,'' he said, almost conversationally, "to pick up exactly where we had left off earlier. Although I realize now''—here his voice held the trace of humor—"that it is no longer necessary to go through the delightful bother of removing your clothing.'' At that, he found the ribband that held the lace covering one of her shoulders. It yielded to his touch, and before Judith could prevent him, he had slid the wisp of lace off her shoulder and exposed a breast to his eager touch. He trailed kisses down her neck to her breast.

Suddenly ablaze, Judith nevertheless had recovered a corner of her sanity. She clung to it. Shaking her head, she tried to release herself from his embrace. In a day that had been marked by unusual events, the present moment was certainly the culmination of the extraordinary. At the same time, the events of the day had so far exceeded anything in Judith's experience that she was suspended in a state of disbelief and wondered now whether she had not dreamed the whole. She might still be dreaming now, and she disbelieved her very senses. She disbelieved every nerve and every pore that assured her it was right and good that Lambert had come to her.

"You're not serious,'' she said.

"I am very serious,'' he replied with conviction.

"Climbing up the wall and entering my bedchamber,'' she said, shrugging her shoulder ineffectually to shake him off. "You are always playacting, Lambert.''

"Ah, but you cannot equate that with not being serious."

She turned her head away as if to escape his nuzzling. She succeeded only in arching her breasts into his chest and exposing more of her lovely skin to his ministrations, to which she was helpless to prevent the flaming response. "I don't understand you," she complained.

"I thought you had learned more today!" he reproved gently and sought the savory contact with her neck again.

Judith laughed, more in exasperation than in amusement. "This has been a day of actors and actresses and stages and theater. You are still caught up in it and are merely playacting."

Lambert ceased his nuzzling. He looked up at her and nodded, once, sagely. "It is the 'merely' that bedevils your thinking. Were you 'merely' playacting while you so effectively convinced Spadaccio of your silly, guilty, defiant, and even, ultimately, noble character? Were you 'merely' playacting when you held out your lovelorn heart for his inspection? Did you not learn the lesson of that experience?"

"Which is—?"

"You are what you play," he said. "It is childishly simple." He smiled down at her. "As I have already told you, you have great potential for shaping an emotional scene to your advantage. I predict, for instance, that your abilities will serve you well when you tell Beecham that the wedding is off."

Judith's eyes opened wide, and her head reared back. "What?" she said.

"Well, you cannot truly be planning on marrying him now, can you?" he demanded, surprised in his turn.

The image of Sir George rose in Judith's mind. It flickered there uncertainly and threatened to extinguish, until her uncle's presence rose up behind him, making him burn straighter and brighter.

Lambert drew a little away himself and regarded her. "Are you?" he asked again.

"I don't know," she answered honestly. "It's all . . . it's all happening so *fast* that I hadn't thought about it!"

"Old roles die hard," he remarked, "ever the obedient daughter."

"You call it obedience," she defended herself. "I call it loyalty and constancy. Are those such bad qualities?"

He ran an idle hand up the bare skin of her arm. "You have been disobedient to your uncle for most of the day—and most helpful to me." For all that the passionate recklessness of his youth still lived within him, Lambert the man was tempered with discipline. The Judith that he wanted, the Judith of flesh and blood, stood within the circle of his arms. She was strong and lovely, desirable and desiring. She was his for the taking, and yet he was not going to take her before she knew her own mind. Or until he was able to show her what her own mind was. "Yes. Very disobedient to your uncle and very helpful to me. I am wondering why?"

Why? Judith gazed up at him. Was it because he had trusted her where her uncle had not? Was it because she had never met a man like Charles Lambert? Was it because she was not her old, familiar self when she was with him? Was it because a mischievous star had crossed all her dealings with him, beginning with the moment she had looked up at him through the pouring rain and had heard him compare her to a drowned rat? Was it because his kisses were extraordinarily sweet? Or was it because, being with him now, so near to him, surrounded by the feel of him, his warmth, and able to taste him in the very air that she breathed, *she no longer knew the reason?*

"Well," she hedged, "you were certainly in deep trouble tonight."

"I was."

"And you had been attacked most unfairly."

"A black eye is always worth a kiss or two," he said wisely. "Now, for bigger concessions," he said, drawing her to him in a firm, purposeful embrace, "it's my experience that something more interesting than a bruise or two is often necessary." He looked at her with intention and ran his hand down her shoulder to her breast. His thumb idly stroked the pink tip.

Judith was succumbing rapidly. She could not prevent her fiery response to his embrace, but she thought herself too strong-willed to give in to him at his casual touch and at his casual words. Or was it that she was enjoying the conversation and savoring the anticipation of what she was rapidly coming to see as the highly desirable completion to this day? With Charles Lambert, of all people—the man she had promised her uncle she would never see again.

Her thoughts were truly disobedient now, so disobedient that they had perversely turned on her and were obeying her body. Her voice was light, mocking, skeptical, provocative. "You have a ploy for every occasion?"

"No, for it depends entirely on the woman. You," he explained, "are partial to poetry, and among the frustrations in the gardens was my inability to conjure the words that would help us put the setting to proper use. I have come to rectify that."

"It's an entirely different setting now," she said, her voice faltering, thereby echoing the weakening of her knees at his long prolonged, arousing touch.

"My point exactly," he said unperturbed, "and with many superior aspects, although I am partial to gardens." He glanced meaningfully at the bed, then back to Judith. "Which is why I came armed with the perfect lines."

"Ah yes, those lines," she said, "but I do not think that they will work now."

The expression on his battered face was smug, masculine, and plainly irresistible. " 'I know a bank where the wild thyme blows,' " he began to quote.

She covered her ears so she would not hear. This gesture left her charmingly defenseless, and Lambert took immediate advantage. He made quick work of the other ribband holding her gown in place, and when the sheer cambric had fallen to her hips, he possessed himself completely of her body, his hands spread on her back, crushing her to him, her legs trapped intimately between his and entwined in the folds of the gown that had fallen between them.

He continued, " 'Where oxlips and the nodding violet grows,/ Quite over-canopied with luscious woodbine.' "

At the shocking, unexpected, and overwhelming response to him as she was pressed naked to him, her knees buckled completely, causing her to take her hands from her ears and wrap them around his shoulders for support. Her mouth found his ear, and she explored the shell-like curves with lips and tongue. His response was explosive. She was pliant and willing. He shifted her weight in his arms and managed to lace her legs in his, separating her thighs

" 'With sweet musk-roses and with eglantine,' " he finished.

He gave up the attempt to speak. His hands roamed at will, over her back and breasts and hips. Where they touched her, tiny flames blazed in his fingertips. He bent to drink in the beauty of her breasts.

"The perfect lines," he murmured, "for the perfect skin."

Perfect. Miss Perfect. Judith Beaufort. Of flesh and blood. Soft, white expanses of flesh, glowing in the moonlight. Blood singing through her veins. And his. Perfect. Perfect breasts. Perfect, pink tips that responded so perfectly to his mouth. Perfect body. Perfectly resistant. Perfectly melting into him.

"I thought that mention of eglantine would surely do it for you." He paused, breathing in more of her neck. He held the weight of her hips with one hand. With the other, he bent to dip in between her thighs that were now open to him. "I see that I was right."

Judith's response was incoherent but conveyed unambiguous agreement with his supposition.

"For me, it was rather the idea of sweet musk-roses," he said. His fingers, at their goal, teased away the lace of her gown that had caught between their legs. That delicate action in itself caused Judith to surge against his probing fingers with the eagerness of discovery and inexperience. He stroked her, easing her thighs farther apart, savoring the feel of her sweet musk-roses.

"Do you see what I mean?" he asked her, low, into her ear.

Judith breathed an inarticulate assent.

He separated the petals of her flower and slid his fingers

deep into the soft, moist center, the fertile pistil that welcomed him as it enveloped him.

Judith pressed her thighs together, in belated protest. "No! You go too far!" she gainsaid, but her argument was weak.

"Not quite far enough," he said, now releasing his treasure, reveling, glorifying, worshiping, stimulating so that Judith protested no more.

Being on fire himself made Judith's weight and her increasing desire all the more difficult to hold. The bed invited, with the covers already rumpled and thrown back, the sheets already slept in. He withdrew his hand from her thighs and possessed himself of her hips so that he could lay her down.

"This is what is called ruin for a woman," Judith said, trapped between the flame of her desire and the cold knowledge of the consequences of that desire.

"What an absurd notion," Lambert replied on a deep chuckle, interpreting her words as capitulation. He stretched himself out beside her. "It is exactly the opposite and will be the making of you. But first you will have to undress me."

"I don't know how!" She laughed, but the sound was shaky, as were her fingers which sought his skin.

"Beecham never asked you?" he queried slyly as he submitted to her attentions. He was not idle, and his hands sought all the interesting points on her body that had captivated him the moment before.

"No," she answered, but not in response to his stroking.

When her hands had found the muscles on his chest and were working to release the lacing on his breeches, she paused, as much in fear as in exquisite anticipation, she asked, "And what of the morrow? What then?"

"You may wish to run away with me," was the simple answer.

She laughed. "Run away with you?"

"I think it an excellent idea."

"Your climb up the wall to a lady's bedchamber has confused you and put you under the illusion that you are nineteen again," she said almost humorously. "You don't want to run away with me."

"Yes, I do."

"But, then, I don't want to run away with you," she said.

"I mean, of course, to elope," he clarified.

"*Marry you?*"

"Your shock, my dear Judith," Lambert said, smiling, and enjoying, in his turn, the pleasurable anticipation he derived from caressing her, "is not flattering to either of us."

"It would be impossible to marry you!"

"It is entirely possible, for I am not presently married," he pointed out, "and neither are you."

"No, you cannot have thought—! No, I mean—" she groped for words "—Diana!"

"Your cousin Diana? Why, she does not come into question. She is already married."

"I know, but I mean, I mean—live at *Speke Hall*? Under my uncle's nose?"

"I was not thinking of living at Speke Hall."

"Oh!"

Judith's head was spinning. A thought occurred to her. "If we are to be married—impossible thought!—should we not wait to do—to do *this?*"

"You make me feel very noble when I am around you," Lambert replied, "but not quite that noble."

"Good God, Lambert!" Judith cried, coming to her senses. "You do not want to marry me!"

"But I do." Lambert explained. His clothing loosened, he relaxed his length against her. With one hand, he continued caressing her. With the other, he picked up a curl from her breast and played with it, drawing her face slowly to him as he said, "It came to me in the gardens. When I realized that I could not have my Judith on oils and canvas, I thought that I must have the Judith of flesh and blood as mine." He kissed her lightly. "Mine."

These simple words were strangely more seductive than

all of Lambert's well-learned poetry. "When do we leave?" she asked.

"As soon as we are done here," he said, "and rested."

He sought and found her hidden flower. She did not shy away from his touch, but gazed up at him, very happy and very desirous and very ready and said for no reason whatsoever, "I think my uncle got the painting, after all."

Since he could not kiss her the way he would have liked, he was content to speak with her, knowing as he stroked her and she returned the compliments, that he did not have much longer to wait. He entwined the curl around his finger. "Did he?" he replied. "A poetic justice, of sorts, I suppose, for he's to lose the Judith of flesh and blood." He smiled. "A fair enough trade, especially since I have the better half of the bargain." Then, idly curious, he said, "How do you know he has the painting?"

"He looked extremely satisfied when I met up with him in the gardens later. Extremely satisfied." Judith chuckled in reminiscence. The glaze of desire shining from her eyes caused Lambert to shift his weight purposefully. "I was with Sir George, by the bye. My uncle must have been very satisfied, for he did not reprimand me or wonder why I had not reported to him Spadaccio's activities, and he did not ask me where I had been when Sir George had been called away to tend to his mother. I could only imagine that he concluded a bargain with Mr. Smith and got the painting."

"Lucky old bastard," was Lambert's entirely indifferent opinion of Somerset's success this night. "I'm glad for him," he said as he positioned himself to possess himself of the Judith of flesh and blood. "I got the better half of the bargain," he murmured thickly, "the much better half."

At that very moment came a pounding at Judith's antechamber door. Lambert checked his movement instinctively but then proceeded, ignoring the interruption.

The pounding became insistent.

Lambert swore, and Judith pushed him away. They struggled, bewildered, to their elbows. "Spadaccio!" she cried, low, in alarm. "Lambert, get up. My God, no!"

Judith heard the shouting in the hallway. Muffled as it was, having to penetrate two doors, she heard her name being called. Her heart leapt to her throat. "Worse!" she exclaimed. "It's my uncle! Quick! Hide under the bed!"

Lambert was already on his feet and pulling together his clothing. When Judith began to rise, as well, he pushed her down gently. "Stay in bed," he advised. "I'll leave by the window." When Judith sat immobile in the bed, he whispered, "Lie back down, I say! You must pretend you're asleep! Refasten your gown!"

The pounding continued.

"Should I not go to the door? He'll be furious if I make him wait!"

"He's already furious, by the sound of it," Lambert observed. "Let your woman wake up and open the door." He was already at the window.

"What could he want at this hour?" Judith groaned in anxiety. She looked over the window. "Lambert!" she cried when she saw that he wore only stockings. "Your boots!"

"I left them down below," he said, adding impudently, "I hadn't forgotten everything about these adventures, and boots can make an awful noise on the floorboards, if one isn't careful." He swung a leg out the window and prepared to descend. The pounding beyond Judith's bedchamber door had ceased, suggesting that Edith had been roused and had opened the outer door. He was shaking his head and muttering angrily, "I had better success at this fifteen years ago! It would be funny if it wasn't so damned *frustrating!*"

"And dangerous!" Judith added, fear flooding her.

"I'm gone," he said, his head about to bob below the casing.

"But what about—?" Judith began.

Lambert cut her off. "There's no time to discuss that now! I'll find some way to come get you, but I don't know how right now!" The last thing she heard him say was, "Be asleep!"

Judith laid her head back down. She closed her eyes, pulled the counterpane across her shoulders, and hugged herself into the position of quiet repose. When she clasped her hands together to lay them against her cheek, she discovered that she was still clutching Lambert's miniature. She quickly slid it under the pillow, where her hand made contact with the parchment she had retrieved from the tapestry.

The next moment Somerset stormed in, holding a branch of candles high over his head and followed by four or five of his retainers.

"Judith!" he commanded. "*Judith!*"

Judith's eyes opened reflexively. She started. Then she sat up. The covers fell forward, revealing her rumpled night shift. She turned her face toward the offending light and dashed her hand across her eyes. She looked tousled and drugged with the sensuality of sleep. She looked infinitely virginal and vulnerable and desirable. She looked impossibly beautiful.

"Uncle. Sir," she managed with blankest incomprehension.

In his haste and rage, Somerset had miscalculated. Seeing Judith, he recognized his error. He turned to the men who had accompanied him into his niece's bedchamber and who were now ogling the luscious picture she presented. "*Out!*" he roared, as if it were their fault they beheld Judith in such a condition.

This byplay had given Judith the edge of a second's thought. She imagined that her uncle had just discovered that the painting he had presumably bought from Mr. Smith was, indeed, no more than the painting of *Judith*. To deflect all possibility of her involvement in tonight's schemes, she snatched the covers to her breasts, as if suddenly aware of her exposure. She said, as if it were the first thing to come to her mind, "It's Sir George, isn't it?" Her voice was fearful. "That's why you have come! To tell me that something bad has happened to him!"

This question checked her uncle, but only for a moment. "No, nothing has happened to Beecham," he said curtly. He was still angry, but when Judith relaxed in great relief, his voice acquired the suggestion of a doubt about this unprecedented storming of her bedchamber. "It's rather that I have just had it on the authority of the Roman envoy that an unexpected guest has attended this evening's masque." Without a pause, he rapped out the name, "Charles Lambert!"

In her most convincing performance to date, Judith looked up at him, confused. As if the thick gauze of sleep still prevented her from following his train of thought, her voice cracked over the syllable, "Who?"

Chapter
17

QUICKER even than the time it had taken her to fall in love with Lambert, Judith found herself on the road to Raglan Castle, bundled in a Somerset coach. She was seated next to Edith who seemed to have as much to say on the journey that took them away from London as on the one that had taken them to London.

Lambert had not again scaled the wall to her bedchamber at Whitehall that night, and when she had arisen the next morning, she had been greeted with the elegantly worded message from her uncle stating that since Judith must have tired of the gay life of the Stuart Court by now, she would welcome a return home. Judith had no difficulty interpreting that gentle effusion for what it was, but she did not think it wise to disobey her uncle, since she had no knowledge of Lambert's movements or intentions.

Judith had further learned that her uncle had already ridden ahead. She could only wonder at the turn of events that had required of him the energy and purpose of a man thirty years younger. She did not see him once on the relatively quick and, therefore, grueling trip from London to Wales.

Judith next saw her uncle immediately upon her arrival at Raglan. She had gone to the Solar ostensibly to attend to all the business she had abruptly left those not very many days before at her uncle's request. Judith had seated herself in a heavily carved chair set at a massive oak table littered with the curling sheaves of the household inventory and other papers. Edith sat across from her mistress in one of the sunny window embrasures of the Solar and was plying an embroidering tambour. Rogue sat at his mistress's feet, tail and ears down, dozing comfortably.

Somerset entered. Judith rose and crossed to him, curtsying low before him. They greeted each other conventionally. He placed a kiss atop her head. Judith rose. He begged her to take a seat and did so himself at the other end of the table. Without further reference to events at Whitehall or her precipitous return to Raglan or anything else in the world, he began calmly to sort through the correspondence that was awaiting him.

It was a quiet, cozy scene, one that had been played a thousand times. However, this day was different. A cloud had settled between her and her uncle. The shadow it cast was so long and so cold that the thought had crossed Judith's mind, upon receiving her uncle's salute, that she had just received the kiss of death. She hastily dismissed the thought as a lingering reaction to his strange behavior in her bedchamber at Whitehall. In retrospect, she had found that the bedroom scene had frightened her profoundly, for she had never seen her uncle when he was not rigidly in control of himself.

"You are engaged in finishing the invitations to your wedding, I perceive," was how Somerset opened the conversation after a few, quiet minutes. His voice was placid and congenial.

Judith was doing nothing of the kind. She looked up and over at him. "Indeed," she said with seeming acquiescence.

"You will want to have them all delivered within the next fortnight," he said. "Do I understand correctly that you have not yet begun to send out any of them?"

"You understand correctly," she said and thought inevitably of how all the intrigues of the past days had been shaped by her innocent decision to deliver the first wedding invitation by her own hand to Monmouth.

Her uncle nodded and smiled and returned his attention to the letter in his hands whose seal he was just then breaking. He glanced down at it and, upon the instant, exclaimed mildly.

Judith looked up, an inquiry in her eyes.

"This is most unexpected," Somerset commented with a hint of distaste. "I have just received a quite incomprehensible communication from Charles Lambert." He paused. "You do remember the man now, do you not, Judith?" Without waiting for Judith's reply, he continued smoothly, "He wishes to call at Raglan." Somerset glanced up the page at the date and confirmed, "Today, in fact." He put the missive down, placing it to one side of his correspondence as if it were slightly soiled. "Most incomprehensible."

Judith's heart had leapt in her breast at the thought of Lambert coming to see her at Raglan; and she had not been deceived for a moment by her uncle's apparent surprise at receiving the communication.

Judith busied herself with her papers and asked, casually, "Is Charles Lambert, perhaps, in residence at Speke Hall?"

Somerset laughed softly. It was a ghostly sound. "No, my dear, you were mistaken. Quite by chance, I learned that Speke Hall has not changed hands, that the squire's heirs have not sold it to anyone, and indeed have no intention of selling it to anyone."

Judith bit her lip uncertainly. "How strange that I should have heard the wrong information, then," she said.

"Strange indeed, my dear." Somerset picked up the next piece of correspondence and made as if he were perusing it. His voice was a trifle bored when he said, "It is unlikely that a man of Charles Lambert's background would have the money to make the purchase of such a house—modest though it is, by certain standards." Somerset shook his head. "No, it is unlikely that a man who has misspent his noble, though impoverished name on the Italian stage—I believe that he has been reduced all these years to earn his living as an actor, if one can call it a living—has fifty pounds to his name at any one time.''

Judith had the stray memory that upon asking Lambert where they were to live if they had run off together, he had discounted the possibility of residing at Speke Hall. He must have known the Hall was empty and had chosen to squat there for the night. For the first time ever, she considered what life would have been—would be—like without wealth and comfort. It was an alien concept.

"Why is he wishing to call?" she asked logically.

"A trifle over a painting," he answered, glancing down in some ironic amusement at Lambert's message. He looked over at Judith, his expression unreadable. "Did I tell you that I succeeded in buying a painting in London before my departure?" Judith shook her head. "No? It must have slipped my mind. It is nothing important. Simply a painting I took a fancy to." Somerset waved this away negligently. "For some reason Charles Lambert wishes to speak with me about this painting. How he came to learn of my purchase of it, I shall never know. I suppose that impecunious men no longer in their first youth must ferret out what information they can in order to make their living in dubious ways."

Judith's first elation upon hearing that Lambert was to come to Raglan this day turned into an uneasy happiness. She remembered clearly the passionate circumstances under which she had divulged to Lambert the knowledge that her uncle had gotten hold of the painting. Surely Lambert's message to her uncle was merely an excuse to come to Raglan. Surely he was coming for her and not for the painting—wasn't he?

"I do not understand," she said evenly. "How can a discussion of a painting you have already bought bring him any profit?"

"My dear, I am sure that I do not know. Perhaps he wishes to sell me something associated with the painting. A certificate of authenticity, for example."

Judith suddenly realized that her uncle must think that Lambert had retrieved the parchment that had been hidden in the tapestry along with the painting. Her uncle must think that Lambert was coming this day to strike a bargain with him. Judith had had no intention of meekly handing over the parchment to her uncle, but at her uncle's mention of the painting, Judith felt a spasm of guilt—or was it triumph?

When she had had an opportunity to wade through the heavy Latin scrawled across the parchment, she had discovered that Lambert's conjecture had been right: it was a gracious invitation to King Charles from the Vatican for the Church of England to become one again with Rome. Uncomfortable questions now occurred to Judith to cause her uneasiness: How had Lambert known of the existence and contents of the parchment? What was Lambert's *real* interest in the painting? Why was he coming to Raglan today?

Judith had not lived all these years with her uncle without having learned a trick or two from him. Her face betrayed nothing of her thoughts, and she was calmed by the knowledge that, even in his wildest imaginings, her uncle would never guess that the dangerous, volatile parchment stamped and sealed by the Vatican lay innocuously under the pillow in her bedchamber at Raglan.

"A certificate of authenticity?" Judith replied, in dismissive accents. "Why, that would not bring him more than several pounds in any case, and I would hope your reputation as a collector is wide enough to prevent anyone from thinking you would need one—or be fooled into buying one."

Lord Henry regarded his niece with approval. "Perhaps you are right, my dear. Indeed, now that I come to think of it, I am sure you are right. Even so poor a man as Lambert would need a somewhat more compelling reason than a few pounds to have returned to England after all these years." Somerset's voice conveyed utter indifference. "A reason very much worth his while."

Judith felt her stomach plummet. What her uncle said rang sickeningly true. Just as her uncle did not know who possessed the Vatican's invitation, neither could Lambert suspect that it was Judith who held it, for he knew her uncle had the painting. Lambert must have had a reason very much worth his while to have returned to England after all these years, a reason that was highly compelling. If he was as poor as all reports indicated, Lambert could profit handsomely from his knowledge of the parchment. Judith's uneasy happiness sank into depression.

Judith's mind tried to capture conflicting images and blend them into a coherent whole. What had Lambert said about having fallen in love with the painting? Surely she was not so big a fool as to believe that! Was it not more likely that he was gambling that her uncle might somehow be coerced to pay him to keep silent about the dangerous document that had come with the painting?

The horrible possibility occurred that Lambert was using her. When she looked back on all of her encounters with the man, they could all be interpreted as his having used her: at the theater, the night of the masque, in her bedchamber at Whitehall. Perhaps he intended using her today, as well— but how? To get her to divulge the whereabouts or particular contents of the parchment—as if she would know?

Judith was suddenly aware of a familiar sensation deep inside her which she had never before named. She recognized it now as her lacing. In Lambert's presence, she had been expanding, loosening. In her uncle's presence, by contrast, she felt the laces pulled again, ever so lightly, but perceptibly, tightening around her. She was caught in the middle, neither fully laced nor fully unbound, between two selves and two existences and two men. Were the laces keeping her proper and in place, or suffocating her? Were they anchors, or weights? To which man should she give the parchment?

"Shall you receive him?" she asked noncommittally.

Somerset stroked his neatly clipped beard. "Oh, I suppose I shall receive him," he said, his boredom pronounced. "I shall even listen politely to his proposition—if he has one to offer me."

"I confess that I am curious. Where is the painting, sir?" Judith said. "I should like to see it."

"I am having it hung in the gallery," Lord Henry replied.

"Is it beautiful?"

"That, my dear, is a difficult question to answer. As you know, I am not one who wavers on matters of taste. This time, I find, however, it is quite different! I shall wait until I can appreciate the painting in its intended setting. If Charles Lambert has come to buy the painting—which I doubt! for I paid quite an interesting price for it—I may just sell it to him. You see, I was deceived"—he emphasized the word delicately—"in the artist. The painting was not, as I had first thought, by Gentileschi, that is Orazio Gentileschi, a master painter, as you know." Somerset's brows drew together. "The painter and the painting may be . . . inferior. I have not yet decided."

"Speaking of paintings, I am reminded of that handsome man—what was his name, now?—oh yes, Signor Spadaccio," Judith dared to say, "and his misplaced piece of artwork. What became of him the night of the masque? I kept my eye on him as you had requested, but you never asked me to divulge what I had discovered about his movements."

Somerset smiled like the cat who swallowed the canary. "Signor Spadaccio discovered that urgent business called him back to his native Rome," he said smoothly. "He was desolated to have to leave the pleasures of the Stuart Court. Perhaps, it was precisely his enjoyment of those pleasures that persuaded him that he had lost effectiveness as an envoy." He paused. "I, myself, found him most uncooperative."

"Oh, and Mr. Smith?" she inquired artlessly. Brightly, she said, "Was it he who sold you the painting after all?"

Her uncle did not reply directly to this. Instead, he said with a chilling finality, "Mr. Smith shall not be heard from again."

Before Judith had grasped the possible horror that lay behind that statement, Judith's cousin Caroline bounced into the room to greet the newcomers. She kissed her father obediently and greeted Judith with her usual warmth and happiness. When questioned gently by her father of her activities in the past week, Caroline displayed every evidence of daughterly submission.

"And have you heard from your future mother-in-law, my dear?" Lord Henry asked at length.

Caroline lowered her pretty eyes, blushed charmingly, and answered, "Yes, Father." She proceeded, with becoming hesitation, to describe her pleasure at the most pleasant letter from this noble dame and the anticipation she felt at meeting the handsome man who was this lady's son.

Judith was still detached enough, still unlaced enough, to witness with new eyes this exchange between Caroline and her uncle. Is this how easily she, Judith, acquiesced to every wish and whim of her powerful uncle? Watching Caroline's blushes and lowered lashes, Judith was put in mind of Caroline's impassioned letters, written hardly the month before, on behalf of her True Love, James Lambert. *Remember Diana!* Caroline had written, and Judith had been almost moved.

Judith was now thoroughly disgusted. Remember Diana, indeed! Remember how Diana had crumbled when the thought of disobeying her father had translated into deed. Remember how Diana had capitulated so willingly to the thwarted elopement. Remember how Diana had bent herself to life with the very respectable and very dull Simon Stephens these past fifteen very respectable and very dull years.

"And my only regret now," Caroline was saying, evidently addressing Judith, "is that I must wait until my cousin is married off before anyone can think of my marriage! Oh, how grand it will be!" Caroline sighed.

Judith was jolted out of her rebellious reflections. She forced herself to smile and wave her hand across her work on the table as if immersed in the pleasurable industry of writing out the wedding invitations.

At that, Somerset finished reading his correspondence and rose from his chair. "Yes, my love," he said to Caroline, "Judith is making haste to wed the man of her choosing and to prepare the way for you." He paused first to regard his daughter, then his niece, and an expression came upon his face that suggested he was a man twice blessed and unable to decide which young woman he loved the more. "I shall be leaving on the morrow for London," he announced.

"You return on the day after your arrival?" Judith said quickly.

"Yes, is it not extraordinary?" He held up a piece of parchment from his pile of correspondence. Judith would have said that he chose it at random. "My son has written me the most fascinating letter. Edward, as you know, has been commissioned to provide the water works for a festival two weeks hence in London. At the King's request, of course. Edward left Raglan last week, as you know, and is engaged in setting up his mechanical inventions now in London. He asks for my assistance. That is all." When Somerset turned to address Judith directly, he smiled, but the expression did not reach his eyes. "After all the attention I have given lately to my two, most lovely daughters," he said, "I would feel remiss if I did not attend to my son just now. Oh, and Judith, in case that I do not see you again before the morning—I shall have much to do today and will leave before dawn—I have been informed by Sir Robert that your horse, Barbary, has developed an unfortunate quirk and is apt to bolt. She is, therefore, most unreliable. Even dangerous. I will ask you not to ride her."

Judith could not fail to comprehend the message. She was not to ride out on Barbary or any other horse in the Somerset stable, and Sir Robert had the orders from the master this time.

"It is for your own good," Somerset said, taking his leave of Judith. He kissed the top of her head when she curtsied before him. "I am sure that you understand."

Judith understood that she was to be a virtual prisoner at Raglan.

Judith presently learned that her uncle was spending the afternoon in the gallery where he would presumably give audience to Charles Lambert. Judith was determined, even burning, to see Lambert, to dispel the doubts about him that her uncle had wittingly, or unwittingly, planted in her brain. She was alert to the possibility that her uncle might still suspect her of having a liaison with Charles

Lambert. Apparently, however, no servant had been set to watch her this day, and she thought that perhaps her uncle was secure in the knowledge that no harm could come to her within Raglan walls, if she cared to engineer a meeting with the visitor.

She did. She knew the moment Lambert arrived. She found a place between the stables and the main Stone Court which was hidden from the view of any upper window. Waiting there for him in the shadows, doubts shook her. Was Lambert expecting to see her this day? Had he come for her? Or had he come to bargain disreputably with her uncle?

Lambert turned the corner and came face-to-face with Judith. She saw that his bruises had faded and were discoloring. The effect was not as hideous as before, but he still bore the visible results of his battering. She fell in love with him all over again.

A happiness filled her when she saw a spark light his eyes upon seeing her. Dared she hope that his stated desire for her was genuine, and not playacting? She was confident that she had just the method for finding out, and she renewed her determination just then to discover the real reason why he was here today, his real interest in the painting. When she had forced his confession she would forgive him all and beg him to take her away with him. However, she would insist that he not use the parchment against her uncle. She had it all worked out.

Something in Judith's manner caused Lambert to be on his guard. The light in his deep gray eyes quickly quenched. "Miss Beaufort," he said politely. He bowed.

The gesture struck Judith as slightly distant. Perhaps Lambert feared being seen and overheard. She greeted him in kind. "You have come to see my uncle?" she asked.

"That, and other things."

"What other things?"

Lambert was suddenly wary. He had not imagined their meeting to be quite like this. In fact, he had hoped—almost assumed—that she would meet him *outside* the castle, either before or after his visit with her uncle and be prepared to flee with him. What ailed her? "That, of course, remains to be seen."

"My unclc is a very rich man," she said.

His caution deepened. "Indeed, he is."

"And you, sir?" she asked. "Are you in need of money?"

"A man in my position," Lambert bantered lightly, "always needs money."

All Judith's doubts and insecurities seized on what she took to be an admission. "Does money figure among 'the other things' that you have come for?"

He had come, quite simply, to take her away. Lambert was confused. Had she reverted to following her uncle's rules and regulations after only a few days? Had she changed her mind about running away with him? Being a passionately impulsive man himself, he had not seriously considered the possibility that she would be so constrained. It seemed now that she regretted her strong impulses at Whitehall. He hardly wished to look the fool.

"What do you think I have come for?" he returned.

The conversation was going awry. He was confessing to nothing. Judith was suddenly anxious and impatient. "Have you come to bargain for this?" she inquired. Her voice had come out a little breathless in fear of what his answer might be.

She had withdrawn her hand from the folds of her skirts. In it she was holding up the parchment she had retrieved from the painting. She had repaired the Vatican's large seal which she had broken and was holding the letter so that Lambert might see the impression left by the papal ring in the red smear of wax.

"And what might that be?" he inquired coolly.

"The parchment from the Vatican," she answered, her voice wavering, her hand shaking slightly. "The one you suspected was there all along. I have it, as you see. It's worth a lot of money . . . to someone."

"To myself, for instance?"

"Why, yes, to yourself." Judith was realizing in one horrible, continuous unfolding of a second, that she was making a mistake. She tried to repair it. "You are not a rich man, I believe—"

One of Lambert's mobile brows arched.

"—and something compelling must have brought you back to England after all these years," she dared to continue, feeling herself sinking deeper into an ugly morass. "Perhaps you wished to bargain for this, or perhaps to . . . to coerce my uncle into paying you to keep quiet about the message from the Vatican?"

Both Lambert's brows were now raised.

"But that won't be necessary," she said quickly. "I'm a rich woman." He knew that. Then why did it feel so terrible to her to say it? "If it's money you want . . ." she began but stopped short of openly accusing him of using her to get to her wealth.

She did not have to state it. It was clear enough. After a moment, he said, without emotion, "What remarkably ignoble motives you attribute to me."

"You can't . . . you *can't* be offended!" she said quickly.

"Offended? No." He almost laughed. "Confused. Yes. What are *your* motives, Miss Beaufort, in telling me all this?"

She gestured with the parchment for emphasis. "So that there are no mistakes! From the beginning! If we were . . . to go off together, I would want you to know where you stand! I would want you to know that *I* know you need money, but that I have more than enough for the both of us!"

Lambert's brows had snapped together, and his eyes had narrowed. Was she using the parchment and his possible interest in it as a club over his head? Had she confused him with George Beecham? Did she think him so submissive? Did she think he would like life under her thumb?

"No mistakes," he said. "I see."

However, Miss Perfect had made a mistake. A fatal mistake. In his feelings for her, Lambert had suppressed the fact that she was the niece of Somerset. He had seen her strength and intelligence and had thought her cured of her blind obedience to a man who was at best a rigid authoritarian and at worst a ruthless murderer. He had believed that Judith had committed her flesh and blood to him. Now he realized that her flesh had been long since molded by her uncle whose poison ran in her veins. She was more than Henry Somerset's niece: She was his spiritual daughter. A skillful manipulator. A feminine tyrant. A bargainer for his body and soul. A strong, intelligent, beautiful woman, but one who knew nothing of whimsy or caprice or giving or love.

He had had no use for Somerset fifteen years ago, and he had no use for his niece now.

Lambert's next words confirmed Judith's dawning realization that she had drastically overplayed her hand. He shook his head slowly, his eyes never leaving her face. "In my far from illustrious career," he said, cool and dignified, "I have played the part of many a creature." His glance was sharp, and it cut her. "But never the four-legged variety who sits up and begs." He bowed. It was an uncivil gesture. "You have mistaken your man."

He turned on his heels and left her.

Stunned and humiliated, Judith stood there. She had thrown herself at him, and he had refused her. It seemed that she had been right all along: He had not come to Raglan for her. With the part of her brain that could function, she supposed that he went to the gallery for whatever it was he wanted to see her uncle about. However, she was never to know, for she had no control over her limbs and had seemingly forgotten how to walk. She stood there, shivering. Some time later, she was aware that Lambert passed by again. She glimpsed him depart on his horse and heard the thundering of hooves across the bridge over the moat. The shadows lengthened, and the lights of the day went out.

Her uncle left early the next morning, and as he had predicted, Judith did not see him again before his departure. She was not to learn what business, if any, had been transacted with Lambert.

The next week passed miserably.

Then Caroline received a message from Court, a gay, gossipy letter from Lucy, Countess of Carlisle. "Oh, lovely! Judith," Caroline chirped one morning, "listen to this!"

They were in the Solar. Judith was busy with some castle matter or another, and Edith was separating her embroidery threads. Caroline had been idle and dreamy, until the arrival of the letter.

"It's about Charles Lambert," Caroline continued happily. "You know him, do you not?"

Judith did not look up. Nor did she need to prompt her cousin to read on, for Caroline needed no prompting.

"Lucy says here that Charles Lambert, yes, uncle of James—James was a *dear* boy but rather unsteady," Caroline opined. "Anyway, Charles Lambert is reported to be paying court to the lovely Elizabeth Marston. Do you know her, Judith? I wouldn't think so. Well! Her father is head of the Merchant Adventurers Company. And it says here that Charles Lambert's pursuit is very assiduous." Caroline scanned further. "Although Elizabeth Marston has no title, of course, Lucy reports that no one is quite pronouncing the word 'mismatch' because the lady is so very beautiful and because Charles Lambert had the reputation of being extravagantly expensive in his youth and does not seem to have any more money now than he did years ago." Caroline put the letter down. "Now, what do you think of that?"

What Judith thought was that she had not felt so bereft, so sad, so forlorn since the moment of learning the cruel death of her happy, laughing mother. She had not felt so angry, so bitter, so helpless since having been delivered, at the tender age of five, into her uncle's cold care and the strict, censorious household of Raglan Castle. The hurt and anger she had buried nearly twenty years ago were suddenly vibrant and fresh, as fresh as yesterday, as fresh as torn flesh still bleeding. And into that raw wound twenty years ago, her uncle had thrust his gilded needle. He had sewn her gut and laced it tightly.

During the next few days, Judith indulged savage thoughts. The sky had turned a summer's overcast with the approach of August. The gray furrowed patterns of clouds appeared to her as spilled brain matter. With the sun blotted out from the sky, she imagined the gray expanse in a wash of red. She spent more than the usual time in the kitchens, overseeing the skinning and gutting of the catches from Somerset Park. She savored the sight and smell of the blood and offal from the eviscerated animals. She spent many long hours in Raglan's justly famous gallery, gazing at her uncle's latest acquisition, the painting of *Judith Slaying Holofernes* and lost in profound admiration of the biblical Judith's arms, the sword she held, the cobalt of her dress, the carmine of her maidservant's, the deeper red of Holofernes' spurting blood.

An inferior composition by an inferior painter? Hah! It was a defiantly brilliant work—but not a man's work. Even the great Orazio Gentileschi would have been incapable of such a representation. No, it was a woman's creation, that of Orazio's daughter, and Judith imagined that it had been composed when Artemisia Gentileschi had been young, possibly unmarried and undoubtedly disgraced—by a man. It was a chilling, violent representation, but there was more, for mere violence, after all, was a convention of the great art gracing Raglan and the Stuart Court. This *Judith* offended and shocked in its portrayal of unthinkable violence, the murder of a man by a woman, unredeemed by hesitation, distaste, or fear. Artemisia had uncovered beneath the biblical story a lawless reality too horrible for men to contemplate. Holofernes was not just an evil patriarch who threatened the weak, feminized Israel. He was Everyman. Judith and her maidservant were, together, the most dangerous, the most fearsome forces on earth for man: women in control of his fate.

The Judith of flesh and blood relished the painting, was enwrapped in it and unable to distinguish herself from it. *She* was the Judith of the feminine arms clutching the sword, spilling the blood, and severing the head from its masculine body. *She* was the heroine, strong and disobedient, who risked her life for freedom. *She* was the woman who bent her arms into the task without flinching or looking away.

On these occasions, Judith would sigh deeply and wonder: Whose head was it that she wished to carry out of the tent in a basket?

Chapter
18

JUDITH was able to answer her bloodthirsty question a
few days later and in a most unusual way.

She was seated in the Solar, mercilessly attacking the
household accounts, slaying numbers with the point of her
pen. Her only happiness was that Lord Henry was gone and
that she need maintain no mask of obedience before him.
Rogue, faithful hound, lounged at her feet. Edith had
learned, in one painful episode this week, to be quiet.

Judith's attention was claimed by a distant, muffled sound
that resembled a muted explosion. She glanced up from her
work. Ears cocked, Rogue whimpered. Judith rose and
crossed to the open window and looked down into the Stone
Court. There she saw a noisy tangle of human bodies and
castle dogs making its way toward the wide stone staircase
that led to the Solar.

Moments later, an excited throng consisting of three
bodies and several dogs tumbled into the room.

The words "Miss Judith! Miss Judith!" rose above the
barking, along with a babble that vaguely resembled "The
tower!" "It's the Devil!" "Lord Edward is gone, just when
we need him most!" "I've been to chapel every day this
week and have not sinned in a month!" and "Raglan will be
washed away before the day is done!" and "Water!"

Rogue was contributing his most enthusiastic, high-pitched yelps to the canine conversation. Judith quieted the animals who were happy to obey a well-loved mistress. She next stemmed the tide of human confusion with an astringent, "Owen and Marshall, hush! Let Llewellyn speak!"

Llewellyn, a canny black-haired Welshman, pushed past his cohorts and said simply, "Melin-Y-Gwent is filling with water fast. It's the waterworks. The boiler burst."

Owen, the most God-fearing of the group, was not easily silenced. "It's a flood!" he cried in dark, portentous tones. "It's a judgment on us all!"

These words had the unfortunate effect of putting the less God-fearing but generally timorous Marshall into a quake; of provoking Edith into one of her most disjointed series of exclamations which borrowed amply from Owen's pronouncements of "The Devil!" and of causing Llewellyn to wag an accusatory finger at Owen and to say, "Aye, it's a judgment! On you! It was your job to have repaired the boiler last week!"

Pandemonium threatened in earnest. Perceiving words to be of no avail, Judith efficiently dealt with the situation by grabbing Llewellyn's arm and pulling him toward the door. She had often entertained thoughts of the magnificent disaster that would happen when one of Edward's inventions went awry, but in her wildest imaginings she had never thought that Edward himself would not be there to fix it. Since the task of repairing the mess had plainly fallen on her, she reckoned that she needed at least one able-bodied man and all her wits. For the first time since her disastrous meeting with Lambert, she felt the poisons of anger and regret festering in her veins ease and ooze away.

Judith had the presence of mind to turn and to command the other three who were following after her, "The rest of you, Edith, Owen, and Marshall! Stay here! Tend to the dogs! I'll be back when I can!"

"But, no, mistress! We're coming with you!" Edith wailed. "You need our help!"

Thinking fast, Judith said, "Right! You can help me most by going to the Chapel and *praying*!"

Judith's suggestion found a welcome audience. She left the room then with Llewellyn in tow and descended the stairs with all due haste.

"How bad is it, Llewellyn?" she asked when they were halfway down the stairs.

"Oh, aye, it's praying we need, miss," he answered with the suggestion of a smile.

"And the Chapel is also the *farthest* point from the Tower," she remarked with an answering smile. "If the disaster is as bad as I fear, I will need no distractions! Now, is the Tower going to crumble into the moat?"

"No, ma'am, surely not," was Llewellyn's reassuring response. "Not today, at least."

Nevertheless, Judith had some indication of the magnitude of the event when she reached the bottom of the stairs. The rest of the castle dogs had gathered there, barking frantically and vying for her attention.

"Dear me!" she said and shooed the dogs. "Not now, you naughty creatures!" Then she lifted her skirts above her ankles, and with Llewellyn, ran across the Stone Court and under the vaulted archway between the two courtyards. There they skirted the stairway to the cellars and took the wooden steps, two at a time, up to the main fortified wall that rose from the moat. At the wide landing on top, they did not pause for breath. Neither did they stop to speak to any of the Raglan rank and file who had fled to the comparative safety of the castle proper to witness events when it had seemed that the entire Tower was going to explode.

Judith and Llewellyn charged across the drawbridge which gave internal access to the Yellow Tower. Another two flights of wooden stairs led them down into the Tower and to the cellar where stood the boiler. On the way down, Llewellyn grabbed a torch from the wall to light the way, but Judith's eyes had hardly adjusted to the dim light. She was just about to descend the last steps when Llewellyn grasped her arm to pull her back.

When he extended the torch over her shoulder to illuminate the chamber before her, she saw the reason. A smooth pool of water covered the entire floor and lapped up to the top of the bottom step. Across the chamber, which measured not more than seven feet by five feet, stood the boiler, now with a gaping rent in its side.

"Is it dangerous?" Judith inquired cautiously, gesturing to the boiler which was still slobbering benignly.

"The fire underneath it is out," Llewellyn informed her, "and can do no more harm."

Judith rapidly assessed the situation. "There's not but a half foot of water on the chamber floor," she estimated. "The boiler's out. So all we have to do is to pump the water out." She turned to Llewellyn. "It's been an age since I've been down here, but I do recall that Edward installed pumps here, did he not?"

Llewellyn affirmed this by pointing to the far corner of the cell where stood an unlovely snarl of pipes and gears and pistons and valves.

"Then it's not so bad!" Judith pronounced with heartfelt relief. At that, she took off her silk slippers and placed them on a step. "Nothing for it but to crank them up." Not bothering to lift her skirts, she waded into the water which rose above her ankles.

Llewellyn waded in behind her. "There's something you should be knowing, mistress," he said in an ominous voice.

Judith turned, her brows lifted.

"We're below the level of the water in the moat here. There is water still coming in," he explained. "Slowly, but it's still coming."

"Ah."

"Yes, ma'am. It was the young master's idea to build the waterworks below the level of the water, you'll be remembering, so that he would have a continuous supply for the boiler without having to rig more pumps. It has something to do with pressure, I think, but I'm not rightly sure where it is."

Judith waded over to the boiler to inspect. "Pressure?"

Llewellyn cleared his throat. "The young master kept pointing to it when he took me about the nether chambers, explaining everything to me. 'See there, Llewellyn,' he said. 'There's pressure. It's the pressure that moves the water along.' I'm sure that what the young master said, and he kept pointing to it, but I didn't see a thing and I did not like to contradict him!''

"Ah yes, Edward's explanations!'' Judith said knowledgeably. "I myself have heard all about water boilers and the virtues of steam as a mechanical agent. Steam!'' she ejaculated in disgust. "Steam as a mechanical agent! I begin to think my cousin is quite mad!''

To which comment Llewellyn wisely did not respond.

Judith gave the conversation a practical turn by saying, "Well, if you can't tell me where the pressure is, perhaps you can tell me where the water enters the cell.''

"Through the pipes,'' was Llewellyn's unhelpful response.

"I gathered as much,'' she replied. "The question is, how—or where—does the water get into the pipes in the first place?''

Llewellyn was sorry to say that he had not understood *that* part of Lord Edward's explanation either. All he knew was that there was water in the moat where it was supposed to be, water in the pipes where it was supposed to be, and water all over the floor of the cell where it *wasn't* supposed to be.

Judith did not have her cousin's mechanical mind, but she did possess her portion of common sense. Thinking aloud, she said, "Now, if we can pump the water out a little faster than it is coming in, we can avert disaster.'' She paused. "I think.''

Llewellyn coughed into his fist. "The young master was explaining to me before he left last week—just before your return, ma'am—and very proud he was, too, of the idea—to have the water come in faster than he had before. He said he was increasing the pressure. He said it would improve the ability of the boiler to keep the machine working that runs the Stone Fountain. He called it an ex—an ex—'' Llewellyn groped for the words. "—an experience. No. An . . . experiment!''

"I see. Well, that does sound remarkably like Edward's version of a good idea. However, for the experiment to work, the boiler must also be working and, yet, it is not. The water is still coming in,'' she pointed out, ''and we are in trouble.''

''Perhaps if we found the pressure and removed it, the water would stop flowing,'' Llewellyn suggested.

Judith frowned. ''I don't know about that,'' she said. ''The first task seems to be to find the point where the water comes in and to stop it. If we don't, the entire moat could empty into the Tower.''

Standing ankle-deep in water in a cold, dank cell with the water level rising imperceptibly with every passing second, Judith willed herself not to panic. After bursting forth with ''But how am *I* supposed to know anything about this?'' she felt measurably better.

She briefly inspected the cell, Llewellyn in her wake, and asked a few questions, none of which was he able to answer. At Llewellyn's manifest ignorance, Judith finally asked, ''What on earth was in Edward's mind to have you running the boiler all this time while he is gone?''

''The young master said it was good for the pipes to have the water flowing through them continuously,'' Llewellyn explained. ''The master said that nothing could go wrong if we kept the proper fire beneath the boiler.''

''Nothing could go wrong—!?'' Judith exclaimed. ''Unfortunately, I have no time now to curse Edward as he deserves, but I shall certainly do so later, at my leisure! In the meantime, I suggest that you go above and find several men to help you get the pumps to working. Even if water is coming in at a faster rate than you can pump it out, it's still worth the effort to get whatever water we can out of the waterworks. Before you go, though, hand me the torch, if you please.''

Llewellyn did as she requested and turned to go.

''Oh, and if you have difficulty persuading any of them to enter the Tower,'' Judith added, ''I think you can offer them the usual inducements. But use your discretion and don't offer too many coins! That may lead them to think it possible that the Tower might blow up—which I devoutly hope is not likely!''

Llewellyn nodded understanding and sloshed his way out of the cell and up the stairs. Judith was left to look about her in a watery blackness relieved only by the pool of light cast by the torch she held overhead. She expelled her breath at length and looked down. The water seemed to have risen a little more up her calves in the few minutes she had been there.

"Don't panic," she muttered to herself, peering into the various corners of the cell. "Don't panic. That's a good girl. It's a simple matter of stopping the water from coming in. All I have to do is stop it. The pumps will be working in a few minutes, and all I have to do is—"

She had reached the fourth corner of the cell and discovered a low archway leading, evidently, into another cell. She knew there was a series of chambers in the waterworks, although she had never before explored them and had only visited the present cell on several occasions, years ago. Stretching her torch out before her, she bent down to see through the archway. There was a hallway, at the end of which she could scarcely discern another archway, most likely leading to another cell.

She had no choice but to take the hallway. She hesitated, however, for it seemed that she would have to take several steps down into deeper water. She was afraid, and then she thought of the wonderful *Judith* painting and took heart. But she was no heroine, she thought with a wry twist to her lips.

She plunged resolutely down the steps. The water quickly swirled above her knees. Once in the passageway, she pushed her way through the water that was moving perceptibly in the direction of the boiler room. At the other end of the hallway, she climbed as many as ten steps and found herself in shallower waters.

At the top of the stairs she discovered a second cell. Although it was much larger than the one where the crippled boiler stood, the vaulted ceiling of this room was so low that Judith's head brushed the ceiling stones. To Judith's right, along one wall, stretched a bewildering maze of metal wheels with teeth like combs that intermeshed one with another. The wheels were lying horizontally and formed a zigzag line across the room, beginning with the smallest wheel nearest Judith and ending with the largest wheel at the opposite wall of the cell.

Judith headed across the room to inspect the line of wheels but tripped and nearly fell headlong into the water when her foot stubbed against a pipe on the floor which had been obscured from her view under several inches of water. One or two more experimental steps informed her that the floor of the room was crisscrossed with pipes. The water was only a few inches deep in this cell, but Judith could see, by the water rippling over the pipes, that the water was moving away from her and down in the direction of the boiler room. She surmised that the water coming into the waterworks was entering from somewhere directly ahead of her.

Because of the hazard of the pipes, her progress across the cell was slow and when she reached the end of the toothed wheels, she saw that they continued their zigzag line down a little passageway that was too small and narrow for a human being to explore. She craned her neck as far down that passageway as possible but could not see the end of it. She could, however, see that water was flowing in through it.

She thought a moment and turned back around. She picked her way carefully back to the archway through which she had entered this cell so that she stood in front of the smallest of the wheels. This last wheel was fitted with a handle sticking straight up from its outer rim. Judith gripped it and moved it experimentally. She turned it a half circle, exerting very little effort, and was surprised to see each successively larger wheel move in turn. Emboldened, she turned the little wheel again, completing one or two circles. Hardly had she completed a third circle when a perceptible gush of water came into the cell, rushing across the floor past her knees and down the steps. For a wild moment, it seemed likely that she would drown.

Seized by panic, Judith attempted to undo the damage she had just caused. With both hands she reached out to grasp the handle on the little wheel and consequently dropped her torch at her feet where it sizzled and fizzled in the rushing water. She paid no attention to the utter blackness and concentrated instead on turning the handle furiously in the opposite direction. She completed a dozen turns of the crank before the wheel would turn no more, at which moment she heard a decisive noise which echoed eerily for several moments.

Then silence. She looked about her but saw nothing, of course, since she had no more light. She was aware, however, that water was no longer rushing in. She also had the distinct impression that it had stopped moving all together and was standing still, suggesting that she had dammed the point of entry of the water from the moat to the cells.

The immediate danger past, Judith stood, transfixed, images washing over her just as the water had done; images of events rushing together, threatening to wash her away. There was the rainstorm in Somerset Park; the visit from Lady Beecham when Lambert and Sir George had tumbled out of her bedchamber in a disaster of embarrassment; the pleasant drowning she had experienced at The Red Bull Theater in Lambert's arms; the tight embrace in the alcove when Lambert's life, and hers, had been in true danger; their flight through the silvery gardens; Lambert's climb to her bedchamber where she had thought, pressed to him fully, that the great tide of warm, tangy saltwater would finally engulf her, submerge her, drown her and happily so; her uncle's brutal banging on her door; the realization that she had dramatically misinterpreted Lambert's reasons for coming to Raglan and that she had disastrously misplayed the scene with him in the courtyard.

Rebellion clamored deep within her, and anger filled her. Suddenly her invisible stays and spiritual harness burst. Her inner lacings snapped to unravel, irretrievably. Her nausea vanished. She felt steady and rock-solid. She knew what was right. She knew what was good. She knew what she needed, and it was not her uncle's approval or protection or clutching love.

Of her uncle, she uttered, aloud, "He has played me for a

fool." Her words echoed back at her. They rang with conviction.

Of Elizabeth Marston, she exclaimed, "She can't have him!"

In the pitch of the cell, her blood flowing fresh, her thoughts cleansed and cleared by this strange scare in the depths of Edward's godforsaken waterworks and standing knee-deep in water, a dazzling idea flooded her brain.

"And I know just how to get him!"

Chapter
19

JUDITH'S liberation in the dark, dank cell of Raglan's waterworks was swift, thorough, and irreversible. She was free. She had lifted, metaphorically speaking, the biblical Judith's sword and severed in one blow the thick cords that had tethered her all these years to Raglan and her uncle's regimen.

She would burn her bridges, and there would be no going back. She knew it. She foresaw all the difficulties ahead of her, and she was undeterred. She would depart and never look back. She might have felt less joyous had she known that civil war would soon sweep the country into an orgy of fanaticism and bloodshed on all sides. She might have felt less exultant had she known that her uncle would suffer and die for his loyalties and that her mechanically minded cousin Edward would spend the greater part of his adulthood in prison. She might have felt a pang to leave her splendid home had she known that it would become a principal royalist center and be the first castle to fortify itself for the king and the last to surrender. She might have spared a backward look at Raglan in all its grandeur had she known that within a few years it would lie in waste, plundered and looted, never to be reoccupied or restored.

She might have felt differently, but not necessarily, for her emotions now unlaced and unleashed were passionate and uncompromising; and, to be sure, neither she nor anyone else in the realm had foreknowledge of the magnitude of the tragedy that would soon engulf the nation and cause the king to lose his head.

Judith's resolve was firm, her preparations calm, even methodical. The curious, liberated spirit that moved and breathed behind her eyes was not the same one that had held center stage the month before, or even the day before. Outwardly, however, the old Judith was still firmly in place. She had certainly learned enough of the art of acting to maintain, for the few days it took her to execute her plans, a role that she herself had perfected over the years.

Not a gesture or a word betrayed the new Judith to Edith or to Caroline or to anyone else in the Castle. Judith would have been gratified (though not at all surprised) to have learned, the morning after her escape when her absence at Raglan became noticed and confirmed, that not a soul was able to account for this extraordinary phenomenon: not Edith who cried at incoherent length that all the dresses still hung in her mistress's wardrobe save the one she had been wearing the day before and who was prone to blame the work of malevolent fairies; not Caroline who offered the neat pile of Judith's handsomely written wedding invitations as evidence of the fact that Judith had no intention of eloping (not that Sir George was likely to have conceived or executed such a romantic plan) and who wondered anxiously what Judith's disappearance would do to her own plans to marry; not Sir Robert who threw open the doors of the stables in the Fountain Court to demonstrate that all the Somerset horses were in their stalls, even Barbary.

And when, several days later, the wherry that Judith had used to transport herself across the moat in the dead of night was discovered hidden under the bridge, still no one guessed that the little boat had done anything more than strayed from its moorings. Even when Downy Don was reported missing from the village, no one guessed that he had fled with Miss Judith from the Castle. Since Downy Don was the stupidest and brawniest young man for miles around, there was no telling what notion might have led him to stray away. It was generally agreed that he would turn up sooner or later.

Simply no one would have credited the idea that Judith had roused Downy Don from his childlike slumber in the wee hours of the morning and invited him to escort her to London. Downy Don had never been to London, and he was not sure that he wanted to go now. He was not precisely sure what London *was*, but after Miss Judith explained to him that he was soon to have a job at a theater where he would see many fine and funny plays and laugh a lot, he was persuaded that the idea was a good one. He had never intended refusing his mistress, anyway, and he certainly did not balk at the prospect of having to accomplish the first part of the journey on foot, nor did it even occur to him that this was an odd way to begin such an adventure.

After several days (by which time Judith and Downy Don had got as far east as Trellich and Judith thought it safe enough to procure two horses with one of the lesser jewels from her mother's legacy which she had kept hidden and treasured away all these years and taken with her from the castle), the combined rank of Raglan determined that Somerset must be notified of his beloved niece's mysterious disappearance. It would be difficult; his lordship would be sorely grieved.

Judith had known from the start that her uncle would have to be informed, eventually; however, far from imagining him despondent, she was the only one to predict correctly his reaction to the extraordinary news that his niece had vanished off the face of the earth. She imagined that he would hunt her down in London, and she knew that if she valued her life and Lambert's, she would have to work fast.

Judith did not let up the pace, nor did her resolve waver, and the journey was consequently rough and uncomfortable. Still, Judith's spirits did not flag. The rigors of this new way of life affected her only to the extent that she realized that from now on she would pretty well have to get used to them, and Downy Don traveled without complaint.

Her arrival in London early one morning was far less dignified than it had been less than a month ago in July.

What it lacked in dignity, it more than made up for in appeal. After she and Downy Don had stabled their horses at a foul-smelling posting inn and were making their way to the hamlet of Clerkenwell, she discovered that she was far less annoyed by the jockeying and jostling in the crowded streets and unsanitary alleys than she had been on her last visit to the same locale. The stew that was working London suddenly struck her as pleasing, almost appetizing, and she wondered, idly, if one could readjust aesthetically to poverty, if not outright squalor, given enough time.

Making her way down St. John's Street, Judith experienced her first qualms since standing knee-deep in water in the nether cell of the Yellow Tower at Raglan. She quickly suppressed them. A thousand difficulties arose in her mind, and real fear overtook her until she remembered, with a kind of dazed relief, that the old Judith who was used to unquestioning command could solve those thousand difficulties and more. And how did she know that there would not be other, undiscovered and equally useful selves who had dwelled, bound, inside of her all these years?

Soon enough she stood in front of The Red Bull Theater and was gazing up at the banner proclaiming the day's performance. In real delight she recognized it to be one of Henry Webster's confections. She was in luck. She smiled broadly at Downy Don who stood behind her and motioned him to follow her around to one of the theater's side entrances. At that door a most dissipated-looking man stood sentry.

Far from being undone by his seamy mien and demeanor, Judith uttered not a word of her intention to enter but simply froze the man with a regard that was worthy of Judith Beaufort, the niece of Henry Herbert, Lord Somerset, fifth Earl of Worcester.

It worked like a charm. The man fell back. Judith snapped her fingers for Downy Don to follow her, and the two of them ducked behind the dirty woolen curtain that was held aside for them.

Judith had a hazy recollection of the backstage intricacies of theater. She made her way through the darkness of the central hallway, heading toward the voices coming from the stage where evidently a rehearsal for the afternoon's performance was in progress.

She stepped onto the apron stage in time to witness a fine-boned figure standing at the center, his breeches stuffed carelessly in his boots, his doublet hanging awry, gesturing with ink-stained fingers and exclaiming, "No, you dolt! My great lines should scan: 'I want that glib and oily art/ To speak and purpose not.'"

My first entrance! Judith thought. She took a deep breath, squared her shoulders, and swept out from the shadows and into the sunlight of the stage, saying brightly, "Mr. Webster, give you good day!" She nodded and greeted the players. "Tom. Allan. And Robin. Ah. Play you a man today? Very handsome!" She turned back to the playwright, glib-tongued herself. "How pleasurable it is to come to The Red Bull and to hear the players rehearsing with lines from *Lear*!" She smiled and added, "I fear that I had not fully appreciated those lines—or the play—until this very moment! But tell me: Are you not readying yourselves for this afternoon's performance of your comedy *The Widow's Lament*?"

Judith's entrance and her speech were dramatic enough to halt the rehearsal. Mr. Webster gaped momentarily before replying with chilly dignity, "Miss Beaufort. I might inform you that *my* lines are entirely original—" but his defense of this latest piece of theatrical larceny was swallowed in his subsequent exclamation, "Eeek! It's a monster!"

At that, Downy Don, who had been agreeably ambling behind his mistress and was also now standing onstage, turned to look behind him in alarm. "Monster!" Downy Don cried. "Monster!" He threw himself at his mistress's feet, grabbing onto her knees and nearly toppling her in the process.

Mr. Webster, Tom, Robin, and Allan watched, immobile and wide-eyed, as Judith swayed. By some miracle, she remained standing, and when she had her balance, she surprised the troupe by breaking into a delighted laugh and turning to help the monster to his feet. "No, Don!" she soothed. "There is no monster! They were funning you! It's a joke!"

"Oh, a joke," Don repeated obediently but doubtfully. He essayed a laugh. It rumbled eerily. "A joke."

Something in this extraordinary exchange prompted the players to rally around Judith and the monster, offering support and greeting and curiosity in their mixed exclamations of "Miss Beaufort, is that really you?" and "The master told us we would not be seeing you again!" and "From *Lear*? So *that*'s where I'd heard those lines before!" and "I hardly recognized you at first, so changed you are, Miss Beaufort!"

"It's to be Judith henceforth, if you please," she offered and replied to the last of the exclamations first. "Yes, indeed, I am *very* travel-stained," she acknowledged, "after so many days on the road." She touched her disheveled curls and displayed her dirty dress. "I am in great need of repair, although I confess that I have never been happier!"

It was true, and it was Judith's changed countenance and not her rumpled aspect that was responsible for her altered appearance. No one had an opportunity to develop that interesting subject, for Will, who had been deep in a very successful flirtation with a serving wench from The Old Dun Cow, was drawn from the shadowy wings by the commotion onstage. He entered at that moment and demanded in blunt surprise, "Miss Beaufort! What are you doing here?"

Judith smiled at him and answered the question that was uppermost in everyone's mind. "I am come in search of the trunk."

"The trunk?"

"The trunk with the women's clothing. The costumes," she clarified. "You remember! The one you had with you the day I met you! I will be needing some men's clothing as well—a variety, in fact, to cover all contingencies. Can you help me?"

Will was understandably confused. "Costumes?"

"Yes," Judith said, "I mean to take up the theater. Only temporarily! Lambert always said that I would have a gift

for comedy, and I mean to show him as soon as possible!''
Judith looked about her. ''Is he, by chance, here?''

Will frowned. ''Have you not heard?''

The words *too late!* flashed through Judith's mind, momentarily stopping her heart. She pulled herself together.
The risk had been there from the beginning, she reminded
herself, and she had burned her bridges. ''About Elizabeth
Marston, you mean?'' she inquired calmly, determined to
carry off her rôle at all costs.

Will nodded slowly.

''Has he married her?'' Judith asked. She was pleased
that her voice betrayed none of the cold fear that clutched
her.

''No, ma'am,'' he replied, ''but it's as near a thing as
ever I've known with him, for I've never seen him in the
grip of temper as what he returned last week from Wales,
and so I'm thinking—'' Will broke off, unwilling, or unable, to complete the thought.

''Exactly,'' Judith said. ''It appears that we've no time to
lose. Will you help me?''

While Will considered the request, the others went to
retrieve the trunk, the search party headed by Mr. Webster
who claimed to know just where it was.

''How can I help you?'' Will replied finally.

''By telling me first where Elizabeth Marston lives,''
Judith answered directly. ''Is Lambert there presently, paying
her court?''

His brow lowered. ''The master's not expecting to see
you.''

''So he *is* there!'' Judith said, satisfied. ''And, no, he is
not expecting to see me or, rather, he is not expecting to see
the female character who is soon to appear on the lovely
Elizabeth's doorstep.'' To Will's doubt and hesitation, the
old Judith smiled her Queen of the Castle smile and said
authoritatively, ''Well, I am glad to have that settled. Now,
on to more essential matters. Downy Don,'' she continued
smoothly, ''I might ask you to—''

Before she could complete her request, Mr. Webster
wandered back out onstage, followed by Allan and Dick

who bore the trunk in question on their stout shoulders. "Here it is, Miss Beaufort, as you requested, but I really must ask you," the playwright said, referring to Judith's gentle monster, "who—or what—is *that*?"

Judith turned back to the playwright. "Your new stage-hand!" she informed him. "A professional troupe such as yours should not have to carry its properties or costumes from theater to theater. Now, let me see if you have what I am looking for," she murmured as she knelt down to lift the thongs of the trunk that had been deposited at her feet. She began to rummage.

"A stagehand?" the playwright repeated.

"Indeed, and I have brought him all the way from Wales in order to serve you," Judith explained, looking up from her task. "Downy Don thinks that working in the theater will be great fun! Don't you, my dear?"

"Do I, ma'am?" Downy Don inquired, secure in the knowledge that his mistress would answer all difficult questions for him.

"Does he?" the playwright echoed, still skeptical.

"Of course he does," Judith answered brightly.

Will was not the canniest man alive, but he was able to perform simple sums and found a satisfactory answer when he added the fit of ungoverned passion that had ruled his master this week to Miss Beaufort's sudden appearance at The Red Bull. "You brought him with you all the way from Wales, you say?" Will asked. "And would it be a difficulty to return him there?"

Judith smiled congenially. "A great difficulty," she acknowledged. "Impossible, in fact! Ah! Here they are!" she exclaimed and held up the items of clothing that she had been looking for. In her search through the trunk, she had also found a lady's tapestry bag and into this ratty pouch she stuffed the selected items of clothing.

Will blinked. "Never *that*, ma'am!" he protested.

"*Exactly* that!" Judith stated, rising from her knees and slipping the handles of the tapestry bag onto her wrist. "Now for your help, Will. Your immediate task is to escort me to a bath! I'm in great need of one. Should you like one, too?''

Since Will had as great an aversion to bathing as his master did to blood, a look of mute horror came over his face, and he took several involuntary steps backward.

Judith laughed, crossed to his side, and linked her arm in his, saying, "But not a Turkish bath, mind. I've a preference to water over steam. Let us try a bagnio and hope that they have already set the fires under the barrels!" With Will in tow, she exited on the lines, cast over her shoulder to the assembled troupe who was gaping at her in lively astonishment, "I shall return after the bath. In the meanwhile, you may dig up the men's costumes, for I've a notion that I'll be needing some of those, too! Take good care of Downy Don, and who knows, Mr. Webster, but that he might not provide you with inspiration for a new character in your next play!"

She and Will left then, followed by the calls of encouragement from the troupe and the speculations of the playwright.

"A new character?" Mr. Webster mused, regarding Downy Don thoughtfully. "Well, I might make him a hunchback and have him fall in love with a perfect angel of a woman and have him carry her off— No," he said, shaking his head. "That won't work. Let me see . . . he could grow to truly monstrous proportions and cause mayhem in the City of London, leaving death and destruction in his path— No," he said again, waving the idea away. "Too farfetched. There must be some perfect role for a— A *gatekeeper*!" he exclaimed, suddenly struck. "Say, *there's* an idea! A half-witted gatekeeper." Mr. Webster smiled with great satisfaction. "I," he pronounced, "am a genius."

On the way to the bath, Judith engaged Will in a most fascinating and highly satisfactory conversation. It was a fortunate thing that Judith learned all she needed to know from that conversation, for on the way back from the bath, Will was not speaking to her.

Clean and confident and properly cloaked, Judith left The Red Bull some time later with her tapestry bag bulging. Will had recovered his temper and had accompanied her to Covent Garden. He left her in front of the arcade before a tall house on the "piazza," extremely fashionable in its lack of ornamentation, save for the flat stone pilasters and the first floor which faced the street with an open, vaulted, and arched loggia.

"Here we are," Will said cautiously, still a bit apprehensive about what Miss Beaufort had in mind and what his master would have to say about it.

"Here we are," Judith repeated cheerfully, her heart suddenly beating with excitement and the desire to get on with the show. She gazed up at the house and fell into character. "Oooh!" she cooed. "It's a lovely establishment. Why, it's almost a palace!" She turned to smile saucily at Will. "And thank you, dearest Will, for all your help!" She leaned forward, grasped his doublet, and pulled him toward her. She kissed him then, in broad daylight, smacking him soundly on both freshly shaven cheeks. "You smell heavenly!" She winked. "Wish me luck!"

"I will."

"And send the message I have given you straight around to Whitehall. Promise?"

"I promise."

"And will I be seeing you again?"

Will's nod was a little watery. Overcome, he was unable to resist winking and kissing her in return. He watched as she trod the stone steps to the front door, plunked her tapestry bag down, and pulled the bell so that it clanged loudly, more than once.

Judith raised a silent prayer to Thespis: *On the body of my mother, let inspiration visit me!*

Presently the front door swung open, and Judith was smiling cheekily up into the face of a senescent steward. *If it isn't Uncle Henry's Sir Albert to the life!* she thought with an inward laugh. Aloud, she said, "I've come to see Charlie Lambert." She covered her mouth with a quick, guilty hand. "*Sir* Charles Lambert," she corrected with a giggle.

The steward looked down at the unescorted young woman on the Marston doorstep with all the speechless indignation that a man of his age and respectability would assume if propositioned by a doxy from the Strand.

Judith's eyes twinkled mischievously, and she wagged an admonishing finger. "Now, don't tell me that he's not here, for I'm a particular friend of his, and I know that he's been giving the Lady Elizabeth his special attention." When the steward did not move or make any other indication that the caller was to enter the fine house, she continued, "And I surely would hate to have to put it about in the piazza— that's a square, you know—that I was not granted the request of speaking a few words with Lady Elizabeth's beau!"

"Who may I ask wishes to speak with him, ma'am?" the steward asked politely on the sheer strength of force of habit.

"Why I'm . . . Charlie's cousin!" she said, adding brightly, as if she'd just thought it, "Yes! His cousin! We're *kissing* cousins, you might say! Tell him it's Judith who's come. Just Judith!"

The steward nodded gravely and stepped back to permit Judith's entry. She picked up her tapestry bag and stepped nimbly across the threshold and into the two-storied entrance hall. She gasped, with eyes popping, and cooed, "Oooh! It's a palace, it is!" Undoing the large buttons that fastened her cloak, she lowered her voice confidentially, "Old Man Marston has the gingerbread, hasn't he?" She nodded wisely. "I hear he's thick with the Mayor Garraway. I know *him* as Hank, of course." With these disclosures, she slid the cloak off her shoulders in a swirl and remarked, "Why I'm sure to like setting my glaziers on Old Man Marston!"

To this vulgar comment the steward was incapable of reply, for the effect of Judith's toilette had struck him dumb. She had chosen for the occasion the theatrical costume cut from a loud purple figured velvet that she had worn the evening she had first spent with Lambert at Speke Hall. Its hue was all the more overpowering in the daylight, and she had increased the garishness of the costume with a stomacher of ruby red. A strand of her mother's garnets was all that covered the immodest expanse of alabaster bosom she displayed.

She fluffed her puffed sleeves and twitched her bodice as if to pull it up but succeeded only in lowering it another perilous fraction of an inch. "Never fear," she whispered to the steward with a wink, "I've got what it takes to keep it up."

When she made as if to nudge him, the steward shook himself of his immobility and bade Miss Judith to follow him across the elegant entrance hall to the Great Hall at the center of the house. Down the stairs that led from the far end of the Great Hall to the Long Gallery she saw three figures descending as she was ushered in and "announced" as the cousin of Sir Charles Lambert.

Judith stepped into the room and waited in all her garish splendor for the three people making their way down the stairs and across the room. Judith spared a brief glance for Lady Elizabeth and was relieved that this very beautiful woman did not recognize her. She mentally thanked her uncle for having prevented her being introduced to Miss Marston at the Banqueting House. She did not even glance at Lambert at all, for fear that if she met his eyes now she might spoil her entire plan. She ogled instead "Old Man Marston" with what could only be described as venal speculation. Judith weighed a delicate point: Would it be overacting to smack her lips? She decided that it would.

Upon their approach, Judith curtsied low, causing the two gentlemen to wonder if she was going to fall out of her bodice. She did not, but bobbled up pertly and, looking the master of the house unblushingly in the eye, said, "Please to make your acquaintance, your lordship, sir!" She turned to the Beauty. "And you, ma'am, too, I'm sure!" Then to Lambert, she said boldly, "Charlie! You weren't expecting to see me, were you? Just a social call!" and before he could adequately respond to that, she rolled her eyes and sent him a look that conveyed the ill-concealed message: *I've something of great importance to discuss with you!*

"Miss Judith," Master Marston greeted in return and

looked to his guest for explanation. "Sir Charles?" he asked with an expression torn between curiosity and pain.

Lambert's face gave nothing away. "Perhaps I might have a word with my, er, cousin?" he replied to this and took Judith by the elbow and led her a few steps away. "And now, dear cousin?" he began, holding her a little roughly.

Judith met Lambert's eye with a laughing one of her own and said, in a plainly audible stage whisper, "I'm not up the spout this time—not *pregnant!*—if that's what you're thinking, Charlie!" She shifted her glance back and forth, as if not wanting anyone to overhear her. "It's just a little matter of *business*—a painting that you said you were wanting." She attempted to shake her elbow free of his hand and turned back to the understandably astonished father and daughter and said, "But I wouldn't want to be taking you from your amusements here, Charlie, and it's a rudeness to speak when others can't hear, and that's the truth!"

"I have one word to say to you," Lambert murmured into her ear in true sotto voce, "and that is 'outrageous.' " He let her elbow go and stepped out of her stage space, apparently deciding to give her room to play the scene as she chose. He took up a position behind Master Marston and wore an expression that suggested that he was prepared to enjoy her performance. Judging from the look in his eye as he surveyed her in that dress, Lambert found much to enjoy.

"So!" Judith said with a blinding smile for the man of the house. Her expression was expectant of the hospitality she assumed would be forthcoming.

Judith looked about her to take a seat and was about to flounce into a chair, when Elizabeth Marston said in the sweetest voice imaginable, "Won't you be seated, Miss Judith?"

"I don't mind if I do," Judith replied happily, finding a nearby chair, seating herself and bobbling unselfconsciously as she did so. She looked up, and her face fell. "But I'm the only one? Won't you be seated, too, Miss Elizabeth?" When Miss Marston took a seat, more from astonishment than any considerations of courtesy, Judith bent a smile on her and said, "Well, now, that is very fine, and it's a kindness you're showing me, with me so ill at ease and in such fine company!"

"And you are Sir Charles's cousin?" Master Marston made as his first attempt, visibly at a loss, for he was hard-pressed to discover anything ill at ease about the expansive young woman before him.

"Why, in a manner of speaking, yes!" she answered. "You see, in the theater, we are all family! And, of course, I've known Charlie for years—since his theater days!"

Judith paused momentarily to interpret the perplexed expressions on the faces of her host and hostess. Miss Marston was looking up at Lambert, her face compounded of longing and incomprehension. *She doesn't deserve him!* Judith thought. *Worse! He would make her miserable inside a month!*

Judith continued cheerfully, "But he hasn't been onstage in a long time, as I'm sure you're knowing, and took up another line of work entirely. But I'm thinking now, of course, that he won't be having to work at all—" Here Judith cast her eyes significantly about the well-appointed room. "—and I'm happy for him, too, that his money worries will soon be over! I've already congratulated him on *that*, but it's a rudeness to mention it, and that's the truth!"

Miss Marston was plainly floundering. "Are you married, Miss Beaufort?" she asked, rather desperate to find an acceptable topic of conversation.

"Married?" Judith echoed, astonished. "Why, no! Why would you think that? I'm an independent lady," she said, fingering the garnets at her throat suggestively.

"But you have some . . . connections to the theater?" Master Marston tried again.

"Yes—that is, no! That is, no, your lordship, sir, not directly," Judith assured him seriously, "although I have met my share of the theater folk, pursuing as I am my independence, if you see what I mean! But let me assure you that I am a respectable lady, and I have never been to France! La! I wouldn't want you to think that Charlie knows what people he shouldn't. Never that! But I do like to sing. Do you care for a ditty?''

Judith rose and fussed with her skirts and her bodice to draw the maximum attention to her amply displayed charms. She took a deep breath and opened her mouth.

"That won't be necessary, my dear!" Master Marston broke in hastily. Completely at sea, he asked, in an echo of his daughter's desperation, "May I offer you some refreshment?"

Judith closed her mouth, a little surprised, but instantly recovered her composure and said gaily, "Why, I don't mind if I do, and isn't *this* a fine establishment?" Still standing, she looked about her, suddenly frowning. She placed her hands on her hips and said, "Say, where is my tapestry bag? Don't anyone move! I have several sets of jewels in there, and my favorite necklace from—" She broke off and cocked a sapient brow at Master Marston. "—but you might be knowing the fine gentleman, and I'm too discreet to divulge his name, I'm sure! Now, about that bag...." Her gaze traveled over to the door where she had deposited it. She beamed and looked back at Master Marston and the lovely Elizabeth, excusing them with her indulgent smile. "*There* it is! It was there all along! Well! Now, about that refreshment?"

Lambert had heard enough. She had made her point, and he was thoroughly seduced. It was time to get her out of the house. And out of that dress. He stepped forward. "Judith," he said, smiling calmly, "perhaps this is the moment to discuss the business you have with me, hmm?"

"It's a private matter," she rebuked him with dignity, "and I'm not wishing to embarrass Master Marston and his daughter with discussion of what's not for public ears."

"Then perhaps we should leave the house."

She easily read his tone but was having too much fun to stop now. "After I've just been offered refreshment from this kind gentleman?" she demanded. She looked over at Master Marston as if she thought him good for a jewel or two and stated her unwavering code of social behavior, "Why, I would never come to a house—especially such a fine house!—and leave just like that! That would be a rudeness, and that's the truth!''

Master Marston rose to the occasion. He quickly seconded Lambert's suggestion. "No, my dear, do not let that weigh with you. You can run along and conduct your, er, business with Sir Charles, and do not give us another thought!"

Judith bestowed on him one of her blinding smiles. "Well, if you're thinking that I won't stand in your bad graces, your lordship, sir, Charlie and I will leave on the instant!"

Lambert bowed to his host and hostess and bid them a correct adieu before taking Judith's elbow in a firm grip and steering her out of the room.

Judith looked back over her shoulder and promised to return. "For I'm sure to be coming to visit often—once Charlie has set up a more permanent residence here!"

Lambert wasted no further time propelling her out of the Great Hall.

"But, no, Charlie," she protested, trying unsuccessfully to break free of his hold, "don't let me forget my bag, now. Stop, will you! Yes, there. Now, I have it. There is really no need to hurry!"

She cast a last, blinding smile over her shoulder and, in interpreting the looks on the faces of Master Marston and his lovely daughter, Judith was confident that she had just performed a great service to the Marston family.

The well-trained steward was already at the front door, holding it open, her cloak across his arm. When she took her coat from that eminently respectable worthy, she could not resist it. Yes, she pinched him on the cheek, saying to Lambert, "He's cute!" and left the house on the carrying words, "Oooh! It's a fine establishment, it is! Almost a palace! Why, you're the luckiest man in the world, Charlie! I'll plan to visit you here often!"

Chapter
20

"**P**UT that cloak on!" Lambert commanded when they were safely outside the house and descending the steps into the street.

"But, Charlie—" Judith protested and got no farther.

Lambert snatched the cloak from Judith's arm and placed it around her shoulders, saying, "You're likely to start a riot in that dress!"

"You didn't like my performance, Charlie?" Judith asked, apparently hurt. Then, batting her eyes, said, "I'd appreciate your professional opinion of my comedy."

"Very broad," he answered dryly. "Now, where's the painting?"

"What painting?"

"The *Judith*, I suppose."

"You do?"

They had crossed under the vaulted arcade and had started across the "piazza." Lambert stopped and looked down at Judith curiously. "Doesn't your coming today have something to do with the painting?"

"Indirectly, you might say," she answered.

"You told me that you had a painting for me. I assumed that you had revised your reading of my motives for wanting the *Judith* and were attempting to demonstrate that your opinion of my character was as high as ever.''

"It was never *high*," Judith reminded him, "but I *am* trying to make amends! However, I don't have the painting for you.''

"Then why did you say so in there?" he inquired, cocking his head back in the direction of the Marston house.

"It was a ploy," she confessed, "to get your interest.''

"It certainly did that!''

"Then it worked," Judith said, with a smile of satisfaction.

Since Lambert was giving all his attention to the strange turns in this conversation, he was not attending to their path through the city. Judith was leading him down a little-used alleyway that wound behind St. Paul's church, and they seemed to be heading in the general direction of the Strand.

"It worked?" Lambert asked. "I suppose it was your intention that I never see Elizabeth Marston again?''

Judith nodded. "That is exactly right," she said, adding confidently, "You certainly will not be seeing her again.'' Before Lambert had an opportunity to fully assimilate Judith's statement, she was on to the next topic. "Oh, good! I wasn't sure whether or not the garden that I saw on the way over from The Red Bull extended this far, but it seems we're in luck." Judith stopped in front of an iron grille leading into one of the many public pleasure gardens and open-air resorts dotting London where the newly emerging leisure class would come for gambling or lounging or drinking or wooing. She pulled the latch. "Let's go through here. This should make a shortcut."

They stepped into an ornamented garden that seemed to be more of an orchard of fruit trees, with lawns and a bowling green. Judith chose the main path, and she and Lambert were immediately surrounded by the warble of bird song and flowering hedgerows of red currants and roses. In the neat beds lining the path were raspberry brambles and vegetables, and the borders were edged with flowers. There were several strolling couples, and a maid or two, going leisurely about her business.

"A shortcut?" Lambert asked. "Where are we going?"

"First, to Clerkenwell," she explained.

"You've had enough theater for one day, I think."

She laughed up at him. "I agree, and we are not bound for The Red Bull, if that's what you're thinking, but for a place of business called The Rose."

Lambert searched his well-informed memory of the vicinity. "That is a posting inn, if I am not mistaken."

"And hardly worthy of the name," Judith averred, wrinkling her nose in memory of the unsanitary conditions.

"An observation unworthy of the remarkably vulgar-Judith who is my cousin," Lambert said with a sly glance.

"Unjust!" Judith protested at once. "She is a woman what loves perfumes and powders, your lordship, sir, and in the course of pursuing her independence, so to speak, she has seen to it that many a well-to-do man has patronized the baths, the Lord Mayor not excepted!"

Lambert laughed at that. "By the way, do you sing?" he asked on a tangent.

"Not a note."

Lambert looked down at her in admiration. "You really were prepared to make a complete fool out of yourself, weren't you? I find your willingness irresistible, and I'm all the more sorry that Master Marston stopped you when he did. That part of the performance would surely have added a finishing touch."

"Well, I *was* hoping for my song to be the, er, low point of the performance," she acknowledged humorously.

"And what do we do at The Rose?" Lambert asked, reverting to the original topic of discussion.

"That's where I've two horses stabled," Judith informed him.

"Ah!" Lambert had taken an increasing delight in the day since first laying eyes on Judith in a toilette that stood at dramatic variance with the Marstons' tasteful Great Hall. "And the horses are taking us . . . where?"

Judith was suddenly serious. "I don't know yet," she said. "Italy, perhaps?"

"Ah, Italy! What a charming idea! And what shall we do in Italy?" he pursued, content to play along.

"We may decide to get married."

"Then my suggestion in your bedchamber at Whitehall found favor with you, after all," he stated, nodding wisely. "This is an elopement."

"No, no, Lambert," Judith corrected, "this is an abduction."

"This is no abduction!" he dismissed scornfully.

"Why not?" Judith fired back.

He gestured about him. "Well, for one, we're on foot and, for another, it's broad daylight!"

"I will admit that you have had more experience with abductions than I have," Judith said with dignity, "but this one has all the elements. I tricked you out of a house, and I am coercing you to leave with me."

"But that's just it! The key element seems to be missing: coercion. A true abduction means carrying off the woman—and it is traditionally a woman, but I won't quibble about such irrelevant matters!—against her will and in such a way that she cannot escape." Lambert stopped abruptly, causing a crunch of fine gravel underfoot. They had arrived at the intersection of two pathways. Down one was a butt for archery practice, down the other a bathing pond. "What's to prevent me from simply walking away?"

Judith had stopped as well. "I thought of that!" she said. "I knew that I could not heave you over my shoulder and carry you off, but I did see to the small matter of coercion."

"In that case, then, this may qualify as an abduction," Lambert said agreeably. He asked politely, "And the precise method of coercion?"

Judith's face was pained. "This is the ignoble part. I'm afraid I had to resort to a rather risky method!"

"Why do I have the feeling that you have put my life in danger?" Lambert mused, purely rhetorically.

"I've put mine in danger, too, if it comes to that!

Besides, I owe you! And if you really must know, what I did was to send an anonymous message to my uncle at Whitehall to inform him that you had the Vatican message to King Charles in your possession. The message also said that you could be found at either the Marston residence or at The Red Bull."

Lambert considered this. "I see. Does that mean that your uncle did *not* get the parchment along with the painting?"

"Not exactly," she hedged.

"You mean, you had it all along?"

Judith nodded and explained how she had retrieved the parchment from the tapestry.

"I was wondering how it had come into your hands. I naturally thought your uncle had put you up to it."

Judith was about to deny it, but then said thoughtfully, "I suppose he did—beginning when I was five years old! My uncle bred me to a life of luxury and poisoned me with the idea that I must marry a very rich man. He gave me wealth and love in return for unquestioning obedience. Only since meeting you have I come to realize that his price was too high!" She ran her eye over Lambert's dress which was, as usual, undistinguished and careless but infinitely more attractive than the most fashionable cavalier. She smiled. "I am happy, even eager, to marry a poor man."

Lambert opened his mouth to speak but apparently thought the better of it, for he refrained from commenting on this diagnosis of his financial health.

"Which reminds me," Judith said, "*did* you come to Raglan last week for me and not for that hateful parchment?"

Lambert had, of course, come for her. However, if he admitted that, he perceived that the effect of Judith's present maneuvers would be spoiled, and he wanted nothing to thwart the initiative she had so charmingly established. He could reject a woman who wished to dominate him; he could not resist the woman who had risked all for him. He shrugged and avoided the question by saying, "More to the point now is that the old bastard will be after my blood, as a result of your anonymous letter, and there will be no place for me to hide in London.''

Judith nodded, pleased with his ready understanding. "You have no choice, in fact, but to let me get you out of London.''

"And how do you propose to do that?"

Judith smiled with satisfaction and patted the tapestry bag dangling from her arm. "I've costumes in here with which we shall disguise ourselves. Oh," she added on an afterthought, "and if you're thinking of wresting the bag away from me—and I can hardly stop you, you know—I might add that the ostlers at The Rose have strict instructions to deliver the horses only to me! I bribed them handsomely! So, you can't get away without me, since your horse will be under surveillance as soon as my uncle receives my message. Indeed, I am sure that he has received it by now!''

"And how will we get out of London, if Somerset sets his guards at every gate? They might be prepared for disguises.''

Judith smiled complacently. "With my mother's jewels— which is all I took with me from Raglan! Don't worry. Even if we do have to bribe the sentries, I've plenty of jewelry to trade for the journey. I have no idea the style in which you and Will traveled from Italy to England, but I shall no doubt wish for something better. And since I am abducting you, I don't want you to assume any monetary burden on my account.''

"That's a relief," Lambert commented conversationally. "You said you had two horses available. What of Will?''

Judith had taken care of that consideration, too. "Will and I came to an agreement. Yes, I saw him along with the rest of the troupe before venturing to Covent Garden. Will has conceived a great attachment to his homeland, and wishes us luck. He says that he will come and visit sometime soon. He assured me that he will know where to find you in Italy.''

Lambert was regarding Judith meditatively. A light had kindled deep in his gray eyes, a light combining affection and something of a warmer nature. He was not yet touching her with his hands, but his gaze was a caress. "And that parchment from the Vatican? Have you concealed it somewhere on my person, to insure that my life is in your hands?"

"I did not go *that* far, Lambert," Judith replied with a cluck of her tongue. "I left it conspicuously placed among my uncle's papers in the Tower Library before I escaped Raglan last week. However, I am counting on the fact that he has already received word of my disappearance and will attempt to track you down first—or perhaps he will suspect that we are together!—before returning to Wales. I am also counting on the fact that once he does return and finds the parchment that is so very dear to him, he will end his interest in our movements."

"And so both the parchment and the painting fall into his tender care in the end," Lambert remarked.

"I owed him that much," Judith said, serious now.

"I'm not so sure, but we'll leave it at that." Lambert placed his hands lightly on Judith's shoulders. "However, I will congratulate you on a very neat stratagem and agree that your abduction is nearly a complete success. You have made a flight to Italy entirely feasible, and you have almost coerced me into allowing you to abduct me."

Judith regarded him steadily, blushing a little now at the solemn intention she read in his eyes.

A fashionable couple passed them, hardly raising a brow at the intimacy implied by their stance, for such was the general run of business in the gardens. No, the couple who passed by Lambert and Judith gazing at one another in silence and desire spared not a glance for them, for the unknown couple was eager just then to find their own leafy bower. However, the passing couple did prompt Lambert and Judith to move on. Their progress did not suggest that they were anxious to leave London or felt pursued by the fearful forces of Somerset. They chose to amble down a side path this time, one thick and lush and over-grown.

"Yes, it's nearly a complete success," Lambert repeated

lazily, smiling down at Judith, "and you've almost coerced me. . . ."

Judith wrinkled her brow. "What could be lacking? Given that your experience in abductions is superior to mine, what, in your opinion, have I failed to consider?"

"In an abduction," Lambert instructed her, "it is customary to have designs on the virtue of the person being abducted."

"Oh?"

"Yes, and you'd pretty well better have designs on my virtue," Lambert stated categorically, slowing his pace to another halt, "or I am not going another step."

"Let me assure you that I do!"

The warm light in Lambert's eyes became a challenging gleam. "Prove it."

"Let me see," Judith said gamely. "Would an expression of love be appropriate?"

"Entirely."

"Well, then," she said, "I love you."

Lambert shook his head, indicating that this expression was not good enough.

"Madly!" she added, with emphasis.

He laughed. "Why is it that when a woman uses the term 'expression,' she means words, and when a man uses the term, he means action? It is very curious!"

Judith was a little put out. "I have just abandoned my home and my inheritance and my family *and* my dignity for you!" she retorted. "Yes! My dignity! For you were so chivalrous to point out that I was willing to make a *complete fool* out of myself not half an hour ago! If *that* is not action, I don't know what is!"

"But we were speaking of your having designs on my virtue," Lambert reminded her, "and I am asking you to prove it—with actions." While Judith grappled with his meaning, he smiled his very charming smile and said, "You perceive now the true complexities of abduction. It is no simple undertaking!"

Judith could not quite have said how it happened, but they were no longer on a path, not even the narrow side path. Somehow, they had penetrated a small gap in the hedge and found themselves in a lovely little thicket deep in the garden which, with its charming stone bench and rambling roses, was contrived to all the advantages of gallantry.

"I await a demonstration that your intentions regarding this abduction are serious," he said gravely. He did not touch her, but his presence was as intimate as any contact with him she had previously experienced.

Judith's eyes had widened. "You really do mean for me—that is, that I should—that *I* should be the one to—!" She could not untangle her thoughts or her tongue.

"The word is 'seduce,'" he said helpfully, "and, yes, I really do mean for you to seduce me."

Judith gaped slightly, unable to move for all the delicious emotions swirling through her breast.

"This abduction *is* your idea, after all," Lambert said in low, provocative tones.

"But I don't know the first thing about it!" she managed to protest. "I am completely inexperienced!"

Lambert was plainly enjoying himself and the situation. "I have confidence in you. I note that you did not know anything about proper abductions before this day and have contrived admirably!"

"And I can't quote a word of poetry!" she added, as if to clinch her argument. The denial, however, recalled to her the last time Lambert's poetry had worked its magic, and the memory caused the first flowering of musk-roses deep inside her.

"If you will permit a suggestion," he said, "you might get the proper start by shedding that cloak, which will be poetry enough for me."

It had become a *very* warm day, Judith was discovering, and she obediently unbuttoned the cloak and let it slip from her shoulders. Suddenly, in the privacy of this bower, Judith felt more exposed in the dress than when she had worn it as a costume.

"I have always admired that dress on you," he said, his eyes lingering.

"No, you have not!" Judith said, partially to cover her

embarrassment. "When I wore it that first night, you said something uncomplimentary about it!"

"It's not your color," he said. "However, you do have the figure for it, which was immediately apparent to me that first night, and I do think that the garnets add a certain sort of something! I must enjoy the sight of the combination while I can, for I fear you will soon be losing the jewels to the various bribes you will be forced to pay in order to get us out of London."

He was teasing her with words, with his eyes, with his smile, hoping to gentle her into relaxing. He would do everything he could think of, but he was not going to make the first move to touch her.

"Speaking of which," Judith said, uncertain of herself and attempting to forestall the inevitable, "I think we should be making haste."

"So do I!" Lambert agreed promptly.

Judith flushed. "To leave London!" she answered. "There's no telling whether you or I or both of us are being sought after at this very moment!"

"Good point," Lambert said. "On previous similar and ill-fated occasions," he said, reaching an arm into the shrubbery and pushing aside the branches, looking about, "we've been interrupted by any number of people lurking behind bushes." He searched the greenery. "I don't expect that your uncle could have tumbled so quickly to our movements, but I wouldn't put it past Harry Webster to be in the wrong place at the wrong time! No! No one!" He turned back to Judith. "You are free to proceed."

Judith froze.

Lambert was a perceptive man and recognized Judith's condition as that of stagefright. "A remarkable young woman came to the Marston House," he said persuasively, "not a half hour ago, I think we were agreed, wearing that very same dress." In his reminiscence, his voice conveyed all the seduction he had felt at watching her comic performance. "A remarkable young woman. Not a raving beauty but infinitely desirable, wreathed in jewels and humor and stories of her amorous exploits!" On a professional note, he held up a hand and asked, "What would that woman do with this?"

Catching on, Judith took the hand he offered her and placed it at the edge of her bodice between her breasts. The look she summoned was entirely in character for Judith of the purple dress. "She would need it to help her calm her heart which is fair to swooning in the August heat." She spread his fingers so that they covered her breast and sighed with lusty exaggeration so that her flesh swelled against his palm. "The heat is making me weak," she said. She dipped slightly, as if her knees had buckled and maneuvered such that his fingers slid under what little fabric covered the tip of her breast. "La, sir!" she sighed, coy, but only half of her sigh was a product of artifice for a passion had surged through her at his touch. "What must you think of me?"

Lambert had been wanting her out of that dress for many long minutes—even weeks, now, if he thought back on the first night they had met at Speke Hall. However, he was a patient man who would not force the pace. "I think you have made an excellent beginning," he encouraged, enchanted by his seduction, "but it is only a beginning. And then?"

She looked into his eyes on a question and met only a blaze of passion in his as her answer. With the warmth and delight of his hand caressing her breast, she was emboldened to improvise. She took his other hand and placed it at her waist, and when she sidled against him, his hand slid to her buttock. Judith felt Lambert's unmistakable response as she pressed herself against him, but still he made no further move.

"And then?" he prompted again, less distinctly this time.

"It being such a hot day and all," Judith continued, lifting her hands to his doublet, "I'm sure that the kind gentleman is wishing for some relief." She began to unlace, very slowly and with great attention, the garment to expose ever more of his chest. Her fingers traced circular patterns down the ropes of muscles of his torso to the top of his breeches. Her fingers paused at the lacings. She looked up, her eyes bright and avid and laughing. "If we are really to play the scene according to our rôles," she said, and her voice held all the seduction of well-articulated desire, "it would help me to know what kind of a gentleman I'm dealing with." She loosed his breeches and pressed herself against him. She wrapped a leg around him, sliding it up and down. "I wonder, your lordship, sir, if you're a man who fills a woman's . . . heart with love—a man like Master Marston."

"Or the Lord Mayor?" Lambert suggested.

"Or him!" Judith breathed. "A woman's heart desires . . . love, above all else." She reached up to pull Lambert's face down to hers. "And security, of course. Some proof to show her that his love is the equal of hers."

Lambert laughed silently as he kissed her, and Judith's lips had never tasted so delicious a flavor as shared laughter. "You are quite right," he murmured. "To find the true inspirational center for your rôle, think of me as a man who owns a vast villa on the Tuscan hills overlooking Florence that is surrounded by a garden more lovely and seductive than even this corner of paradise. Think of me as a man who could replace the trumpery trinkets at your neck a dozen times over."

Judith was delighted that he was playing along so perfectly, and she was blazing with the rôle of the seductress, eager to explore it fully. "Oooh, sir, I think it's love! Yes!" Her leg continued to rub its silk along his. "We must discuss it at length."

"Willingly," Lambert said against her lips.

"Perhaps on the bench?" Judith broke the kiss long enough to look behind her. She eyed the stone slab with disfavor. "No," she said, shaking her head, "I do not think discussion could flourish on that hard surface." She removed Lambert's hands from the soft spots on her body, for he had managed to part her bodice and spread it away from her breasts. She took his fingers in hers. She led him to a grassy spot behind the bench, in a dark shadow, and pulled him down to the ground with her and replaced his hands on her breasts to bring that glorious sensation back.

"In your professional opinion, Lambert, do you think the

woman who has possessed me for the afternoon enjoys such scenes?''

''She revels in them,'' he assured her with heat.

He had stretched out next to her, and Judith drew him closer by wrapping one leg around him, as she had done earlier, and nuzzling her body into his. In between kisses, she said, ''You know, I must be a fast learner.'' Her hands had drawn his doublet off and had slid down his back to the top of his breeches. They gave way easily. ''The more I get to know this very vulgar and very lusty and very wonderful woman, the more I realize how generous she is.'' Here her breathing became labored, for she had pulled her skirts up to her knees and pushed one of Lambert's hands down to her thigh that lay across him. ''She's a generous woman.''

''Generous and open?'' Lambert queried, his fingers traveling a natural course up her thigh. He shifted his legs so that hers would spread delicately, voluptuously around him.

''Ooh, yes. Generous and open and able to distinguish between giving her favors to a man who can help her pursue her independence, so to speak, and giving herself to a man whom she hopes desperately to please. Ooh. That's right. Please.''

''Please?'' Lambert murmured thickly, having found the center of earthly pleasure, drenched in desire.

''Yes,'' she replied. ''For her, there will come a man that she *wants*, pure and simple. To please.'' She kissed him as deeply as his fingers sought and explored her. ''No villa, no jewels. Just a man. Just *this*. Please.''

She moved to make a definitive gesture, the final act that would prove to him her intention to pleasure him, but found that she had lost the initiative in this encounter.

Lambert had restrained himself as long as he was able. Her seduction had succeeded far beyond his expectations. Surrounded by the scent of her, her hair, her skin, her humidity, her words, he wanted her now on his terms, and he was happy to instruct her with his hands and certain quiet commands spoken into her ear, what those were. In an instant, she was beneath him fully, caressing him as he desired, desirous herself as he caressed her, and aware that she had imagined this moment for days now, dreamed herself repeatedly available to him and ready and generous, her naked below him, him naked above her, him naked within her, with purpose and desire and love.

In the deep enchantment of the garden, reality met the fantasy, gave it shape, filled it, fulfilled it, far exceeded it. They sustained each other, satisfied each other, fused with each other in a molten crucible. Afterward, they played, stroked, laughed, and were as pleased with themselves as any pair of giddy young lovers intoxicated by the slick heat of a summer's passion and the salty perfumes of the earth.

"Elopement is our only course," Lambert remarked at length.

"This was an abduction, Lambert," Judith corrected.

Lambert was idly fondling her breast. "Abduction," he agreed on a satisfied chuckle, "up to a point." He considered it. "One good abduction deserves another, but you can't return modestly to Raglan after this one as you did after the first." He rolled over so that he was on top of her again. He looked deeply into her languid pools of brown that still glowed with satisfaction and desire. "Your uncle would take one look at you and cast you out for the strumpet you have become."

"Always were," she corrected again. "The Judith of the purple dress has been *wantonly* corseted all those years." She stretched luxuriously under him on the grass. "How happy she is to have escaped!"

"I take that," he said, kissing her, "as an invitation."

Judith laughed. The sound muffled against his lips. "Speaking of invitations and abductions, do you know why I was traveling through Somerset Park the day Will pulled me off the path?"

His tongue found hers. "No, cunning woman, why were you in Somerset Park?" His fingers sought another point.

"To deliver the first of my wedding invitations to Monmouth!" Judith sputtered, then whispered aghast, "No! Not again!"

"A woman of foresight," Lambert said, "and, yes, again

and again!'' He plucked her lips with his. ''But I don't know how you knew then that you were to marry me.''

''I didn't,'' she gasped. ''That wedding was to Sir George.''

''I told you he was a dullard,'' Lambert remarked.

''You did?''

''I didn't? I certainly thought it! Thank me prettily that your marriage to him is off.'' He took her hand to show her how she could thank him. ''There's a good girl.''

Judith's eyes had popped open. ''But the marriage is *not* off, Lambert!'' she cried.

Chapter
21

"**WHAT?**" Lambert exclaimed, propping himself on an elbow and looking down at her. "Oh, no, my lovely wanton! I am afraid that you have learned your part *too* well! You are not going to leave me dangling on a string, dancing for your favors, while you marry your rich and respectable cavalier!"

"How I love a masterful man," Judith murmured provocatively, evidently not cowed by his harsh words.

Lambert's eyes had narrowed, and his expression was fierce. "You had better get used to it," he said. "Beecham might have wagged his tail to your command, but I will not! You are not marrying him!"

"Of course not, you idiot!" Judith laughed. "I have no intention of it. All I meant was that the wedding to Sir George has yet to be called off!"

"What does that have to say to anything?" Lambert wondered.

"Until this very moment, I had forgotten all about him, you see," Judith explained, "but now I realize that I cannot just leave without a word to him! Sir George does not deserve such shabby treatment!"

"Oh, but he does!" was Lambert's opinion.

"No, he does not," Judith insisted. "He may be dull—

314

oh, all right, I admit it!'' she said, noting the look on Lambert's face, "but that does not mean that he should be treated inconsiderately! He should hear of the broken engagement from me!''

"You wish to speak with him?'' Lambert asked, somewhat surprised.

"Well, maybe not *speak* with him,'' Judith admitted. Then, brightening, said, "I could send him a message!''

Lambert shook his head. "He is bound to learn of your disappearance before too much longer, and the gossips will be linking our names soon enough. Not communicating with him under the circumstances will be the greater kindness.''

"How is that?'' Judith asked, unable to follow the reasoning.

"Because it will be proof to him of your poor character, and he can console himself with the thought that he is well rid of you.'' Lambert considered the matter from another angle. "In addition, I predict that his mother will derive a perverse satisfaction from this turn of events. She will, no doubt, be highly successful in convincing her son that he has had a narrow escape.''

Although Judith was relaxed in her nakedness and insensibly enjoying the feel of being wrapped sensuously around Lambert's body, she said with an admirable dignity, "Your habit of being right is *not* what I find most endearing about you, Lambert! And, I do believe, that in his own way, Sir George is very devoted to me.''

"I don't doubt it, but I maintain that his particular devotion is most unworthy of you!'' Lambert said and took to fondling her boldly, as if to prove his point.

"Which is what I thought about the lovely Elizabeth,'' Judith retorted.

"To think,'' Lambert mused, shaking his head in disbelief, "that he did not even have the wit to climb to your bedchamber. By the bye, did he ever kiss you?''

When Judith was about to respond in the affirmative, Lambert put his lips to hers, causing her to reinterpret the meaning of "kiss.'' "No,'' she said after a long, pleasurable moment, "I do not recall that he ever did. Did the lovely Elizabeth ever attempt to abduct you?''

"No abduction, no seduction," he said. "Does that satisfy you?"

Since Lambert had found other points on Judith's body to explore, his question was ambiguous. So was Judith's response. "Say, now, *there's* an idea!" she said as she moved against him and as her hands strayed absently into his unruly curls.

Lambert had found the tip of Judith's breast responsive to his touch. "How rewarding that our ideas converge," he said, bending his lips to explore the crease in her neck which had been tantalizing him for the last few minutes. "How I love gardens!" he remarked into her warm, sweet-smelling skin.

She pushed his head away and attempted to untangle herself from him. "No, not *that*!" she said. "I had a different idea. *This* shall tire you of me before we leave England!"

"Me, tired?" Lambert replied, deliberately misinterpreting her and favoring her with a very warm look. "The word is for old bucks. Don't worry! I haven't felt this young and eager since my rawest manhood."

"That's not what I meant!"

"I know. You bring out my better side."

"I am afraid that you shall tire of *me* before we reach Italy," Judith tried again.

"Women have such strange notions," Lambert commented. "I don't know where they come by them." He shook his head. "Everything up until now has been but—my pardon—foreplay," he said, the warmth in his eyes deepening, "in preparation for the real scene."

"The *real* scene?" Judith said in a strangled voice. The look in his eye had deepened to fire, and Judith made a further effort to slide away from him but was unsuccessful. She was hampered by the precise location of one of Lambert's hands.

Lambert chuckled, pleased with his little treasure. "Yes, the real scene. You, my vulgar, lusty, wonderful Judith, were until a very few moments ago a virgin." He smiled, rather smugly. "Not a mental one, however, I am happy to say.'' He fondled his treasure, bringing a flush to Judith's cheeks. He bent to whisper into her ear, ''This gentle sport is as least as mental as it is physical, I hardly need to tell you. You lost your mental virginity to me—'' He broke off, in fond reminiscence. ''When was it I wonder?''

''In my bedchamber?'' Judith suggested.

''No, before that,'' he said.

''You, sir, are conceited.'' The effect of Judith's response was, however, blunted by the moan of pleasure she gave at Lambert's ministrations and the movement she made toward easing her legs around him again.

''Not at all.'' Lambert had moved so that Judith could relax against him. He propped his head on one hand and continued a leisurely exploration with the other.

Judith's lids lowered, and her lashes brushed her cheeks.

''Look at me,'' Lambert commanded.

Judith opened her lids. She regarded him steadily and with growing passion, her eyes lovingly tracing the outlines of the bruises on his face which had faded to mere shadows, the delicate expression on her face communicating to him all her desire. It was, indeed, a highly stimulating idea that she had given herself to him mentally long before the episode in her bedroom. It had the further merit of being true.

''And when did you lose your mental virginity to me?'' she was emboldened to ask. ''Provided, of course, that you did not lose it first to Diana fifteen years ago.''

He smiled in fond reminiscence, and could find nothing in that experience to compare to the rich web of love he felt for Judith. ''That was a pretty picture,'' he said, ''but was no more than a sketch, a pale outline.''

Judith, profoundly gratified, kept to her teasing. ''Provided you have lost it to me, of course,'' she pursued. ''Was it five minutes ago?''

''You are cruel,'' he said. He smiled at her and touched her and held nothing back. ''Don't you know a man is not likely to fall in love with a woman after he has possessed her? But as for losing your mental virginity, I asked you first, and you have yet to answer me.''

She was loving the wordplay that was part of the foreplay. "Well, then, I suppose," she said breathlessly, sportingly, "that I lost my virginity to you at just about the same time you had the idea to do . . . this."

"Early on, then," he replied lazily. "At Speke Hall."

"No!" she scoffed low.

"Yes!" he assured her.

Judith was lost in mental and physical delight. "Could you—are you saying that you believe in . . . but, no! It is not possible!"

"Hmm?"

"Love at first sight?" she asked, incredulous.

He thought of the painting he had seen that fateful day in the Palazzo Strozzi in Florence and of all his subsequent adventures which had led him to this particular, paradoxical moment. It was both a dream and vividly real for Lambert, as if the most beautiful painting in the world had come to life, with a sea of blue above and a bed of green beneath; as if the strong, heroic Judith had stepped off the canvas, out of the dark shadows and into the light, into his arms so that her wide, warm expanses of alabaster skin could feed his hungry hands and the deep pools of her passionate brown eyes could slake his thirsty soul. Yet the Judith of flesh and blood he held was not the vengeful, determined Judith of oils on canvas. His Judith was laughing and loving and shimmering in the heat, but from the strength of her lovely, unlaced passion for him he was able to infer the depths of the savagery in her that had rent her relationship with her uncle. It pleased him deeply. She was his, his heart, his love, his woman, his wife, his heroine. As for having fallen in love, he realized that he had been hers even before leaving Italy.

"Yes," he said slowly, with a disbelief that partially echoed Judith's. "Or, perhaps, passion at first sight." He added, almost dreamily, "It was the best deal I ever lost. The very best."

Although this last comment was a non sequitur to Judith, she hardly quibbled that logic did not guide this delightful conversation. Instead she said, "Does this mean that you think we are finally playing the scene right?"

"Finally," he said definitively. "Finally. To think it only took fifteen years to get it right." And that was the last that either of them spoke for quite a while.

They lazed and dozed languorously; and when next Lambert did speak, it was to ask idly, "What, my profound heart, was the excellent idea you had before I convinced you of my excellent idea?"

Judith had to make a distinct effort to think of anything but her passion for Lambert. "I don't recall, but it might have had something to do with Elizabeth Marston."

Lambert shook his head. "No, it had rather to do with George Beecham."

Judith laughed and drew Lambert's head down to hers. She kissed him with abandon. "I am *sure* you are mistaken—*he* is insignificant, and *she* is so very beautiful! But, no!" she said, remembering now. "We are *both* right!" She raised herself partway to a sitting position and shielded her eyes with a hand to gauge the course of the sun. The afternoon was at its ripest. The perfect, glorious day promised a perfectly glorious sunset and evening. Judith stretched and yawned with deep pleasure. Lambert had never seen a movement more sinuously appealing.

Judith hitched together the halves of her bodice and began to pull it up. She smoothed down her skirts, saying, "My excellent idea concerns them both." She turned to Lambert to explain. He was rising and arranging himself as well. "It seems a shame to leave London without doing something for Sir George. If I am not to write him a note of apology—and I see the inconveniences of that action, since it will only potentially alert my uncle to where I am and what I am about!—I thought Sir George might appreciate a different kind of gesture. Not that he would know the gesture had been initiated by me, of course." She smiled. "I thought of Miss Marston as the perfect balm to soothe his wound."

Lambert briefly reflected on the match. It appealed to his aesthetic sense, in a detached sort of way. "Perfect," he pronounced, as if considering a painting whose composition and technical skill he admired but did not care to have hanging in his private collection. "Yes, it has all the correct elements," he agreed.

Judith interpreted Lambert's comment as acceptance of her idea. She was on her knees and sitting back on her heels, fiddling with the laces of her bodice. "We need to get them to fall in love," she said, looking up. "Why, what could be simpler! All we need to do is to arrange that they meet face-to-face! They are sure to fall in love at first sight!" To Lambert's chuckle, she said on a frown, "But I don't know how to insure their meeting." Then, brightening, she said, "However it shall be done, we shall need our costumes." She reached over to her tapestry bag and held it up. "While we are getting dressed, we may as well use the occasion to change into the costumes."

Lambert was arranging his clothing now, too, and asked with mild curiosity, "And what rôles have you chosen for us?"

She withdrew several garments. "I am to be a boy, and you," she said and smiled mischievously at her love, "are to be a monk!" His expression was all that she could have hoped. She choked on a laugh. "Yes! Are they not the perfect disguises for us?"

" 'Outrageous' was rather the word I had in mind," he said, his tone very dry, indeed.

"But these were really the only costumes available," Judith defended herself, "and the only ones Mr. Webster thought he could truly part with."

"So your choices have the further appeal of innocence, I note." Lambert did not intend to let her off easily. "It's a difficult time for Catholics in England, Judith," he pointed out.

"Yes, of course, you are right, and that is why you shall be an Italian monk," she returned in triumph, holding out the plain brown habit to him.

"A Franciscan," he remarked. "How thoughtful! Unfortunately, my Latin is not what it should be."

"No one will question you about it. Just keep your mouth

shut and look pious." She smiled sweetly. "That should test your acting abilities."

"And you, my far-from-innocent actress, shall never convince anyone that you are a boy," Lambert was moved to observe as he watched Judith don the loose shirt and jerkin of a boy.

"It's been done before," was Judith's coolly confident reply. After she had hidden her hair under a felt cap with a cocky feather, she continued, now fully transformed, "If Robin and Mr. Smith and others can pass themselves off as women, why can't I be a boy for an hour or two?"

"Stand up and walk a few paces to convince me of it," Lambert bade her as he slipped the monk's habit over his clothing. Judith did so, with no success whatsoever. "Before you ever even leave the garden," he said, watching her lips, "you will be arrested for a violation of the sumptuary laws which the king in his infinite wisdom thought fit to revive. We'll never make it out of London, for you'll be in the darkest cell of Ludgate for the crime of having tampered with your essence."

"Hah!" Judith said over her shoulder with what she hoped was boyish bravado, "My essence can't be altered with a change of clothing."

"That's not the opinion of the current law," was Lambert's comment. He took a few tentative steps around the leafy enclosure himself, trying out a religious gait.

Judith had turned to watch his interpretation of the new character. "I won't be alone at Ludgate," she said. "You'll be right there with me—on the crime of blasphemy!"

Lambert had placed his hands together in a prayerful attitude, looked heavenward with respectful eyes, then bowed, thereby bringing his cowl up over his head. From the depths of his hood, his adaptable voice intoned low the syllables of what sounded like a Latin chant and finished with the solemn words, "Then I shall pray for our swift release. Amen." He raised his head, and his eyes held the gleam of his old acting days. Stepping out of character, he said, "I like it! I've always thought that you had a curiously enno-bling effect on me, but I had never imagined it would go this far!'' He laughed in sinful delight and regarded the boy who would never grow to be a man. ''And, as for urging you to disobedience all this time, neither could I have imagined you would far exceed my boldest promptings!''

Judith returned to him. ''Do any of these developments truly surprise you?''

They regarded each other for a long moment, the monk who was no monk and the boy who was no boy. He shook his head. ''Perhaps one part of delight might be surprise, but mostly I feel satisfaction. Abiding satisfaction.''

Reading the light in his eye, she said quickly, ''Let's be gone before we're arrested for public prurience and indecency!'' She grabbed her tapestry bag into which she had stuffed her strumpet's clothing and turned to leave the bower.

''A swagger, Judith, a swagger! Not a sway!'' Lambert admonished her provocatively as he followed her out. Looking up and down the path, he said with humorous relief, ''Either for public prurience, my love, or for sodomy, dressed as we are!''

Judith turned to him, eyes wide. ''A monk and a boy! Dear me! I hadn't thought of *that*!''

''You might not have, but anyone wandering along just now would have!''

They proceeded down the path, continuing in the direction they had taken before their interlude in the alcove. They would be leaving the garden by the gates opposite to where they had entered.

Judith laughed. ''Since you have been away so long, you cannot know that the worst we could be accused of in this instance is bad taste. In the prosecution of such matters, Charles has shown himself to be remarkably tolerant. Come,'' she said, ''help me contrive a way to arrange the meeting between the lovely Elizabeth and the handsome Sir George.''

''I think we'd best be leaving London, Judith.''

''I thought you said my idea was perfect,'' she objected.

''The idea for the match, but that does not mean that your involvement in bringing it together is equally perfect.''

"But no!" she protested. "We can't depend on fate or chance. We can't leave London without bringing them together—at least once. It is our responsibility!"

Lambert shook his head.

"But they did us no harm," Judith argued, "and they are perfect for each other."

"Already you betray your costume," Lambert said. "I confess that I have never imagined a boy to take on the rôle of matchmaker."

"The fair Cupid of myth," she said, "was a boy."

"True enough," Lambert conceded, "but you, as I know to my greatest happiness, are neither mythic nor a boy."

"But—" Judith began to protest.

"I rather see the hand of Somerset guiding you in this action."

"My uncle? No! I am not wishing to . . . to *destroy* anyone or bend him to my will!"

"But you are manipulating people, just the same, which is the particular specialty of the Somerset household."

"I wish to bring two people together who will love each other on sight. My intentions are noble, my motives pure," she said with dignity.

"Worse and worse!"

"Well, bringing them together would ease my conscience, if you must have a baser motive," Judith retorted. She turned, laid a hand on Lambert's arm, and smiled up at him. "Please?"

Lambert was lost in her plea, in her smile, in her eyes. It took him a moment to realize that for the first time in his life he was at the command of a woman. It took another moment for him to accept it. Then, quite irrelevantly, he asked, "Do you speak Italian?"

"No," Judith answered, understandably puzzled.

"Good," he said, then began to move forward. "All right, then. I bow to my lady's wishes. As our last act of volition before leaving London—and I *do* hope we will be leaving today!—we shall facilitate the meeting of Elizabeth Marston and George Beecham."

"Wait!" Judith called out and hurried to catch up with

him. "You agree?" When Lambert nodded, she demanded, "And *what* does that have to do with my *not* speaking Italian?"

"Figure it out," he tossed back.

"I don't see what—" Judith began and then broke off. "I don't suppose I shall so easily get my way in a country where I do not command the language! Well, let me tell you what I have to say about that!"

Judith was never to have her opportunity for they had reached the gates that led them out to the street, and Lambert said softly, "In character, my boy! In character! Feminine pique is not what fills your breeches!"

Judith had no choice but to rein in her temper. Through her teeth, she managed, "And you, Brother Charles, are going to tell me that there is no devil in you?"

Lambert's attitude was all that was serene as they strode the street. "I will tell you nothing of the kind, my boy." His eyes strayed heavenward. "It is precisely the devil that we men of the cloth must wrestle with at all times."

"Attempting sainthood, Lambert?"

"Canonization," he said solemnly, "is a goal devoutly to be desired."

"Your chances will be greatly increased," said Judith the woman, her own devil dancing in her eyes, "if you would show my soul the way to Paradise."

Judith's regard and her words made Lambert's very bones ache with desire. "I would be happy to show the novice the way," he said piously with an impious look in his eye.

Realizing that the only satisfactory conclusion to this exchange would be a long interlude in the deep green recesses of another London garden, Judith chose instead to concentrate on the matter at hand. "Your first—that is, second—step to sainthood may be taken tonight," she said, "but first we need to devise a way of bringing Elizabeth Marston and George Beecham together without exposing our identities or jeopardizing our lives." Judith was inspired. "Lady Margaret Beecham is the answer to all of our prayers!"

Lambert crossed himself and murmured an *amen*.

As they made their way to The Rose to retrieve the horses, Judith devised her plan. It was extraordinarily simple. She would compose and deliver a letter to Lady Beecham at Whitehall, claiming it to be from one of Lady Beecham's kin who was known to Judith. Judith would disguise her handwriting and explain it to be the result of a minor hand injury. In the letter, she would allude to Elizabeth Marston and extol the young woman's virtue, beauty, and modesty. She would even hint, ever so delicately, that Elizabeth Marston had seen Sir George at the recent masque at the Banqueting House the night, in fact, of Davenant's *The Temple of Love*, and had subsequently been known to have spoken of Sir George's elegance.

More than that Judith did not think was necessary. "And I shall deliver the message myself!"

"Is that wise?" Lambert asked.

"Wise, no," she admitted, "but an irresistible test of my acting abilities!"

"You've had one success today, so leave it at that," Lambert recommended.

"Ah, but that was merely as a woman!" Judith pointed out. "That was far too easy! Besides, if we are henceforth to make our livings on the stage—and you did tell me the first time we met that there are women actors in Italy, did you not?—then I think it best to practice my craft, to develop my range. Starting immediately."

Lambert looked pained.

"There! You see!" she said. "You look perfectly *religious* just now, as if you were contemplating mortal frailty—"

"Something like that!" Lambert interjected.

"—and I see no reason why you should . . . should upstage me! I want a chance to prove myself!"

Lambert took a vow of silence.

The monk and the boy were soon enough on their way to the royal village. The afternoon had progressed, but there was still time enough to accomplish this errand and make it past any one of the dozen city gates before the curfew. In addition, since leaving The Rose, they were both emboldened by their disguises, for no one had regarded them with suspicion or accorded them anything other than the treatment and respect that might be expected of a humble monk traveling with what must be a postulant.

The excellence of their disguises and acting abilities was put to a further test. After approaching Whitehall through St. James's Park, they brought their horses up to the edge of the park that bordered on the ornamental gardens whose green carpet unfurled to the terrace of the Banqueting House. At this end of the gardens, there was a tempest of activity, with noblemen and servants and laborers and work carts and mules hovering about a garbled series of constructions which were, no doubt, designed for some royal entertainment. Judith had no notion what it might be, but when they had dismounted and tethered their horses to the posts where several other horses shuffled, she saw with a start that her mechanically minded cousin Edward stood in the eye of the storm.

Surrounded by several men, brick masons and coopers by the look of them, Edward was holding a large piece of paper, alternately gesturing to the paper and pointing to the low brick wall which was being built between two large stone fountains. These fountains defined the end of the gardens and were centrally placed. Viewing the fountains from the park, she surmised that the purpose of the brick wall being built was to hide a veritable snarl of pipes and pistons and valves and cylinders which were visible to her but would not be from the garden side.

In a flash, Judith saw that Edward must be setting up a waterworks display for the fountains. Could the Court festival that her uncle had alluded to before he left Raglan be scheduled for this evening? Judith could not be sure, but from what she now knew of such mechanical monsters, she reckoned that the festival must be imminent. Her eye followed the low brick wall which ambled up a gentle slope and meandered over to a clump of trees under which squatted a huge copper vessel and to which were connected all the pipes. The vessel simmered over a fire which must have been excessively hot, for even in the shade, the three men who were stoking it were sweating profusely. Judith guessed the vessel contained water. She also guessed that the vessel was connected to a further series of pipes and pumps that, no doubt, ran down to the Thames.

As had been decided beforehand, Lambert retired to the shade, where he sat on a bench distant from the activity and absently fingered the beads hanging from his brown rope belt at the end of which was attached a wooden crucifix. No one paid the good friar the least attention, save for the occasional man who had to pass by that shady spot for some reason or another and was moved to greet the man of the cloth with a respectful, uninterested nod.

Not skirting the activity, Judith picked her way among the men, deliberately passing close by her cousin. Lord Edward looked up briefly at the moment she crossed into his line of vision but gave her no more recognition than he would a fly. Neither did anyone else accord this boy any more attention than the other lads laboring on the waterworks. Judith made so bold to hop over the wall—a boy's trick, she hoped—in order to proceed to the palace. She cast a look back over her shoulder at the work in progress and, off to one side, recognized a maze of metal wheels with teeth like combs that were interlaced one with the other. She saw that they were similar to the gears she had operated in the neither cell of the Yellow Tower at Raglan; these toothed wheels were lying horizontally in a zigzag line between one set of pipes that ran to the copper vessel and another set which was rigged to the two fountains.

Judith made haste to the palace, quickly found Lady Beecham's chambers, and delivered the letter into Lady Beecham's very hands. With her hat pulled down low over her brow and ears, Judith could hardly suppress the grin that curved her lips when Lady Beecham bestowed on her a most niggardly reward for the errand. Judith slipped the cheap coin into her breeches pocket and thanked the "kind leddy." Judith left Lady Beecham's company on a truly boyish swagger, thumbs thrust insolently into the waist of her breeches, cocky in her success.

Perhaps it was this overconfidence that came close to undoing her and Lambert. Or perhaps it was simply because she had played her part too well. Whatever the reason, by the time she had returned by way of the garden to the edge of the park, she had caught the eye of a noble gentleman who was also crossing the garden to the park and whose voice calling her caused a thrill of alarm to raise the hairs along her nape.

"You, there, boy!" Somerset hailed from behind. "Boy! I say! I have an errand for you! There's a coin in it for you!"

Acting as if she had not heard, Judith increased her gait and was almost at the low brick wall connecting the two fountains to the copper vessel, when her uncle called out again, this time in a voice that would brook no disobedience, "Stop in the name of the king!" When she did not slow down, she heard the angry threat, "Your hide wants tanning, boy! *Stop!*"

Chapter
22

JUDITH'S alarm was sliding into panic. Her only hope was to lose herself in the confusion at the work site. Fortunately, that confusion was increasing, for in addition to the men laboring on the waterworks itself, a small army of footmen were setting up chairs in a semicircle about thirty feet from the fountains. Evidently the spectacle was intended to be held this night.

Judith darted in and among the footmen. She headed straight for the thickest part of the activity around the waterworks. So far, her uncle had not yet made a sufficient clamor to have attracted anyone's ears but hers, and she hoped she could elude him and be off before he had raised a hue and cry to arrest everyone's attention. Or, perhaps, if she were quick enough and nimble enough, he would simply give up and find some other lad to do his bidding.

This happy possibility was out of the question. Such was Somerset's deep-seated fear for the future of the king's rule that even the insignificant infraction of obedience by a rough lad spurred him to the kind of murderous fury that had snuffed the talented Mr. Smith's life.

Somerset's voice rang out again, and this time it held enough of a stinging whip to cause a number of heads to turn. In another second or two, Judith would be identified as the offender and apprehended. It would be a small step from there to complete unmasking, for she did not think that her disguise would survive more than a minute under her uncle's scrutiny.

Fortunately, although seeming to meditate on his rosary, Lambert had been keeping a sharp eye out for Judith's return. He had spotted Judith's progress through the garden, and his eyes had widened at seeing the man who followed in Judith's wake. At sight of Somerset, Lambert had already untethered their horses and, with utmost decorum, had begun to lead them forward, in Judith's direction.

In that next instant, however, when he saw to his own alarm that Somerset was seeming to call after the lad, Lambert improvised hastily. There were several other horses tethered. What Lambert did was to release them. He gently slapped their rumps so that they would wander off and not be immediately available to their riders in the event that he and Judith, first, should manage to mount their horses and, second, should be pursued.

Then came the decisive moment. To both Judith and Lambert, it was as if the tableau of the activity around the fountains had frozen, to be fixed and framed in an infinite moment. All the men had halted mid-gesture—some with hammers raised, others hoisting wheelbarrows, still others laying bricks—to remain immobile for that fraction of a second, when Somerset had called out to the lad for the third time and had not been obeyed. Judith saw the men stop and turn toward her, in the direction of Somerset's pointing fingers, and gape slightly in question and wonder. Even her cousin Edward stopped issuing orders, she noted, as if the animation had suspended just for her so that she could analyze every facial expression and bodily movement. At hearing his father's cries, Edward had lowered the sheet of paper that held his mechanical drawing and turned to regard, openmouthed and brows raised, the lad who was darting through the work site.

The next moment, the men sprang back to action, and Judith would be caught. It needed only a couple of men to reach out to catch her and stop her progress.

In an act of supreme desperation, Judith knew what to do. She ducked an outstretched arm or two and made her way over to the horizontally zigzagging line of gears. Watching her movements and on cue, Lambert had made his way over to Judith, circling wide around the commotion, for he had the horses in tow. His movements were unhampered by virtue of the fact that no one was paying attention to him or in the habit of questioning the movements of foreign-looking monks.

Lambert reached Judith's side at the very second she grasped the handle sticking straight up from the outer rim of the smallest of the wheels. Lambert thought she had lost her mind, for it seemed to him as if she was trying to turn the wheel.

She was, and the wheel was not responding to her effort. When he demanded, harshly, "Good God! What are you doing?" she turned to him and said with fierce determination, "I'm trying to turn it, but it's stuck!" Then, equally incomprehensibly, Judith hissed, "There had better be some pressure here, or we are lost! But I don't see a thing! *Turn* it!" she cried while she took the horses' reins from Lambert's hands.

Lambert did not argue. His very unmonastic muscles turned the wheel easily, and that wheel turned the next, then the next, and the next after that. At Judith's continued urgings, he kept turning the smallest wheel, a dozen times or more, before anyone had the wit to attempt to stop him.

By this time, Judith's strategy was already proving its merits. Several ghostly, bone-chilling creaks echoed eerily from the bowels of the mechanical monster, effectively checking the steps of the men who were closest to Judith and Lambert and in a position to grab them. Judith might have been struck with the fear of God herself had she not been accustomed to the wrenching groans. In fact, this time she had been anticipating the melancholy wheezing and even welcomed it as the first sign of success. Fortunately, it was she ·who was holding the reins of the horses, for Lambert, in his surprise, would have dropped them, and their horses would have bolted. The other, untethered horses Lambert had earlier loosed were now pawing and neighing and stamping wildly.

The miracle happened. With a great shout of steam forcing itself through the pipes, Edward's brainchild came to life. Its birth was attended not only by this painful scream but also with a rush and a gush of water from the two fountains. The first, intemperate spray showered none other than Somerset himself whose angry cries and commands were drowned into incoherent and watery gobblings.

The untethered horses were running madly. One was charging the brick wall, causing men and tools and materials to scatter everywhere. No one was concerned any longer with the disobedient lad who had caused this mess, or the unmonkish monk who was abetting him, for all was chaos. The pandemonium of cursing humans and stampeding animals and screeching machines was heightened by the continuous spray from the fountains whose jets of water were chugging now with a mechanical regularity. Even the rotators in the center of each fountain to which were affixed buckets were turning steadily. However, the design for this revolving apparatus was imperfect, and the buckets, on their circular course around the center column of the fountain, tended to dump the water outside of the fountain rather than in the basin. Consequently, several men who happened to be standing nearby received a soaking.

Judith and Lambert wasted no further time surveying the extraordinary scene. After a brief exclamation of "Good God! What *is* this child of Satan?" Lambert tossed Judith into the saddle, lifted the skirts of his habit, and swung his long legs over his horse.

Judith replied, having to shout, "It's my cousin Edward's handiwork, and I'll explain it all later!"

As they wheeled their horses around, Judith became aware that one person, at least, was so far from fear or anger as to be positively joyous.

"'Streuth!" carried a voice through the cacophony and confusion. "It works! It *works*!" This was evidently Lord

Edward. "Now, the buckets are a problem. Yes! I quite see that! But what if I were to reset the angle of vanes of the float wheel and narrow the apertures in the upright pillar through which the steam escapes?"

Judith did not wait to hear her cousin resolve his hydraulic problems. She and Lambert spurred their horses forward, and their escape was aided by the fact that no one was able to follow them on horseback, nor was anyone in sufficient command of himself to alert the castle guards to the flight of the monk and the boy through the thick woods of St. James's Park.

Judith did spare a backward glance, once it was apparent that they would not be caught. She saw her uncle stalking with haste and sodden dignity away from the fountains, toward the palace, cutting a path for himself through the bewildered footmen and overturned chairs.

She saw Somerset through the sprays and spouts of water, crystalline drops soaring to explode and evaporate in the hot summer sun, misting the sky and framing the roof and chimneys of the royal palace with a pastel rainbow dancing on the tips of the highest jets. It was a contradictory image. Judith felt her hate for her uncle soften as he strode toward the palace and she rode away from it. She no longer loved him or craved his good opinion, but she did admire him: for his resolve, for his effectiveness, for his skillful politics, even for his brilliant manipulations. However, the wall of water that separated them now might as well have been a river or a channel or a gulf or a sea, so wide was the spiritual distance between them. As the tall, erect, dignified figure of Lord Somerset receded, Judith felt something shrivel inside of her to the size of a withered pea, and that was her opinion of Somerset's soul. She felt no answering ache in her own soul. Yet it was a loss all the same, but a loss of what never was.

Cantering next to Charles Lambert, she turned back around and grinned at him broadly, it being impossible to exchange words above the thunder of the hooves.

The next time they had an opportunity to speak was when they had slowed their horses and were exiting the royal park in a most undignified manner. Lambert remarked, "This escape, my dear, lacks something of the majesty of the liberation of Israel the original Judith achieved."

Judith laughed. "I got us out of it, didn't I?"

"You also got us into it," Lambert observed.

"Details, details!" Judith said dismissively, and then a thought struck her. "Say, you're not disappointed that I am not a *painting*, are you?"

It was Lambert's turn to grin. Broadly. He thought of the many splendid paintings he had bought and sold in his time. He thought of his magnificent collection gracing the walls of his villa. He thought of the *Judith* which had driven him with a rare passion. None of those experiences had brought him a fraction of the happiness he now felt, fleeing for his life in a monk's habit beside his love dressed as a boy.

"No," he said, "I'm not."

"That's good," Judith said with a nod. "By the way, it is a superb piece, your *Judith*."

"Do you think so?"

"The most gorgeous painting I've seen in a long time," she averred. "Well, we've left it behind, along with everything else." She said it without regret, and Lambert felt a remarkable equanimity knowing that the painting had remained behind with Somerset.

"On to Italy?" she said.

"On to Italy," Lambert said. With a great inner laugh, he realized for the first time that he could have chosen no better partner than Judith Beaufort, Somerset's niece, to take back home with him. Home. Italy. Florence.

First came the small matter of leaving London. Flush with excitement and triumph and love, Judith and Lambert did not, for all of that, underestimate Somerset. Judith had no way of knowing whether her uncle knew yet about her disappearance from Raglan but, once he did learn of it, she did not think it would take him forever to figure out how an insignificant lad had understood the mysteries of hydraulic machinery. In any case, it was also clear that Somerset was going to be making a thorough and determined search of the City and environs for a boy and a monk.

Lambert had an excellent idea for covering their tracks. They first left the City as monk and boy by Tyburn Brook and reentered the same gate dressed as man and strumpet. They exited as monk and boy by Turnmill Brook and reentered the same gate dressed as man and strumpet. They did the same at the exits to Islington, Hackney, Stratford, and Stepney. They even, daringly, crossed the City and the bridge, to perform the same ruses at the gates to Nervington and Deptford. Although this was an extremely time-consuming process, it proved to be very effective in frustrating Somerset's pursuit. The positively confirmed and wildly conflicting reports he received of the direction of the pair's flight sent him into a furious rage, and he dissipated his forces by sending men in all directions at once. Consequently, Lambert and Judith spent a safe and heavenly night hardly a mile east of London walls, undisturbed by the royal guardsmen.

They left England with no difficulty, but still they kept their wits about them, knowing just how far Somerset's arm could stretch. They alternated between traveling as man and wife, debauché and whore, monk and boy, brother and sister, and never once encountered problems. They made their way through France, rather than following the Antwerp-Augsburg axis along which Lambert was well known. He even resisted the impulse to do any business in Paris.

They were two weeks into their journey. One fine, hot late summer day, Judith, happy and boyish in her breeches and her felt hat with the cocky feather, turned to Lambert, the pious monk, and asked with some concern, "What shall we do when my jewelry runs out?"

Lambert shrugged indifferently.

She touched the locket beneath her shirt. "I certainly do not want to give up my *Judith* miniature," she informed him.

"I hope it won't come to that," Lambert said. "Perhaps by then we shall be in Italy."

"But we shall still need money in Italy," Judith argued.

"True, but then I know more people there."

As if knowing people would buy them food and shelter, Judith thought. Still, if Lambert was not worried, she saw no reason to accept that burden. Besides, it did not fit her boyish mood.

"Speaking of knowing people in Italy," she said, "what of Spadaccio?"

"What of him?"

"He might take exception to our presence in Italy."

"Italy is a large place," Lambert replied, "and he might not have any interest in our movements."

"But the world is not so very large, when all is said, and after his defeat in London, he might be *very* interested in our movements."

"I imagine that his influence in Rome, and thus his effectiveness in bringing revenge on me, will have been greatly diminished."

"All the more reason for him to be after your blood," Judith said.

"Then I will expect you to continue to protect me from him with your acting abilities," Lambert tossed back.

"Not only my acting abilities," Judith said, showing teeth, adding at her most bloodthirsty, "I would *kill* for you."

Lambert was perversely pleased. "I thank you for the sentiment," he said. "However, since it will not add to my happiness to have you languishing in an Italian prison—the Italians do have a curious sense of justice—I might have to call on the protection of the Duke of Florence, if Spadaccio threatens." He turned to her with an innocent smile. "The duke is a particular friend of mine."

Judith was confused. She did not know whether he was teasing her or not. "Then there is my uncle," she pursued, apparently caught up in serious thoughts for the day.

"Yes, there is."

"He is bound to put two and two together, you know," she said. "We left a pretty mess behind us. He will not take it lightly."

"No," Lambert agreed slowly, "he will not take it lightly. However, I would guess that Somerset will have his hands full with affairs of state at home." His gaze traveled ahead, between his horse's ears, into the haze and dust of the middle distance. His mind was lost in abstraction. "But it's only a guess," he continued after a moment, "and I cannot foretell my fate or yours, much less your uncle's, the king's, or the nation's."

They pondered that profundity for half a league, before Judith asked, "Shall we never return?" Her voice held a certain wistfulness only. The question held no remorse.

"Some day," he assured her.

"That reminds me!" she said, having called to mind the green glories of her native Gwent. She was more cheerful now and questioning. "Did you really buy Speke Hall or were you just squatting there for the night?"

"Squatting?" he asked with real surprise and some indignation but quickly recovered. He had determined that Judith should enjoy for a few days more the romance of her imagined poverty. He chose to deflect the question. His eye lit, and he slanted her a glance she had come to know well.

"My lad!" he said, chiding. "Such unseemly questions from a beardless youth!"

Judith had the answer to that. She met his glance with a challenging one of her own and said with pointed reference to his monk's habit, "Such unseemly answers from a man in womanish skirts."

"I'm still wearing my sword," he said. "Do you care to see it?"

Judith blushed and laughed. When she did not immediately decline the treat, he drew rein on his horse and put a hand on her bridle as well. They were traveling a shaded road that rambled beside a brook. Lambert gestured to the green, shadowy depths and quoted, " 'This green plot shall be our stage, this hawthorn-brake our tiring-house.' "

Judith had yet to resist one of his quotes. "To show me your sword?"

"To give it to you, my lady," he said with gallantry, "to lay it at your feet."

Judith blinked. "Surely not *there*, sir!"

Lambert laughed and pulled her off her horse.

With only the least strenuous of resistance, Judith struggled. "And what else do you have to offer me?"

Lambert's gesture encompassed the earth and the sky and the woods and himself. "All this, my heart."

GET LOVESTRUCK!

AND GET STRIKING ROMANCES FROM POPULAR LIBRARY'S BELOVED AUTHORS

Watch for these exciting romances in the months to come:

December 1990

AND HEAVEN TOO
by Julie Tetel

January 1991

INTIMATE CONNECTIONS
by Joanna Z. Adams